Renewed By Dawn

*September 1871 –
January 1872*

*Book # 17 in The Bregdan
Chronicles*

Sequel to Courage Rising

Ginny Dye

Renewed By Dawn

Copyright © 2020 by Ginny Dye

Published by
Bregdan Publishing
Bellingham, WA 98229

www.BregdanChronicles.net

www.GinnyDye.com

www.BregdanPublishing.com

ISBN # 9798640423686

All rights reserved. No portion of this book may be reproduced in any form without the written permission of the publisher.

Printed in the United States of America

For all those enduring the 2020 Coronavirus Lockdown – but especially for the health care workers and 1st responders who put their life on the line every day.

THANK YOU!

A Note from the Author

My great hope is that *Renewed By Dawn* will both entertain, challenge you, and give you courage to face all the seasons of your life. I hope you will learn as much as I did during the months of research it took to write this book. I have about decided it is just not possible to cover an entire year in one book anymore. As I move forward in the series, it seems there is so much going on in so many arenas, and I simply don't want to gloss over them.

When I ended the Civil War in *The Last, Long Night*, I knew virtually nothing about Reconstruction. I have been shocked and mesmerized by all I have learned. Every moment of research emphasizes my belief that every action has lasting repercussions throughout history – in both good and bad ways. Each book pulls me forward to the next one, increasing my eagerness to know what will happen next.

I grew up in the South and lived for eleven years in Richmond, VA. I spent countless hours exploring the plantations that still line the banks of the James River and became fascinated by the history.

But you know, it's not the events that fascinate me so much – it's the people. That's all history is, you know. History is the story of people's lives. History reflects the consequences of their choices and actions – both good and bad. History is what has given you the world you live in today – both good and bad.

This truth is why I named this series The Bregdan Chronicles. Bregdan is a Gaelic term for weaving: Braiding. Every life that has been lived until today is a part of the woven braid of life. It takes every person's story to create history. Your life will help determine the course of history. You may think you don't have much of an impact. You do. Every action you take will reflect in someone else's life. Someone else's decisions. Someone else's future. Both good and bad. That is the **Bregdan Principle**...

**Every life that has been lived until today is a part of the woven braid of life.
It takes every person's story to create history.
Your life will help determine the course of history.
You may think you don't have much of an impact.
You do.
Every action you take will reflect in someone else's life.
Someone else's decisions.
Someone else's future.
Both good and bad.**

My great hope as you read this book, and all that will follow, is that you will acknowledge the power you have, every day, to change the world around you by your decisions and actions. Then I will know the research and writing were all worthwhile.

Oh, and I hope you enjoy every moment of it and learn to love the characters as much as I do!

I'm constantly asked how many books will be in this series. My answer remains the same - I guess that depends on how long I live! My intention is to release two books a year – continuing to weave the lives of my characters into the times they lived. I hate to end a good book as much as anyone – always feeling so sad that I have to leave the characters. You shouldn't have to be sad for a long time!

You are now reading the 17th book - #18 (*Journey To Joy*) will be released in Summer 2020. If you like what you read, you'll want to make sure you're on my mailing list at www.BregdanChronicles.net. I'll let you know each time a new one comes out so that you can take advantage of all my fun launch events, and you can enjoy my BLOG in between books!

Many more are coming!

Sincerely,
Ginny Dye

Chapter One

Late September 1871

Carrie breathed in deeply, filling her lungs with the first cool air of fall. The day was going to be warm, but after a brutally hot summer, she was grateful for a morning that whispered autumn was just around the corner. Lured by the James River, she had risen early to watch the sun rise over the sparkling blue waters that flowed placidly.

Not wanting to disturb anyone in the house, she had left Anthony sleeping soundly in their bed and slipped through the tunnel to the banks of the river. She was settled on the log that held so many of her memories. She closed her eyes against the still fresh pain of the image that coursed through her. On Granite's last day, she'd been sitting in this very spot when he came up behind her and rested his head on her shoulder, his warm breath repeating the promise he had made earlier that day.

Later that night, she had held that same beautiful head as he gazed into her eyes, closed his own, and took his last breath.

She allowed the tears to flow as more memories flooded her.

The first moment she had seen him when she was thirteen; a prancing, rambunctious gelding whose gray coat glistened and gleamed in the sun like burnished pewter.

How he had immediately calmed when he saw her, lowering his head to come over and accept her caresses. Everyone had been astonished when he'd pressed his forehead against hers with a gentle nicker.

Long rides through every inch of the plantation.

Endless hours of talking to him about all the things she couldn't tell anyone else, even Rose.

Their escape from the Union soldiers.

She thought of the agonizing year when she'd feared both Robert and Granite had died during the war.

More images appeared in her mind.

The glorious sight of him carrying Robert home on the spring afternoon they'd returned to her.

Her father riding off on Granite at the fall of Richmond, and then returning to rebuild his life.

Granite had been a vital part of every moment of her life for almost seventeen years. No matter how hard she tried, even though she knew he was gone, she still couldn't envision life without him. She'd known this time was coming, but knowing and *experiencing* were two completely different things.

She couldn't walk into the barn without her eyes flying to his stall, waiting for his head to pop over the wooden door as he whinnied his joyful greeting. She had ridden a little since his death, but it only deepened her sense of loss. There would never be another horse like Granite.

A flock of geese startled her out of her reverie. Their loud honking was another sign that fall was almost upon them. The early migrants formed a perfect V as they followed the curves of the river, their silvery wings flashing in the sun as it crested the horizon.

"Anthony said I would find you here."

Carrie smiled but didn't look away from the geese. "He must have gotten up right after I left."

"He did," Rose agreed as she sat down. "Annie told him last night that she would be making cinnamon rolls this morning."

Carrie chuckled. "He wanted to make sure he got some before Moses and John invaded the kitchen."

Rose nodded. "Those fellows of mine can eat."

"Enough for ten men," Carrie said lightly. She was glad for her best friend to join her, but she didn't want to talk about what she was feeling.

As always, Rose understood. "It's a beautiful morning," she said calmly. "When I left, Annie had carried a huge platter of steaming buns out onto the porch. The aroma woke up everyone in the house."

Carrie was more than happy to talk about the weather and cinnamon buns. She swept away stray hairs from the long, black braid that cascaded down her back and returned her emerald green eyes to the sky. "The geese are coming in early this fall."

"Annie told me it's a sign that we'll have a hard winter."

Carrie raised a brow. "Annie is predicting the weather now?" She had never heard Rose's mother-in-law talk about the weather, other than to complain of hot or cold. Her domain was the kitchen.

Rose's eyes filled with amusement. "Well, Miles is predicting the weather. Annie is just repeating him."

"Then it's true. I've never known Miles to be wrong about the weather. If he says it's going to be a hard winter, we need to be ready for it. When I was little, he tried to warn my father a hard winter was coming. My father didn't believe him."

"The one and only time he didn't believe him?" Rose guessed.

"The one and only time," Carrie acknowledged. "We ran out of firewood that winter. It was freezing in the house for almost a month before spring came. More wood was cut, but it was too green to burn well. Father and I have gotten good at recognizing the signs of a hard winter, but Miles seems to know before there is even one smidgen of evidence. It's like he feels it somewhere deep inside him." That was most likely true. The elderly man, who had spent the majority of his life on the plantation as a slave before he escaped to Canada and stayed gone for eight years, had an innate wisdom that belied any rational explanation. She was grateful every single day that he'd chosen to return to the South and to Cromwell Plantation to live out the rest of his life. Aside from how much she loved him, he played an integral role as an employee of Cromwell Stables.

"Moses is taking Miles seriously. He hired extra men to start cutting firewood while everyone else brings in the harvest this year."

Carrie kept her eyes on the glistening water. "It's going to be another good crop."

"It is," Rose said proudly. Then she changed the subject. "I talked to Susan last night when I went down to pry John out of Cafi's stall."

Carrie smiled. It was no secret how much Rose's son, John, loved his chestnut gelding. "Let me guess. He wanted to skip dinner again."

"He did," Rose replied. "He insisted he wasn't hungry. Which makes it all the more miraculous that he polished off an entire chicken, along with a massive mound of mashed potatoes, green beans, and two pieces of blackberry pie." She shook her head dramatically. "He's only eight!"

"With a daddy who is a giant," Carrie reminded her. "Most people think John is at least twelve. He's determined to be as tall as Moses. He doesn't seem to understand he doesn't have to accomplish that before he's ten." She was repeating a discussion they'd had many times before, but she was determined to keep Rose from steering the conversation in the direction she was certain it was headed.

Rose nodded but didn't take the bait of a new line of conversation. "Susan told me more horses are arriving today."

Carrie kept her voice casual. "Yes. She purchased ten new broodmares from a stable in Kentucky. Clint went to pick them up in Richmond. They arrived very early this morning on the train. We thought it best that they unload when the Broad Street Station was quiet. The train can often be stressful for horses, but it's much better than riding them from Kentucky or paying for the expense of transporting them in horse vans." She was well aware she was providing more information than Rose cared about, but she hoped it keep her friend from asking more questions about her emotions.

"Susan told me there are some extremely fine mares arriving," Rose answered, once again not rising to the bait. "She told me several of them would be excellent riding horses."

"Probably," Carrie replied, turning back to stare at the river. A slight breeze kicked up, creating a flurry of ripples and small, dancing whitecaps. She took another deep breath, not wanting to lose the magic of the morning.

Rose remained quiet for several moments, but finally said what she had really come to say. "Don't you miss riding, Carrie?"

"I can ride any time I want to," Carrie said quietly. "Cromwell Stables has plenty of excellent horses."

"And yet, you rarely do."

Carrie knew distractions and changing the topic of conversation weren't going to work. She turned away from the river and met Rose's shining, dark eyes. "I can't." Her voice caught as she blinked back the tears that threatened. "Every time I get in the saddle, all I can do is think about Granite." She took a deep breath against the pain that wanted to explode inside her. She knew that Rose, and everyone else on the plantation, was aware of how much she had loved Granite, but...

Rose regarded her steadily. "It took John time before he could think of another horse replacing Rascal."

Carrie nodded but she knew the situations weren't the same. John lost his horse, Rascal, after the gelding was badly injured in the flood that nearly killed him and Moses. John had carried too much guilt to accept another horse, until Miles brought Cafi to the plantation.

She couldn't quite explain her reluctance to tell Rose what was really in her heart. The two best friends talked about everything, but she couldn't find a way to communicate what she didn't really understand herself. More importantly, she couldn't allow anyone to ridicule or disbelieve what she would say. The hope that she was right was the only thing enabling her to deal with the pain.

"The two of you had a very rare connection," Rose said gently.

Again, Carrie just nodded. She knew Rose loved her own mare, but it was nothing like the connection Carrie had shared with Granite. She didn't expect anyone to understand it. As she thought back to their last day together, she allowed Granite's promise to buffer the pain that engulfed her.

Rose reached out to take her hand. "I know I don't understand what you're feeling," she said softly. "I'm trying to," she added.

Carrie gulped, her friend's compassion close to shredding her last bit of self-control. "I miss him," she whispered. Much to her chagrin, the tears began to flow again.

Rose gripped her hand. "I know."

Carrie could feel the words Rose wasn't saying. *It will get easier. Another horse will come that you'll love just as much.*

Carrie knew that wasn't true. Suddenly, the words she was unwilling to say could no longer be contained. "Granite is coming back." She said it so quietly that she wasn't sure Rose would hear it over the lap of waves against the shore.

"Yes."

Carrie whipped her head around. "What did you say?"

"I said yes."

Carrie stared at her for several long moments, trying to read the inscrutable expression on Rose's face. "You don't think I'm crazy?"

"I think that life has mysteries we'll never truly understand. One of those mysteries is the connection you and Granite had." Rose's eyes brightened with curiosity. "Do you know *when* he's coming back?"

Carrie, amazed to be having this conversation, shook her head. "No. On top of all the grief, the not knowing makes it much harder. I don't know when he's coming back, and I don't know how I'll know." Her tears fell harder.

Rose laughed lightly. "If Granite is coming back, I'm fairly certain he'll know how to let you know. It seems to me that little issue is the smallest part of the equation."

Carrie wasn't certain whether having this conversation was making her feel better, or if it had diminished the power of the secret she'd been keeping tucked close to her heart.

"Does Anthony know?"

Carrie's long silence provided the answer.

"Why not?"

Carrie ducked her head and turned away to the river. "It's crazy to believe Granite is coming back," she blurted. "Except that I completely believe it." She was aware of the desperation in her voice. "It was the last day he was alive. Miles and I took the children down to my special place. While we were there, Granite and I had a..." She trailed off as she struggled to give voice to her thoughts. "... A moment." She smiled slightly. "We had a moment when it was as if we were the only two beings on the planet. He told me then."

"That he's coming back?"

Carrie listened closely for a hint of ridicule or disbelief in Rose's voice but heard nothing except curiosity. "Yes."

Rose gripped her hand more tightly. "I hope it's soon," she said softly.

"Me too," Carrie said softly. She turned away from the river. "Thank you."

Rose cocked a brow.

"Thank you for listening. Thank you for believing me...at least the best you can. Thank you for not making fun of me." She thought of all she'd been through with the woman perched next to her. "Thank you for being the best friend anyone could ever have."

Rose's response was to wrap her in a warm embrace. "I love you, Carrie." When she finally released her, she added, "Does this mean you're ready for a cinnamon roll?"

"Excuse me?"

Rose reached behind the log and pulled up a picnic basket. "Annie didn't want you to feel left out," she said, depositing a large cloth bundle in Carrie's lap.

Carrie smiled genuinely when she peeled back the cloth to reveal still warm cinnamon rolls. "Bless her," she murmured, inhaling the delicious aroma. "Want one?"

Rose snatched one quickly. "I'm starving," she announced. "It took all my self-control to not eat one on my way through the tunnel."

Silence enveloped them as she and Carrie attacked the treats.

When the rolls were devoured, Rose turned again to meet Carrie's eyes. "How do you feel about going to Philadelphia?"

Carrie frowned slightly. "I hate to leave the plantation right now, but Dr. Wild needs me. I would never tell him no after all he's done for me. Not to mention the fact that he's a good friend." As she spoke, she thought of the good-natured physician that had opened the doors of medicine to her during the Civil War and accepted her as an intern so she could obtain her surgical certification years later. He'd written to ask if she would come train his new assistant in the homeopathic remedies she'd used when she was with him. "I'm looking forward to seeing him, and Anthony and the girls are thrilled we're going as a family." She smiled. "Thank you for letting them miss school, Mrs. Samuels."

"Frances and Minnie are two of my best students," Rose said sincerely. "They'll catch up quickly. And if they don't, I'll be able to tutor them." Her lips quirked into a smile.

"That's what they're afraid of," Carrie laughed. "I'm not sure they're always thrilled with having their teacher under the same roof."

Rose shrugged. "They'll survive…and thank me in the future."

Carrie knew that was true. "While we're there, Frances and I are going to work together at the Moyamensing Clinic. I'm also looking forward to spending time with Faith."

"Have you heard from Faith?"

"I received a letter yesterday," Carrie said. "I'll share it with you when we get back to the house. Faith is doing well but says she can feel herself getting older. She doesn't think she'll live as long as Biddy did." There weren't many days that passed without her thinking about Biddy, the lively Irishwoman who had won her heart and taught her the power of the Bregdan Principle. "I hope she's wrong."

"I do too," Rose said fervently. "Faith is a special woman. Is she still helping at the clinic?"

"She helps with the books and keeps the patients full of Irish oatmeal cookies," Carrie said. "Frances is excited to spend time with when she's not working with me at the clinic."

Rose shook her head. "It's a shame that little girl can't just go ahead and be a doctor. She'd rather be with you at the clinic than at school. She talks constantly about homeopathic remedies and insists on collecting herbs for medicines during her walks to and from school. Some of the children are even coming to her when they feel unwell."

Carrie glowed with pride, remembering the day she'd rescued Frances from an Ohio orphanage. "She knows much more than I did at that age. She has a lot to learn, but I've never known anyone more passionate."

"Except her mama," Rose observed. "Frances gets her passion from you."

Carrie shook her head. Her adopted daughter had lost both parents to a flu outbreak in Ohio. "I believe she was passionate in the beginning because of me, but she has learned to truly love medicine because she's passionate about helping people. Losing her parents to the flu shaped who she is now. The more she learns, the more passionate she becomes."

"She recognizes the power she has to make a difference."

"Yes," Carrie agreed.

She fell silent as she thought about traveling to Philadelphia. They were leaving the plantation the next morning, spending the night in Richmond, and then taking the train the following day.

"What's bothering you?"

Carrie briefly considered denying that she was bothered, but then realized how futile it would be. She knew she couldn't hide anything from Rose, any more than Rose could hide things from her. "I don't know," she admitted.

"But something is bothering you?"

Carrie hesitated. "I'm feeling uneasy about something," she acknowledged. "But I don't know what. Janie is going to handle everything here at the plantation clinic. I'm excited to stay with Jeremy and Marietta. I'm eager to work with Dr. Wild, be at the clinic with Frances, and spend time with Faith. There is absolutely nothing to be uneasy about."

"Nothing that you know of," Rose offered. "Which changes nothing about how you feel."

Carrie sighed. "You're right. It doesn't really matter, however. We're leaving tomorrow. If there is something in Philadelphia to be uneasy about, I'll discover it in time."

Carrie and the others had barely finished lunch when they heard the sound of wagons rolling down the long driveway.

Susan pushed back her chair and stood, her blue eyes flashing with excitement. A long, blond braid swung across her shoulder as she spun toward the door. "Clint is here with the new mares! Come on, Carrie!"

Carrie jumped up to join her, eager to see the new broodmares. Somehow, telling Rose about her belief that Granite would return had freed her ability to embrace the horses being raised at Cromwell Stables. They'd had an extraordinarily good year, with their profits increasing steadily as the number and popularity of Eclipse's foals continued to grow.

Carrie stood on the porch, Abby and her father by her side, as they waited for the wagons to get closer.

Clint had taken two of the plantation men with him. Three horses were tied to the two wagons driven by the other men. Clint, at the front of the long line, had four horses secured to the wagon bed. The trip, normally a four to five-hour journey, had taken all morning because they had mostly walked. After a long journey on the train, they'd been careful to not add additional stress to the horses.

"They'll be glad to be here," Abby commented, her gray eyes shining with compassion. "What a long journey they've had."

"We have a pasture set aside for them," Carrie assured her mother. "They'll have plenty of time to recover."

Amber, her dark eyes sparkling with enthusiasm, ran up onto the porch to join them. "I can hardly wait to get my hands on them!"

Carrie laughed, understanding how Amber felt. The little girl who had saved Robert's life twice—once during the war and once right after the war—had turned into a tall, slender young woman who was arguably one of the finest horse trainers in the country. A large part of Cromwell Stables' success was due to Amber. Foals that she trained were in high demand.

"Will they be bred right away?" Abby asked.

"No," Amber said quickly. "Horses have an eleven-month gestation period. It's too late to breed them this year. We'll do that next spring."

Annie cocked her head. "I don't pretend to know much about them horses out in that barn, but I done been learnin' some things from Miles. Why you gonna be feedin' them horses all through the winter? Seems like it be better to buy them in the spring."

Thomas reached out and put a hand on her shoulder. "You may not know a lot about horses, but you obviously have a head for business. You're right."

"You and Father are both correct," Carrie acknowledged. "Normally, we would have waited until spring to make the purchase, but when we found out about these mares we couldn't pass up the opportunity to add them to the herd."

"Why?" Annie asked.

"Because their bloodline is exceptional," Amber replied, her entire body tense with anticipation.

Carrie knew the girl wanted to dash off the porch and run down the driveway to meet her brother and the horses. It was taking every bit of Amber's growing maturity to keep her where she was.

"Their sire is Lexington," Amber continued. "Robert taught me about him when he was recovering during the war. He laid in bed and told me stories about what a great horse Lexington is."

Carrie expected the twinge that came with the mention of her first husband, who had been murdered while saving Amber's life. She would feel it for the rest of her life. She had learned to live with it, glad to know the connection she and Robert had shared would never die. Her love for Anthony wasn't any less than her love had been for Robert, it meant she had room in her heart for both of them.

"Lexington was born in 1850. He's a Thoroughbred who won six of his seven race starts," Amber gushed. "He didn't race very many times, but they were grueling, four-mile races. When he was five years old, he ran a race in New Orleans where he set a record running four miles in seven minutes, nineteen and three-quarters seconds. He was the best racehorse of his day!" Her eyes grew sad. "Unfortunately, he had to be retired that year because of poor eyesight. His sire, Boston, also went blind."

"That's horrible!" Abby exclaimed. "What a loss."

Amber nodded. "Yes, but Lexington is still one of the greatest horses ever." A ringing neigh from the stables made her laugh. "Except for you, Eclipse!" she called loudly to the stable stud. "You'll always be my favorite!" Another ringing neigh filled the air.

"Anyway," Amber said, returning to her recital when everyone quit laughing, "Lexington has been the leading stud in the country for the last ten years. Robert used to dream of having horses with Lexington's lineage. His sons and daughters are among the most coveted horses in America. Robert would be so proud of what is happening today."

Abby leaned forward as the horses drew closer. "These ten horses are Lexington's daughters?"

Susan entered the conversation. "They are. I found out their owner is in financial trouble and had to sell all his stock. I made him an offer he couldn't refuse." She grinned with satisfaction. "Of course, I told him it was contingent upon the horses being the quality he said they were." Her grin broadened. "Evidently they are or Clint wouldn't be leading ten horses right now."

Carrie grinned along with her. "I love having a brilliant partner," she said happily. The profits from Cromwell Stables made it possible to continue to expand the clinic and treat patients who couldn't afford to pay for care. She spent time in the barn every day, but it was Susan who oversaw all the operations. Clint was the stable manager.

Suddenly, a chorus of whinnies split the air. All the horses that had been grazing moments before in the verdant green pastures were now rushing to press up against the white fencing that lined the drive.

"They're saying hello," Amber cried. Her patience worn thin, she leapt from the porch and raced the last several hundred yards up the driveway to meet her brother and the mares.

Carrie and Susan followed at a more measured pace.

Carrie's heart pounded with excitement as the horses drew closer. Even after their arduous journey, it was obvious these were quality mares. Their conformation was perfect and their heads were up, their eyes alert as they took in their new surroundings. They were curious but not alarmed. Carrie knew they had endured a long trip, but there was no place in the world that would give them better care than Cromwell Stables. "Welcome home," she said softly.

Amber was already walking from horse to horse, examining them as she went.

"They're gorgeous," Susan breathed. "I can hardly wait to see the foals that will come from their breeding with Eclipse."

"Welcome home, Clint!" Carrie called. "Did everything go well?"

"Without a hitch," Clint drawled, his smile gleaming against his dark skin. "The station master was surprised when a black man came to collect these fine mares, but Thomas' letter did the trick. Either that or he didn't really care what happened at four o'clock in the morning."

Carrie sighed. There were days when the ignorance and prejudice in the South made her weary beyond words, but she chose to be grateful there had been no trouble. "They're magnificent," she said as he pulled the lead wagon to a halt.

"That they are," Clint agreed cheerfully. "Perfect conformation, and they all have a sweet disposition."

At that moment, the bay mare closest to him snorted loudly and stomped her foot as she pulled back on the rope latched to her thick leather halter. Her eyes were locked on Carrie.

Carrie and Susan laughed.

"You're right to be impatient," Carrie said soothingly as she stepped forward to untie the mare, reaching up to stroke her neck. "You're home now, girl. You're home." She attached a lead line to the halter and walked the mare forward. "I'll get her some water, groom the dust from her, and then take her to the pasture." She glanced up at Clint. "What is this beautiful lady's name?"

"No Regrets."

Carrie turned and stared at him. "No Regrets?"

Clint shrugged. "It's the name on her registration papers. The stable manager came with the mares to make sure they were cared for during the train ride. I asked him about the name. Evidently, the owner's wife had a thing about living with no regrets. This mare was hers."

Carrie smiled with delight and then sobered as she thought about how bereft the woman must have been to lose her mare because of finances. Carrie would write her to let her know her horse was in good hands. "It's a perfect name." No Regrets snorted again and bobbed her head before she turned in the direction of the barn. "I'm coming," Carrie assured the eager mare.

Within an hour, all the mares had been untied, watered, groomed, and turned out into the pasture that would separate them from the other horses until they had a chance to adjust to their new home. Within a week, they would be introduced to more of the horses.

Once the work was done, Carrie joined Susan and Amber in the pasture. They wanted the mares to get to know them. The moment Carrie stepped through the gate, No Regrets stopped grazing and walked over to her, greeting her with a gentle whinny.

"She likes you," Susan observed.

"She's a beautiful mare," Carrie responded, drawn to the gentle yet spirited sparkle in No Regrets' eyes. Carrie stroked her neck softly and raised her hand to rub around her ears, before caressing the white star that was the only marking on her dark body. The mare closed her eyes and sighed.

"She's in heaven," Amber said with a giggle.

"Will you ride her?" Susan asked carefully.

Carrie surprised herself when she nodded. "I will." She wanted to laugh at Susan's look of relief. She would never have another horse of her own until Granite returned, but No Regrets was a fine mare. It would be fun to introduce her to the plantation. It was time.

"I'm going to be gone for a little while, girl," Carrie said regretfully, suddenly sad to be leaving.

No Regrets opened her eyes and stared at her in protest, but then closed them again in resignation.

"I'll be back before you know it," Carrie said gently. "You'll be fine." She didn't understand the instant bond she felt with the beautiful mare, but she knew better than to deny it.

Susan cleared her throat when the three of them stepped back into the cool interior of the barn. "I have some news to share. I want you two to be the first to know."

Carrie pushed aside her thoughts of Philadelphia and gave Susan all of her attention. She could tell by Susan's tone of voice that whatever she had to say was important. "I'm listening."

"Me too," Amber said. "You sound serious."

"More like seriously happy," Susan replied with a wide grin. "It appears that Harold and I are going to be parents."

Carrie laughed and pulled her into a hug. "You're pregnant? What wonderful news!"

"A baby?" Amber squealed. "That's fantastic!"

Susan continued to grin. "We've wanted a child ever since we got married. We're not getting any younger, you know. We're quite excited!"

"Thirty is not too old to have your first child," Carrie assured her. "Janie and I will take good care of you."

"I have no doubt of that," Susan answered with a laugh. Then she looked serious. "Don't either of you think I'm going to stop working, though. My mother rode horses until the day I was born. I intend to do the same."

Carrie tensed, remembering her desperate ride back to the plantation when Robert was dying. She would always wonder if it had been the long, hard trip that had killed her daughter Bridget before she was born. Carrie tried to keep her voice light when she responded. "May I recommend moderation?"

"You may," Susan said quickly. "I'm not going to be foolish, but I don't want everyone fawning over me like I'm a weakling."

"My mama says any woman that can have a baby is the strongest person she knows," Amber said. "No one could ever think you're weak, Susan."

Carrie could tell by the expression on Amber's face that she was remembering Robert and Bridget's deaths, too.

Sudden understanding spread over Susan's face. "I'm sorry!" she cried. "I didn't realize how selfish and thoughtless I was being."

"Hush," Carrie said firmly. "There isn't a selfish or thoughtless bone in your body. You're excited. Just as you should be. I know you'll be wise, and we'll be right here to help you through everything. We'll support you in everything you want to do, and we'll take care of the things you think you can't." She laughed lightly. "Seems like you should give birth about the same time as our current herd of broodmares. It will be an exciting time."

Susan looked anxiously from Carrie to Amber and let a broad smile spread across her face again. "Thank you both!"

A sudden flurry of activity sounded outside the barn. Moments later, fourteen-year-old Frances and nine-year-old Minnie burst through the door.

"Mama!" Minnie called.

Carrie felt a moment of alarm, hating that she was always anticipating trouble, but the looks of joy on her daughters' faces quickly dispelled any worries. She smiled down at the freckled-faced redhead as she skidded to a halt. "Hello, Minnie. How was school?"

"Fine," Minnie said dismissively. "We want to go riding! Peaches is going to miss Frances while we're in Philadelphia, and I would surely love to go for one last swim before summer is over," she said persuasively, her blue eyes growing wide for emphasis." Will you go with us for a long ride?"

"And have a picnic down by the river?" Frances added eagerly.

Carrie pushed aside thoughts of everything she had to do before they left in the morning. It would all get done. How could she turn down her girls? She had chosen to close the Bregdan Clinic in Richmond so she wouldn't have to be away from her daughters. "Absolutely," she replied. "I can't think of anything I would rather do."

The girls clapped their hands happily.

"Do you want to come with us, Amber?" Minnie asked.

"Not this time," Amber said. "I've still got to work with three of the horses but when you come back, I'll show you the new mares that came today."

"Yippee!" Minnie cried.

Carrie laughed as she watched her daughter twirl with delight. She could hardly believe this was the same little girl who had lost her entire family to a fire in a Philadelphia tenant building just nine months earlier. Minnie lived life with a vibrant joy that infected everyone around her. Though Frances was five years older, the two girls were best friends, as well as sisters. Minnie's infectious enthusiasm was a perfect balance to Frances' serious passion.

"Who are you going to ride, Mama?" Minnie asked.

Carrie turned to Amber. "Who needs exercise?"

Relief crossed Amber's face. "Please take Queen. I was going to ride her later. She's coming along well. Her new owner will be here to pick her up next month."

Carrie felt a surge of remorse. Her reluctance to ride had put more of a strain on Amber's time. The girl never complained, but it had to be exhausting. Carrie thought quickly and then turned to Frances. "The two of you need to go change. Ask your daddy and Abby to join us. She'll love spending time with you before you leave in the morning, and it will be two fewer horses Amber will have to exercise."

Amber laughed. "In that case, I'm going to join you."

"Me too," Susan said with a smile. "It's a perfect afternoon for a ride and swim. Fall will be here soon. We should make the most of these warm days while we still can."

Carrie was thrilled, but the talk of leaving in the morning pulled forward that same uneasy feeling. She shook her head impatiently. Whatever was in Philadelphia would have to be dealt with when they arrived. Right now, she was going to create memories with the people she loved.

Chapter Two

The sun was perched atop the trees when Carrie rode up to the barn. The afternoon had been a glorious success. After a long ride, their troop had ended up on the banks of the James River, where they spread out quilts on the shore, and plunged into the sparkling waters. Still warm from the long, hot summer, the water was both embracing and exhilarating.

Even Abby had joined in the fun, splashing into the water in her riding breeches, and then dancing with her granddaughters, who laughed and shrieked with joy.

Anthony and Thomas had found a deep hole in the calm river and thrilled all the girls by tossing them high in the air so they could splash back down.

They ate the picnic Annie had quickly packed for them as they dried off on the riverbank. Mounds of fried chicken and ham biscuits had been devoured. They were all looking forward to the blackberry cobbler Annie had waiting for them at the house.

"I'm tired, Mama," Minnie said woefully as they dismounted outside the barn. She leaned against her mare, Wisteria, and yawned.

"I'm sure you are," Carrie answered sympathetically. "So is Wisteria. You can go up to the house as soon as you groom, water, and feed her.

Don't forget to put your saddle and bridle in the tack room."

Minnie made a pitiful face. "But I'm real tired, Mama. Could you do it for me this time?"

"Was I the one who rode her?" Carrie asked gently. Minnie was only nine, but that was plenty old enough to be responsible.

Minnie looked away. "No," she admitted.

"I'm sure everyone is tired after such a fun time. Should I take care of all their horses, too?" Carrie could see Minnie struggling with her answer. What the little girl really wanted to say was that her mama should take care of hers because she was the youngest, but she knew better.

"No, Mama," Minnie finally said. "I should take care of Wisteria myself."

"That's my girl," Carrie said warmly. "I'm proud of you for being so grown up." Minnie didn't look any happier, but Carrie was glad when she saw her daughter's shoulders straighten with determination. "Annie has blackberry cobbler waiting for us when we're all done," Carrie reminded her.

Minnie released the last of her self-pity and smiled brightly. "I can hardly wait!"

"Me either," Carrie assured her, deciding to turn it into a game. "Let's race to see who gets done the fastest. Whoever makes it to the house first will get the first bowl of cobbler."

"That will be me!" Frances called as she disappeared into the tack room with her saddle and bridle. "I'm ahead of both of you."

Carrie exchanged a look with Minnie. "Which only means we need to start moving really fast."

Minnie laughed and sprang into action.

Rose and Moses were settled into rocking chairs on the porch when Carrie and the rest converged on the house. John and Hope were on the lawn, chasing the last fireflies of the season as they rose from the grass and the forest floor. Bright flashes of light emanated from the dusk that was rapidly claiming the plantation.

"I'm going to miss this," Anthony said quietly.

"Me too," Carrie responded as she gazed up at her tall, lean husband. "Having second thoughts about going to Philadelphia?"

"Not a chance," Anthony assured her. "I wouldn't miss the trip with you and the girls for the world, but it doesn't mean I won't miss Cromwell Plantation. As far as I'm concerned, it's the most beautiful place on the planet. We'll only be gone two weeks, but I'll be eager to come home."

Carrie agreed with him. She paused to gaze at the columned, three-story house that glowed white in the encroaching darkness. The oak trees she had grown up with spread wide arms across the lawn. The cool weather had produced just the tiniest hint of yellow in the leaves. Soon, they would be clothed in magnificent color. Manicured boxwoods lined the drive. Cromwell Plantation had been home her entire life. It was thrilling to know she was now raising her daughters here. "After this trip, we'll be home for the rest of the year," Carrie promised him. "Except for your trips to Richmond, of course."

Anthony nodded. "Willard and Marcus are taking over more and more of the operations at River City Carriages. I won't have to leave as much as I used to."

Carrie squeezed his hand happily.

"Annie left a big pan of cobbler on the kitchen table for y'all," Moses called out lazily.

"You mean you and John left some?" Anthony called back.

Carrie shook her head. The competition for Annie's cooking had simply become part of life on the plantation.

"Only because we didn't know it was there," Moses replied good-naturedly. "She told John that it was a sad day when she had to hide food from her grandson just to make sure others could eat."

Carrie chuckled. "I might have forgiven him, but I don't think Frances and Minnie would have."

"Nor would I!" Anthony retorted.

"Nor I," Abby added. She climbed the steps to the porch slowly, her arm linked with Thomas'. "Since I'm the oldest female in this group, does that entitle me to be served here on the porch? I'm quite certain I can't take another step until I've been strengthened by Annie's cobbler." Without waiting for an answer, she sank down in a comfortable rocking chair, leaned her head back, and closed her eyes.

Carrie gazed at her with sudden concern and took a step forward.

Without opening her eyes, Abby spoke again. "You can stop looking at me like that right now, Carrie Wallington. There is nothing wrong with me. I'm tired. I'm also not above using my age to get waited on by my daughter." She opened her eyes slightly and smiled. "Go get me some blackberry cobbler."

Carrie laughed loudly as she stepped forward to plant a kiss on the top of Abby's head. "Coming right up," she promised. She waved her hand at the chairs. "Everyone have a seat. I won't have any trouble bringing everything out."

Anthony shook his head. "You bring out the cobbler. I'll bring out lemonade and tea for everyone."

"Hot tea for me," Abby said. "This day is going to cool off quickly."

"Your wish is my command, good lady," Anthony said gallantly.

It hadn't taken long for Frances, Minnie, John, and Hope to go up to bed after eating their cobbler. Carrie leaned back in the rocker and took a deep breath. "We have great husbands."

"We do," Rose agreed. "It was wonderful of them to tuck the children in. I don't have the energy to move right now." She shook her head. "Moses should be more tired than I am, but he insists I have the easier job."

"He's right," Carrie said lazily. "Riding out in the tobacco fields all day is much easier than handling a school full of rambunctious children."

"That's what he says," Rose replied. "But I love doing it."

"Loving something doesn't make it any less exhausting," Carrie answered. "I love working in the clinic, but there are days it takes everything out of me." She changed the subject. "How is Hazel doing?"

Rose smiled brightly. "Hazel is a godsend. I thought having to separate the schools would be a nightmare, but Phoebe is doing a wonderful job with the white students, and all my students have fallen in love with Hazel. She connected with them instantly. Most importantly, she's a good teacher. It's still completely ridiculous that our children can't all learn together, but I'm not willing to risk the Board shutting us down."

Carrie scowled. "That still makes me so angry I could spit nails."

"Careful. When my wife is ready to spit nails, dangerous things can happen." Anthony appeared out of the darkness with Moses.

Carrie smiled at him when he claimed the rocker next to her. "Thank you for putting Minnie to bed."

"I was happy to," Anthony said. "Of course, that means it's your job to wake the girls in the morning."

Carrie groaned. "I didn't think that through very well. They're going to be less than thrilled to be awoken so early."

"Just bribe them with the promise of May's apple pie when they reach Richmond," Abby suggested.

Carrie brightened. "That should do the trick." She pulled a blanket up to snuggle under. "Regardless, I'm happy I didn't have to move tonight."

"You'll have to come to bed at some point," Anthony teased.

Carrie pretended to pout. "Won't my wonderful husband carry me to bed?"

Anthony laughed. "I'll do my best, but I won't be responsible if I drop you while going up the staircase."

Carrie stuck her tongue out at him playfully.

"What are you ready to spit nails about?" Moses asked.

"Stupid people," Carrie said bluntly as she returned to the conversation she'd been having with Rose. "I still can't believe the Board of Education has mandated segregation of the schools. All that's doing is making things harder for black children. Most of them won't have access to schools like the one we have here. The Board of Education says there will be equal facilities, but it doesn't take a genius to know that won't happen," she said angrily. Talking about it raised her ire even more. "The separation will also make it harder for blacks and whites to develop relationships that could end their prejudices." Weariness pressed down on her.

"All true," Moses said evenly.

"You don't sound angry," Carrie observed.

"Oh, I'm angry," Moses replied. He paused for a long moment. "I just figure I have to put my focus on what I can change. We've changed things here on the plantation. Our children are in different buildings, but they come together every day at the community playground and picnic shelter. We're following the letter of the law, while doing what we know is right."

"But what about all the other children here in Virginia?" Carrie demanded. She wasn't sure why she was pushing this issue so hard tonight. They'd discussed it many times since the mandate had come down from the Board of Education during the summer.

Moses eyed her, obviously wondering the same thing. "What has you so riled up, Carrie?"

Carrie sighed heavily. "I don't know," she admitted. "Perhaps it's our trip to Philadelphia. Marietta wrote me about the upcoming election." As soon as she said the words, she knew why she was uneasy about going to Philadelphia. "She's afraid there will be violence. I'm just so sick of the prejudice and fighting."

"I understand," Moses replied. "All any of us can do is to just do our part. My part is to run a plantation that provides good-paying jobs to good men. Rose's job is to create the best school she can for the children around here. Your job is to provide medical care and let people know they matter."

Carrie sighed again. "You're right. I realize this is something we've discussed many times. Why don't we change the subject?" She was grateful when Abby reached beneath the blanket to grasp her hand. Her mother always knew when her emotions were in turmoil.

"A letter came from Elizabeth today," Rose said promptly.

Her fatigue and anger forgotten, Carrie sat up straighter. "What did it say?"

"I have no idea," Rose answered. "It's addressed to you and Janie. I didn't open it."

"Did Janie?"

"She hasn't been to the house today. Annabelle has a bad cold, so she went straight home to care for her."

Carrie was so grateful the guest house was finished. The main house had been packed to capacity before it was completed. It was only a hundred yards from the main house, but it was so tucked away in a thick grove of trees that you couldn't see it, providing privacy for everyone.

Janie, Matthew, and their children, Annabelle and Robert, had moved into two of the bedrooms. Hazel and Phoebe, the two new teachers who were best friends from Oberlin College, were in the other two rooms. Matthew had begun work on a new home for his family now that Janie had chosen to stay on the plantation to work at the clinic, but it wouldn't be ready for another month or so.

As if summoned by her thoughts, Matthew appeared at the foot of the steps. "Mind some company?"

"You're always welcome," Anthony said. "We miss having all of you in the house. We also happen to have enough blackberry cobbler left for you."

Matthew ran lightly up the stairs. "Well, I had some while you were out riding, but I'll never turn down Annie's cobbler."

"How is Annabelle?" Carrie asked. "I didn't know she was sick until a few moments ago."

"Better," Matthew assured her. "Janie is treating her with the onion compresses, and she set a bowl of onions next to her bed. If Robert is thinking about getting this cold, the onions will scare him right out of it." He wrinkled his nose.

Carrie laughed. "It doesn't matter what it smells like as long as it works!" She turned back to Rose. "Where is the letter? I can't wait to see what Elizabeth has to say. It's the first letter since she returned to Boston."

Rose smiled, reached into her pocket, and pulled out a thick envelope. "I knew you would feel that way."

Anthony turned up the flame on the lantern and placed it on the table closest to Carrie. "This should do the trick."

Carrie tore open the envelope quickly. Aware of the eyes fastened on her in anticipation, she scanned the first page and then began to read.

Dear Carrie and Janie,

Greetings from Boston. What a joy it is to be home with my family again. And, yes, I will admit it's wonderful to be out of Richmond's prejudice and violence...not to mention the summer heat and humidity! It was such a hard decision to leave all of you, but I know I made the right choice. I suppose the Richmonders were right all along. I'm a true Italian Yankee!

Carrie waited until the quiet laughs died down before she continued.

My parents adore Peter, just as I knew they would. My father told Peter that if he was brave enough to take me on as his wife, then he already had all his respect. The thing is, I completely agree. I'm not sure my wonderful fiancé has any idea what he's really signing up for, but I've never been happier.

We've set a date for the wedding! It will be Saturday, April twenty-seventh. I'm counting on all of you being there as promised. Yes, I'm going to hold you to your promise. If it were up to Peter and me, we would have gotten married at the plantation before we left, but that would have broken my mother's heart. She's already told me she didn't think I would find a man who could handle my independence, but since I did, she's going to plan the most extravagant wedding of the season. I'm overwhelmed by the thought, but at least I'll be busy working with Father. Mother promises she'll take care of almost everything. I have no problem letting her!

I'm working with Father at his practice. I love treating our patients with him. We've created a wonderful blend of traditional and homeopathic medicine. More women are coming now that I'm here. I see the same kind of connection among our women patients that I saw at the Bregdan Clinic. I will always be grateful for the things I learned there.

Carrie paused for a moment. She felt the same gratitude. She knew they had all made the right choice to close the Bregdan Clinic, but she still had twinges of sadness for what they had walked away from in Richmond. She would forever be grateful for the things the experience had taught her.

Dr. Rebecca Crumpler sends her greetings.

"Isn't she the black doctor from Boston who worked for the Freedmen's Bureau here in Richmond until this spring?" Matthew asked. "Peter wrote a series of articles that included information about her."

"Yes," Carrie responded. "Rebecca is a delightful woman and a magnificent doctor. She also happens to be the first black woman to become a physician in the United States. She told us she had grown weary of the South. I know she's happy to be back home."

Carrie picked up the letter again.

One of the first things I did was visit Rebecca at her new clinic. She opened it in her house. Her practice is solely for women and children, regardless of whether or not they can pay. My father was so impressed with what she's doing, that he's making donations so she can treat more patients.

"How perfect," Abby said happily as she cast a sideways glance at her husband.

Thomas laughed, his silver hair glowing in the lantern light. "Yes, my dear, I agree that we should send funds to Dr. Crumpler's clinic. I also have connections in Boston that I believe I can persuade to help."

"Thank you!" Carrie cried. "Rebecca will be thrilled." She turned back to the letter.

Peter is leaving for Chicago for a journalists' conference on October second. While he's there, he's also traveling up to Peshtigo, Wisconsin to visit an old college roommate. They haven't seen each other in years, so he's quite excited. He wanted me to join him, but I don't want to leave the clinic so soon after returning home. I know I'll miss him, but I also have to get used to the lifestyle of a journalist.

"I'm happy those days are behind me," Matthew said ruefully.

"Janie is even happier," Abby replied. "She quite loves having her book author husband home with her most of the time."

"No more than I love it," Matthew responded. "I don't regret all the years I spent roaming the country to cover stories that needed to be told, but I'm glad it's over. At least I thought it was…"

Thomas leaned forward when Matthew's voice trailed off. "Meaning?"

Matthew shook his head and waved his hand. "Finish the letter from Elizabeth, Carrie. What I have to say can wait."

Carrie hesitated but knew her friend wouldn't budge. His stubbornness was as legendary as his red hair. The faster she read the letter, the sooner they would learn the meaning of Matthew's cryptic comment. "I'm almost done," she said as she turned to the last page.

I hope all is going well. While I don't miss Richmond, I dearly miss the plantation. It does my heart good to think of all of you there, working and living together. I know the winter here in Boston will be brutal, but I've learned a shorter, less brutal winter doesn't make up for the prejudice and narrow-minded thinking I found in the South.

I admire and respect both of you for your commitment to create change in the South. I'm going to do my part up here and count the days until you all arrive for the wedding.

All my love,
Elizabeth

"She sounds happy," Rose said. "I'm so glad for her. And for Peter. They're perfect for each other."

Carrie nodded as she folded the letter and slid it back into the envelope. "Elizabeth struggled to make the decision to leave because she thought she would be letting us down. I believe we're all exactly where we're supposed to be." She handed the letter to Matthew. "Please take this to Janie."

"*After* you tell us what your comment meant," Thomas added.

Matthew smiled. "I've received an offer I might have difficulty refusing."

"You have us intrigued," Abby said. "Don't even think of dragging out the story for creative value."

Matthew laughed out loud. "I wouldn't think of it. Besides, I know so much about this because of you and Thomas." He leaned forward in his chair. "When you returned from New York City in July, you told us about Boss Tweed."

Thomas frowned. "That arrogant, corrupt politician who is doing his best to bankrupt New York City by fulfilling his own greedy desires? What has he done now?"

"He's been arrested," Matthew said bluntly. "Have you ever heard of Thomas Nast?"

"Wally Stratford told me something about him," Thomas replied. "He's a political cartoonist for *Harper's Weekly*, a publication in New York."

"Thomas Nast is also a friend of mine. We met when I spent an extended time in New York City several years ago. We've stayed in contact."

"Wally told me his political cartoons have played a huge role in exposing Boss Tweed," Thomas said. "If I remember correctly, Tweed said that he didn't care about newspaper coverage because his constituents can't read, but he hates Nast's cartoons because they're pictures that people can understand."

Matthew chuckled. "That's true. Thomas Nast's mission in life is bringing down Boss Tweed. Tweed tried to buy him off so he would leave the city, but it only made him intensify his attack."

"Evidently he succeeded in his mission," Moses said. "I don't see what Boss Tweed's arrest has to do with you, though."

"Nast wants me to come to New York City for the trial," Matthew revealed.

"Why?" Thomas asked.

"Because Matthew has spent so much of his career exposing corruption and pressing for change," Abby said proudly. "Nast wants him to see that change can happen."

Matthew smiled and reached out to take her hand. "You're right, Abby."

"Of course I am," Abby said. "Don't forget that I've watched your career since before the war. Your articles helped save me when Philadelphia businessmen attacked me for taking over my first husband's factories. I couldn't have made it through without you, my dear." She cocked her head. "Are you going?"

"I don't know," Matthew said. "I have a house to finish building, and I'm not quite done with my newest book. I can't miss my deadline."

"Surely the trial isn't starting right away?" Thomas inserted.

"No," Matthew acknowledged. "It probably won't start until the end of October."

"Do you *want* to be there?" Carrie asked, curious about his hesitancy. She had witnessed his passion for journalism over the years. She had also, as had everyone else, seen the stories he was covering almost destroy him.

Matthew remained silent for a long moment. "Yes," he finally acknowledged. Then he shook his head. "I still must have a home for my family before winter." He glanced at Thomas. "I know you said we could stay in the guest house for as long as needed, but I'd like to have Janie and the children in our own home before winter hits."

"My men can help with that after the harvest," Moses offered. "We start harvesting the tobacco next week. I figure the last wagons will head to Richmond by the middle of October. I can assign three men to help you after that."

"That's very generous of you," Matthew said warmly.

"I'd give you more men, but Miles is sure this winter is going to be harsh. With so many more people on the plantation, I'm going to have a lot of men cutting firewood to make sure we have a big enough supply through the winter," Moses said.

"Three will be all I need," Matthew said quickly. "I'll get as much done as possible in the next two weeks. If the house is finished and my book is completed in time to make a trip to New York, I'll go. It would be nice to see Boss Tweed brought down, and I would love to visit Thomas Nast."

"Hello!"

Everyone on the porch startled to attention as a call came from the darkness.

Carrie knew it was too late for visitors, which could only mean there was trouble. She pushed aside her fatigue and waited to see what was in store.

Chapter Three

Moses and Anthony stepped forward to the edge of the porch, their tall bodies outlined by the lantern light.

"Who's there?" Moses called, his deep voice ringing out authoritatively.

"It's me. Franklin."

Franklin was Moses' assistant, well-loved and much respected.

Carrie remained tense. Franklin's appearance this late in the evening was unusual. Her thoughts flew to his Navajo wife, Chooli, and their two children. She mentally prepared herself to spring into action.

"What's wrong?" Moses called as he walked down the steps.

Franklin emerged from the darkness, accompanied by two other men. It was too dark to see anything but shapes. "My friends need some help."

No one asked whether it could have waited until morning. If Franklin was here late in the evening, it was because he believed it was necessary.

Franklin looked toward the porch. "Are any of the children still up?" he asked quietly, just loud enough for his voice to carry.

"They're all in bed," Moses assured him.

"Then everyone should hear this," Franklin said, his voice a mixture of anger and resignation.

Moses turned and beckoned for them to join him. The two men with Franklin hesitated for several moments before they slowly climbed the stairs.

Carrie barely controlled her gasp when the two men drew close enough to the lantern light for their faces to be seen clearly. Both of them had been severely beaten; their faces swollen and disfigured.

"This is Morris and Vincent," Franklin began.

Morris was tall and scarecrow slender, with bowed shoulders that broadcast a sense of defeat. Vincent was shorter and rounder, his body radiating both despair and defiance.

"Welcome to Cromwell Plantation," Abby said warmly.

Thomas stood, walked forward, and extended his hand. "Welcome to Cromwell Plantation," he echoed. "My name is Thomas Cromwell. Everyone here is family or friends. You're safe," he said firmly. He waved an arm toward three empty rocking chairs. "Please have a seat."

"Can't be takin' your seat," Morris muttered as he shook his head. Fear radiated from his whole being.

"I'll stand," Vincent said.

Carrie looked at Vincent closely. Even with his swollen face, and what seemed to be a badly mutilated eye, she could tell he was well-spoken. Her curiosity and horror grew.

"Tell us what happened," Moses said simply. "Why are you here?"

Franklin was the one who answered. "Morris and Vincent are from South Carolina. One week ago, they were attacked by the KKK."

Carrie tensed as anger coursed through her. "Why?" she asked through gritted teeth. To her surprise, it was Vincent who responded.

"The situation in South Carolina is out of control," he said clearly. "The KKK is out to destroy the Republican Party and all the blacks who support it."

"Including Robert Scott?" Matthew asked keenly. "My understanding was that as a white Republican from Ohio, Governor Scott was going to do the right thing for the blacks in South Carolina."

Vincent shrugged. "I believe he wanted to. The problem is that while Governor Scott and the Republicans supposedly hold the authority, the leaders of the white community hold the real power in South Carolina. The Governor worked hard to protect the black folks for a while after he took office three years ago, but the KKK has gotten too powerful. He won't declare martial law, and he's holding back the militia because he's afraid of more bloodshed."

"He's not protecting you?" Matthew snapped.

Vincent met his eyes. "Things have gotten worse since last November. The KKK schedules nightly rides to terrorize all the black folks so they won't vote."

"And to make real sure we know our place," Morris added thickly, forcing the words through still swollen lips.

"What about the Ku Klux Klan Act that Congress passed back in April?" Anthony asked. "That was supposed to stop the violence."

Vincent shrugged again. "Back in March, the governor disbanded the black militia units in several counties. It was a compromise to the whites who said they would do everything in their power to try to restore law and order."

Carrie winced. The way he said it showed just how ridiculous an attempt it had been. Even with his swollen face, and what seemed to be a badly mutilated eye, he was well-spoken. This was a man who had an education

"They took away your ability to protect yourself and made you vulnerable to attack," Matthew said sharply.

"That's the truth of it," Vincent replied. "The federal government sent down some troops, but the KKK greatly outnumbers them. A few months back, President Grant threatened to send more, so the KKK *officially* called off the nightly raids."

"*Officially*, meaning the KKK is still doing them," Thomas said angrily.

"All the reports we received said they were still happening," Vincent responded.

"Somethin' sho'nuff happened a week ago," Morris said wearily.

Carrie watched as he swayed in place, and she could see the same bone-deep weariness etched on Vincent's face. She stood abruptly. "Enough questions and talking," she said crisply. She strode forward and took Vincent's hand, and then grabbed Morris' hand, aware of the shocked expressions on their faces when she touched them. She could feel the fever scorching their bodies. "My name is Dr. Carrie Wallington. Both of you are in pain and exhausted. You have fevers, which means there is infection. You need help. Any other questions can be answered after I've treated your wounds and you've gotten some rest."

Carrie turned to Franklin. "How did you get here?"

"We walked," Franklin admitted.

"Where are Vincent and Morris staying?"

"We're still figuring that out," Franklin answered. "They only got here an hour or so ago."

Miles appeared at the base of the porch. "You put those men up in mine and Annie's room," he stated. "We'll come on over here for the night. I heard me enough to know they need you to take care of them and get some good rest."

Carrie smiled her gratitude at him. "That will be perfect. Y'all help them over to the barn. I'll be right over with my medical bag and supplies." She saw Vincent open his mouth to argue, but then his shoulders sagged with relief. She could only imagine what these men had been through to get to Virginia from South Carolina in one week.

"Thank you," he said quietly.

Carrie rushed into the house, her fatigue forgotten.

Matthew was right behind her. "Do you want me to get Janie?"

Carrie thought quickly. "No. At least not now. I believe I can take care of things. She'll need to care for them when I leave for Philadelphia. She needs to be at home with Annabelle in case she gets sicker. I'll take care of them tonight. Rose and Abby can help me."

Anthony walked in just in time to hear her comment. "You're going to be exhausted if you stay up to care for these men. We can delay our trip to Philadelphia."

Carrie forced a smile. "Dr. Wild is expecting me. I won't delay our trip, but you have nothing to worry about. Don't forget I was a doctor during the war. I know about exhaustion, my love. One night won't kill me."

Anthony locked eyes with Matthew. "We both know that tone of voice. Carrie is going to do what she believes is right, which means she's going to treat those men." He turned back to Carrie. "Is there anything we can do to help?"

"Bring me some nightclothes for them to wear. I'll need plenty of hot water so they can bathe after I clean and treat their wounds. All we could see were their faces, but I'm afraid the rest of their bodies were just as badly beaten." She grabbed up her medical bag, checked it quickly to make sure she had everything she needed, and then turned toward the door. Just before she reached it, she swung back around. "Will this ever stop?"

Not waiting for an answer that no one had, she turned and left.

Carrie ached for the fear and resigned uncertainty she saw on Vincent and Morris' faces when she entered Miles and Annie's cozy room above the barn.

Rose and Abby were waiting for her.

"Annie is already heating water for you. She'll send it over as it gets hot." Abby smiled gently. "We're here to help you any way we can."

"Tell us what you need," Rose said.

Carrie understood the worried anger in her friend's voice. Moses and Rose gave everything they could to improve life for their people. Tonight was more evidence of how achingly far they still had to go. They knew the plantation buffered them against the stark reality of what most blacks dealt with all over the South.

Carrie turned to the two men. "I know you're exhausted, but I want to treat your wounds before you go to sleep. Will you allow me to do that?"

"You don't have to do it tonight, Dr. Wallington," Vincent protested. "Having a bed to sleep in will be miracle enough."

Carrie appraised him. "You were beaten a week ago?"

Vincent's face tightened as a look of horror filled his eyes. "Yes, ma'am."

"And I'm assuming the beating wasn't limited to your faces?" Carrie kept her voice gentle.

Vincent and Morris shook their heads at the same time.

"It ain't pretty," Morris muttered, his face a mixture of anger and agony.

Something about the way he said it made Carrie steel herself for what she would find. "I'm used to treating things that aren't pretty," she said calmly. "It's important I treat you now, though, because there's too much risk of infection," she said, knowing their fevers indicated the infection had already begun. "I have to leave in the morning to catch a train for Philadelphia. Dr. Janie Justin, my partner at the clinic, will take care of you when I'm gone, but

I will treat you tonight. Infection can be very dangerous."

Vincent nodded reluctantly.

Carrie turned to Morris next. It was obvious Vincent was the leader, but it was important that Morris feel respected as well. "Morris, may I have permission to treat you?"

Morris eyed her with surprise but nodded slowly. "I reckon that be alright, Dr. Wallington. I'm real grateful for what you be doin'."

Carrie chose to start with Vincent because she was alarmed with the condition of his eye. She saw that Rose had already covered the one bed in the room with clean sheets. "Vincent, please lie down on the bed." She looked toward Franklin, who was hovering next to the door. "Please bring up enough blankets from the tack room to make a bed for Morris. He needs to rest until I'm ready to treat him."

Franklin nodded and left the room.

Carrie watched as Vincent lay down, not missing the twist of pain that crossed his face when he did. "What is hurting you?" she asked.

Vincent hesitated but met her eyes. "My back is in pretty bad shape."

Carrie thought about how he had moved coming up the stairs. There had been no evidence of muscular injury. Her lips tightened. "It's obvious lying down is painful. Please sit back up. What happened to you?" If she was going to effectively treat him, she needed to know the truth about what had happened to the two men.

Silence filled the room as the men exchanged a long look.

"We done got whipped," Morris said. "Vincent be at my house to get me to register to vote. The Klan done busted in right through the door." His voice faltered before he could continue. "They shot my wife right in front of me. Then..." He choked and brushed at the tears shimmering in his eyes.

Vincent picked up the story. "They hauled us out into the woods and made us strip. Then they forced us to lie face down on some big rocks..." He shook his head, unable to continue.

Carrie held a hand to her mouth to control her cry of horror. She saw Rose and Abby do the same thing.

"They whipped us," Morris managed. "They pulled out a big 'ole whip and laid right into us. They was shoutin' that no black man gonna vote in South Carolina. Yelled that we gotta know our place."

Carrie couldn't stop the tears streaming down her face. "My God," she whispered.

Rose knelt down and took Morris' hand in hers. "I'm so sorry."

Carrie settled into the chair next to the bed, took Vincent's hand, and echoed Rose's words. "I'm so sorry." She knew she needed more information, though she was terrified to ask. "What about your arms and legs?"

Morris answered her question. "They didn't do nothin' to them. I reckon they figured whippin' our backs would make their point."

"What happened to your eye, Vincent?" Carrie asked. It was so swollen she couldn't examine it until she cleaned it.

Vincent grimaced. "Evidently, since I was the one there to register Morris to vote, they thought I needed more persuasion. After they whipped us, one of the men picked up a big stick and poked it into my eye."

Carrie pushed down her nausea. "Can you see out of it?" She knew the answer, but just in case...

"No," Vincent said. "I'm kinda...hoping it's just still too swollen."

Carrie suspected it was far worse than that, but she wasn't willing to give words to her concern yet. "It's going to take time for you to heal, but I promise you're both safe here."

"For now," Vincent managed to say through his gritted teeth. "We don't plan on staying in the South. It's been eight years now that we've been free. I don't see things getting better. We stopped here because we knew we needed help, but we're headed north."

"Yep. We's headed north," Morris repeated. "We figure things gotta be better up there. My boy ain't gonna grow up in the South." His voice was staunch and determined.

Carrie whirled around. "You have a son? Where is he?"

"He's with Chooli and the children," Franklin said, hearing the questions as he walked in the door with an armful of blankets.

"Jed be ten," Morris said. "He was out back in the outhouse when the Klan busted in. He ran and hid in the woods until Vincent and I crawled back to the house. He done been a big help gettin' us this far. He's real smart. Just like his mama was."

Carrie ached for the little boy whose mother had been murdered. She set her teeth and turned her attention to Vincent just as a quiet knock sounded. Anthony and Matthew entered, carrying large pots of hot water. Annie followed close behind with armfuls of cloth and bedclothes for both men.

"Thank you," Carrie said before she started issuing orders. "Matthew, please go get Janie. I'm going to need her, after all. On your way over, ask Father to stay with Annabelle and Robert." She turned to Anthony next. "Please help Annie and Miles mash up enough onions and garlic to make a large amount of honey paste." She already knew she was going to find infection when the men took their shirts off. "Franklin, I want you and Moses to keep bringing me hot water. I'll need your help bathing them before I can treat their wounds."

Unanswered questions mingled with her burning fury, but there was no time for either. She pushed down every emotion and focused on her patients. "We'll be right back," she told the men. "Don't take your shirts off yet."

Not waiting to explain, Carrie beckoned to Rose and Abby. She led them down to the tack room. Together, they pulled out two large metal water tubs. It would be enough to catch the water as they bathed the men, but before they could bathe they would have to wet their shirts enough to lessen the pain they would feel when the cloth was peeled away from their lacerated backs.

None of the women said a word about what they'd heard. They seemed to all know that if they gave voice to their feelings, they would never be able to do what needed to be done that night.

Janie arrived just as they began to climb the stairs. Her face was tight with outrage and worry.

"Janie..." Carrie began.

Janie held up her hand. "Matthew told me. Let's go treat our patients." She grabbed hold of the tub Carrie was carrying and helped haul it up the stairs.

It took only minutes to realize they would have to cut the men's shirts off them. Carrie swallowed tears as she imagined the pain they had endured as they traveled from South Carolina. She knew they couldn't have walked that far in a week. They must have gotten carriage rides or snuck onto a cargo train, but those questions would wait. Every second of their journey had to have been torture.

While Carrie and Rose tended to Vincent, Janie and Abby worked on Morris. They slowly removed the men's shirts, continually wetting them as they pulled the cloth away from their puss-filled wounds as gently as they could.

Neither man made a sound, but the agony that twisted their faces spoke louder than words as they stood motionless in the tubs that collected the bloody water. Both their backs had been flayed into a mass of open wounds and stripes. Infection had created massive swelling and redness.

Carrie didn't know how it had been possible for the men to move, much less walk. Anger and pity threatened to overwhelm her. Treating soldiers during war had been one thing; treating men who had been whipped and tortured just for being black was quite another. The senselessness of it was more than she could bear.

Except that she must.

Carrie swallowed hard and locked eyes with Rose as they pulled away the remaining shreds of cloth. It somehow helped that she saw the same helpless fury in her friend's eyes.

Just as they finished, the men arrived with more pails of hot water. Anthony carried a large bowl of onion and garlic poultice.

One look at Morris and Vincent made all of them stop in their tracks. Their eyes widened and then narrowed with the same fury and pity Carrie was feeling.

"Thank you," Carrie said, amazed her voice could sound so calm. "I'd like y'all to help Vincent and Morris finish bathing. Their lower extremities aren't wounded. Once they have clean pants on, let us know. I'll wash Vincent's face when you're done. I have to be very careful of his eye." She took a deep breath. "We'll be downstairs."

Carrie had known what she would find when she cleaned Vincent's face, but her stomach still twisted when she looked at his mutilated eye.

Vincent watched her closely with his good eye. "You can't fix it, can you?"

Carrie never lied to her patients. She believed they deserved to know the truth. "No," she said. "The damage is too extensive. I'm sorry."

Vincent took a deep breath. "What are you going to do?"

"I have to remove your eye," Carrie said steadily.

Vincent stiffened but didn't look away. "You ever done it before, Dr. Wallington?"

"I assisted in two enucleation surgeries when I was obtaining my surgical license," she said with confidence. She knew Vincent needed to trust her ability. "It's a fairly straightforward surgery."

Vincent considered that for a moment. "What will you do?"

Carrie understood he was a man who would do best with thorough information. "I'll begin by giving you anesthesia. You won't feel a thing," she promised him. "Then I'll detach the muscles from the eyeball and remove it from the eye socket. After surgery, I'll apply a pressure bandage over the socket to reduce bruising and swelling."

Vincent swallowed, looking away for a moment. "How long will the bandage be on?"

"One week, at the very least. It's imperative that I be the one to remove it," Carrie said firmly. "You will not be able to head north until I've done so. If it's removed too soon, the wound can become infected and kill you," she said bluntly.

Vincent nodded. "I hear you." He paused. "How bad is it going to hurt?"

Carrie knew the pain he was feeling at the moment must be intense. "For most people, the pain is minimal. I have no reason to believe yours will be any different. Once the eye is out, most of your pain will go away. Any pain you do experience is usually associated with the pressure that comes from the eye patch. I have remedies I will give you for pain while it's healing." She glanced at Morris. "The pain remedies will help both of you while you're recovering from the lashing, as well."

"And once my eye socket heals?" Vincent asked.

Carrie could tell he was trying to absorb and process the reality that he was going to lose his eye. Surely, he'd been holding onto hope that it could be saved. "Most people wear a patch. When you're able, you can buy a glass eye."

Vincent's one eye widened. "A *glass* eye?"

Carrie nodded. "They're really rather amazing." She thought back to the research she'd done, hoping it would provide a brief distraction for Vincent. "When they first started making glass eyes in the 1500s, they were made of gold and then painted. They were rather uncomfortable," she admitted. "Over the years, they've been improved. There are special glass blowers who create the eyes now. I'm sure they'll keep improving the technique, but the eyes are far more comfortable."

Vincent looked skeptical. "Ain't likely a black man is going to be able to afford a glass eye," he said dubiously. "I think I'll have to get used to a patch."

Carrie didn't argue with him. She knew the challenges he would face. "You never know what the future will hold," was all she said. "My job right now is to remove your eye and treat your back, so that you and Morris can leave here with Jed and head north." She wanted to keep his thoughts focused on the future.

She and Janie had talked about the procedure to treat their backs when they were down in the barn. "I won't pretend that both treatments aren't going to be painful. Your backs are terribly infected, so Dr. Justin and I have decided to put both of you under anesthesia while we clean your wounds. It will make it far easier for you."

"The infection gonna kill us?" Morris asked keenly. "I got my boy to think about."

"Not if I can help it," Carrie said. She knew better than to guarantee anything. She could tell a fever was climbing in both men. "We should get started."

Carrie straightened and stretched her back after two long hours of surgery. Adrenalin was pumping through her, but she knew bone-crushing fatigue wasn't far behind.

She looked over to see that Janie had finished treating Morris. She and Abby were filling the lash wounds on his back with onion, garlic, and honey paste. The paste would work to pull out the bacteria and infection, as well as battle the fever that had gripped the men.

Janie looked at her grimly. "One day more, and we might not have been able to save them."

Carrie knew she was right. She worked with Rose to prop Vincent on his side with blankets and pillows. He shouldn't be lying on his back, but being on his stomach would put too much pressure on the eye socket. The surgery to remove his eye had been fairly simple, but only because she didn't have to worry about attempting to preserve his eyesight. She had packed his eye socket with the same paste that Rose was now applying to his back.

Though many of the lashes would have benefitted from stitches in the beginning, the infection had become too great to close them. She thought about the massive chest wound Moses had sustained toward the end of the war. They had barely saved him. They'd been forced to leave the chest wound open, packing it with the poultice they were using on these men now. Moses had healed completely. She believed Vincent and Morris would too, as long as the infection didn't enter the rest of their bodies.

She pulled out a bottle of tea leaves she'd created from a mixture of willow bark, poplar, lady's slipper root, and skullcap. Once the men were awake, Janie would make sure they drank it on a regular basis to control their pain.

The wounds on their back would have to be cleaned twice a day with a fresh paste applied each time. Each application would draw out a little more of the infection and fever. She frowned as she thought about traveling to Philadelphia and leaving all of this to Janie and Polly.

"Why are you frowning, my dear?"

Carrie looked up to see Abby watching her closely. "I'm wondering if I should postpone my trip to Philadelphia," she admitted.

"Why?" Janie demanded. "Do you think I'm not qualified to handle this?" she asked in a teasing voice.

Carrie smiled. "We both know you are, but you're being left with all the clinic patients, and now two men who are going to require a lot of care."

Janie shrugged nonchalantly. "Polly and I can handle it."

"And I'll help," Abby said quickly. "You and Janie did all the hard work. I'm capable of cleaning wounds and applying paste. Annie and I will make sure there is plenty of it. I can hardly wait to stand in the kitchen and cry over a counter of onions and garlic."

Carrie chuckled. "I agree that there are more enjoyable things in life." Then she frowned again. "I feel selfish leaving all of this to you while I go to Philadelphia."

"Yes," Abby said. "It's so selfish of you to leave for a trip where you're going to be teaching homeopathic treatments and working at the Moyamensing Clinic to give Carolyn a break. It's rather shocking how self-absorbed you've become."

"Shocking..." Janie echoed in a sad voice.

Carrie laughed in spite of her fatigue and the horror of the night. "Alright, alright. I suppose you have a point." She sobered. "Vincent and Morris might not make it," she said grimly. "Their wounds were enough to kill them. Add a massive infection and rising fever to the situation, and it doesn't look good. We've given them a fighting chance. I hope it's enough." She shook her head. "It's beyond a miracle that they made it to the plantation. I have a feeling that their concern for Morris' son was the only thing that kept them going."

Rose settled into a chair as her shoulders drooped with fatigue. She shook her head, gazing up at them with deep vulnerability in her eyes. "How could a human being do this to another person? I've seen the results of men who have been beaten with a whip before, but this goes beyond anything I could even imagine." Her voice trembled. "Why? Will it ever stop?"

Carrie knew none of them had an answer to her questions. There could never be a reason for such torturous cruelty. All of them were holding onto the hope that violence against blacks in the South would get better, but there was no evidence of it happening yet. All she could do was sit down on the floor next to Rose and grasp her hand. Her best friend worried every single day about Moses and their children. No black person in the South was truly safe from what was happening. Neither were the whites who supported and helped them. The plantation offered a haven, but attacks in the past, and Robert's murder, revealed just how vulnerable they still were.

They couldn't go anywhere until the men woke up from the anesthesia. All four of them needed the support they could give each other.

When Anthony stuck his head in the door a short while later, Janie and Abby had joined Carrie on the floor. They were all holding hands silently, knowing words had no real meaning. All they could do was surround each other with support and love.

Anthony pulled Carrie into his arms when they finally crawled into bed. "You're only going to have three hours of sleep before we have to get up again."

Carrie yawned and snuggled close into her husband's warmth. "The same is true for you."

"I didn't spend the night saving lives," Anthony said wryly. "The world won't fall apart if we delay our trip by one day."

Carrie knew he was right. She considered it and then shook her head. "I want to go today," she mumbled as sleep reached out to grab her.

Whatever was waiting in Philadelphia, she wanted to get it over with so she could come home.

Chapter Four

Rose waved good-bye to Carrie, Anthony, and the children, and then walked over to where her mare, Maple, was tied to a hitching post.

Moses stepped out onto the porch, a cup of hot coffee in hand. "Where are you going?"

"To meet Jed. That little boy has been through so much in the last week. I want to check on him before I leave for school. I know Franklin and Chooli are taking good care of him, but I want to meet him."

Moses nodded solemnly. "Do you know how Vincent and Morris are doing?"

"Janie was here before Carrie left. Both of the patients are awake. They're hurting, but the herbal tea they're drinking is helping with the pain. Vincent said his eye doesn't hurt nearly as much as it did. I'm certain that he's not completely processed that it's gone, but it will sink in a little more each day." Rose paused, gripped once again with the fury that coursed through her like a wave ever since she had seen the lashes that were inflicted on the two men.

"Are their fevers going down?"

"Vincent's seems to be responding to the treatment well. It will take time, but he's headed in the right direction. Janie and Annie kept wet rags on their heads for most of the night. Polly is coming to help in a little while so Janie can check on Annabelle and get some rest. Your mother insists she is fine and doesn't need any sleep." Rose shook her head. "Your mother is quite a remarkable woman."

"Morris isn't getting better?" Moses asked keenly.

Rose shrugged. "Morris' fever is still as high as it was last night. Carrie warned us it would take time for it to go down, but there hasn't been any response at all. All we can do is keep cleaning his wounds and treating them with the poultice. And pray," she added. "I doubt he was as strong as Vincent when the beating happened. It truly is a mystery how he made it to the plantation." The urge to meet the little boy who had inspired his father enough to make the long journey grew stronger. "I've got to go. I'll see you when you're done in the fields tonight."

Moses looked at her closely and then strode down the stairs, his tall body blocking out the morning sun as he wrapped her in a warm embrace. "We're safe here on the plantation, Rose," he said.

Rose leaned back in his arms and gazed at him, saddened when the sight of his strong face and reassuring eyes did nothing to ease her angst. "We both know that could change," she said. She tried to blink away the image of the bloody, puss-filled wounds, but they seemed ingrained in her brain cells. Every time she closed her eyes, the horror revealed itself in the darkness. She hadn't slept, even when she'd finally come to bed. "Vincent and Morris weren't here looking for a job," she said. As she spoke, she realized she wasn't feeling fear. It was more of a warning sounding in her heart and mind. "They needed help, but they're on their way north because Morris has vowed his son will not grow up in the South. Both of them are convinced things won't get better for blacks." Her voice quavered. "I can't blame them."

"Rose..." Moses began.

Rose pushed back from his arms and took a deep breath. "I don't have time for you to tell me all the reasons I shouldn't be afraid. I want to go check on Jed and see if he needs anything." She stretched up, kissed him lightly, and turned away.

Rose swung into Maple's saddle and trotted off down the road. She took deep breaths of the crisp morning air, trying to settle her emotions. Regardless of what had happened—and was still happening—in South Carolina, there were things she had to do now. It took only ten minutes to reach Franklin and Chooli's cabin. The couple lived in the home that had first been built for Rose and Moses when they married.

Rose smiled as she rounded the last curve. Bright flowers bloomed in the yard. A still lush garden was full of summer bounty. It would be several more weeks before the first frost would end production. She knew Chooli had been hard at work canning and drying food for the winter.

Rose had just dismounted when the cabin's front door opened. Chooli stepped out, holding two-year-old Dakota in her arms. Her four-year-old daughter, Ajei, broke into a grin when she realized who their guest was and raced across the yard.

"Miss Rose! Good morning, Miss Rose!"

Rose knelt down just in time to open her arms wide before they collided. "Good morning, Ajei!" She never failed to be astonished at the little girl's beauty. Her black and Navajo heritage made her truly lovely. "How are you today?"

Ajei leaned back and beamed up at Rose. "I'm real good, Miss Rose." Her voice dropped to a soft whisper. "We got company."

"We have company," Rose corrected automatically. It was a plantation joke that everyone's speech had to go through the *Rose Filter*. She would never apologize for making sure the plantation children spoke correctly. In a world where being black or Indian was already hard, there was no excuse to not speak correctly.

Ajei nodded solemnly. "We *have* company, Miss Rose."

As Ajei spoke, Rose saw movement out of the corner of her eye. She turned to see a little boy framed in the doorway. Her heart caught as soon as she saw him. A mass of short dark curls framed dark skin. Jed was small for his age, but his eyes gleamed with intelligence and determination. And grief.

"Good morning, Rose," Chooli said. "Are you here to meet Jed?"

Rose nodded, her eyes never leaving the little boy. "Good morning, Chooli." She walked forward slowly. "Good morning, Jed. My name is Miss Rose." The children were required to call her Mrs. Samuels at school, but here on the plantation, the children knew her as Miss Rose.

Jed eyed her cautiously. "Yes'sum."

"Your father told me you're a fine young man. I came to meet you."

Jed's eyes shot up to latch onto her. "You seen my daddy?"

"I have."

"How is he?" Jed demanded.

Chooli cleared her throat. "Let's go inside where we can sit and talk."

Jed nodded reluctantly and stepped back.

Moments later, Rose sat across the table from him. "Your daddy is staying in a room above the barn right now."

"Why?"

Rose was certain Morris had never let Jed see the extent of his injuries. "His back was hurting him," she said carefully. "We have a doctor who lives in the house and another one who lives in the guest house. They took care of your daddy and Vincent last night. They're going to need to rest and get well."

Jed nodded solemnly. "They think I don't know."

Rose's pulse quickened. Surely... "Know what?" she asked calmly.

"Know how bad they got beat," Jed said, his voice trembling as he said the words. "I be in the outhouse when them men first came, but I saw them takin' my daddy and Vincent, so I followed."

Rose wanted to close her eyes and groan, but she forced herself to focus on the little boy. Obviously, this was the first time he was telling the truth about that night.

Tears filled Jed's eyes. "I done saw them masked men beat them," he whispered. "I didn't tell Daddy, though. He and Vincent tried to hide from me how bad they were hurtin', but I knew." His lips quivered. "Those men killed my mama, too."

Rose controlled the sob that yearned to escape her lips. Morris and Vincent had been so sure Jed didn't know the truth of what had happened to them. They had told him they were simply leaving because of his mama's murder, and that it was time for a new beginning. She reached out to grasp his hands. "I'm so sorry that happened, Jed," she said softly.

Jed took a deep breath and squared his shoulders.

Once again, Rose's heart threatened to break. A ten-year-old boy shouldn't have to be so brave.

"How be my daddy and Vincent, Miss Rose? I know they be real sick."

Rose wouldn't insult his bravery by being anything less than honest. "I believe they're going to get better, but it will take time. It took several hours last night to clean their wounds, but the doctors made sure they felt no pain while they did it."

"How they do that?"

"They used a thing called anesthesia to put them to sleep until it was over."

Jed nodded knowingly. "My mama told me about that."

Rose looked at him with surprise. "Your mama did?" Where had his mama learned about anesthesia?

"Yes'sum. My mama lived up north during the war. She was born free in Pennsylvania. She helped treat black soldiers when they got hurt. She told me about how them doctors would put them to sleep before they done treated them."

"I see," Rose said, exchanging a look with Chooli over Jed's head. He answered her next question before she had a chance to ask it.

"She met my daddy during the war. He wanted to come back home to South Carolina when it was all over. He told her things would be lots better now that ever'body be free." His eyes darkened. "That ain't true."

"No," Rose said. "It's not true for everyone."

Jed fixed his eyes on her. "Do things be bad around here, too?" He glanced at Chooli. "Miss Chooli told me it ain't like that here, but..."

Rose didn't blame Jed for not believing her or Chooli. She prayed that when she answered, she would sound more convincing than she actually felt. She wanted Jed to feel safe. "Things are different here on the plantation, Jed. You'll be safe," she said. "So will your daddy and Vincent. Nothing else is going to happen to hurt you."

Jed eyed her for a long moment as if he were peering into her soul, and then nodded. His posture and eyes relaxed slightly. "When can I see my daddy?"

"You can come back to the house with me now if you would like," Rose offered. She glanced at Chooli.

"I'll come up to the house to get you later," Chooli said quickly. "You won't want to leave there right away, though..." She let her voice trail away mysteriously, her dark eyes glittering with humor.

Jed switched his attention to her. "Why not, Miss Chooli?"

"Because Annie makes the best cinnamon rolls in the world."

Jed frowned as his eyes deepened with sorrow. "No, ma'am. My mama done made the best cinnamon rolls in the world. She only did it a couple times 'cause we didn't have much money, but I reckon they be the best thing I ever had."

Rose fought the sadness and fury swirling through her. "I'm sure she did. I bet you'll like Annie's too, though. John does."

"John?"

"John is my son," Rose told him, making the immediate decision to keep John and Hope home from school that day. "He's eight. My daughter Hope is five. She'll be six in December."

Jed looked interested for the first time. "I'd like to meet them."

"And you shall," Rose promised. She had a sudden thought. "Jed, do you go to school?"

"No, ma'am. My mama been teachin' me how to read, but..." Jed's voice quivered again. He blinked furiously to control the tears welling in his eyes. He remained silent for several moments before he could continue. "Ain't no schools out where we lived. I be hopin' there will be some school up north when we get there."

"You could go to school here while your daddy gets better," Rose said.

Jed's eyes widened. "There's a school around here for nigger children?"

"We don't say that word around here, Jed," Rose said gently.

'What word?"

"We don't say nigger."

Jed looked confused. "That's what everybody call me down there. At least, all the white folks."

"Not here," Rose answered. "The word nigger means ignorant. Not a single one of my students—black or white—is ignorant. Neither are you."

Jed's eyes widened further. "You're a teacher?"

Rose smiled. "I am."

Jed continued to stare at her. "And there be white *and* black children you teach?"

Rose knew now was not the time to attempt to explain school segregation to Jed. "Yes."

Jed considered this new revelation. "How come John not be in school if he's eight?"

"He is," Rose assured him. "It's just that I think it would be better for him to spend time with you today. Both him and Hope."

"Hope is in school, too? She only be five."

"Yes. Hope loves school." Rose repeated her earlier offer. "Would you like to go to school while you're here?" She knew it would help distract him from what had happened.

Jed was silent for several moments. "I reckon that would be fine. I know it would make my mama real happy."

"I'm glad your mama would be happy. You'll start school tomorrow," Rose promised. "As long as your daddy agrees," she added.

"Oh, Daddy will want me to go," Jed said with conviction. "He tells me all the time that he wants me to be smart like Mama." He locked eyes with her. "Mama told me that Daddy be just as smart as her, but he don't know it because it's not book smarts. She told me smart is smart."

"Your mama was a wise woman," Rose said. She stood and held out her hand. "Let's go. You can ride on the back of Maple with me."

Jed gaped at her. "Ride on a horse?"

Rose smiled. "That's right. When we get to the house, you can see the other horses." She already knew the little boy was going to be overwhelmed by the Cromwell stock. "Let's go see your daddy."

Jed nodded eagerly, took her hand, and turned to Chooli. "Thank you, Miss Chooli, for takin' care of me."

Rose answered the question in Chooli's eyes. "We'll keep him at the house until his father is well. He can stay in John's room. I think they'll both like it."

"And I'll be close to Daddy," Jed added, his voice both eager and determined.

They were mounted, Jed's arms tightly around Rose's waist, before he spoke again. "John has his own room?" It was obvious he couldn't comprehend that reality.

"That's right," Rose said. Jed had no way to comprehend what he was about to experience with the plantation house, so she decided to distract him. "We're passing all the tobacco fields right now." She knew South Carolina was best known for cotton.

"Yes'sum," Jed said politely. "I done seen it once before."

"What did your daddy do in South Carolina?"

"He started out being a slave pickin' cotton. Then he escaped and went up north to fight in that big war," he said proudly. "After that, he came back down here..."

Rose waited for him to finish, but Jed remained silent. She could feel the tension in his body pressed against hers. "What did he do when he came back?"

"Nothin'," Jed said. "He tried to get work on one of them plantations, but they told him they didn't have no use for a nigger who fought for the Yankees. He ain't never done nothin' else, but he was learnin' how to make bricks so he could work. My mama worked in the big house of one of those places, though. She be a maid." Jed paused. "*Was* a maid," he amended in a thick voice.

Rose knew Jed was still trying to comprehend that his mama was dead.

"Mama told me things be a lot better up north," Jed revealed. "I reckon Daddy finally figured ain't nothin' gonna get better down here. He and Mama been talkin' about movin' up north. She was real excited."

Rose could feel the sob that wracked Jed's small body.

"I sure wish she was gonna be with us when we get there."

"Me too," Rose said tenderly, taking hold of one of his hands that was wrapped around her waist. "You know, your mama is real proud of you for helping your daddy and Vincent get this far."

A lengthy silence was followed by a tentative question. "You reckon she really knows?"

"I do," Rose said firmly. "I believe she knows."

Another long silence.

"That's good," Jed said, his voice a little firmer.

As Rose rounded the last curve, the house came into view, gleaming white in the sunshine.

"What's that?!" Jed gasped.

"That's our home," Rose said.

"You *live* there?" Jed obviously didn't believe her.

"We do," Rose said. "My husband and I actually own half the plantation." She could feel Jed shaking his head.

"That ain't right. Ni—" Jed stopped himself just in time. "Black folks don't own nothin' like that."

"We do," Rose assured him. "I told you that you're safe here, Jed. You are." Gazing at the solid splendor of the place she called home, she felt it a little more herself.

"Who owns the other half?"

Rose smiled. The little boy didn't miss anything. "Mr. Thomas Cromwell."

"How you know him?"

Rose knew her next statement was going to be more than he could possibly understand, but he would in time. "Mr. Cromwell used to own Moses and me. It turns out that Thomas is my half-brother." Jed remained silent as they drew closer to the house. Rose knew he was thinking.

"This sure be a strange place," he finally said.

Rose laughed. "You're right, Jed. Strange...but wonderful," she added. "I'm glad you're going to be with us for a little while." She wanted the little boy to understand that all of life didn't have to be what he had experienced so far.

Annie was waiting on the porch when they rode up. She rushed down the steps to help Jed off Maple, and smiled at the little boy. "Hello, Jed. I'm Annie. Welcome to Cromwell Plantation."

Jed appraised her solemnly. "Hi, Annie. You the one that makes the cinnamon rolls?"

Annie chuckled, her round face creased with a broad smile. "That's me. How 'bout you come on in my kitchen, and I'll give you one. I just pulled a fresh pan out of the oven."

Jed looked tempted but shook his head quickly. "Thank you, but I wanna go see my daddy." He gazed up at Annie. "He's been real sick. He needs me." He turned to Rose. "Can I go see Daddy now?"

"You can," Rose assured him.

Jed smiled up at her. "Thank you." Then he turned back to Annie. "Can I have one of them cinnamon rolls later? I reckon they gonna make me think of my mama, but maybe she'll know I be eatin' one and be real glad about it."

Rose understood the tears that misted Annie's eyes.

"Yes, Jed. You go on over and see your daddy. The cinnamon rolls will be waitin' along with a glass of milk."

Rose smiled. "Please tell John and Hope they aren't going to school today. They get to stay home and play with Jed."

Annie nodded, understanding immediately.

Rose took Jed's hand and walked him to the barn.

His mouth gaped open as he took in the horses grazing in the pastures. "All them horses belong to you?"

"No, my best friend, Carrie, who is also the doctor who treated your daddy and Vincent, owns them along with another friend."

Jed stared at her. "You tellin' me a lady owns all them horses? And that she be a *doctor*? A *lady* doctor?"

"Actually, two ladies own the horses," Rose answered, knowing he was experiencing a life he never dreamed could exist. "Miss Carrie is gone right now, but you'll be able to meet Miss Susan today."

Jed ground to a stop as he stared out at all the horses. "They be real pretty," he murmured. "You reckon I could pet one of them while I be here?"

"Oh, I think we could do better than that," Rose replied. "How about if you go for a ride on one of them?" There was something about this little boy that tugged at her heartstrings.

Jed swung around to look into her eyes. "You mean all by myself? Really?" Hope mingled with disbelief.

"We can make that happen," she assured him. "But right now, I have to take you up to see your daddy so that I can get to school."

Jed followed her into the barn.

Janie was just coming down the stairs from Miles and Annie's apartment. "Good morning, Rose." She smiled down at Jed. "I bet you're Morris' little boy, Jed."

"Yes'sum," Jed said earnestly. "My daddy doin' alright?"

"Jed, this is Dr. Justin. She's taking care of your daddy."

"Pleased to meet you, ma'am," Jed said politely. "He doin' alright?" he repeated, his voice strained with worry.

"He's eager to see you," Janie said warmly.

Rose realized Janie didn't directly answer Jed's question, but she couldn't question her more thoroughly until they were alone. "I've got to get to school. The students will be arriving soon."

"You go on," Janie told her. She took Jed's hand. "Let's go see your daddy. He's lying on his stomach right now because he hurt his back."

"The whips cut him real bad," Jed said sadly.

Rose nodded when Janie looked at her with alarm. *He knows,* she mouthed. *He saw it.*

Janie's lips tightened, but she forced a smile. "Yes, they did," she agreed, "but we fixed him up. It will be a while before he can lie on his back, but he can turn his head to see you and talk to you."

"Same with Vincent?" Jed asked. "They hurt him real bad, too."

"Vincent is lying on his side," Janie said. "He'll be able to talk to you, too."

"Is that 'cause of what they did to his eye with that big stick?"

Rose's heart sank as she realized Jed had seen the act that had stolen Vincent's eye.

"That's right," Janie said steadily. "His eye doesn't hurt like it used to, though. It's just best for him to be on his side right now."

Jed held her gaze, looking far older than ten. "What did you do to fix it?"

When Janie looked up, Rose nodded. It was important that Jed be told the truth. He had to be able to trust them.

Janie stooped down to Jed's level. "We had to take his eye out," she said.

Jed considered this, his face crinkled with worry. "So, he ain't gonna see out of it again?"

"I'm afraid not." Janie answered honestly, "He's not going to be in pain from it though, and he can still see with his other eye."

"That's good," Jed said thoughtfully. "He was hurtin' real bad the whole way here."

"Both of them told me how much you helped them on the way here. You're a very brave boy."

Jed shrugged. "My mama always told me that you just gotta do what you gotta do. That's all I did."

Rose blinked back the tears that once more flooded her eyes. Jed had no idea how extraordinary he was. Impulsively, she wrapped him in a warm hug. He stiffened for a moment and then seemed to melt into her embrace. "Have a good day, Jed. I'll see you when I get home."

"Thank you, Miss Rose," he whispered.

Janie led Jed into the small apartment. She had opened the windows to allow in fresh air and to diminish the smell of the pungent paste filling her patients' wounds.

Jed's eyes flew to Morris. "Daddy!"

Morris opened his eyes and managed a weak smile. "Jed... Son... How you be?"

"I be real good," Jed assured him. "Franklin and Chooli took real good care of me last night. Annie has cinnamon rolls waitin' for me. And I'm gonna play with John and Hope today."

Janie answered the question she could see on Morris' face. "John and Hope are Rose's children. They'll all have fun playing together."

"That's good," Morris said, gritting his teeth against a fresh spasm of pain.

"Roll to your side so you can drink some more tea," Janie said encouragingly. "It will help with the pain."

Jed's face puckered with worry. "You gonna be alright, Daddy?"

Morris forced another smile. "You bet I am, Jed. Just gonna take a little while."

"And then we're going to head north and leave the South behind?"

"That's right," Morris assured him.

Seemingly satisfied, Jed turned to Vincent. "Howdy, Vincent. You be alright?"

"I'm going to be," Vincent said, his voice stronger than Morris'.

"You ain't gonna see again, though," Jed said sadly.

"No, I reckon I'm not going to see out of the one eye, but I've still got a good one," Vincent told him. "And I'm going to live. I'm real grateful for that."

Jed nodded quickly. "Yep. That be real good." He stared hard at both of the men. "And then we're gonna keep goin'? We're gonna head north?"

"You bet we are," Vincent replied.

Janie had heard enough of the story to understand why Jed was so eager to leave the South.

Jed turned to look up at her. "How long 'fore we can all leave?"

Janie was determined to be honest. "I don't know. I don't want to make a promise I'm not sure I can keep. I can promise you, though, that we're doing everything we can to help them heal as fast as possible."

"What can I do to help?" Jed asked, his eyes boring into hers.

Janie had to remind herself the little boy was only ten years old. At that moment, his eyes burned with a wisdom and knowing far beyond his years. "Your daddy and Vincent need to rest, but it would be wonderful if you came to visit them twice a day. I know that will mean a lot to them. When you're not visiting them, I want you to have fun."

"Fun?"

Janie understood that Jed felt guilty about the idea of having fun while his daddy and Vincent were so sick. She also knew he was grieving his mother.

"That's right. It will help your daddy get well if he knows you're not worrying about him all the time."

"Listen to the doctor," Morris said gravely. "She be tellin' the truth." He paused and took a deep breath, gathering the strength to continue. "Your mama would want that, too."

"Mama's gone," Jed said sadly.

"Yep." Morris' voice broke with the single word, but he reached out to take Jed's hand. "Just the same, it's what she would want. Your mama done always wanted the best for you. Ain't that the truth?"

Jed nodded uncertainly. "I reckon."

"Your mama be in heaven, Jed. She ain't hurtin' no more. She lookin' down on you wantin' just what she always wanted for you. The very best. It be alright for you to go play and have fun with Miss Rose's young'uns." Morris collapsed onto his pillow, his energy spent after his speech.

Janie knew he had reached the end of his endurance for now. She took Jed's hand. "They need to rest now, Jed. I'm going to take you back over to the house so you can have those cinnamon rolls Annie promised you."

Jed nodded uncertainly. "I love you, Daddy."

"Love you too, Jed," Morris whispered.

Jed was almost to the door when he turned back around. "Get better real soon, Vincent."

Vincent smiled and nodded. "Absolutely, Jed. We're heading north soon."

Harold was on the porch talking to Thomas and Abby when Janie reached the house. She introduced Jed to everyone and ushered him into the kitchen.

Annie looked up from a huge vat of beans and fatback that she was stirring. "Hello, Jed," she said cheerfully. "You be here for your cinnamon rolls?"

Jed nodded vigorously, looking around the kitchen with obvious disappointment.

Just at that moment, the door burst open. John and Hope dashed into the kitchen.

"We're here, Grandma!" John announced. He skidded to a stop when he saw Jed. "Hello. Are you Jed?"

Jed nodded.

Janie bit back her smile as she watched Jed appraise John.

"I'm John. This is Hope."

Jed glanced at Hope before staring back at John, who stood at least a head taller than him. "You really only eight?" he asked suspiciously.

"Yes," John said, a smile lurking on his face. "I'm big for my age."

"That be for sure," Jed muttered.

The back door swung open. Moses strode into the kitchen, talking as he approached. "Mama, I came back for one or two more cinnamon rolls."

Annie chuckled. "You don't think half a pan was enough?"

Moses shrugged. "It's your fault they're so delicious." He noticed Jed standing beside Janie.

"Hello." He smiled down at the boy. "You must be Jed."

Jed continued to stare up at him but finally found his voice. "I ain't never seen no man as big as you."

Moses laughed easily. "I don't suppose you have. It's all because of my mama's good cooking."

"John must eat a lot, too," Jed observed.

Everyone burst into laughter.

"I'm going to be as big as my daddy someday," John said proudly. Then he turned to Annie. "Can we put some cinnamon rolls in a basket, Grandma? I want to take Jed over to the barn to meet Cafi."

"And Patches!" Hope added, her luminous eyes glowing with excitement. "We're going to get Grandpa to go riding with us, Jed."

Jed looked at them uncertainly. "Us?"

"You'll get to go riding, too, Jed," Janie said. "Annie's husband works in the barn."

"Grandpa used to run the entire stable," John told him. "Back when he was a slave. Now he works there and gets paid."

Jed had one more question. He looked back at Moses. "You the one that supposedly owns half this place? That really be true?"

Moses nodded solemnly. "It's true," he replied in his deep voice. He knelt down so he could look Jed in the eye. "Cromwell Plantation is different from most of the South."

"Sure diff'rent than where I be from," Jed responded.

"I know," Moses said gravely. "I'm sorry about that. I know you've had a lot of terrible things happen. I'm sorry about your mama."

Jed took a deep breath but remained silent.

Janie could see the tears shimmering in his eyes.

"I also heard about how brave you were after what happened to your daddy and Vincent," Moses added. "It took a lot of courage to help them get here."

Jed shrugged but his shoulders straightened. "It weren't really much," he said modestly. "I talked some men into givin' us rides, and I found food for us. That's all."

John looked at Jed more closely. "You did all that? Are you sure you're only ten?"

Jed grinned suddenly. "Yep."

"Want to go for a ride?" John asked.

Moments later, gripping the basket of cinnamon rolls Annie had given them, the trio burst out the back door.

"They be best friends by the time they get back here for lunch," Annie predicted. "It be just what that little boy needs." She turned her eyes to Janie. "How is his daddy?"

Janie frowned. "He still has a high fever. I'm trying to bring it down, but the infection had taken hold of him more than it had Vincent." She decided to leave unspoken what she was thinking. *I'm not sure he'll make it.*

She refused to give voice to words that would tear Jed's life apart even more.

Chapter Five

Thomas, Abby, and Harold watched as Jed raced across the yard with John and Hope.

"What's going on down in South Carolina?" Thomas asked.

Harold frowned. "I thought North Carolina had the worst of the violence against blacks." He shook his head. "I was wrong." He thought of the brutal murder that had brought Daniel Blue and his daughter, Angel, to them the year before. The Klan murder of the rest of Blue's family still enraged him, but what he'd learned about South Carolina sickened him.

"Worse?" Abby asked, her gray eyes dark with concern as she watched the children disappear into the barn.

"The KKK has ramped up its attacks since the election last year," Harold said. "I was in Richmond last week and ran into Joe Holly, a reporter who has been covering Klan activity in South Carolina for a paper in Baltimore. Both Matthew and I have worked with him over the years. He told me the Klan riders have been doing raids almost nightly, terrorizing as many black families as they can to try to keep them from voting. Or even *thinking* of voting," he growled. "Many families are sleeping in the woods or the swamps in hopes of staying alive."

"Why isn't the government stopping them?" Thomas demanded. "That was the whole purpose of the Ku Klux Klan Act that passed earlier this year in April."

Harold scowled. "South Carolina is like a world unto its own. As far as my friend can tell, there isn't as much violence in South Carolina's Lowcountry. Klan brutality is much worse in the counties of the Upcountry."

"Why?" Abby asked.

"Politics and money," Harold said bluntly. "It's the same story everywhere, but it seems to be worse in South Carolina. The whites are enraged that blacks have any say in how their state runs. They ratified the Fourteenth Amendment because it was the only way to gain their seats in Congress again, but they're determined to maintain white dominance. They're also trying to force the freed slaves back into working like they worked before the war."

"Slavery has been abolished," Thomas snapped.

"Yes, but farmers who have never known anything but that way of life are struggling with the change. They're losing money because the blacks will no longer work the way they used to. Most of them won't even agree to sharecropping. They're demanding rental agreements."

Abby shook her head. "I'm afraid I don't know what you're talking about."

"I'm learning, too," Harold assured her. "Sharecroppers basically have no rights under Southern law. Most of them live in terrible poverty. Under South Carolina's lien law, renters actually qualify as owners of the crop they're growing. What that means is they can use the value of their crop to get the supplies they need to farm and live. Sharecroppers are dependent on the landowner for everything. The whites are furious because blacks have figured out how to gain more autonomy now." He paused as he remembered everything Joe had told him. "The whites are also alarmed because the freedmen seem to prefer politics to farming."

"Who can blame them?" Thomas asked. "For the first time ever, they have a voice in what happens to their lives."

"And they're taking advantage of it," Harold replied. "The blacks in the Upcountry are far more politically astute. They're flocking to Union League meetings where Republican Party organizers are educating them about their rights as free men, as well as their duty to the Republican Party." He paused. "In the beginning, the Union League meetings were secret."

"Because everyone was afraid," Abby said wryly.

Harold nodded. "Southern whites—all over the South, not just in South Carolina—see the Union Leagues as dark and sinister organizations that need to be eradicated. Combine that with the reality that the freedmen would rather attend political rallies than work in the fields, and you have the foundation for a mutual distrust that explodes into violence." Harold paused. "Whites in Charleston, and the rest of the Lowcountry, seem to have taken a more patient course of action. They hate blacks in politics as much as anyone, but they believe that the government will eventually leave the state to them, and that the superior whites will take control again."

"Whites in the Upcountry aren't so patient?" Thomas asked.

"No," Harold said with a sigh. "I'm disgusted that the Lowcountry believes it's just a matter of time before they can force the blacks back into submission. It doesn't portend well for the future, but what's happening in the Upcountry is horrifying. They believe that murder and torture will force the blacks back into their place. They also believe the only thing that will return peace is the absolute political subjugation of the blacks."

Thomas scowled with frustration. "I don't understand why Governor Scott isn't stopping it. He's a Republican governor. It's his job to protect the blacks during Reconstruction."

"It is. He formed a state militia two years ago," Harold replied. "It ended up being all black because he couldn't find whites who were loyal to the state government. Whites in the Upcountry view the presence of a black militia as an intolerable affront, and an insult too grievous to bear," he drawled, trying his best to mute the Yankee accent that overlaid his West Virginia upbringing.

"I take it that is a direct quote," Abby observed with a slight twitch of her lips.

"It is," Harold agreed. "In all fairness, the black militia did not always act with wisdom. I completely understand their feeling that they finally had some control over their lives, but their actions were also guaranteed to frighten every white person in the state. They enjoyed drilling and firing their guns late into the night. They insisted on marching down the streets through the middle of town, shoving white people out of their way." He shook his head. "The resentment is rather intense."

Thomas looked thoughtful. "I thought Vincent told us that the militia had been disbanded?"

"It has been," Harold replied. "But the fear and hatred haven't disappeared. The Klan gained support by convincing every white person in the state that they're in mortal danger of being killed by blacks. It didn't take much to appeal to white paranoia that was nurtured through centuries of slavery."

"The militia was formed because so many of the freedmen were being killed," Abby protested.

"I believe people have conveniently forgotten that," Harold replied. "Ordinary Klansmen tend to be poor whites who are as ignorant and illiterate as the blacks they attack. Whites who would prefer to not be involved have been pressed into service through threats and night attacks on them, as well. The beatings haven't been limited to blacks. The Klan hates white Republicans and has brutalized many of them into renouncing their Republican Party membership."

"So they can pretend to have a unified white front," Thomas growled.

"Yes. The unity gives the Klan the freedom to terrorize blacks at will. For the most part, the outrages go unreported and unpunished." Harold thought about what he'd learned. "The Klan bursts into Republican homes, both black and white. They pull them from their beds and whip them mercilessly."

Abby covered her face with her hands. "I saw just how mercilessly last night." Her voice trembled. "I don't know how Vincent and Morris survived."

"Two hundred and thirteen whippings have been documented in Spartanburg County," Harold informed them. "The number for York County is estimated to be six hundred."

"No!" Abby gasped.

"That's just what has been documented," Harold said grimly. "There are certainly many more whippings that have been unreported, like Vincent and Morris'. There's more, though. The Klan commits robbery, rape, arson, and murder." Bile rose in his throat. After his months in North Carolina the year before, he had hoped to never be confronted with such atrocities again. "The nightly visits combine contempt for the black man, fear of an armed black militia, and the desire to suppress the Republican Party. They seem to be equally and inextricably intertwined."

A heavy silence hung over the porch. Harold tried to focus on the soft breeze carrying the promise of fall, and the sound of geese honking overhead on their migratory route, but it was impossible. The laughter from the barn was the only thing that offered him respite from what he was feeling.

Thomas shook his head with disbelief. "President Grant suspended the writ of habeas corpus in April," he protested. "How is this still happening? Surely there are South Carolinians who are appalled by the Klan's behavior?"

"Probably," Harold conceded, "but my friend told me that white South Carolinians prefer to live with Klan activity over the government of law." He struggled to explain what he was only just beginning to understand, despite the fact that he would never accept it. "There seem to be two distinct legal systems in South Carolina. One is the established Southern white perception of what justice is and how it should be accomplished. The other system is dominated by Yankee values, which the Republican administration has attempted to force on the state."

"I believe we fought a war over this not too long ago," Abby responded. "The North won."

"I remember," Harold said heavily. "Let's not forget, however, that South Carolina was the first to urge secession. They may have lost the war, but their defeat didn't alter their beliefs. Basically, the white residents believe the Klan's raids are a necessary, if unfortunate, means of enforcing law and order, and defending the South's traditional values."

"Maddening," Abby muttered. She turned to Thomas. "Is it possible to understand Southern white men?"

Thomas grimaced. "I understand them all too well," he admitted. "I've changed, but I haven't forgotten what drove me."

"Please explain it to me," Abby implored. "I find myself quite incapable of comprehending what is happening."

Thomas looked out over the pastures for several moments before he began to speak. "The Southern white man believes honor is everything. It defines his self-worth, which is completely dependent upon the opinion of others. Instead of being led by conscience or guilt, he is controlled by the fear of being shamed." He paused, searching for the right words. "Southern honor stresses family and kin, the sanctity of white women, and the necessity of defending your good name."

"But most of the Klan is made up of poor whites," Harold argued.

"It doesn't matter," Thomas replied heavily. "They believe the practice of slavery bestowed honor on *all* white men because it proves their supremacy. The Klan takes pride in the fact that they're neither slaves nor black. They believe those two facts legitimize the principles of honor that they espouse. At its core, the Southern code of honor embodies white male values and demands conformity from women and blacks because they're excluded."

Abby stared at him. "Their *white honor* is worse than any animal behavior. Actually, I'm quite certain there are no animals on the planet that act so abhorrently. How did you ever break free from such a mind-numbing, ridiculous belief?"

Thomas smiled slightly, his eyes deeply troubled. "I happened to have an amazing daughter who both forced me to see the truth *and* gave me the time to change." He frowned. "I shudder to think who I would be now if Carrie hadn't shown me the truth of my prejudices."

Abby looked thoughtful. "Carrie told me your neighbors gave you a hard time because you allowed her to be so independent when she was growing up."

Thomas sighed. "That's true. I suppose I had begun to change a little before the war happened. Many of my neighbors and friends told me I was ruining my daughter. The Southern code of honor includes certain gender expectations. White men demand absolute chastity from their unmarried daughters, and submission and unerring faithfulness from their wives. Most men consider their women to be both physically frail and childlike.

They prefer them that way because they're easy to manipulate and morally weak. Southern whites believe it is their duty to both protect and control their women, but rarely do they see them as more than property." He shook his head. "The belief is a complete disservice to Southern women."

Abby reached out and squeezed his hand. "Thank you for becoming a different man," she said. "It's not only *Southern* men who believe women are their property. Women are fighting that perception all over the country."

Harold could feel the pain and embarrassment in Thomas' voice. Though he could understand the shame Thomas felt about who he had been in the past, he was mostly impressed Thomas possessed the courage to become someone totally different from who he had been. It gave Harold hope for others.

Thomas turned to Harold, obviously wanting to steer the conversation away from himself. "Back to what the Ku Klux Klan Act has accomplished. Is it doing *anything*? My understanding was that President Grant passed it so that he could send federal troops, with or without the state's request. The purpose was to provide protection to those being terrorized by the Klan and other white supremacy groups."

"That's true," Harold answered, but instead of answering right away, he asked Thomas a question. "Do you know Attorney General Ackerman?"

"The head of the United States Justice Department that was formed last year?" Thomas nodded. "I'm familiar with him. I don't know him personally, but I understand he was born and educated in the North before he moved to Georgia to teach and to open a law office. He fought for the Confederacy but changed his allegiance to the Republican Party at the end of the war. He was the first Confederate to serve in President Grant's Cabinet."

"Ackerman has been put in charge of what's happening," Harold replied. "Joe told me he has amassed a huge amount of information on Klan activities. He's been in South Carolina interviewing victims and is sending that information back to Congress."

Thomas tightened his lips. "Because if the government is going to send troops into the South again, they want to make sure they have the evidence necessary to justify the action."

"Yes," Harold replied. "I suspect we're only a few weeks away from the suspension of habeas corpus."

"And the arrests that will go with it?" Abby asked.

"Yes."

A long silence fell over the porch.

Annie bustled out, carrying a pot of hot water. "Could one of you fine gentlemen carry this over to the barn for me? I know Miss Janie about to clean them cuts again. She gonna need it."

Harold reached for it without a word, achingly aware that the need for it was more evidence of the violence ripping lives apart in South Carolina.

Jed peered up at Miles. "You really gonna let me ride one of them horses?"

"I reckon I am," Miles said gravely, his wrinkled face creased by a smile. "You ain't never been on a horse before?"

"Only ridin' on the back of Maple with Miss Rose this morning," Jed answered. He wasn't sure how he felt about riding one all by himself, but seeing John astride Cafi gave him a yearning so powerful he could taste it. Watching five-year-old Hope expertly saddle her gleaming black and white pony, Patches, made him determined to do the same thing. "I reckon I can do it, though," he added, hoping he sounded more confident than he felt. He turned when a tall, blond-haired woman strode into the barn.

"You must be Jed."

"Yes'sum." Jed appraised the woman with shining blue eyes and decided he liked her.

"I'm Miss Susan. It's a pleasure to meet you."

Jed cocked his head. "You the other lady who owns this place?"

"That's me," Susan confirmed with a smile.

"It's a real nice place," Jed said, still unable to comprehend a woman owning a whole barn full of horses.

"Thank you. Are you going riding with John and Hope?"

Jed nodded, hoping he wouldn't embarrass himself by falling off. "I ain't never been on a horse before," he said, realizing he sounded more nervous than he wanted to.

"All of us have to get on a horse for the first time," Susan told him, and then addressed the fear he hadn't spoken. "We've all fallen off before, too."

Jed narrowed his eyes. "Does it hurt real bad?" Maybe if he was ready for it, it wouldn't be so bad when it happened.

Susan smiled the kind of smile his mama had given him when she was saying she understood something he was feeling. "It can sometimes, but you get up and get on again. That's the hardest thing about learning to ride—having the courage to fall off and get back on."

Jed felt a tug in his heart. "My mama told me there ain't nothin' wrong with makin' a mistake as long as you do it right the next time." Thinking about his mama made a rock lodge in his throat.

"Your mama was a very wise woman," Susan said gently. "You were a lucky boy to have her."

Jed nodded but couldn't push out any more words.

Miles came to his rescue. "What kind of horse you want to ride, Jed?"

Jed jerked his head around. He'd never thought about choosing a horse. "Uh…one that ain't as big as Cafi, but not as little as Patches?"

Miles chuckled. "That sounds like a good place to start." He opened a stall door and led out a horse that shone like a bright copper penny. "This is Copper."

Jed's eyes widened. "She's beautiful!"

"And really gentle, too."

A strange voice made Jed whirl around.

A slender black girl entered the barn and walked over to give Copper a kiss on her nose. "Hi, Jed. I'm Amber."

"Howdy," Jed muttered. He didn't know how he was supposed to keep up with all the new people he was meeting. He liked the warm smile on her face, though, and the way her eyes shone with enthusiasm. "What you do aroun' here?"

"She and her brother, Clint, train the horses," Miles answered. "Clint is also the barn manager. I reckon Amber be the best horse trainer in the country. She's got a magic touch when it comes to a horse."

Amber ducked her head with modesty as a loud neigh rang out in the barn. Moments later, a massive head appeared over a stall door. A snort and a loud stomp accompanied the first call.

Jed stumbled back, nearly falling as he scrambled to escape the huge horse that seemed as if it could escape the stall and attack him.

Amber smiled and moved over to stroke the horse's head. "You scared Jed, Eclipse. That wasn't very nice." The horse gentled immediately, closing his eyes in ecstasy as Amber rubbed his face gently. "Jed, this is Eclipse. He's the barn stallion. That means he's the daddy to all those young horses you see out in the pasture."

Jed, reassured by her easiness with the horse, edged a little closer. "He be the most beautiful horse I ever seen."

"He's special," Amber agreed. "Do you want to pet him?"

Jed was shaking his head before he was aware of the motion. He flushed but stayed where he was. "Maybe another time?" he asked weakly.

"You got plenty of time for everything," Miles said. "Right now, we gots to get you on a horse. Come on over here. I'll start showin' you how to put on a saddle and bridle."

Jed scampered to Miles' side, glad to put some distance between him and the massive stallion.

Twenty minutes later, Miles led Jed to the mounting block in the spotless barnyard. Jed watched closely as John climbed the steps and slid onto Cafi's back. It looked easy enough. Miles showed him how to gather the reins, talk softy to Copper to get her to stand still, and then ease himself into the saddle so that he didn't hurt the mare's back.

Moments later, Jed was on a horse by himself for the first time in his life.

"Well done, Jed."

Jed sat straight in the saddle, a brilliant smile on his face as he basked in Miles' praise. Actually sitting on top of a horse on his own was a feeling like nothing he had ever experienced. The feeling faded, along with his smile.

"What's wrong?" Miles asked keenly.

Jed glanced up at the window of the room where his daddy and Vincent were. It felt wrong to be having fun when his daddy was in pain and sick. "My daddy..." he muttered.

Miles shook his head. "Janie told me your daddy wants you to be havin' fun while he be gettin' better. Ain't that right?"

Jed nodded reluctantly, drawn to the old man's kind eyes and open smile. "Yes'sir. That be what he told me, but it just don't feel right."

"Well then, I reckon that's what you oughta be doin'," Miles said firmly. His voice softened. "Of course you be worried about him. That's only right. You love your daddy. But it be alright to ride this horse and have fun." He paused and glanced up at the window. "You goin' up to see your daddy later?"

Jed nodded quickly. "Yes'sir."

"Then you's gonna have a right good story to tell him, ain't you?"

Jed considered the question. "Yes'sir." He let the smile bloom on his lips again. "Where we goin'?"

Susan walked from the barn, leading another tall horse. "I've got Ascent ready for you, Miles."

Miles smiled his thanks, mounted easily, and then turned to the children. He fixed his eyes on John and Hope. "We ain't doing nothing but walkin' until I say. Are we clear on that?"

"Yes, Grandpa," they said in unison.

Jed could have burst with pride and excitement when Copper fell into place beside Miles' horse. He listened closely as Miles instructed him on what to do, doing exactly as he was told. He started out feeling awkward and uncomfortable, but it wasn't long before he seemed to fall into a rhythm with Copper.

About twenty minutes later, as they were moving down a road that ran through the tobacco fields, Miles gave him an approving nod. "You're sittin' in that saddle like you done it before, Jed. How you feel about doin' a trot?"

Jed looked at him. "What's a trot?"

Miles chuckled. "It just means we gonna go a little faster. Would you like that?"

Jed wasn't at all sure he would like it, but the excited looks on John and Hope's faces wouldn't allow him to say no. "I reckon so," he said, holding back a gasp as Copper immediately broke into a bouncy gait that made him grip tighter with his legs.

"That's right," Miles said. "You just gotta relax your upper body and move with your horse. Grip with your legs but let the rest of you dance with your horse."

"Dance?" Jed sputtered.

"Ain't you ever danced before, boy?" Miles asked.

Jed remembered the times his mama had whirled with him around the cabin as she hummed a song. "Yes'sir."

"Ridin' a horse is a lot like dancing. You learn how your horse moves. Then you just move with her."

Miles continued to give instructions as they moved side-by-side down the road.

Jed quickly decided he liked the trot. He felt like he was on top of the world as they rode through the tobacco fields. Following John and Hope's example, he waved to the workers in the fields, luxuriating in the breeze that caressed his face.

While he rode, he thought.

"You lookin' real serious over there," Miles said.

"I be wishin' all the South could be like this," Jed replied. "My mama would still be livin', and my daddy wouldn't be hurt so bad. I ain't never dreamed of a place where a black man could own some of all this." His thoughts continued to whirl. "Women own a fancy barn with real pretty horses. A black girl trains them horses. And I can go to school." He gazed around. "It don't seem real."

"No, I reckon it don't," Miles said thoughtfully. "It is, though. I used to be a slave right here on this plantation. I took off right before the war started. Escaped and went to Canada. I liked it up there just fine, but my heart belongs down here on Cromwell Plantation, so I came back. Best thing I ever did."

"And y'all be safe here?"

Jed stiffened when Miles hesitated.

"As safe as we can be," Miles finally said. "We done had some bad things happen, same as in the rest of the country, but not too many. Right this minute, there be guards watching the plantation and the school. We ain't never gonna let anyone sneak up on us, Jed." He paused. "All any of us can do is be real careful. The thing is, bad things can happen anywhere. I figure you got to choose where you want to be, and then do your best to live there."

Jed thought through what the old man said. "I reckon that sounds right."

John rode closer. "You don't have anything to worry about, Jed. My daddy and his men take care of us. My daddy is bigger and stronger than anyone who could try to hurt us," he boasted.

Jed nodded, remembering the giant of a man whom he'd met earlier. "I reckon that be true enough."

"My daddy saved me from a flood last year," John confided.

Jed's eyes widened. "A flood?" He listened as John launched into his story. One story flowed into the next, with Hope adding stories of her own. Jed relaxed, amazed that he could feel so at ease on the massive animal beneath him.

He didn't know how much time had passed before he saw the barn and the big white house appear in the distance. Their ride was over.

"Are you hungry?" John asked.

Jed nodded. Even though he'd already had more food to eat than he usually ate in a whole day, he couldn't deny he was starving.

"My Annie will have a good meal waitin' for you," Miles promised. "Once we take care of the horses, that is." His eyes flashed. "Whenever you ride a horse on Cromwell Plantation, you also take care of it, Jed."

"Yes'sir. I want to do ever'thin' just right," Jed said earnestly. He meant it with all his heart. He didn't know how long he would be on the plantation or how long it would be before his daddy and Vincent got better, but he hoped he could ride every single day. It would probably be the only time in his whole life that he would be around horses like this. His mama used to tell him to take advantage of every opportunity that came his way. He intended to do just that.

"Mr. Miles?"

Miles swung down from Ascent and showed him how to dismount from Copper. "Yes, son?"

Jed gazed up at the old man. "You figure maybe I can ride again?"

"Of course you can!" John answered. "You can come riding with me every time I go. Isn't that right, Grandpa?"

Jed waited anxiously for the answer, thinking about how differently John talked than he did. He felt more comfortable around Miles because the old man talked more like him, but he was curious as to why John sounded different. Of course, Miss Rose and Mr. Moses sounded the same way. It must have something to do with the plantation.

"I know your mama let you stay home from school today, John, but that probably ain't gonna happen again." Miles swept his eyes over both boys. "You two got to go to school each day, then you can go for a ride. Deal?"

"Deal!" John replied.

Jed nodded vigorously. He would do whatever it took to be able to ride a horse again.

He turned when Janie appeared from the barn. "Hello, Dr. Justin," he called, all his worry and fear returning. "How be my daddy?"

Janie smiled reassuringly. "I think he's a little better, Jed. He ate some of Annie's soup and had some bread. He's resting now, but he's looking forward to seeing you later. Vincent, too."

Jed sagged with relief, glad to know his decision to have fun hadn't made his daddy sicker.

"Did you have fun riding?"

"Yes'sum." Jed's smile bloomed now that his worry had been alleviated. "I reckon it's the best thin' I ever did in my whole life!"

Carrie could feel it the instant she stepped down from the train onto the station platform. She glanced up at Anthony. The expression on his face said he felt it as well.

"Mama! We're here!"

Carrie smiled down at Minnie and gripped her hand firmly. "Yes, we are," she said cheerfully.

Frances edged closer to them. Her oldest daughter wasn't comfortable around large crowds. The plantation and the open spaces were perfect for the sensitive girl. She insisted on joining them on trips, but she was happiest when she was home.

Anthony disappeared into the crowd to go collect their baggage, while Carrie led the girls outside and looked for a carriage to drive them to Jeremy and Marietta's. They had wanted to pick them up at the station, but Carrie had refused. Jeremy was busy at the factory, and Marietta would have her hands too full with the twins.

Carrie had secured a carriage by the time Anthony appeared, loaded down with their bags. She didn't miss the way his eyes constantly moved, scanning the crowd as he looked for trouble.

Tension vibrated in the air. She could feel it as easily as she could feel the humid air flowing in from the Delaware River.

Anthony and the driver loaded the carriage while Carrie got the girls settled, smiling at their excited chatter. She wanted to drill the driver for information, but she didn't want to alarm her daughters. Jeremy and Marietta would know what was going on. They would be able to talk later that evening.

"I'm hungry," Minnie announced.

"I'm starving," Frances said dramatically, pretending to swoon.

Carrie laughed, determined to focus on the girls.

Whatever was going to happen, was going to happen.

Chapter Six

Dinner had been devoured and the children put to bed before Marietta turned to Carrie and Anthony. "Are you too tired to have company tonight?"

In truth, Carrie was exhausted, but she had managed to sleep several hours on the train despite the clanking and swaying of the cars. There had been no opportunity to share with Marietta and Jeremy what had happened the night before on the plantation. While she wanted nothing more than to crawl into bed, knowing Anthony must feel the same way, there was something about the excited shine in Marietta's eyes that made Carrie shake her head. "We're fine. Who's coming?"

Marietta smiled mysteriously. "Come help me with dessert. They should be here any minute."

Carrie stifled a yawn and followed, eyeing Anthony enviously as he settled into a chair across from Jeremy.

Marietta looked at Carrie more closely as they cut generous slices of apple pie and placed them on delicately patterned china. "Are you sure you're not too tired?"

"I'm assuming whoever is coming to visit must be very special," Carrie said casually, choosing to avoid the question. "I'm eager to see who it is."

Marietta stopped setting out coffee cups and narrowed her eyes. "What is going on? I know it's a long trip on the train, but you're not usually this tired. You're utterly exhausted." She frowned. "I apologize. I've been so excited to have you all that I haven't paid close enough attention."

Carrie didn't bother to stifle her yawn this time. "I was treating patients until almost three this morning." She explained the situation, confident Anthony was doing the same thing with Jeremy in the other room.

Marietta's face grew more and more horrified as she heard of Morris and Vincent's wounds and infection. "That's terrible!" she finally cried. "Do you believe they'll get well?"

Carrie shook her head. "I don't know. Believe would be too strong of a word. I *hope* they'll get well, but only time will tell. We're giving them their best chance. I know Janie and Polly will take excellent care of them. Jed will be their best medicine, though."

"Jed?"

Carrie realized that in her fatigue, she had neglected to tell the whole story. "Jed is Morris' ten-year-old son. I haven't met him yet, but he must be special. Somehow, he helped those two men make it to the plantation from South Carolina, even after his mother was murdered. I don't know how either of them survived. It could only have been their determination to get Jed to safety. That's why I believe he's their best medicine. They will want to get well so they can keep traveling and bring him north. Morris is adamant that he won't raise Jed in the South."

Just then, a knock sounded through the house. Marietta's troubled eyes flew to the kitchen door as she hesitated. "They don't have to stay long, Carrie. You need rest."

"I'll be fine," Carrie said staunchly, eager to see who was visiting.

Marietta pulled off her apron. "Let's go greet them. We'll bring out dessert in a little while."

The moment Carrie walked through the door, her fatigue vanished. "Florence!" She flew across the room and flung her arms around her friend. "It's really you!"

Florence hugged her back as she laughed loudly. "It's so good to see you, Carrie. I've missed you!"

Carrie finally pulled back and gazed at her friend. Florence, tall, angular, and as red-haired as ever, glowed with happiness and confidence. Her harrowing experience during the Paris Revolution obviously hadn't harmed her in any permanent way. "I've missed you, too. You look wonderful."

Florence smiled. "As do you." She stepped back slightly. "I'd like you to meet my husband, Dr. Silas Amberton."

Silas stepped forward, his dark good looks catching Carrie by surprise. "Please, call me Silas," he said warmly. "If we all start using our titles, it will be a rather strained conversation."

Carrie laughed, liking him immediately. "I completely agree." Ignoring his outstretched hand, she wrapped him in a heartfelt embrace. "I feel as if I know you through the letters we've received, and anyone who can make Florence look so radiantly happy is already a friend of mine."

"We mere mortals don't have to worry about titles, do we Jeremy?" Anthony's voice was mournful.

"Nope. Just plain old names seem to work for the rest of us here," Jeremy agreed. "I suppose everyone should be grateful we're not complicating things more. There is much to be said for mere mortals without fancy titles."

Carrie erupted in laughter at the look of concern on Florence and Silas' faces. "They're teasing," she assured them. "Besides," she said nonchalantly, "you shouldn't let them bother you. It's best if they accept their lower position in life."

Anthony leapt from his chair and advanced on her. "You will pay for that statement, Dr. Carrie Wallington!"

Carrie dodged away and ran into the kitchen. "If you want dessert, you will not touch me!" Laughing, she disappeared behind the swinging door.

Peals of merriment followed her.

Laughter continued around the table as the apple pie and coffee were consumed. There was much to catch up on, but by unspoken consent, they stayed away from unpleasant topics.

"Do you really have two daughters now?" Florence asked.

Carrie grinned. "Two beautiful daughters. You've met Frances. Minnie has been with us for nearly a year." She shook her head. "It's hard to believe she's been with us such a short time. It's as if she's always been ours." Carrie shook off the sadness that enveloped her as she thought of Deirdre and the rest of her children dying in the fire that destroyed their tenant house. "Minnie's bright, funny, and full of energy."

"That little girl is going to change our country," Anthony added. "She's passionate and strong-willed."

"Deirdre, her mother, was an extraordinary woman," Carrie continued. "She emigrated from Ireland and managed to raise her children after her husband died. She was our cook, but mostly she was our friend. Minnie and Frances have been best friends since the day they met. We are fortunate to have her as part of our family."

"Do you have a limit?" Florence asked with a smile.

"A limit?"

"Our country is full of orphaned children who need a home," Florence said.

Carrie exchanged a smile with Anthony.

"I don't know about a *limit*," Anthony replied, "but we are certainly open to more children. Frances and Minnie are like rays of sunshine. Why wouldn't we want more?"

Carrie felt an almost overwhelming surge of love for her husband. Her longing to birth a child would never disappear, but she was well aware it was too dangerous. She'd almost died giving birth to Bridget. Anthony assured her often that her life was far more valuable to him than a child who bore his blood. He was excited to adopt more children.

*****

It was Marietta who changed the tone. "From what I've heard, your time in Paris was horrible. Have you kept abreast of what's happening there now?"

Silas nodded, his face growing grim.

Florence's expression reflected the same pain.

Carrie's heart ached at the anguish she saw etched on their features. After her years at Chimborazo Hospital during the war, she knew what they had experienced and what they were feeling. While she waited for them to respond, she reached out and took Florence's hand.

Florence gave her a smile of gratitude and squeezed tightly.

"Communication is still sparse, but I received a letter from a colleague last week," Silas responded. "It was only because of Minister Washburne that we were able to leave the city so quickly after it fell. Thank God we missed the government's revenge on the Communards that held Paris for the first months of this year."

"Revenge?" Jeremy asked.

"The latest reports say somewhere between twenty to twenty-five thousand Communards were shot in the days following the fall of Paris," Silas said grimly.

Carrie shook her head, unable to make sense of what she was hearing. "They just...killed them?" Even though prison camps during their own war had been horrible, nothing like that had happened once the conflict was over.

"They lined them up and shot them," Florence choked. "Dozens. Hundreds. Thousands." Her face tightened. "I suspect the men we saved in the final days are dead now."

"The ones who weren't killed are now suffering in a massive prison camp. My colleague told me the death rate from disease and starvation is staggering."

A heavy silence fell over the room as everyone tried to absorb what they were hearing.

Carrie was glad the children were upstairs, sound asleep. She wouldn't be able to protect them from all the horrors of life, but they were too young to hear of the depravity humans were capable of.

"More men were executed in those days than were killed in any battle during the war," Silas added. His face settled into heavy lines. "It wasn't limited just to men, however."

Carrie covered her mouth as Silas finished his statement.

"Women and children were also killed."

"Why?" she cried.

"Because the French government believes that only complete subjugation will keep it from happening again."

"Yet the history of revolutions reveals their acts did nothing but create martyrs that will inspire future revolutions," Jeremy said.

Carrie looked at him with surprise. Rose's twin, and Carrie's half-uncle, was incredibly intelligent, but she didn't realize this was an area he had studied.

Jeremy managed a smile. "I don't have to be a doctor to keep learning," he teased, his eyes heavy with sadness.

"Unfortunately, you're completely right," Silas replied. "Many of the Communards who weren't killed have already fled to other countries. Their hatred for the government will grow during their exile. The troubles in France aren't over."

"Which is why we came home," Florence added. "If we're going to rebuild a country, we decided it would be our own."

Carrie wanted to hear their future plans, but her mind was still whirling with what she'd heard. "Is Paris rebuilding?"

"Yes," Silas answered. "It will take decades to return the city to its former glory, but they're making great progress. They've demolished and taken away the rubble from all the burned structures. Construction has begun. Many of the magnificent buildings will take several years to rebuild, but at least it will provide income for people who were impoverished during the war with Prussia and the revolution."

"The trees, though," Florence said sadly. "The trees in Paris were so beautiful. They were one of the first things I fell in love with when I arrived last year. They were all cut down and turned into firewood during the brutal winter. When we left, the city appeared naked." She shuddered. "Skeletal remains of buildings. Thin, shell-shocked people. Barren, muddy streets. I still can't believe I was looking at what had been so opulent and beautiful just months ago. It will take decades for it to look as it once did."

Carrie thought about the desolation wrought throughout the South by the war. Sherman's March had decimated Georgia. The Shenandoah Valley had been destroyed. Six years later, they were still struggling to recover.

"War is disgusting," she whispered. "It takes away so much, and for what? The lives lost. The families destroyed. Paris can rebuild its structures, but they can't rebuild the lives that have been forever changed, or their country that has been forever altered."

Florence was the one who took her hand now. "What else is going on, Carrie? What happened in Paris is horrible, but I sense there is something else."

Carrie sighed. "The war is over in America, but only because the government says it's over. The armies have gone home, but as far as I'm concerned, it's still being fought." She told them about Vincent and Morris' horrible beating at the hands of the Klan. "The South hasn't stopped fighting." Her eyes flashed with anger. "And our government isn't doing anything to stop it."

"They passed the Ku Klux Klan Act," Jeremy reminded her.

Carrie scowled. "I can't see that it's doing any good. Besides, what happens when the Federal Government removes the troops they may *eventually* get around to sending down there? Will it really change anything? Or will the South just wait for them to disappear so they can go back to terrorizing and killing the people they don't believe deserve to live?"

Jeremy opened his mouth to argue, but then closed it again.

Carrie noticed the frustration sparking in his eyes at the same moment she thought about the strain she had felt in the air when they arrived in Philadelphia. "What is it, Jeremy?"

"We feel the tension," Anthony said somberly. "What's happening? The city feels like a powder keg getting ready to explode."

"That's a fairly accurate description," Jeremy acknowledged. "The city's first election with black voters takes place in about a week."

Carrie thought about Morris and Vincent's belief that moving to the North would make them safer. "You're afraid of violence?"

"Do you remember meeting Octavius Catto and his fiancée, Caroline LeCount?" Marietta asked.

"Of course," Carrie said. "They are such lovely people. They both have done much for black equality."

"They have," Marietta agreed. "Several months ago, Octavius predicted violence. Now, the blacks in the city are preparing for it."

Anthony frowned. "Let me guess. Moyamensing, and the clinic, will be at the center of the violence."

Jeremy hesitated only briefly before nodding. "I suspect the violence will be citywide, but the tension in Moyamensing is growing on a daily basis. There have already been attacks by white Democrats against black Republicans registering citizens for the vote. The Democrats are determined to do whatever they can to stop Republican William Stokely from beating the incumbent, Mayor Daniel Fox."

"And William McMullen is behind all of it," Silas added. "I haven't been in Philadelphia very long, but it's obvious McMullen has power over what happens in Moyamensing."

"A power he's losing," Jeremy growled. "As an alderman, McMullen believes he is above the law. He's been receiving kickbacks for political favors for years. All of that is being threatened by Republicans who are trying to eliminate aldermen. The Republicans are making great strides toward reclaiming the city by using the Registry Act to register massive numbers of blacks to vote in this election. Liquor law enforcement is hurting the business at McMullen's bar, and educated blacks are moving into Moyamensing and voting. He's watching the life he's always known crumble around him."

"As it should," Anthony snapped. "It sounds, though, that the scene has been set for a violent election day."

"You can count on it," Jeremy conceded. "It's clear that the outcome of this election is going to determine party dominance in Philadelphia for at least the next decade. I can assure you that Democrats aren't going to loosen their control easily. They'll do everything they can to limit the black vote."

Carrie couldn't stop the sick feeling that threatened to overwhelm her. "Is there any place in this country where it's safe for people to be black?" she cried. The fatigue from the last forty-eight hours pressed in on her as she blinked back tears. "I'm sorry. This is all sometimes too much to bear."

"There's no need to apologize," Marietta said soothingly. "Anyone with a heart is disturbed by what's happening in our country."

Carrie took deep breaths, fighting to bring her emotions back under control.

Florence and Silas stood. "It's time for us to be going."

"No," Carrie said. "Please don't. I don't want to ruin our time."

Florence leaned down and hugged her fiercely. "You have hardly ruined it, Carrie. It's been wonderful being with all of you, and I'm planning on seeing you often while you're here. Right now, you need sleep."

Silas laid a hand on Carrie's shoulder. "It's been wonderful to meet you, Carrie. Florence was right when she told me how passionate and caring you are. Just remember, you're not alone. There are many people fighting to make America better for everyone."

Carrie blinked up at them. "I still have so many questions for both of you," she whispered, aware of how pathetic she sounded but unable to stop it.

Florence smiled gently. "I have a lot of questions for you, but I would prefer you get some sleep so you have a functioning brain when you answer them."

Carrie smiled despite herself. "That sounds fair."

Anthony stood and held out a hand to her. "Let's go upstairs, Carrie. Sleep is calling both of us. The world will be waiting for us to change it tomorrow."

Carrie gazed up at him, took his hand, and followed him up the steps.

A brisk wind was blowing early the next morning as Carrie and Frances hurried to the carriage that waited outside. Carrie felt refreshed after a good night of sleep. She was eager to accomplish what she had come to Philadelphia to do.

The driver, standing on the road next to the carriage, turned around with a broad smile. "Good morning, Miss Carrie."

"Sarge!" Carrie laughed with delight as she hugged him. "I asked Anthony to request you, but I had no idea if you were still driving or if you would be available."

Sarge grinned. "What else am I gonna be doing, Miss Carrie? Driving a carriage suits me just fine. I was tickled when my boss man told me you was coming to town." He paused and looked down at Frances. "Who is this pretty little thing?"

Carrie smiled proudly. "This is my daughter, Frances."

Sarge tipped his cap and smiled warmly. "It sure be a pleasure to meet you, Miss Frances. Your mama be a real special lady."

"I know," Frances agreed. "It's a pleasure to meet you too, Mr. Sarge."

Sarge laughed heartily. "Just Sarge will do fine, Miss Frances. Me and your mama go way back."

Carrie nodded, appreciating the fact that Sarge immediately accepted Frances as her daughter. He'd known she had no children when they first met, but he wouldn't ask questions. If they had time alone during her visit, she would explain the miracle that had given her Frances. "He's right. I met Sarge three years ago when I was working here in Philadelphia. He drove me back and forth to Moyamensing while I was working at the clinic and finishing school. He became a good friend."

Frances smiled broadly. "Any friend of my mama's is a friend of mine."

Sarge eyed her with approval. "You going to the clinic with your mama this morning?"

"She is *working* with me at the clinic," Carrie corrected. "Frances wants to be a doctor. She already is invaluable to me. She's going to be a fine physician when she's old enough to go to medical school."

Sarge appraised Frances. "Fifteen?"

"Fourteen," Frances corrected him. "By the time I get to medical school, I hope to know more than my instructors," she said seriously.

Sarge threw back his head with a hearty laugh. "I like you, Miss Frances. You sho'nuff be just like your mama. I reckon you'll know more than your instructors, for sure."

Carrie smothered her smile. "Frances is well on her way," she assured him. "She's got a head start on where I was at her age. She's in the process of reading all my medical books."

Sarge nodded his approval and then changed the subject. "Miss Faith sure be looking forward to seeing you, Miss Carrie."

"How is she doing, Sarge? *Really* doing? I know she'll tell me she's doing just fine, no matter what she's feeling. I worry about her."

Carrie answered the question in her daughter's eyes. "Faith and Sarge are neighbors. He looks in on her when he can."

"Pretty much every day now," Sarge acknowledged.

Carrie felt her heart quicken. "*Every* day? Why? Is she sick?"

"Not sick," Sarge allowed, "but she be movin' a whole lot slower than she used to. She be getting older, you know. She was eighty-three on her last birthday. Dr. Carolyn takes good care of her, but she has to spend an awful lot of time at the clinic."

Carrie frowned. Carolyn loved Faith, and also loved living with her, but she couldn't always be at home. Faith's life had been different. She had been there for Biddy all the time, right up to her death, making sure her friend was never in want of anything until she passed away just short of her hundredth birthday.

"Now, you wipe that frown right off your face, Miss Carrie," Sarge scolded. "Dr. Carolyn can't be there all the time, but the rest of us be pickin' up the slack. We take turns checkin' in on her, and the womenfolk fight over who gonna take her the next meal. She don't got to do much of anything, but there ain't a day that goes by when Miss Faith ain't making batches of her famous Irish oatmeal cookies." He smiled at Frances. "You ever had any of her famous cookies, Miss Frances?"

Carrie met Frances' eyes, hoping she would read the silent message being broadcast. Whatever Frances might understand about the *secret* of the famous Irish oatmeal cookies, she didn't want her daughter to diminish Faith's pride in giving what she had to give. Carrie especially didn't want Faith to know that Annie used her recipe. Pride among black cooks was legendary.

Frances shook her head. "Not yet, Sarge. I've heard an awful lot about them, though. I'm looking forward to having some."

Sarge nodded with satisfaction. "Ain't nobody in this whole city can make cookies as good as Miss Faith. You just wait and see."

Carrie leaned back in the carriage seat and inhaled deeply. Despite the layer of soot that covered the city. She coughed, longing for the plantation's fresh air. Pushing that thought aside, she focused on the beauty around her. The trees lining the streets were beginning to turn gold and orange, and blooms still filled the flowerboxes hanging on almost every window they passed. She suspected they were less than a week away from the first hard frost that would kill them, but they were celebrating the last days of summer with all the vibrant color they could.

The streets were packed with wagons and carriages, their drivers yelling to each other as they jockeyed for position. The clatter of wagon wheels on the cobblestones added to the cacophony of sounds.

Carrie understood the look of distaste on Frances' face as she gazed around. Her daughter wasn't meant for city living any more than Carrie had been. Frances would have to survive it when she was ready to attend medical school, but she still had many years on the plantation before she had to worry about that.

"Mama, what's wrong down here?" Frances asked. "Everyone looks worried and upset."

Carrie didn't bother to deny her daughter's observation. She'd felt it as soon as the carriage entered the outskirts of Moyamensing. The tall, wooden tenant buildings seemed tired. The streets were thronged with people, but the usual laughing and calling were absent. People hurried about their business, but their faces were strained and worried.

"Sarge? What's going on?" Surely, worry about the election wouldn't be enough to cause the dread she felt pulsing in the air.

Sarge remained silent as he glanced at Frances.

Carrie understood his reticence to say anything in front of Frances, but if they were rolling into trouble, she wanted to know. "Go ahead," she said quietly.

Sarge still hesitated, his leathery hands twitching on the reins as he stared ahead.

"I'm not a child, Sarge," Frances said. "It's obvious something is wrong. I'd rather know the truth. I can't help people if I don't know what they're going through. I've already seen trouble in Moyamensing. This is just something new."

Carrie stared at Frances with the same amazement Sarge was staring at her with. Her daughter had become a young woman. She knew Frances was mature for her age because of all she'd gone through, but Carrie hadn't realized until now how much she'd grown up.

"Tell us, Sarge," Carrie urged. The longer he stayed silent, the more concerned she became.

Sarge sighed, his kind face creased with trouble. "A man got killed yesterday, Miss Carrie." He shook his head. "All he be doin' was registerin' some new folks to vote. He'd done finished for the day and was walkin' home. He went down one of the alleys to get to his house. They followed him there and cracked his head with a brick. He was dead by the time folks found him."

Frances covered her mouth in horror.

Carrie was sickened by the story, but her first thought was for Frances' safety. "And today?"

Sarge understood immediately. "Things be calm right now," he assured her. "It's kinda like things had reached a blowin' point. The killin' done let some of the pressure off."

"Aren't the police doing anything?" Frances cried. "Did they catch the man who did it?"

Sarge hesitated again, his eyes seeking out Carrie's.

Carrie nodded. Her daughter was mature beyond her years. If she was driving into danger, she had the right to know what might happen.

"Well, Miss Frances, the police don't be much help down here. I don't reckon they gonna do anything to find that man who killed our friend."

"Why not?" Frances asked indignantly, her eyes flashing with anger.

Carrie listened closely, wanting to understand every bit as much as Frances did.

"The police in Philadelphia are all Democrats," Sarge replied. "They all got hired by a Democratic mayor. That be Mayor Daniel Fox. If he don't win this election, none of them gonna have jobs anymore. They ain't got no reason to stop the violence down here. They figure if enough blacks be too afraid to vote, then maybe their man gonna stay in office. That means they get to keep their job."

"So the police aren't going to try to stop the violence? That's wrong!"

Sarge nodded his head, his eyes heavy with resignation. "I reckon it is, Miss Frances. Just ain't nothin' we can do about it."

Carrie gritted her teeth against the fury and helplessness raging inside her. She understood what Sarge *wasn't* saying. Not only were the police not stopping the violence, but if they were fighting to protect their jobs, they were most likely *responsible* for some of the violence.

What would election day be like?

The morning flew by. Carrie had decided to spend the first day at Moyamensing Clinic with Frances before she split her days between the clinic and Dr. Wild's medical practice. Her original plan was to have Sarge bring Frances to the clinic each morning, while she walked to Dr. Wild's office. Frances would work with Carolyn in order to gain more experience. The conversation that morning had changed those plans. She wouldn't allow Frances to be in Moyamensing without her.

Carrie was glad Minnie was happily back at the house with Marietta and the twins, baking bread and making a large pot of soup in honor of the first chilly, fall-like day. It was a relief to know she was safe.

After a long morning of treating patients, Carrie looked up to see Sarge at the door.

"Miss Faith sent me to get you," Sarge announced.

Carrie hesitated, thinking through the patients that still needed to be seen.

"She done told me to not take no for an answer. Miss Faith baked cookies this morning. My wife took over a big pot of stew and some of the best biscuits you ever tasted in your life."

Frances stayed quiet, but Carrie could see the yearning in her eyes. Her daughter had worked tirelessly all morning. Certainly she was hungry. Carrie smiled. "How can we turn down an offer like that?"

Frances' smile was all the reward she needed.

Carrie was surprised to see the carriage out front. "We can walk down to Faith's house, Sarge. It's not far."

"Yep," Sarge drawled, his eyes scanning the crowd. "Just not today."

Carrie stiffened, knowing he was watching for trouble, but she kept her voice cheerful. "Looks like we're being treated like queens today, Frances."

Frances' expression revealed she knew something was wrong, but she played along. "I'm happy with whatever gets me to Miss Faith's cookies the fastest."

Once again, Carrie was warmed and astonished by her daughter's maturity.

Faith Jacobs waited for them on the stair landing. Carrie was alarmed by how much she seemed to have aged since Carrie last saw her, but the tall, elderly black woman remained erect, and her eyes snapped with enthusiasm.

"Carrie Wallington!" Faith called. "You are a sight for sore eyes." She held out her hands in welcome.

"Faith!" Carrie hurried up the stairs and swept the woman into a warm embrace. "I've missed you. It's so good to see you."

"You wipe that look off your face right now," Faith said sternly.

Carrie's eyes widened. "What look?"

"That look that says you recognize how old I'm getting and that you're worried about me," Faith said sternly.

Carrie remained silent. She'd never been good at hiding her feelings. Why try to pretend differently?

"There isn't anything wrong with me but old age," Faith continued. "None of us are going to live forever, Carrie, but I suppose I have some years left. People around here treat me like I'm a china doll. The only thing they'll let me do is bake cookies." She broke off from her complaint and smiled at Frances radiantly. "Frances, it's wonderful to see you again. My you have grown up. I'm getting older, but you're growing up and looking more beautiful every day."

Frances grinned and rushed forward to give Faith a hug. "I haven't seen you since the day Minnie got hurt at the factory, Miss Faith."

Faith peered at the carriage. "Where is that little sister of yours?"

"Making soup with Marietta," Frances explained. "She doesn't want to be a doctor like I do. She claims the clinic is boring." She rolled her eyes. "I'll never understand how she can feel that way!"

"We all have different things we're passionate about," Faith responded. She stepped back to beckon them into the house. "Lunch is waiting, ladies."

The stew and bread disappeared quickly. Until they started eating, Carrie hadn't realized how hungry she'd been. She sat back when her bowl was empty and took a deep breath. "That was delicious."

"The people around here take good care of me," Faith said. "There are times when I want them to let me cook and take care of things the way I used to, but mostly I'm grateful."

"You mean so much to the people of Moyamensing," Carrie said. "The clinic has changed so many lives. People couldn't get medical care before. They can now."

"Biddy was the one who did that," Faith scoffed. "It's her money that opened that clinic."

Carrie shook her head firmly. "No, it was her money that made it possible for *you* to open the clinic. She knew she was putting her money into the hands of the woman who could make everything happen. She was right." Faith ducked her head, but not before Carrie saw the flash of appreciation in her eyes.

"Thank you," Faith murmured.

"How is Paddy doing?" Frances asked.

Faith's eyes brightened. "That boy is really something. Once he had the chance to go to school, he proved what I knew all along, which is just how smart he is. He's talking about going to college someday now."

Carrie smiled with delight. Paddy had been one of the first children she'd met in Moyamensing. During the cholera epidemic, he'd been key to helping her save hundreds of residents. The bright blue eyes that flashed beneath his red hair had never failed to cheer her. The fact that she had saved his little brother's life after he had lost his father to an earlier cholera epidemic ensured his loyalty and love. His mother had been hired by Jeremy to work at the factory. For the first time, his family didn't go hungry. "I'm so thrilled to hear that. Have his leg and arm healed completely?" She could still remember the agony on his face when he'd been carried into the clinic with a broken arm and leg after being almost crushed by a fire truck a year and a half ago.

"Paddy is just fine," Faith assured her. "It was like trying to keep a creek from running to keep that boy still, but we did it. There were lots of days they made him sit right here in my house so I could keep an eye on him." She smiled proudly. "I pretended my eyes were bad so he would read to me. I let him choose the books out of my library. By the time he got out of here, he had learned to love to read. He borrows books from me every week."

Carrie laughed with delight. "You are a brilliant woman, Faith!"

Faith shook her head. "Nonsense. I love that boy like a son. He is a light in my life. Of course, his red hair, freckles, and white skin could never have come from me, but that doesn't matter."

"It really doesn't," Frances said earnestly. "I didn't come from Mama, but I couldn't love her any more than I do. Minnie and I both feel the same way."

Carrie smiled lovingly at her daughter. "Your father and I are the lucky ones. I'm amazed every day that I get to be your mama."

Carrie turned to Faith. "Does Paddy know what he wants to do if he goes to college?"

"He certainly does. He's seen how Jeremy has improved the lives of so many people with the factory here. He wants to start businesses and employ as many of the folks in Moyamensing as possible." Faith's eyes flashed with pride. "I've promised there will be money to pay for his college when he's ready, as long as he makes good grades. He comes over for me to tutor him two or three times a week."

"That's wonderful," Carrie exclaimed. "You've been such an inspiration to him."

Faith shrugged. "Perhaps, but his real inspiration is Octavius Catto."

"Octavius?" Carrie asked with surprise. "How does Paddy know him?"

"Octavius came by to meet me last year. To say thank you for starting the clinic and caring for so much of the black population in Moyamensing. Paddy came by for tutoring that day, and he and Octavius hit it off immediately." Faith shook her head. "Octavius has that boy studying *Latin*. And geometry." She laughed. "Can you imagine?"

Carrie thought of the impulsive young boy who had been almost impossible to keep from running wild in the streets. "It gives me hope that any child can change if given the right motivation," she murmured. "He's always been extraordinary, but I never would have pegged him for a scholar."

"And I bet you never would have pegged me for a doctor when you met me on the Kansas plains during that blizzard," Frances said.

"That's true," Carrie admitted. "I knew you were special, but I also knew it would be hard for you to have the opportunity to go to school, much less to college."

"And then my life changed," Frances said. "You never know what a person is capable of when they're given the chance."

Carrie's mouth dropped open. "When did you become so wise?" she finally managed.

Frances shrugged. "I couldn't stay a child forever, Mama." She grinned. "Besides, you and Rose have been preaching these things to me since you adopted me. I suppose some of it had to stick."

Faith chuckled and pushed back from the table. "On that note, I'm going to get some cookies. Did you leave room for some of my cookies, Frances?"

Frances nodded quickly. "Of course, Miss Faith. I've been hearing about your cookies for a long time. I'm eager to have some."

Besides being a wise young woman, Carrie gave her daughter credit for also being an excellent actress. Anyone listening would have sworn Frances had never had an Irish oatmeal cookie in her life.

The rest of their lunchtime passed quickly as the plate of warm cookies disappeared, washed down by hot tea.

Carrie finally stood. "It's time for us to go," she said regretfully. "I promised we would be back to see more patients before the end of the day. We only have two hours before Sarge is scheduled to drive us home."

Faith nodded her head toward the window. "Sarge is waiting outside for you now."

Carrie swung around to gaze through the window. Sarge was leaning back against his wagon seat, his eyes watching the sky. "Has he been out there the whole time?"

"Yes."

"That wasn't necessary," Carrie protested.

"It was necessary," Faith said, her eyes communicating more than her words were saying.

"It's that bad?" She saw Faith glance sideways at Frances. "She knows what is going on. You may talk freely."

Faith frowned. "I've seen Moyamensing like this before."

Carrie nodded. "The night I met you and Biddy." She would never forget the night McMullen's men had set fire to the hospital where they were setting up to treat the cholera patients that were overwhelming Philadelphia hospitals. Terrified the illness would spread to other Moyamensing residents if the hospital became a reality, McMullen's men had burned the building to force them to leave. She had nearly died that night. Biddy's nephew had rescued her and brought her to Biddy and Faith for safety.

"Yes," Faith agreed. "McMullen isn't thinking right. When he's like this, anything is likely to happen. The Irish down here will follow his lead like they always have. If he tells them to keep the blacks from voting, which he will, they'll stop at nothing to make that happen."

Carrie scowled. She knew what that meant. "Riots."

Faith nodded grimly. "I'm afraid so."

"You should come stay with Jeremy and Marietta until after the election," Frances said. "They'll keep you safe."

"I'm sure they will," Faith replied with a grateful smile. "But my home is here with the people of Moyamensing."

"They'll worry about you if you stay," Carrie argued.

"Probably," Faith agreed. "But people count on me being here. My presence will let them know they haven't been abandoned."

Carrie hesitated only a moment before deciding to speak her mind. "You do realize it's mostly the Irish of Moyamensing who will attack the black voters, don't you? The same people who take such good care of you?"

Faith's eyes glistened with sadness. "I know," she admitted. "I can only hope the presence of one old black woman they love will make them think twice about attacking other blacks."

Carrie very much doubted that was true. She'd seen what unreasoning passion could do when ignited with prejudice and fear, but she also recognized the determined look in Faith's eyes. She had made her decision.

"She looks like you right now, Mama."

Carrie swung her gaze to Frances. "Excuse me?"

Frances had her eyes locked on Faith. "She has that look that says, *I know I'm doing something dumb, but I'm going to do it anyway because it's the right thing to do.*"

Faith's mouth dropped open with astonishment and then she started laughing.

Carrie stared at Faith, swung back around to stare at her daughter, and joined in the laughter.

Soon, the three ladies were laughing uncontrollably.

When they finally regained control, Faith reached out and took Frances' hand. "You are absolutely right, my dear. It's probably dumb, but I'm staying here because I believe it's the right thing to do."

"And we will respect that," Carrie said. The laughter had cleared away the fear and angst. Old Sarah and Abby had told Carrie over and over that worry never changed a situation; only action could do that. [*prayer and/or*] "We'll also be down here that day to help take care of people who are injured."

Faith shook her head firmly. "You will do no such thing. You can't put Frances and yourself in danger."

Carrie wasn't concerned about herself, but she was definitely concerned for Frances. She realized, however, that her daughter was now a young woman. If Carrie had been in her shoes at the same age, she would have wanted to be in the midst of the trouble, no matter how unsafe it might be. Frances would be needed to treat victims if the riots everyone predicted actually happened. "We'll be fine," she said.

"Thank you, Mama," Frances said quietly. She smiled over at Faith. "Now you know why I recognized the look you had a few minutes ago. It's the same one Mama has now."

Faith opened her mouth as if to argue, but snapped it closed. "You're right," she muttered. "We'll all do what we believe is the right thing, and deal with what happens."

Chapter Seven
October 8, 1871

Peter stood on the far side of State Street and examined the hotel he had called home for the last four days he'd been in Chicago. He planned to write Elizabeth that night and wanted to describe it as accurately as possible. He would be home before the letter arrived in Boston, but he had promised to write about his experiences during the reporting conference. He had stayed in luxurious hotels, but nothing like the Palmer House. At seven stories high, it had cost two million dollars to finish the hotel and furnish its five hundred rooms. The architecture was stunning. The front, built of highly wrought stone, was imposing and rich. The center was adorned with a colonnade of eight detached stone columns, each two stories in height.

Earlier that day he had learned what a caryatid was; a stone carving of a draped female figure. The upper story of the hotel had four such caryatids, topped a cornice and circular pediment.

He looked toward the south corner of State Street and admired the large pavilion, finished with columns that matched the ones at the front of the building. The end of the building that fronted Monroe Street had the same round pavilion, adorned with identical, richly executed stone columns.

The grand entrance was an elaborate marble archway, twenty-four feet in height. The rotunda it led to was equally opulent. From the rotunda, grand marble steps led to the hotel parlors and dining rooms. If you weren't inclined to take the stairs, you could utilize the baggage and passenger elevators. Five hundred rooms, along with public apartments and stores, had filled up as soon as the hotel was ready.

The beauty of the hotel was truly breathtaking.

"Peter Wilcher!"

Peter spun around, his brown eyes flashing with pleasure when he identified who had called him. "Conrad Hawkins! When did you get here?"

"This morning," Conrad answered, his light blue eyes shining beneath a thatch of sandy blond hair liberally streaked with gray. He pulled at the coat stretched tightly over his stomach and smoothed down his handlebar mustache.

Peter gazed at his old friend, whom he hadn't seen in almost a decade. The war years had obviously aged him, but his eyes still reflected kindness and keen intelligence. "So, you're still a reporter?"

Conrad nodded. "My days of reporting are nearing an end, but I decided I would come to the Chicago conference to see old friends before I close my illustrious career."

"We'll be sad to see you go," Peter said sincerely. "You were a godsend to me when I first got started. I would have made far more mistakes than I did if you hadn't been there to help me out."

Conrad chuckled. "From what I hear, your career has thrived. I've read many of your stories. You've done well."

Peter flushed with pleasure. "Thank you. I'm going to meet some friends for dinner. Would you care to join us?"

"I'd love to." Conrad gazed around with appreciation. "The Palmer House is quite a hotel. It's been at least a decade since I've been in Chicago. My last visit here was just before the war. I barely recognize the city."

"It's my first visit," Peter acknowledged. "I've wanted to see the city for quite some time. Had I visited earlier, however, I would have missed out on staying at such an opulent hotel. The Palmer House has only been open for thirteen days."

Conrad nodded. "Potter Palmer built the hotel as a gift for his wife, Bertha Honoré. The two have been married less than a year. She's twenty-one. Palmer is forty-four, and quite the successful businessman here in Chicago."

Peter whistled as he once again took in the sight of the hotel against the skyline. "That's quite a gift. I'm afraid Elizabeth can't expect anything like that."

Conrad raised a brow. "Elizabeth? I heard about the flu taking your wife and daughter five years ago. I'm so sorry."

"Thank you. I will never quit missing them, but a wonderful woman has agreed to be my wife. Elizabeth Gilbert is a doctor. I met her in Richmond this year, but she has returned to Boston, where she is in practice with her father. I have moved there, as well. We're to marry in April. I would have loved for it to be sooner, but her mother has her heart set on a spring wedding for her daughter."

Conrad gripped Peter's hand tightly. "I'm happy for you, old man."

Peter glanced at his watch. "It's time for us to meet my friends in the dining room."

Peter was stuffed when he finally laid down his fork and knife. His meal had been as sumptuous as the hotel itself. A thick steak had been complemented with fluffy mashed potatoes, green beans, and steaming rolls. Fragrant coffee was placed in front of him as he pushed back from the table and gazed around at his three companions.

"I've heard so much about Chicago, but seeing it for myself is quite illuminating."

"In what ways?" Peter asked. Mike Perry, tall and lean with jet black hair, was a new acquaintance, a reporter from Baltimore. He looked to be in his mid-twenties.

"There have been many rags to riches stories in this country, but Chicago has to be at the top of the list. Even the Civil War didn't stop its growth," Mike replied. "Less than forty years ago, Chicago consisted of a government fort and about one hundred fifty residents living in wooden cabins on a patch of soggy marshland. The mud was so thick that wagons got stuck in it up to their axles, and starving wolves roamed the streets at night for food."

Mike waved a hand toward the windows as if to embrace the entire city. "Now? There are three hundred thirty-four thousand residents. Chicago is the largest city in the West, and the fourth largest in the nation. It's a city full of elegant hotels, theaters, and marble-faced department stores."

Gerald Banker, another new acquaintance added to the description. "I read there are sixty thousand buildings spread across thirty-six square miles," he said enthusiastically. "Every major railroad comes through here, and the harbor welcomes more ships than the ports of New York, Philadelphia, Baltimore, San Francisco, Charleston, and Mobile, Alabama combined!"

Peter was impressed. He'd known only a portion of that information.

"It came at a great price," Conrad said wryly.

"What do you mean?" Mike asked.

"I was covering the story out here before any of you were old enough to even think about being reporters," Conrad answered. He appraised Mike. "Probably before you were born son." He chuckled and continued. "The main reason Chicago is so wealthy now is because of the network of connected waterways. When the Erie Canal was built, it opened up waterways to the East Coast and Europe, but they wanted to open up the route from the Mississippi River, as well. In order to do that, they had to build another canal that would connect everything into one big web of waterways. It opened in 1848."

"The Illinois and Michigan Canal," Peter said. "I read about it."

"Did you?" Conrad asked. "Did you learn about Chief Black Hawk?"

Peter hesitated and then shook his head. "No." He knew he was about to.

"Before that canal could become a reality, there was a problem that had to be solved," Conrad said grimly. "The land surrounding the dreamed of canal—and really, much of the land in Illinois—was occupied by Indian tribes. Our government took steps to change that fact. One of the things they did was to cite an earlier, *disputed* treaty with the Sauk and Fox Indians."

Peter could tell by Conrad's expression that the dispute had most likely not had merit.

"The federal soldiers escorted Chief Black Hawk and his community of Sauk and Fox Indians across the Mississippi River into Iowa and warned them not to come back." Conrad's lips tightened. "That didn't sit well with Chief Black Hawk. Now, this was a man who was used to fighting. In fact, he joined with America to fight the British during the War of 1812, but by the time this happened in 1832, he didn't want to fight anymore, and he didn't want to use force to regain the homeland of his people. He tried a different approach. He convinced his tribes to return to Illinois and peacefully resume farming. His plan was that they would return with old men, women, and children, carrying seeds for harvest to prove they meant peace." Conrad paused. "He believed that by quietly planting their crops instead of fighting, they would prove that these fertile plains were still their lands, just as they had been for hundreds of years. They would show they meant no harm so that the militia would leave them alone."

"It didn't work that way," Peter said quietly, remembering the many stories he'd heard from Carrie and Chooli about the near destruction of the Navajo people.

"It didn't work that way," Conrad agreed. "His tragic miscalculation led to the fifteen-week war known as the Black Hawk War." His expression bore a mix of resignation and anger. "The very morning when Black Hawk and his tribe returned, the governor called out a group of militiamen to protect the state. The next night, about four hundred of these men were camped at White Rock Grove, drinking from a barrel of whiskey. While the party was going on, a small group of Black Hawk's men approached with a white flag of truce. They had completely peaceful intentions, but the militiamen panicked and fired at the flag bearers, killing two of them instantly. Then they seized them and killed two more."

Peter grimaced, envisioning the scene that he knew was being played out all over the country, even now.

"Chief Black Hawk, sickened and infuriated, sounded the war whoop and attacked the militia. His men killed eleven of them and sent the rest into a chaotic retreat."

Peter already knew what was coming next.

"The government mobilized seven thousand soldiers," Conrad continued. "Black Hawk's warriors didn't stand a chance. They were forced into a retreat, but were slowed down by their sick, their elderly, and their children. They were at the Bad Axe River attempting to cross back into Iowa when the militia caught up with them."

Peter could see the pain etched on his friend's face. Many Americans believed in the concept of Manifest Destiny. They believed the expansion of the United States was both justified and inevitable, because they were the superior people. Anyone who got in their way had to be annihilated by any means necessary. Peter was glad to see his friend obviously didn't share that sentiment.

"Many of those who were killed were women attempting to swim across the river with children on their backs," Conrad said between gritted teeth. "Many of the victims were scalped by the soldiers. Those that made it to the other side were pursued by the Sioux Indians and killed. It was a slaughter," he said flatly.

"They should have stayed in Iowa when they were told not to return," Mike said, his expression showing he was bewildered by Conrad's obvious anger. "They were given more land. They should have stayed there."

"Would you accept it if the government told you and your family to leave the house you're living in?" Peter asked. "And killed you if you refused?"

Mike still looked confused. "They're *Indians*," he said, as if that explained everything. "They simply have to make room for the United States as it grows."

"Manifest Destiny?" Conrad growled.

"Yes. It's happening all over the country," Mike protested.

"And it happened here," Conrad continued, his eyes broadcasting his weary disgust. "After Black Hawk's defeat, the remaining tribes were too dispirited to resist the inevitable pressure to sell the remaining five million acres around the area that would become the canal. They were given a tract of land farther west that our government had determined was too poor for snakes to live on," he snapped.

"But they have a new home," Mike pointed out.

Peter understood when Conrad opened his mouth but remained silent while his fists clenched on the tabletop. People who believed in Manifest Destiny had no willingness to understand or empathize with the suffering of others. As long as America got what it wanted, opening the door for more citizens to claim the land that had once belonged to Indians, they didn't care how it happened. He thought again about everything Carrie and Chooli had told him.

Until he'd met Chooli, he hadn't really thought much about what was being done to expand America. Suddenly, he had a face and name of someone he cared about. Millions of Indian lives were being changed and destroyed, never to be the same again. America was vast. The situation was incredibly complex, but surely there was a way they could all share it fairly. Peter suspected the time would come when the consequences of Manifest Destiny would return to haunt the country.

Conrad frowned and finally spoke what he was thinking. "So, you believe it's perfectly fine to destroy an entire group of people just so you can do whatever you want?"

Mike shrugged and looked away, clearly uncomfortable with the question. "It's Manifest Destiny," he muttered.

"It's a ploy created by greedy Americans who want to make you feel better about what's happening in our country," Conrad shot back. "I've been covering these stories for more than thirty years. They have become more and more appalling."

Anger replaced the confusion in Mike's eyes. "I didn't create Manifest Destiny, Conrad, and I'm certainly not responsible for it."

Conrad shook his head. "You choose to believe that. The truth is that every time you use Manifest Destiny to defend some atrocity by our government, you're as responsible as they are for the consequences."

Peter was reminded of the frank conversations he'd had with the old reporter at the beginning of his career. Conrad had challenged his thinking, exactly as he was now challenging Mike's. Peter realized he was well on his way to being as disillusioned with America as his mentor. He didn't yet know what he would do with that realization, but he would be forced to face it in the near future.

Mike swung his gaze to Peter, obviously looking for support. "Do you feel the same way Conrad does, Peter?"

Instead of answering Mike directly, he asked a question. "Are you aware that America ended formal treaties with Indian tribes this year?"

Mike looked confused. "No."

"They did," Peter assured him. "Our nation has obliterated a nearly one hundred-year-old diplomatic tradition in which the United States recognizes tribes as nations."

Gerald chimed in on the conversation, his blue eyes dark with frustration above his thick beard. "I'm aware of it. I also know they've agreed to honor the approximately three hundred sixty-eight treaties that were ratified to date."

Conrad snorted. "For now. Congress has stated that no Indian tribe or nation shall be acknowledged or recognized as an independent nation, tribe, or power."

"It goes further than that," Peter added. "Congress believes that Indian tribes should be considered as wards of the government because they're entirely dependent on the government for survival. They consider them helpless and ignorant." Visions of Chooli swam in his mind, as did all the stories she had told him of the Navajo nation.

Gerald raised a brow. "Aren't they?"

Peter felt a surge of anger. "Do you realize you sound like the Southerners who justified slavery by saying blacks weren't capable of taking care of themselves?" He could feel the tension growing in his body. "Slavery was tolerated in this country for hundreds of years because it served a purpose of free labor. This country was built on the backs of slaves. We fought a war to abolish it, and now we're justifying destroying whole nations of people so we can have what we want."

Peter searched for words that might break through the beliefs the two men had. "These people, that our government believes can't *care for themselves*, have lived in this country for probably thousands of years. They've survived and flourished. Until we came along, intent on destroying their way of life so we can expand our own."

His words became more heated. "It's wrong. I believe Senator Eugene Casserly from California said it best this spring."

Conrad gave him an approving nod before he finished Peter's thought. "Casserly said ending the treaty system will be the first step in a great scheme of taking Indian goods and properties from them by illegal and unethical means. He said it's the first step toward Indians being plundered, corporations and individuals being enriched, and the American name dishonored in history." He shook his head heavily. "He's right."

Peter gazed at Mike and Gerald, wondering if anything they were saying was making a difference. He doubted it very much. Most people who embraced the belief of Manifest Destiny in order to justify American expansion weren't open to seeing it differently. Driven by greed and the need to feel superior, they weren't willing to accept a different perception.

Raised voices at the next table interrupted their conversation. "Did you hear about the huge warehouse fire last night?"

Not wanting to completely ruin their meal together, Peter changed the subject as he tilted his head toward the nearby talk. "Do any of you know about that?"

Mike nodded. "There was a large fire in the warehouse district last night. Most of the Chicago firefighters were out to battle it. They finally brought it under control."

The man at the next table overheard his comment and turned away from his companions to respond. "This whole city is a tinder house waiting to go up," he said.

Gerald sighed. "You could be right. The entire Midwest has been suffering from a drought. There's been no rain since July fourth. I don't think things could be any drier." He frowned. "There have been twenty-eight fires in Chicago this week, but the fire department has been able to put them out."

"So far," the man next to them muttered. "This whole city is built out of wood. The buildings are wooden. The sidewalks are wooden. Even the streets are made of wood blocks instead of bricks or cobblestone. The city leaders have been warned over and over that the city is at a great risk of being consumed by fire."

Peter's pulse quickened. Only ten months ago he had come close to perishing in the Spotswood Hotel fire in Richmond. His friend, Grace Miller, had died in that fire, along with dozens more. He would never forget her final scream before the flames engulfed her at the third-floor window she was looking down from. Her husband, Willard, had collapsed in Peter's arms that night.

He glanced around the luxurious dining room nervously.

"We don't have anything to worry about here," Mike said confidently. "The Palmer Hotel is the first fireproof hotel in the world."

"That's what they say," the stranger muttered. He glanced in the direction of the harbor. "There are hundreds of boats in the river. At least two hundred of them are full of wood. There are huge wood yards everywhere. If they ever catch fire, there will be no stopping it."

Peter stiffened again. Fires were far too commonplace in the United States. A week or so before Grace had died, Minnie's entire family had perished in a tenant house fire in Philadelphia.

The stranger at the next table wasn't done sharing what he knew. "I believe George Train predicted it last night," he said ominously.

Peter swung his eyes toward the short, wiry man with snapping brown eyes. "What are you talking about?" He wanted to block the man out, but his curiosity demanded to be satisfied.

"I went to hear George Francis Train speak last night."

Conrad leaned a little closer. "I heard he was speaking." He glanced at his companions who all wore puzzled expressions. "Train is quite the entrepreneur. He organized the clipper ship line that sailed around Cape Horn to San Francisco, and he played a large role in constructing the eastern portion of the Transcontinental Railroad." He paused, thinking. "Last year he made a widely publicized trip around the globe."

"That's him," the man agreed. "He was giving the lecture last night to a packed auditorium, when he suddenly stopped and looked out at all of us quite solemnly. He told us this was to be the last public address to be delivered within those walls." The man's eyes widened with very real fear. "He told us a terrible calamity is impending over the city of Chicago. He added that he dared not utter more."

Peter felt his heart began to race. He wanted to laugh off Train's warning, but he'd endured too much tragedy in his life. He was achingly aware that calamities happened.

"That's nonsense!" Mike said. "Nothing is going to happen. Chicago is one of the greatest cities in the world. They can handle whatever might come. They have an excellent fire department and I'm sure there are plans in place for every situation."

Peter hoped he was right. Chicago had grown fast. Just that morning, foul odors had mingled with choking clouds of smoke from the endless trains that passed through the congested city, as well as the factories that seemed to run around the clock. When he'd questioned the odor, he'd been told the Chicago slaughterhouses held a hundred twenty thousand animals waiting for their fate. The city may be impressive, but it wasn't a place for him.

The outspoken stranger wasn't done. "Chicago was built quickly and cheaply because of all the wood coming in from the surrounding area. We're the world's largest lumberyard. The problem is that much of the construction is haphazard, shoddy, and crowded." He scowled. "I've tried to warn the authorities, but they won't listen. The poorer section of town is nothing but flimsy wood shanties. The entire area is full of barns and sheds loaded with hay, coal, and wood shavings. Factories are filled with lumber to build things. There are mountains of coal everywhere to provide fuel for the boilers." His scowl deepened. "It's as if the city decided to specialize in combustible materials."

Conrad sighed. "You're right, my friend. Chicago has always had an image problem. About two-thirds of the buildings are made from wood. Many of the buildings that *seem* to be made from brick, stone or marble have secretly been built with white pine frames and faced with a thin layer of some more impressive building material."

"Why?" Peter sputtered.

"Because they're determined to compete with the most magnificent cities in the world," he said bluntly. "They know that rickety wooden structures aren't nearly as grand as the magnificent avenues of old European cities. They aren't as imposing as the heavy brownstones lining the streets of New York." His voice dripped with sarcasm. "To compensate, they build ostentatious buildings that pretend to be what they're not."

The stranger's expression tightened. "Last month, the *Chicago Tribune* finally addressed what I've been saying for years. They warned us the buildings downtown are mere firetraps pleasing to the eye. They're nothing more than shams and shingles."

Peter felt a surge of fear. Just that morning, a strong wind had begun blowing in from the north. Shortly before he'd come down for dinner, he heard it blasting against the windows of his room. He was suddenly very eager to leave Chicago. There was only one day of the conference left. His train would leave the morning of October tenth. He wished it were sooner.

The narrow-faced woman sitting next to the stranger leaned over and grasped his hand. "Dear, that's enough. I'm certain these gentlemen are simply trying to enjoy a pleasurable meal."

"As am I," the man growled. "I find it quite impossible, however." He seemed set on his mission of educating them. "Do you know there were twenty-eight fires already this month? In just the first seven days? Our firefighters have had no time to sleep or even repair their equipment. Last night, four city blocks were burned when a lumber mill went up like quicksilver. Three alarms called out all the city's firemen and engines. They fought like crazy, but if spectators hadn't jumped in to help, they never could have put it out. Some of those spectators got trapped by flames. They jumped onto planks from the lumberyard next to the river and paddled to safety on the opposite shore. The only thing left of those four blocks are smoldering mounds of coal and ash."

"Perhaps the great calamity predicted by George Train has already occurred," Mike commented. "To the people in those four blocks, I'm certain it was a great calamity. I saw the newspaper this morning. They called it the *Great Fire,* but now it's over."

Peter hoped he was right.

"I don't believe that's so," the stranger muttered. The fear in his eyes was real. "There is something more coming."

Peter pushed back from the table. He'd heard everything he could listen to. "It's late," he said abruptly. "It's been a long day, so I'm going to my room. It was a pleasure, gentlemen." He could feel eyes boring into his back as he walked away, but he didn't care. All he wanted was the refuge of his room. Just thirty-six hours must pass before he could board a train and head north to Peshtigo, Wisconsin to visit his friend. He truly just wanted to head home to Boston and Elizabeth, but he'd made a commitment he intended to keep.

Once he reached his room, he walked over to the ornate window framed with luxurious velvet curtains and peered out over the city. A relentless wind continued to assault the glass, but the only light he could see below came from the gas streetlights and the glow of buildings entertaining Chicagoans. Feeling a sense of relief, he prepared for bed, aware he was still partially dressed when he laid down to sleep. He was certain his dreams would be full of the night he nearly died in the Spotswood fire.

Peter didn't know what time it was when he was disturbed from a restless slumber by a pounding on the door.

"Peter! Peter!"

Peter stumbled to the door and ripped it open. "Conrad! What is it?"

"There's a terrible fire on the south side of the river," Conrad said tersely. "I'm assured it won't get this far, but I'm not willing to trust that." He strode into the room. "Your room is higher than mine and looks north."

Peter rushed to the window with Conrad. When he looked down, he could feel his blood running cold.

A glance at his watch told him it was ten o'clock. He'd been in bed only an hour.

Chapter Eight

"My God!" Conrad exclaimed.

Peter stood silently as he watched the orange glow on the horizon. Though the fire was on the other side of the river, he could see roofs being ripped from buildings, tossing flames as it went. Peter thought he saw what must be burning mattresses and furniture hovering hundreds of feet in the air. "What is going on?"

"Fire devils," Conrad muttered.

"What are fire devils?" Peter couldn't look away from the flames.

"The heat is creating them," the older man explained. "I've seen them before. They're superheated columns of air that rise with a tornado-like motion. They're formed by intense heat. I've known heat like that to melt marble and steel, or make trees explode from the heat of their resin. The fire devils are ripping the roofs off buildings and sending everything in their path flying through the air."

As Peter watched, the burning flames suddenly seemed to leap a hundred feet in the air, creating what looked like a solid wall of fire. They watched as the blaze reaching the towering steeple of a nearby church.

"The steeple is on fire!" Conrad yelled.

"The firemen have to put it out. If it burns, it will spread sparks and burning debris that will spread the fire even farther," Peter muttered. He peered across the expanse of city, comforted by the river separating the flames from the business section of town.

"They won't be able to control it," Conrad said tensely.

"The river will stop it from reaching downtown," Peter said, praying he was right.

Conrad remained silent, his eyes scanning the distance.

"Won't it?" Peter asked nervously when his friend didn't respond.

"I hope so." Conrad's eyes narrowed. "It's going to be mass confusion down there. The people who live in those homes are going to try to save whatever they can. They're hauling everything they can out into the streets right now." His voice grew grimmer. "The wind is blowing hard enough that it's going to pick up those items and throw them into the fire. The fire devils will pick up even more."

Peter groaned. "Making the fire even more impossible to put out."

"Not to mention the fact that the firemen won't be able to get their wagons down the streets if they're lined with people and burning items." He peered into the night again. "The fire seems to be heading toward the section of town that burned last night. Once it reaches that area, the fire will run out of fuel and burn out."

Peter wanted desperately to believe that's what would happen. At the same moment, he thought of

George Train's prediction. If this was the great calamity, what was truly going to happen?

"Oh my God," Conrad whispered.

Peter looked in the direction of his pointing finger. He could see hungry flames leaping higher. "What is it?"

"The wind must have shifted away from the burned-out area. Bateman Mills has caught fire."

As Peter watched, he saw burning wood, caught by the wind, drift over the river. Great chunks landed on the ground and on surrounding buildings. Moments later, flames leapt into the air.

"My God..." Peter couldn't look away.

"Nothing can stop it now," Conrad growled. "It's coming."

Peter stood frozen, watching the fire spread. In addition to the debris flying over the river, the very water itself seemed to catch fire. Oil on the river's surface burst into flame, igniting logjams floating in the harbor. The river turned an eerie orange, as one by one the ships began to burn.

The fire was burning brightly enough, and they were stationed high enough, to see what happened when Conley's Patch was ignited. Peter had been told about Chicago's most famous vice district. The wooden maze of shanties was filled with brothels, pawnshops, gambling dens, and saloons. It was where Chicagoans went to sin. From where Peter stood, it seemed as if the flames thrashed it like the very wrath of God.

He groaned as he saw hordes of women and children rush out into the street. He couldn't hear anything, but he could well imagine their screams of terror as they fled from the wall of flame bearing down on them as building after building began to burn. He covered his mouth as he saw a flash of flames shoot the length of a city block and strike a building, encasing it in fire. The next moment, a massive sheet of red fell over an entire street, incinerating what looked to be dozens of homes in minutes.

He watched as tugboats worked to pull ships in a long procession toward Lake Michigan. Many of the masts and riggings were already on fire. He could see the dark shapes of sailors leaping into the water, thrashing toward shore to escape the burning river. His mouth dropped open as the ships neared one of the rotating bridges. He could imagine the agony of the bridge operators. Did they turn the bridge to allow the ships through, or leave them in place so the masses of people fleeing from the fire could cross? Up and down the river, bridges had already burned and been destroyed. The avenues of escape were diminishing by the minute.

The conflagration crept closer. All around the outskirts of the downtown area, men could be seen on rooftops trying to douse the bright orange cinders with nothing but buckets of water and brooms. They swept the embers like a frantic team of chimney sweeps, working feverishly and pausing only long enough to slap out the flames on their clothing.

Peter's gaze shifted to the courthouse, a marble behemoth rising like a castle in the center of the city. With its domed clock tower and five-ton bell, the courthouse was the city's grandest showpiece. Built with iron girders and other flame-resistant features, it was believed to be fireproof. He could see a team of men on the rooftop, working to put out the embers as they fell. He admired their effort but was certain they would fail. The fire was simply too hot.

He watched a firebrand blow into a broken window in the clock tower. Moments later, a blaze poured across the courthouse roof like water. He watched the men dive through the door leading onto the roof, praying they would survive.

"I believe the calamity is upon us," Conrad muttered. "Train was right."

Conrad's voice shook Peter from his dazed stupor. "The Palmer Hotel isn't fireproof is it?" He couldn't control the fear that shook his voice.

Conrad gripped his arm firmly. "Nothing will survive the heat of this fire, Peter. It's time to go."

Peter gazed at him. "Go where?" He wondered if it was anything but a futile effort to attempt to escape the blaze. Surely everyone fleeing the inferno would be devoured. It was just a matter of time. He looked at the window, certain he would choose death by jumping rather than catching fire like Grace had.

Conrad read his mind. He took Peter by the shoulders and shook him vigorously. "We're not going to die," he snapped.

Peter heard him but looked back toward the window, certain a well-placed chair could break the glass easily.

"Elizabeth is counting on you to come home to her," Conrad growled, shaking him harder.

Elizabeth's name filtered through Peter's despair. He envisioned her laughing eyes, wavy black hair, and olive skin. He heard her voice saying she loved him. Her love broke the despair and hopelessness.

Peter took a deep breath and reached for the rest of his clothing on the chair next to the bed that had seemed a haven such a short time ago. He dressed quickly, shoving cash and his watch into his pocket. He glanced at his baggage, but there was nothing he owned that was more valuable than Elizabeth. He glanced out the window once more at the orange glow drawing closer, and bolted for the door. "Let's get out of here!"

Conrad was on his heels as they burst into the hallway. Already it was filled with people pushing toward the stairwell. Peter stared as women rushed from their rooms, dressed in several layers of silk clothing and bedazzled with jewelry they were frantic to save. He was certain their pockets were full, as well. Several men attempted to pull heavy trunks down the hallway. Peter gritted his teeth with frustration. Grace had died because she'd returned to help a frantic housekeeper intent on saving her belongings.

"Leave them!" Peter yelled. "Nothing you can pull from here is worth your life. Get out of the hotel now!" His authoritative voice boomed with both anger and desperation, cutting through the chaos.

Several of the men looked at him and turned away from their trunks. Despite their wives' screams of protest, they hurried toward the stairwell, pulling the women with them. Two men refused to give up their quest, though Peter knew they would never maneuver the trunks down the crowded stairwells.

"Help me!" One man reached out a beseeching hand to him, a desperate plea in his frightened eyes.

Peter shook his head but felt a surge of pity for the man who was valuing possessions over his life. "Leave it! Your family needs you more than they need whatever is in that trunk!" He turned and followed

Conrad into the stairwell that was little more than a mass of people.

Peter felt a surge of regret that they hadn't left the minute they saw the fire jump the river. Mesmerized by its relentless advance, they may have waited too long. A glance at his watch made him realize they had watched for more than three hours as the fire had relentlessly advanced on the downtown area. It had felt like mere minutes. Shocked, he moved slowly down the stairwell, wondering if it would collapse in a ball of flames at any moment. All he could do was continue to move his feet, each inch taking him closer to Elizabeth.

Conrad exchanged a grim look with him but neither man spoke.

The stairwell rang with screams and cries of despair.

The seven floors disappeared beneath them as slow as molasses, but no flames had exploded into the building by the time they reached the grand rotunda an hour later. Screams from outside mingled with screams from inside as they joined the throngs moving toward the gigantic arched entry.

Peter took deep breaths as he fought to maintain control of his emotions. He knew escaping the hotel would do nothing but funnel them into streets becoming quickly engulfed with flames. He thought about Mike, Gerald, and his other colleagues from the conference. He hoped they would make it out of the hotel, as well, but all of them were on their own.

The air was hot, laden with smoke, and sparking with glowing embers when they emerged into the night that was bright as day. Peter looked around him with astonishment. The streets were full of fleeing Chicagoans. Horses fought to pull carriages and wagons loaded with goods through the throngs of humanity. People of every age and every station in life fought against the tide, trying to outrun the flames.

"Where are they going?" Peter yelled. Now that they were out of the hotel, he had no idea which way to go to escape the flames. From his room, they'd seen people run toward the river, but running through the wall of flames headed toward them was clearly not a viable option. "Where do we go?"

"I suggest away from the flames," Conrad yelled back.

Peter managed a grim smile. Chicago encompassed thirty-six square miles. He forced himself to think. It was hard to tell which direction the wind was blowing because of all the heat convections swirling around them, but from where they had watched it spread, the flames seemed to be headed due north. His thoughts cleared. South would take them straight into the fire. North would mean they would continually have the fire at their back. East would deliver them to the shores of the river, with no path for escape.

"West!" Peter yelled. "We have to go west."

The two men took off down the street, looking for roads and alleys that would take them away from the devouring inferno. In the chance the fire eventually consumed the entire city, at some point they would make it to the barren plains that marked the outskirts of Chicago.

Peter didn't dare to think what he would do if the entire city burned, taking the railroads with it. Their prime concern at the moment was to escape the flames. He grabbed the watch from his pocket and looked down.

It was 2:10 a.m.

"All the prisoners have been freed!"

Peter heard a man cry the news as he appeared, bent over almost double under a heavy trunk. "What prisoners?" he hollered.

"From the jail!" the man gasped. "The courthouse is burning. Those poor beggars were locked up tight down there. You could hear them banging on the bars, screaming for help. Just as I was going by, the door opened and they came pouring out." He paused and shifted the weight on his back. "There were a bunch that got led away in chains. My guess is those were the murderers." He swore under his breath as a strong gust of wind filled the air with more sparks, and kept moving.

Peter's lips tightened. It wasn't enough that the entire city seemed to be burning. Now they were escaping with criminals.

A sudden commotion in the street ahead grabbed Peter's attention. Two wagons were stationed in front of a burning building that he quickly identified as a jewelry store. He had passed it earlier that day and had been impressed by the quality of the jewels displayed in the window. The owner and staff were running in and out of the building, loading the inventory into wagons as fast as they could.

As the owner jumped into the seat and slapped the reins for the terrified horses to move forward, a fireman appeared and held up a commanding hand to stop him. Peter couldn't hear the conversation, but it was obvious the fireman wasn't going to allow the wagon to move. A quick look at the road laced with canvas water hoses told him the weight of the wagon would damage the hoses.

The owner's shoulders sagged with defeat for a moment but then straightened. He stepped down from the wagon and waved his hands toward the jewelry. "Take what you want!" he called to the fleeing crowd. "It will do no one any good if it's burned up!"

Many in the crowd whooped and cheered as they surged forward, their hands outstretched to grab the abandoned jewels.

Conrad grabbed Peter's arm. "Come on!" he urged.

Peter spotted an opening in the crowded street as people thronged around the jewelry wagon. He sprinted forward with Conrad, covering almost a city block before the crowds slowed them to a crawl again. They were clearly not the only ones who had decided west was the best direction.

As their progress slowed once again to a snail's pace, an ear-splitting crash sounded behind them. Peter whirled around. "What was that?" he yelled. He held up his hand to shield his face from the blast of scorching heat that rolled over them in a relentless wave, seeming to suck the oxygen from the air.

"The courthouse bell came down!" someone hollered. "Crashed right through to the bottom of the building, I bet!"

Peter thought about the prisoners who had been released just minutes earlier. Any longer and all of them would have perished beneath the weight of a five-ton chunk of heated metal.

As he and Conrad rounded a corner in their circuitous quest to continue moving west, a seven-story white building loomed in front of them.

"That's the Sherman House Hotel," Conrad shouted.

Peter stared up at the white walls, glowing a brilliant rose color as it reflected the flames from the street. The building was smoking but not yet burning. A contingent of firefighters trained hoses on it, struggling to save it.

Suddenly, people began to stream from the hotel, their faces a mix of fear and confusion.

Peter could tell many of them had only just been rousted from their beds. Somehow, they had either not heard the alarm bells or had chosen to ignore them. As he watched, a group of men emerged in pairs, each of them carrying a bundle between them. They hurried to a carriage parked in front of the hotel and deposited the bundles gently. Stepping closer, Peter realized they were elderly women who were obviously ill. As the carriage began to roll forward, a man dashed from the lobby, yelling for the driver to stop. He ran to the side of the carriage, his face growing ashen, even with the golden glow from the fire.

"We're missing one of the women," the man yelled, his eyes wide with distress. "Wait here!"

The carriage driver was already frantically shaking his head. "We've got to go." His eyes reflected his desperate fear.

"No!" the man yelled. "I'll get her!" He spun around quickly.

Peter was powerless to move as he watched the drama play out, feeling exactly as he had ten months earlier when people had been trapped in the Spotswood Hotel. Long, orange flames snapped from the upper window like dragon tongues. He watched as the man grabbed a fire axe from one of the firemen and raced back to the hotel. The firemen yelled at him to stop, but he ignored them and disappeared through the door.

Peter held his breath for the several minutes it took for the man and his assistant to reappear with a water-soaked bundle between them. They rushed to deposit the woman into the carriage and stepped back as it rattled away. The crowd, stopped momentarily by the scene played out before them, cheered loudly.

Moments later, the Sherman Hotel collapsed in a tornado of flying debris and sparks.

Peter and Conrad took off running. Peter spotted an alley on the left side of the road. Realizing they might get trapped, he decided it was worth the risk. The fire was gaining on them. He grabbed Conrad's hand and pulled him into the gap between buildings, which were not yet ablaze.

Both men ran as fast as they could, with the alley acting as a funnel for the sparks that had erupted from the crash of the hotel. They beat at their clothes, putting out the flames sparked by flaming embers.

Peter knew his face and hands were burned, but he didn't stop running. After what seemed an eternity, the sparks stopped flying around them. The darkness of the alley swallowed the flames; it couldn't block out the noise, however. They could still hear the pop and crackle of burning wood. The roar of the flames sounded like ocean waves crashing in a storm. Windows shattered as oil barrels and liquor casks exploded through the night like gunfire. Almost every minute the sound of another building collapsing echoed through the night.

Chicago was dying all around them.

Peter had lost track of time when he looked up and saw a group of grimy-faced firefighters walking wearily toward them. He and Conrad had stopped in a tiny park area to rest, surrounded by perhaps another hundred people who were all staring back at the city. Their attempt to travel west had forced them into circles as they were forced to sometimes double back because of the fire's path. He was aware the flames might turn in their direction again and force them to keep fleeing, but they were both exhausted and overcome with the smoke and fumes. He knew the fire wasn't out because the sound was still hellacious, and the flames still split the sky. He wondered if their attempt to flee was as futile as it felt at the moment.

"Why aren't you fighting the fire?" someone yelled at the approaching firefighters.

One of them, a tall man with a full beard that had been terribly singed, stopped long enough to answer. "The Waterworks burned," he said grimly. "There is no water."

A shocked silence fell on the crowd.

"The Waterworks burned?" Conrad looked as stunned as everyone else. "That's the only source of water for the city. Without it, there is nothing to fight the fires with."

Cries of despair sounded from the people in the park as they absorbed the impact of the new catastrophe.

Peter struggled to absorb the news as he looked at the orange glow in the sky. "You're telling me there's no way to put out the fire?"

Conrad took a deep breath and nodded. "God help us," he muttered.

The fireman's shoulders sagged as they looked over the refugees. "I'm sorry," he muttered as he turned away. "We did our best."

"Wait!" one of the onlookers yelled. "What should we do?"

The fireman shrugged. "I'm getting my family and heading west toward the outskirts of the city." He turned and walked away.

A stunned silence fell on the people huddled in the night.

"We're doomed," a woman cried.

"I've lost everything," another whimpered. Two children clung to her skirt. "We have nowhere to go."

"This never should have happened," a man growled angrily. "The firefighters gave up and left us to perish."

Angry mutters began to rise in the night.

Peter had heard enough. "How were they to extinguish the fire without water?" he demanded. "They've been fighting that fire all night, wondering what was happening to their own families." He thought of the heavy fatigue etched on the faces of the firemen who had just walked by. "They gave everything they had to save the city." He gazed around at the crowd. "Trying to find someone to blame is pointless. It's up to us to save ourselves now."

The man looked away angrily, but the two women who had spoken trained their eyes on him. "What are we going to do?"

One of the women was well-dressed, obviously wealthy. Despite the heavy layer of soot that covered her, Peter could tell her dress was made of silk. There were jewels around her neck. The other woman, surrounded by her children, wore a plain dress and an expression of exhausted fear. The two women had drawn close to each other as the tragedy of the night erased barriers erected by income and societal expectations.

"Yes," others muttered. "What are we going to do?"

Peter took a deep breath and locked eyes with Conrad. His speaking up had evidently targeted him as the leader. Conrad cocked his head and raised a brow, issuing a silent challenge with his eyes. Peter supposed someone needed to take charge of this ragtag group thrown together by the terrible fire. It might as well be him. "We're heading west," he said firmly.

"How do we get there?" one of the group asked.

"Will the fire come there?" a woman asked fearfully.

"I don't know," Peter admitted. "But I know it's not burning right now. The wind is blowing north. Unless the wind shifts, the flames won't come this direction. If they do, we'll be far enough ahead of them to escape." He stared at the group gazing back at him.

"We have to find a bridge that will take us west, but that means we have to travel north a little ways until we find one."

"Mama, I'm tired!" The little girl clinging to her mother's skirt cried out fearfully. "I can't walk no further."

Peter knelt next to the child. She looked to be five or six. "Hello. What's your name?" he asked gently. The child gulped as she stared up at him. Peter knew he must look as dirty and beaten as everyone else. He smiled warmly, hoping he wouldn't scare her further.

The terror on the girl's face eased somewhat. "I'm Sophia," she whispered. She tilted her head. "My brother is Ezekiel. He's eight."

"It's nice to meet you, Sophia," Peter said gravely. "You too, Ezekiel." He focused on the boy. "Do you think you can walk a little farther?"

Ezekiel nodded bravely. "I reckon so."

"I can't!" Sophia wailed, tears pooling in the blue eyes staring at him from her blackened face.

Peter smiled again. "I know. That's why you're going to ride on my back." He turned to the mother regarding him with wide eyes. "Is that alright with you, ma'am?"

"You'd really do that?" she asked.

Peter shifted so Sophia could clamber onto his back. "Sophia has been brave to get this far. I'll carry her for as long as I can."

The man who had growled criticism of the firemen stood abruptly. "I'll take her when you get tired."

Within a few minutes, they were all moving again.

Peter gritted his teeth with frustration as every road they turned down led them to the edge of the Chicago River. "We need a bridge," he muttered.

"The Wells Street Bridge!" one of the men in the group gasped. "I came across it yesterday."

"Which direction?" Peter demanded.

The man hesitated before pointing north. "We'll get to it if we go this direction."

Peter realized walking north would take them closer to the fire, but he was running out of options. If they didn't find a bridge to cross, the fire could eventually swallow the neighborhoods they were walking through. The river was too wide for many of them to swim across. "Let's go!" he shouted with far more confidence than he felt.

Conrad had a knowing look on his face but merely fell in beside him.

Ten minutes later, a bridge appeared in the distance.

"That's it!" the man exclaimed. "The Wells Street Bridge!"

Peter, relief surging through him like a cool breeze, led his group onto the crowded bridge and trudged across. He was aware the flames were drawing closer but he refused to look back.

Sophia, exhausted, clung to him like a monkey but never made a sound. He didn't know how many of the people in his group would be able to find him once they crossed with the masses of other fleeing Chicagoans, but at least he'd given them a chance to survive. He was aware the fire could once more jump the river, but at least they were now free to head west, out of the city.

Ezekiel and his mother were glued to his side. Conrad walked closely on the other side, leaning down to offer Ezekiel encouragement on a regular basis.

Peter knew Ezekiel was as fatigued as his sister, but he never uttered a word of complaint.

Everyone crossing the bridge cheered when their feet touched solid ground on the other side.

They were about a block past the Wells Street Bridge when Peter heard screams behind him. He looked back in time to see the bridge catch fire.

His small group watched as they caught their breath. One end of the bridge was burning faster than the other, but if the blaze jumped the river, they would once more be running from the inferno.

Peter stiffened as the unbalanced bridge ripped apart from the pilings and tipped to stand at a sixty-degree angle in the orange water. The framework coursed with flame like a skeleton with ribs of fire, and then turned a complete somersault and plunged into the river.

Peter blinked back his tears of horror as the screams of victims filled the air. The bridge being swallowed by the river had stopped the flames before they could reach the shore. He could almost feel the buildings breathe a sigh of relief as the bridge slowly sank beneath the surface.

Unable to do anything to help, he turned away and continued walking.

West.

****

By the time the sun started to lighten the sky, fighting to show itself through the thick layer of smoke, Peter and Conrad's group consisted only of himself, Conrad, Sophia, Ezekiel, their mother Penelope, and the wealthy woman, Bertha. Once they had crossed the bridge, small groups broke off and went their own way.

Peter was completely exhausted. He placed each foot carefully, willing himself not to stumble and cause the sleeping Sophia to fall from his back. His throat ached with thirst, and the burns on his face and hands were throbbing. He said nothing, knowing each of them was suffering.

A man walked out into the yard of a large home they were passing. "Hello!"

Peter lifted his head wearily. "Hello."

"Did you come from the fire? What's happening?"

Peter stopped, more because he needed a rest than because he wanted to talk. "It's bad," he said grimly. "The entire downtown district burned. I don't know how much more. It's still burning."

The man's face tightened. "Will it jump the river?"

Peter shrugged. "It's jumped the river twice, but the wind is still blowing north. I don't believe it's coming this way."

The man sagged with relief and then looked at him more closely. "You're a New Yorker?"

Peter nodded. "I'm here for a conference." He paused and then said, "I *was* here for a conference. All the buildings are gone," he said wearily.

The man's gaze swept their ragtag group. "My name is Sebastian Epstein. I'm from New York, too," he replied with a smile. "Come on in the house."

Peter's mouth dropped open. "What?"

"You all look like you're about to drop. My wife and I don't have a lot, but we can give you a meal, a bath, and a place to rest." He looked over his shoulder. "If the fire keeps coming, we'll all leave together."

Peter nodded his acceptance. "Thank you."

It was two days before the Great Chicago Fire stopped burning. It had demolished almost four square miles of the city, destroying all of the downtown business district before the heavens opened and provided rain.

From the moment the Waterworks had burned, there was nothing that could be done to stop the flames. A few of the fire engines had drawn water from the river, spraying it as far as they could reach, but it did nothing to stop the spread of the fire.

The fire had advanced north, burning everything in its path until the cold rains finally put it out. No one had been spared. The inferno seemed oblivious to wealth, status, or position. It reduced mansions to ashes as quickly as it devoured the shanties.

At least three hundred people were known to be dead. One hundred thousand had been left homeless.

The great city of the Midwest had been brought to its knees.

The great calamity had come.

Chapter Nine
October 10, 1871

Peter stood on the station platform and scanned the board for information on the next train toward Peshtigo. He was glad to be leaving the city very early in the morning. He was eager to leave behind the destruction and suffering.

Union Station had miraculously escaped the fire. Chicago was offering free fares to homeless women and children who had family or friends they could stay with while they rebuilt their lives. Chicago men, necessary to rebuild the city, were expected to stay. With winter breathing down their necks, rebuilding the city would be a daunting task.

Peter continued to scan the board, confused when he could find no mention of Peshtigo, Wisconsin. He had the ticket in his pocket that assured him of a seat. He finally turned to the long line at the ticket window. Clearly, an accident of some kind had caused a delay. With the entire city in chaos, it was to be expected. He ground his teeth with frustration but knew tens of thousands were in far worse straits than he was.

Peter watched the crowd while he waited. Most wore desperate, shell-shocked expressions. It was easy to identify the people who had lost everything. He knew Penelope, Sophia, and Ezekiel were somewhere in the crowded station, waiting for the train that would take them to family in St. Louis, Missouri.

He had waited in line all day yesterday to get a simple, two-line telegram to Elizabeth.

I'm fine. Home in four days.

He knew she must be frantic with worry. Reports of the fire had gone to every newspaper outlet in the country. There was no hope of getting a return telegram before he left, but at least she would know he hadn't been harmed.

His hands and face still throbbed from the burns he had endured, but they were healing.

"I thought you were heading to Peshtigo?"

Peter whipped his head around, surprised to see Conrad standing next to him. They'd said their goodbyes earlier that morning when they'd left Sebastian and Carmen's house after showering them with thanks. "And I thought you would already be on your way to New York."

Conrad shrugged. "I doubt a single train is running on time. I've been told there will be a two-hour delay. At least," he added ruefully. "Are you delayed, as well?"

"There's no information on the board," Peter replied. "I'm assuming a delay." He didn't add that he was feeling increasingly uneasy.

A man standing close by overheard them. "Are you trying to get to Peshtigo?"

"Yes. Do you know what's going on?"

The man frowned, his heavy eyebrows knitted together under wiry gray hair. "You from there?"

"No, I'm going to visit a friend."

The man's eyes gleamed with sadness. "Not now," he said. "Peshtigo is gone."

Peter stared at him. "Gone? What do you mean?"

"There was a large forest fire up there in Wisconsin two nights ago, about the same time the fire started here. Word just reached us this morning."

"Us?" Conrad asked.

"I'm here for the reporters' conference," the man explained.

"Us too," Conrad replied. "We haven't heard anything, though."

Peter listened closely. They'd been with Sebastian and Carmen, only venturing out a few times to see the destruction. The Palmer House Hotel was gone, and there had been no way to connect with their colleagues in the confusion and despair.

The man reached out to shake hands with both of them. "Eli Crompton, *Cincinnati Daily Times*. I happened to be in the makeshift office of the *Chicago Tribune* when someone rode in. Evidently, there was a firestorm up there the likes none of us can imagine."

Peter grimaced. He could imagine. "I'm Peter Wilcher. This is Conrad Hawkins." He was still trying to make sense of what Eli had said. "What do you mean *gone*?"

Eli's face tightened. "The fire destroyed the entire town. A fellow who was going there for a job in one of the factories arrived by horseback the morning after the destruction. The town, on both sides of the river, is gone," he said. "If there are any survivors, we don't know about them yet."

Peter's entire body went cold. "No survivors?" he whispered. "Almost eighteen hundred people live in Peshtigo."

"Not anymore." Eli's eyes reflected the pain Peter was feeling. "The fire burned other communities as well, but Peshtigo was the largest." He shook his head. "There was nowhere for people to run. They were completely surrounded by burning woods. They expect the death toll to be somewhere around two thousand, but it will be a while before we know."

Peter stood silently, trying to process what he was hearing. A vivid image of Mark Rivers filled his mind; tall and solid, brown eyes beneath thick blond hair, with a ready smile and laugh. They'd been roommates for two years in college. Mark, lured by the excitement of the Midwestern frontier, had moved to Peshtigo to take over the management of a large lumber factory immediately before the war. He'd invited Peter to visit for years.

"You're sure there were no survivors?" Conrad asked keenly.

The man shrugged. "There could have been, but nothing has been heard. Of course, the telegraph station must have been destroyed, along with all the railroad tracks for the last ten miles into Peshtigo. It will be a while before we'll know. The fellow who brought the news had been riding for two days. He was barely upright when he stumbled into the office." Eli shook his head. "He thought he was coming to Chicago for a refuge. It seems the entire Midwest must have burned two nights ago." He gazed at Peter with empathy. "I'm sorry, old man."

Peter nodded numbly. He would do what he could to determine Mark's fate in the days to come, but he wouldn't be going to Peshtigo today.

Just then, the last person between him and the counter walked away. "Can I help you?" the weary ticket agent asked.

Peter took a deep breath, fighting to control the emotion surging through him. "I need a ticket to Boston, please."

All he wanted was to get home to Elizabeth.

Minnie clapped her hands together happily when Marietta and Carrie brought platters of steaming pancakes and crisp bacon from the kitchen. "Pancakes!" she cried.

Carrie smiled at her enthusiasm as she sat down in her chair, while Frances poured cups of coffee at the sideboard.

Minnie gobbled down two fluffy pancakes before she turned to Carrie. "Mama, are you sure you and Frances have to go to the clinic today? Last night was so much fun. I would love to play some more games today!"

"Last night was fun, wasn't it?" Carrie agreed. They had all been concerned about Peter when the first telegrams came through with news of the Chicago Fire. Elizabeth had gotten a telegram through to them during dinner the night before. Assured that Peter was safe, the evening had turned into a celebration of games, cookies, and hot chocolate.

"I beat Florence in backgammon," Minnie boasted.

"And I beat Jeremy in checkers," Frances added as she finished pouring coffee and sat down to eat her breakfast.

"It's a good thing, because both of you were terrible at charades," Carrie teased.

Minnie waved her hand in the air. "Charades is a guessing game," she said dismissively. "Besides, you should have been better at getting us to guess the right thing." Her eyes glistened with mischievousness.

Carrie laughed, hardly able to debate that issue. "I was never very good at charades," she confessed.

"Grandpa has been teaching me how to play backgammon," Minnie said. "He told me I'm very smart."

Frances raised a brow. "He's your grandfather. He has to say that."

"You're just jealous," Minnie shot back.

Carrie smiled, listening to the banter between her daughters. She knew how much her father loved being called Grandpa. He had given up hope of grandchildren when Bridget was stillborn, and Carrie had almost died. Carrie's own mother had almost died giving birth to her. Everyone knew Carrie would be at grave risk if she were to conceive a child again. Thomas couldn't love Frances and Minnie anymore if they had actually come from her body.

"You're sure you can't stay home?" Minnie asked again, her blue eyes large with longing.

Carrie shook her head. "I wish we could, but no. Frances and I are needed at the clinic." She tried to keep her voice lighthearted, but now that election day was actually here, her nervousness was growing.

"I'll play games with you," Marietta offered. "And you and the twins are going to help me make sugar cookies today."

"Sugar cookies!" Marcus and Sarah Rose cried in unison.

Carrie laughed but felt a surge of sadness. Marietta's last trip to Richmond had resulted in Sarah Rose being threatened because of her obvious mulatto heritage. Marcus, who was red-haired and blue-eyed, had been completely confused by the danger his twin had been in. Jeremy and Marietta had decided it was too dangerous for their children to return. Everyone understood, but Rose especially had been brokenhearted. Southern bigotry was separating her from her own twin brother, as well as her niece and nephew.

Sarah Rose jumped down from her chair and danced in a circle, her arms raised with delight. "Sugar cookies!"

Minnie laughed in spite of herself. She adored the twins, who had turned three a few days earlier.

Sarah Rose chortled, stopped dancing, and ran over to crawl into Minnie's lap. "We're going to make sugar cookies, Minnie," she said, her black eyes snapping with excitement beneath a cap of dark curls. "Will you help?"

Minnie nodded. "Of course, Sarah Rose. Will you let me eat the first one?"

Sarah Rose frowned, taking several moments to think through her response. Finally, she shook her head. "It's always the youngest that gets to eat the first cookie," she explained earnestly. "Since Marcus was born a few minutes before me, that means I eat the first cookie." Her smile flashed with triumph, but her eyes took on a worried shine when she looked at Minnie's sad face.

Carrie bit back a laugh. She wasn't certain theatre was a lucrative profession, but her youngest was certainly well-suited for the stage.

Sarah Rose leaned closer to pat Minnie's cheek. "Don't be sad," she implored. "I promise you can have the first cookie, Minnie." Her lip quivered. "Don't be sad."

"Alright," Minnie said promptly, her pretend sadness evaporating into a large smile. "I'll be happy to eat your cookie."

Sarah Rose sat back, staring up at Minnie. She looked relieved, but there was a reluctant look in her eyes that revealed her suspicion she'd been conned.

Carrie swallowed her laugh and finished her breakfast, glad to know Marietta, Minnie, and the twins would be safe for the day.

Sarge was waiting outside the house, his breath rising in white puffs. The first hard frost of the year had happened overnight. The breeze flowing in off the Delaware River said the day would warm nicely, but Carrie was grateful for her coat as she pulled it tightly around her.

"Good morning, Miss Carrie. Miss Frances."

"Good morning, Sarge," Frances replied. "Do you know how to play checkers?"

"I been playing checkers since I was knee-high to a grasshopper. Why you asking?"

"Would you like to play sometime?" Frances asked seriously. "I must warn you that I'm quite good."

Carrie choked back her laugh. She had to give her daughter points for confidence.

Sarge eyed Frances for a long moment before he nodded. His lips twitched, but he didn't smile. "I reckon we can make that happen, Miss Frances," he said. "But I ought to warn you that I'm real good, too."

Carrie could only imagine the number of hours Sarge had whiled away playing checkers.

Frances appraised him and smiled, holding up a bag that, until then, Carrie hadn't realized she was carrying. "You come inside the clinic sometime today. We'll play a game."

Carrie chuckled. "You brought checkers?"

Frances grinned but quickly sobered. "If as many bad things happen today as you think will happen, Mama, our patients will need something to take their minds off the pain they're in."

Carrie's laugh faded on her lips.

"I read about last year's election," Frances said, all humor gone. "There was a small riot, but federal troops intervened and stopped it. Will the same thing happen today?"

Carrie exchanged a look with Sarge, but his eyes were inscrutable. "I hope so, honey," was the best she could do.

When they got to the clinic, Carrie told Frances to go inside and help Carolyn set up, and then she turned to Sarge. "What aren't you saying?" she demanded.

Sarge frowned. "Things been gettin' more violent, Miss Carrie. You know there's been trouble for the last couple weeks. Two nights ago, on Sunday, I was at a meeting of the Republicans at Union Hall. A bunch of white men rushed in and started throwing rocks. The meetin' broke up, but some of the fellas got hurt." His expression grew grimmer. "Last night, Jacob Gordon, a black fella that lives right here in Moyamensing, went out to buy shoes. He left the store 'bout eight. This white fella rushed up and shot him."

Carrie gasped. "Is he dead?"

"Not yet, but it don't look good."

Sarge's eyes told Carrie just how bad it was. "Is he at the clinic?"

"We brought him to see Doc Blakely last night, but he insisted on going home after she treated him. I could tell by the look on the doc's face that she didn't think he was gonna make it, so she let him go. She knew he wanted to be with his family. Some of the women be there with his wife now."

"I didn't see anything about it in the paper this morning," Carrie protested. "I woke early so I could read it."

"I don't reckon you did. The paper ain't writing 'bout nothin' but that big fire out in Chicago." He peered at her more closely. "You done heard anything about your friend, Mr. Peter?"

"He's fine," Carrie assured him, her mind racing. "How bad is it going to get, Sarge?"

Sarge hesitated before he looked at her levelly. "Don't know, but I reckon it's gonna get bad. I woulda told you and Miss Frances not to come, but I know the two of you done made up your mind to be here." He nodded toward the door. "Go on inside, Miss Carrie. You be the safest in there. These white Democrats hate the blacks, but they ain't gonna attack a clinic that Miss Biddy and Miss Faith built. These Irish boys gonna make sure that don't happen. I reckon you be alright inside." He turned away. "I gotta go vote."

As Carrie watched Sarge walk down the street, leaving his carriage in front of the clinic, she prayed for his safety. She was aware of just how much courage it was taking to go to the voting precinct.

Carrie was working with Frances to prepare supplies and equipment for the day when she heard the door open. She turned around to tell whomever it was that they weren't open yet.

A familiar voice rang out. "Do you need some help, Dr. Wallington?"

Carrie's mouth dropped open as Florence, Silas, and Dr. Michael Wild walked through the door. "What are you doing here?"

Michael answered. "There's going to be trouble today. We know you and Frances are going to be in the middle of it, so we decided we would worry less if we were in the middle of it with you." His cheerful grin matched the dancing green eyes under his thick red hair.

Carrie rushed forward to give them each a hug. "Thank you," she said fervently. Quickly, she told them about what had happened the previous two days.

When Michael looked at Frances, Carrie knew what he was thinking. "She wouldn't hear of not coming to help. If it were me, I would feel the same way."

Michael smiled. "It *was* you, not that long ago," he reminded her. "You worked at Chimborazo, *and* you ran the hospital down in the Black Quarters during the war. You put your life at risk every single day."

"And yet here I am," Carrie replied. "Frances is an excellent assistant. I want her by my side today."

Frances looked up from setting out surgical instruments. "I'm right here, Mama!" Her eyes were bright with determination.

Moments later, Dr. Carolyn Blakely pushed through the front door of the clinic. Her face was flushed and anxious.

Carrie knew whatever was going to happen had already begun. "Are you alright, Carolyn?"

Carolyn nodded, her light blue eyes shimmering beneath salt and pepper hair that had definitely become more salt in the last few years. After accompanying Carrie on the Santa Fe Trail to Bosque Redondo three years earlier, she'd taken over the clinic and now lived with Faith Jacobs. "It's begun," she said flatly.

Carolyn smiled slightly when she saw Florence, Silas, and Michael. "I'm glad you're here," she said. "I predict it will take all of us to care for the patients we'll see today."

"What's begun?" Silas asked.

"They're fighting at Sixth and Lombard Streets."

Carrie frowned. "The voting precinct."

"Yes. The whites are attempting to keep the blacks from voting."

"Will Mayor Fox call on federal troops to stop them?" Frances asked. "That's what happened last year."

Carolyn shook her head sadly. "I doubt it. My understanding is that Mayor Fox went to the scene of the riot and pleaded for voters to remain peaceful." Her lips twisted with disdain. "And then he left."

"Let me guess," Michael said. "The rioting broke out again as soon as he was gone."

Carolyn nodded. "He's determined to win the election. The policemen are *just* as determined that he win. None of them want to lose their jobs."

Carrie looked at her friend more closely. "What aren't you saying?"

Carolyn walked to the clinic window and peered out. "The policemen are leading the assaults," she said heavily. "They're not trying to stop it, because they're the ones leading it. Just before I arrived, I overheard a black man on the street yelling out a warning about the policemen. There's a white mob throwing bricks at the blacks trying to vote. They chased them down Lombard Street."

Carrie bit back a groan as she looked around the clinic.

They were ready.

Anthony and Jeremy could feel the tension in the air when they arrived at the Cromwell Factory in Moyamensing.

George Frasier, the factory office manager, met them as soon as they stepped inside. "There's trouble," he said tensely.

"We can feel it," Jeremy responded. "What's happening?"

"What we expected," George replied. "A lot of the men haven't arrived at work yet."

Jeremy nodded. "They're voting."

"They're *trying* to vote," George corrected him. "From the reports I'm receiving, it's nothing but a melee down there. Lots of people, both black and white, are getting hurt, but the assaults are being led by policemen."

Jeremy ground his teeth with anger and frustration. It was what he'd expected, but he'd held onto a slim hope that Mayor Fox would do the right thing and call in troops to maintain order.

"The Mayor isn't calling in the troops?" Anthony snapped.

"No," George said grimly. "He's not going to."

Jeremy accepted what George was saying. The young man stayed mostly to himself, but that very fact made him a valuable asset when it came to knowledge about Moyamensing. No one viewed him as a threat, so they spoke freely around him, blacks and whites alike

"Where is Octavius Catto?" George asked.

Jeremy sighed. "He's at his school. He's closing the Institute for Colored Youth early, but he insisted he wouldn't let fear keep students away. He beseeched Mayor Fox to provide greater protection for the black voters. Obviously, Fox decided to ignore him."

He turned to Anthony. "Are Carrie and Frances at the clinic?"

It was Anthony's turn to sigh. "They left early this morning." His eyes and voice were full of worry.

Jeremy glanced around the factory. "Are things running smoothly, George?"

"Yes, sir. We're not at full capacity because of the missing men, but what's being done is being done with excellence."

Jeremy was satisfied with that. "Keep everyone here," he ordered. "Going out in the streets to return home will only put them in danger." Then he turned to Anthony. "Let's go."

"Where to?"

"We're going to the clinic to check on your family, and then we're going to find Octavius." Jeremy felt his heart quicken. "I have a very bad feeling this."

Chapter Ten

Less than two minutes after Carrie and the others opened the clinic, a group of black men pushed in through the door, carrying another man between them.

"Doc Blakely!'

Carolyn walked forward calmly and directed them to lay the wounded man on a nearby bed. "What happened?"

"A brick caught him in the head, Doc."

Before Carolyn could open her mouth to respond, the door burst open again. Two men, one of them leaning heavily on another, entered. "Doc Blakely!"

Carrie moved forward. They had agreed to take turns treating patients as they came in, and helping each other where needed. "I'm Dr. Wallington. What happened?"

"A big 'ole rock smashed Ollie's leg," the unwounded man said breathlessly. "I think it might be broke, but I ain't right sure."

Michael moved to help ease the man onto a table.

One look and Carrie knew the man had a fractured ankle. "You walked on this to get here?" she asked with astonishment.

Ollie's face twisted with pain. "Better than being stoned to death," he gasped.

Carrie looked toward Frances. Her daughter, anticipating her request, was already gathering plaster cast supplies to set and cast the broken leg. "Are you hurt anywhere else?"

"I think my arm caught one of them rocks those white boys was hurling."

Carrie's lips tightened as she gently removed Ollie's shirt. A gaping wound was bleeding heavily.

"I'll treat the wound and stitch it together while you set his leg," Michael said quickly.

Within twenty minutes, the clinic was full.

As soon as Carrie finished setting Ollie's leg, she was called to the side of another man who was gasping with pain. She couldn't see any blood, but it was obvious he was in agony. "What's your name?"

"Carter," the man said faintly.

"What happened, Carter?"

"They caught me and beat me real bad. I don't think I be bleeding anywhere, but…" His voice trailed off as he slumped into unconsciousness.

"What's wrong with him, Mama?" Frances asked anxiously.

"I suspect he has internal injuries." A quick glance told Carrie the surgical suite had just emptied out. She looked at the group of men who had been responsible for bringing the patients in. She waved two of them over. "I need your help in moving your friend."

"You ain't Doc Blakely. What you gonna do to him?" one man asked suspiciously.

"I'm going to make him better," Carrie said matter-of-factly. At the rate wounded men were pouring into the clinic, she didn't have time to offer explanations.

Someone standing nearby overheard the question and gripped the man's arm. "Don't you know who this be?"

The suspicious man shook his head. "She ain't Doc Blakely."

Carrie understood his suspicion. Carolyn had worked hard to make sure the black residents of Moyamensing knew the clinic was open to serve them, just as much as it served the Irish who had first inspired it. Now that more blacks were moving into Moyamensing, Carrie wanted them to know they too would be cared for. She opened her mouth to say more, but his friend beat her to it.

"This here be Dr. Carrie Wallington. She started this clinic. She also done saved hundreds of lives when that cholera hit a few years back. She don't live in Philadelphia anymore, but she be here today. You best be counting your lucky stars she be the one taking care of Carter."

Carrie flashed him a grateful smile. "Will you help me move him?" The men lifted Carter gently and transferred him to the surgical suite.

"Thank you." Carrie entered the surgical room and closed the drapes. Frances had already pulled out a fresh supply of surgical instruments, put a clean sheet on the bed, and had a basin of hot water prepared for Carrie to wash her hands.

"We're ready, Mama."

Carrie, despite the seriousness of the situation, stepped forward to hug her daughter. "You're amazing, Frances Wallington."

Frances grinned. "You too, Mama." Her smile disappeared quickly as she stared down at their unconscious patient. "What are you going to do?"

Carrie sighed. "We're giving him arnica." She suspected internal bleeding, but they weren't set up at the clinic to handle surgery that complex. In truth, any type of internal surgery was brand new.

Carrie decided to use the moment to teach Frances. She kept her voice low. "In the past, doctors would have simply used bloodletting."

Frances looked confused. "Bloodletting? Everything I've read in your medical books say it is not effective – at least the more recent books."

"You're right, Frances," Carrie answered, proud that she knew about the procedure that had been used for a long time. Doctors removed massive amounts of the patient's blood in the hopes it would heal them. She grimaced. "As far as I can tell from my studies, very few patients survive the procedure. More doctors are becoming aware of the danger of bloodletting, but surgical techniques are still very new." She shook her head. "Even if I thought we could perform surgery on Carter, the clinic is not set up for it."

"What about Dr. Wild's office?" Frances asked, staring down at Carter with worried eyes.

"I considered that, but I don't believe he would survive the carriage ride. We have to help him now."

"Arnica?" Frances frowned. "Nothing else?"

Carrie smiled, her confidence growing as she analyzed the available options. "Arnica is the best way to stop internal bleeding. It will help with the shock and trauma of the injuries. I can't definitely diagnose what's wrong with him, but I know he's bleeding internally. I hope the day comes when we'll have surgical interventions to help him, but we're not there yet."

Frances looked at the closed drapes and lowered her voice even more. "Why are we back here if you're not going to do surgery?"

Carrie smiled slightly. "Because his friends won't think we're helping him if we just give him arnica, despite it giving him him his best chance at survival."

"What happens when they find out you didn't actually do surgery?"

Carrie met her daughter's eyes evenly. "If Carter dies, they'll never know. If he lives, they won't care."

Thirty minutes later, with instructions given to Frances to administer arnica to Carter every fifteen minutes, Carrie walked out of the surgical suite. The men standing against the wall straightened.

"How is he?"

"Carter is resting," Carrie said. "It will take him time to come out from under the anesthesia." She forgave herself the little lie as she told it. It was most important to give his friends confidence. Arnica was a miracle worker, but it took time.

"He gonna make it, Doc Wallington?" This question came from the man who had so distrusted her in the beginning. His face was tight with worry.

"Are you a good friend of Carter's?" Carrie asked gently.

"He be my brother."

Carrie smiled at him sympathetically. "What's your name?"

"Billy."

"Carter is lucky to have you, Billy," Carrie replied. She might tell a lie about the surgery, but she wouldn't make a promise she didn't know she could keep. "We're doing everything we can for him." She hesitated. "He was gravely injured, Billy." She wanted him to be prepared if Carter didn't wake up.

Billy frowned. "But he got a chance, don't he?"

"Always," Carrie said firmly. She would do nothing to destroy Billy's hope. The truth was that she had no idea if Carter would recover, but she had seen bigger miracles happen to injured men.

"Thank you, Doc Wallington." Billy lowered his eyes and reclaimed his place next to the wall.

As Carrie turned toward another patient, Anthony and Jeremy walked in the door. She hurried to meet them. "Is everything alright?"

"We're here to check on you," Anthony reassured her. "From the looks of things here, you already know the Fourth Ward has turned into a war zone."

Carrie's lips tightened. "It's still bad?"

"It's still bad, but everything seems to be alright in here," Anthony responded. "I had to make sure of that myself."

"We've been promised no one will hurt the clinic or anyone in it," Carrie said. "Faith is confident we're safe here."

"Even though you're treating black patients?" Anthony asked.

"Yes," Carrie said firmly. "Some of the Irish may not like it, but they know their families won't have anyone to care for them if they destroy the clinic." She was holding onto hope that once the election was over, Moyamensing would go back to the mostly peaceful community it had been before politics caused such violent upheaval.

"A lot of the men are being taken to Pennsylvania Hospital," Jeremy reported. "As far as we can tell, hundreds have already been wounded."

"My God!" Silas exclaimed. "Are they all black men?"

"No," Anthony answered. "The blacks are fighting back. Every voting station seems to be rioting."

Billy stepped forward. "We still be voting, though. They ain't gonna stop us."

Another black man nodded. "Carter voted before they jumped him and beat him. We ain't gonna let anyone keep us from casting our vote." His eyes were dark with passion and determination.

"I admire you," Carrie said. "It takes a lot of courage to do what you're doing."

Billy shook his head. "I spent most of my life as a slave. Now that I been given the right to have a vote on what happens in this country..." His lips tightened. "There ain't nothing more important than that."

Carrie wondered how many men would have to give their lives to exercise their rights. She looked up at Anthony, determined to focus on what she needed to do that day. "I have to treat my next patient."

"Of course. I just needed to see you and Frances with my own eyes." Anthony glanced around. "Speaking of which..."

"Frances is with a patient," Carrie told him. "She's fine. What are the two of you going to do now?"

"We're going to find Octavius," Jeremy answered. "I hope he's still at his school. We're going to walk home with him. With so much chaos, I figure there's safety in numbers."

Carrie bit back her observation that their being together might make them a bigger target. She knew how much Jeremy loved Octavius. He would do anything he could to help his friend, and she knew

Anthony would do anything needed to help them both. Part of her longed to beg him not to go, but all of them were taking risks to help people they cared about.

She smiled and kissed Anthony lightly. "Be safe, dear. Minnie is home with Marietta and the twins making sugar cookies for you."

Anthony gave her a knowing look and hugged her tightly. "I'll be careful," he whispered in her ear. "I'll be back in time to ride home in the carriage with you," he promised.

It was almost two o'clock when Jeremy and Anthony approached the polling place at Eighth and Bainbridge Streets. Men were fighting in the road as a steady stream of blacks approached to vote. Some were swept into the violence. Others managed to avoid it and make their way inside to vote.

"There's McMullen," Jeremy said bitterly. He hadn't expected the ward boss to do anything to stop the fighting, but the sight of him standing in the doorway, merely watching, made Jeremy furious. "The man is a fool."

"A dangerous fool," Anthony muttered. "He'll stop at nothing to maintain his power down here."

Jeremy scowled. "Mayor Fox won't win this election. McMullen can do what he wants to try to stop it, but blacks are voting all over this city. Things are about to change." That knowledge gave him a sense of satisfaction, but he was sickened at the price that was being paid to make it a reality.

One of the approaching men caught Jeremy's attention. "That's Isaac," he told Anthony as he pointed him out. "He used to work for me. Let's go meet him. If we're with him, perhaps he'll be safer."

Before Jeremy and Anthony could reach Isaac, two white men ran up and began to yell and punch him. Isaac fought back but quickly realized he was at a disadvantage. Breaking away from the duo, he dashed into a nearby alley.

The two men gave a holler of victory and chased after him.

Jeremy broke into a run, but the men already had a block head start. Just as he and Anthony turned into the alley, the men caught up to Isaac and jerked him to a stop. "No!" Jeremy yelled, sprinting forward as fast as he could.

He wasn't fast enough.

One of the men pulled out an axe, raised his arm high, and brought it down on Isaac's head. "I got you, nigger! That's what you get for trying to vote!"

Jeremy screamed in fury as Isaac crumpled to the ground, a dark pool already forming around him.

The two men looked up at the sound and ran, disappearing around the corner at the next intersection.

Jeremy dropped to his knees when he reached Isaac, debating the fastest way to get him to the clinic. One look into Isaac's sightless eyes told him he was too late. "No," he groaned. He knew Isaac was leaving behind a wife and three children.

Jeremy barely felt Anthony's hand on his shoulder. "He was a good man."

Anthony gripped his shoulder tighter. "We can't help him," he said regretfully. "We've got to get out of here."

"I can't just leave him," Jeremy protested as he looked up. The expression on Anthony's face made him look over his shoulder. A rush of white men, some of them dressed in police uniforms, was running toward them. Their angry faces were evidence enough that they weren't coming to help. Despite the fact that he and Anthony both looked white (although he knew the wrath that would fall on him if the crowd discovered he was mulatto), they were gravely outnumbered.

"We'll come back," Anthony said as he grabbed Jeremy's arm and hauled him to his feet.

As the men drew closer, Jeremy heard a howl of anger from the rooftops surrounding them. Suddenly, bricks and rocks began to hurtle through the air. A quick glance told him the rooftops were lined with blacks doing the only thing they could do to fight back.

The whites skidded to a halt as the projectiles began to fall on them.

"Let's get out of here!" Jeremy yelled. He broke into a run, following Anthony out of the alley onto an almost empty street. He leaned over, gasping for air.

"We've got to get to Octavius," Anthony said grimly. He reached into his waistband and pulled out a pistol. "Are you armed?"

Jeremy's response was to pull out his own six-shot revolver.

Carrie was treating a nasty gash on a man's head when Frances appeared at her side.

"Mama!"

Carrie looked up. "Yes?"

"He's awake! Mr. Carter is awake!"

Carrie smiled as a wave of relief flowed through her. "I'll be right there," she promised. "I just have to finish bandaging this patient."

"I'll do it, Mama."

Carrie looked at her patient. "My daughter is quite experienced, Grady. Are you alright with her bandaging your wound?"

Grady smiled. "You're a right good doctor, Doc Wallington. I heard all about you. If you say your daughter is good, I reckon she is. I thank you for taking care of me and my friends."

Carrie squeezed his hand, gave Frances an encouraging nod, and hurried into the surgical suite that had served as Carter's recovery place for the last several hours while he had received arnica every fifteen minutes.

Carter's eyes were open when she walked into the room, but he still had a dazed expression. "Hello, Carter."

Carter turned his head slightly. "Where am I?"

"At the Moyamensing Clinic," Carrie said soothingly. "You were badly beaten this morning after you voted."

Carter frowned. "I remember that part," he said haltingly.

"How do you feel?" Carrie peered into his eyes and felt his forehead, relieved not to detect a fever. To be safe, she pulled out the thermometer she kept in her pocket. Invented just four years earlier, she was grateful to have a tool that could accurately detect fevers.

Carter looked thoughtful as he considered her question. "I don't hurt like I did," he said finally. "My head feels clearer, but I'm right tired. Am I alright now?"

"Let's just say you're better," Carrie replied. "You were badly beaten and suffered internal bleeding. I want to keep you here for a few more days to give your body time to heal. After that, you're going home to rest until we tell you differently." She didn't see any reason to add that the internal bleeding could still kill him.

Carter smiled. "You got a real fierce look, Doc..." His voice trailed away in confusion.

Carrie wasn't surprised he didn't remember coming into the clinic. "Dr. Wallington."

"You got a real fierce look, Doc Wallington. I figured I was gonna die while them men were beating on me. I reckon if you got me to live, that I oughta do whatever you say."

Carrie nodded. "I couldn't agree more."

"What did you do to me?"

Carrie considered her answer. It was time to tell the truth because a single look would reveal that surgery had not happened. "Before I tell you, I know your brother would like to see you. He can't stay long, though. You need rest more than anything."

Billy entered the room with a deep look of relief. "Carter!"

Carter smiled wearily. "Hello, Billy."

Billy turned to Carrie. "The surgery worked. I'm real sorry I didn't trust you much in the beginnin'."

Carrie met his eyes. "I didn't perform surgery."

Billy stared at her, his eyes full of confusion. "Why not? What did you do?"

Carrie turned back to Carter. "I gave you a homeopathic remedy called arnica. You were bleeding internally, and surgery would have been very dangerous. Arnica was your best chance to get better."

She turned back to Billy. "I apologize for not telling you the truth."

Billy met her eyes, looked toward Carter, and then looked back at her with a shrug. "I reckon it don't matter. Carter looks like he gonna live." He paused for a long moment. "If he had died, I don't figure we would have ever known you didn't do surgery. Since he's still alive, I don't reckon I care."

Carrie smiled. "That's what I told my daughter," she admitted.

Carter chuckled, but it died away with a wince of pain.

Carrie's voice turned brisk. "You need to go now, Billy. Carter needs rest. We're going to continue to give him arnica, but it will be several days before you can think of taking him home."

"Can I still come visit?"

"Of course," Carrie assured him.

Carter held up his hand. "The voting," he murmured. "How is it going?"

"The fightin' ain't let up," Billy responded, "but there still be lots of us voting. I reckon we gonna win this election, Carter." He stepped back when Carrie fixed him with a firm look. "I'll be back later. You do what the Doc says."

Jeremy scanned the streets for his friend as the afternoon wore on. Octavius had already left the school when he and Anthony arrived. A mutual friend, Winston, confided that Octavius was aware of the rioting, and was on his way to a pawnshop on Walnut Street to purchase a gun.

As a Civil War veteran, Octavius was a major and inspector general of the Fifth Brigade, First Division of the National Guard of Pennsylvania. He'd received word that his unit would be activated at six o'clock that evening to stop the violence. The position required him to have a horse, sword, and sidearm.

"Where will he go after the pawnshop?" Jeremy asked Winston. If they didn't get there before Octavius left, they needed to know where to go next. His gut was screaming at him that his friend would need help.

"I don't know," Winston replied, holding his hands wide. "I wish I could help you, but with the city in so much chaos, it's hard to predict."

"Has he voted yet?"

"First thing this morning, before school. All the violence started right after that." Winston tilted his head thoughtfully. "He might go home, Jeremy. He mentioned the ammunition for the gun was there."

Jeremy had heard all he needed to. Spinning around, he began to walk rapidly, headed in the direction they'd come.

"Where does Octavius live?" Anthony asked, his long legs easily keeping up with Jeremy's rapid pace.

"Eight fourteen South Street," Jeremy answered.

"How far is it?"

"Fifteen minutes if we don't get slowed down," Jeremy replied, eying the road ahead. "We're not going near Chase Street again," he vowed. "If the fighting is still going on after Isaac's murder, it's going to be bad." His eyes scanned the road ahead, hoping for a sighting of his friend.

As he walked, Jeremy thought. Octavius had been his first close friend in Philadelphia. When Jeremy had shown up to play for the Pythian baseball team, Octavius had explained it was only for black players. That had begun their discussion about Jeremy's mulatto status, despite his light skin, blond hair, and blue eyes. When Octavius asked why he didn't play for a white team since he obviously could pass as white, Jeremy had explained his commitment to helping obtain racial equality because his twin was very much black. He had to make things better for her.

Jeremy wasn't certain Octavius had believed him until he met Sarah Rose and Marcus. It was obvious his daughter had black blood. Octavius and his fiancée, Caroline, had fallen in love with Sarah Rose, spoiling her every time they were together.

Octavius had smoothed the way for Jeremy to play baseball with the darker-skinned players. In time, they had completely accepted him, but in the beginning, it was only because Octavius did.

The last two years had provided many late-night discussions about racial equality and life. Octavius and Caroline were regular guests for Marietta's delicious meals.

Octavius had made sure all the men who worked at the factory were registered to vote, both black and white. His primary concern was that every male be certain that their voice would be heard. He also had long conversations with Caroline and Marietta about women's right to vote. He was a staunch supporter.

Octavius had changed Philadelphia, but Jeremy loved him because he'd changed his own life by becoming a treasured friend.

"Where is he?" Jeremy growled. A quick glance at his watch told him it was close to four o'clock.

They walked another block before Anthony grabbed his arm. "Is that Octavius? Two blocks up?"

Jeremy squinted, standing tall to be seen over the heads of other people crowding the walkway. Ahead, a streetcar had pulled to a stop to discharge passengers. He felt a surge of relief as he spotted his friend, very much alive. Jeremy walked faster, pushing his way through the crowd, but he was still almost a block away when he stiffened. "It's them," he muttered.

"Who?" Anthony asked.

"Those two men who just passed Octavius. They're the men who killed Isaac," Jeremy said angrily.

"Are you sure?" Anthony demanded.

Jeremy's answer was to walk faster. Octavius was only a few doors from his house. *Go faster*, Jeremy pleaded in his mind. *Go faster.*

They were still a hundred feet away when Jeremy saw the two white men turn. As if it were a horrible nightmare that couldn't possibly be reality, he watched as one of the men pulled a pistol. He saw the spurt of flame and heard the pop.

Octavius staggered backward, clutching his chest.

Jeremy broke into a run, a terrible sense of déjà vu threatening to steal his breath. Would he be too late, just as he'd been too late to save Isaac?

As he ran, he watched his friend stagger behind the streetcar in an attempt to flee his attackers. The man who had fired stepped closer and shot two more times.

Then he turned and ran.

"No!" Jeremy screamed as he watched Octavius slump to the ground, caught by a policeman who was walking by.

Fury and grief threatened to choke Jeremy as he dropped to his knees beside his friend. "Octavius!"

The policeman shook his head. "He's gone."

Jeremy began to weep, shaking his head back and forth as he clutched Octavius' hand. "No... No..."

Anthony knelt beside him and laid an arm across his shoulder.

Jeremy stared down into Octavius' face, willing him to wake up. Willing him to breathe. Willing him to live. He'd done so much in his life, but there was so much more to do. At thirty-two, he still had a lifetime ahead of him. He had to get married...

At the thought of Caroline, Jeremy's grief and anger intensified.

He glared up at the policeman. "Why aren't you going after the man who shot him?" he demanded.

"There isn't any use," the policeman said quietly. "Those two men are gone."

"I saw them kill another black man earlier today." Jeremy spat the words out. He needed a target for his anger. The policeman who wasn't doing anything to catch Octavius' killer was that target.

The officer's face tightened. "I'm sorry. I've known they're nothing but trouble for a long time," he said shortly.

"They didn't just *disappear*," Jeremy argued. "Go get them before they kill someone else."

"They won't kill anyone else," the officer said. "Now that they've been seen, they'll hide out and leave the city. That's what rats do."

Jeremy ground his teeth. "An entire police force can't catch two men?"

The policeman met his eyes levelly. "Not when the police are most likely helping them escape right this minute." The officer sighed. "I know what happened here today. I'm sorry. About all of it."

Jeremy looked at him suspiciously. "Why are you telling me this? You'll lose your job, too, if Fox isn't re-elected."

"Yes, but I'll still have my honor," the policeman said crisply. "Not all Philadelphia police officers are the same." He looked around. "We have to get your friend out of here. Is there somewhere we can take him?"

Jeremy slumped, his anger spent as the grief consumed him again. "He lives right there," he said as he pointed two doors down. "Will you help us carry him?"

The officer's face tightened even more, as he looked more closely. Recognition dawned on his face. "You're telling me this is Octavius Catto?"

Jeremy nodded heavily. "It is." Saying the words caused his throat to almost close.

"Dear God in heaven," the officer muttered. He met Jeremy's eyes. "Octavius was a good man. I'm sorry. This is a great loss to the city. To the nation."

Tears filled Jeremy's eyes again. All those things were true, but what was breaking his heart was that Octavius' death was a huge loss to him personally.

His best friend was gone.

Chapter Eleven

Rose stood on the porch, drawing in deep breaths of clean air. She'd been home from school for only a few minutes. She could hear John and Hope inside laughing and playing. The school guard brought the children home as soon as class ended. Rose stayed longer, working with Phoebe and Hazel to prepare for the next day.

The sound of another laugh made her smile. Jed was inside playing with her children. She'd fallen in love with the little boy during the three weeks he'd been here. He was bright, funny, and eager to learn. He still had moments when grief consumed him, but being on the plantation had been wonderful for him. He'd already begun to gain weight from all of Annie's good cooking.

"Miss Rose?"

Rose was roused from her thoughts. She looked up at the man crossing the barnyard. "Hello, Vincent," she called, watching as he walked across the grass and climbed the stairs. He didn't resemble the man who had stumbled onto the plantation three weeks earlier, badly whipped and close to death. He had a warm smile on his face, and he was walking erect. He would carry permanent horrible scars as a reminder of the night he came so close to death. The black eyepatch he would wear for the rest of his life was another stark reminder of the brutality he had suffered, but he seemed to have accepted the reality of living the rest of his life with one eye.

"Hello, Miss Rose."

Rose nodded pleasantly. "Would you like some gingerbread cookies?" Annie spoiled her by making sure there was a plate of cookies on the porch in the afternoon. She knew Rose needed a little time to herself after a long day of teaching.

"Yes ma'am," Vincent replied, reaching down to take one. "May I ask you something?"

"Of course." Rose sat down in a rocking chair and waved her hand toward the one next to her. "What do you want to talk about?"

"It's going to take Morris more time to get well," Vincent began as soon as he sat down beside her.

"That's what I hear," Rose agreed. Secretly, she was thrilled with that news. She wasn't ready for Jed to leave. She knew the day was going to come, but she wasn't in a hurry for it happen.

"Morris wants me to head north now," Vincent continued. "He told me I should go ahead and look for jobs for both of us. He and Jed will follow when he's ready to travel."

Rose listened carefully. It made sense. Neither of the two men had lost their passion for leaving the South as soon as possible. Still, it was his decision to make. "What do you think you should do?"

Vincent considered the question. "I think it's a good idea, but I feel bad leaving Morris and Jed here without me to help care for them." He looked toward the barn apartment he still shared with Morris.

Miles and Annie remained in the main house, happy to give up their space until the men were ready to move on. Rose suspected they were so accommodating because they loved being that much closer to their grandchildren.

"I've been the one treating him since Miss Janie and Polly both returned to the clinic."

"How often are you changing his bandages?"

Vincent shook his head. "I'm not doing that anymore. Miss Janie told me last night that the wounds have healed nicely."

Rose frowned. "Then what's wrong with him?" She realized she'd been so absorbed with school that she hadn't paid enough attention to Morris' medical condition. Jed went over to see him each morning before school, and then spent time with him every evening before he came back to his bed in John's room.

Vincent looked worried. "They don't seem to know. His wounds are healed up, but he's so weak he can hardly get out of bed. There doesn't seem to be an infection in the wound, but he's still running a fever. Miss Janie has given him everything she can think to give him, but he's not getting stronger."

"He's not any better at all?" Rose demanded, thinking of how much Jed loved his daddy.

"He's better," Vincent said slowly. He turned his gaze toward the horses in the field for a long moment and then turned back. "He's just not strong enough to make a trip yet." He took a deep breath. "I can take Jed with me if he'll be too much trouble."

Rose shook her head decisively. "Jed is nothing but a joy. He is more than welcome to stay here until Morris is well. It sounds like he needs more rest. Having Jed here will be good for him."

Vincent nodded. "That's what Miss Janie says. She told me this morning that if I wanted to go, I should go. I'm not doing much for Morris now besides keeping him company."

"You should go," Rose said encouragingly. "We'll miss you, but I know both of you want to rebuild your life in the North as quickly as you can. We'll take good care of Morris and Jed until they're ready to join you. We'll look for a letter or telegram as soon as you're settled."

Vincent smiled, relief etched on his face. "Thank you, Rose. Everyone here has been so wonderful to us." He hesitated. "Seeing all of you living together here... It's given both me and Morris hope that someday things might get better for blacks in this country."

Rose smiled, not willing to voice her fears of the exact opposite. "Do you know where you're going?"

"Morris and I have talked about Philadelphia. I plan to head there."

Rose couldn't hide the frown that crossed her face. She had been aware of their original intent, but hoped they had changed their minds.

Vincent eyed her closely. "What do you know about Philadelphia?"

Rose knew he deserved honesty. "There's been a lot of trouble there for blacks recently, Vincent. Philadelphia had elections last week. The white Democrats were determined that the black Republicans wouldn't vote. There were a lot of men injured or killed." Her heart filled with sadness as she thought of Octavius Catto. Carrie's letter had reached her the day before. She'd had the privilege of meeting him during her last visit to Philadelphia. Anger mixed with grief at the thought of the tremendous loss his death was. Carrie and Anthony had decided to stay until after the funeral so they could attend the service, but also to continue to care for other men who had been injured.

Vincent frowned, absorbing this news.

Rose knew he'd been whipped so badly because he was registering black voters in South Carolina. Surely, news of the voting violence would make him rethink his destination.

"Did the Republicans win?" Vincent asked after several minutes of silence.

"Yes."

Vincent looked back out over the fields.

Rose left him to his thoughts. She knew him to be a thoughtful, intelligent man. He would consider his options before he made his decision. She was content to munch on cookies while she enjoyed the orange, red, and yellow leaves that had claimed the trees in the last few days. She sipped her hot tea, grateful for the change in season that had released them from the grip of summer, but not sure she was looking forward to a long, cold winter. All she could do was embrace the fall beauty for as long as it lasted.

"I'm going to Philadelphia," Vincent finally said. "Bad things have happened, but that will only make the Republicans more eager to make things right for the blacks that put them in office. It's going to take time for things to change, but at least Philadelphia is a city that has a chance. I believe it will be the best place to start."

Rose didn't like his decision, but she couldn't argue with his logic. "I suppose that's true." Then she added, "My brother is expecting a visit from you."

"Excuse me?"

"I've told you my twin brother runs Cromwell Factory in Philadelphia. If you need a job while you're looking for a position that might suit you better, he's prepared to offer you one. Morris, too. I've written to Jeremy about both of you."

Vincent stared at her for a moment and then grinned broadly. "You couldn't possibly have given me better news, Rose. I've decided I want to go to college when I get there, but I'll have to pay my way as I go. I had quite a bit of savings in South Carolina, but I had to leave it behind when we ran. It doesn't really matter what the work is," he said. "I'll just be happy to have a job. Thank you," he said fervently.

Rose smiled. "You're welcome. When will you be leaving?"

"Tomorrow morning," Vincent replied. "Now that the decision has been made, I'm eager to get there and find a place for the three of us to live."

"That's taken care of, too," Rose informed him. She had hoped to talk him out of taking Jed to Philadelphia, but since he was determined, she would tell him about the arrangements she and Moses had made.

Vincent's eyes widened. "What are you talking about?"

"Moses and I know a lot of people in Philadelphia. We escaped to that city during the war, and lived there until Moses entered the army as a spy and I went down to Hampton to teach school. Now that Jeremy and Marietta live there, we have even more friends. I asked Jeremy to talk to a family we met during a visit. They're willing to put the three of you up in a room until you earn enough money to pay for a place of your own."

"Why are you doing all this, Rose?"

Rose hesitated but then decided to be honest. "Both you and Morris are fine men, Vincent, but my main priority is Jed. I love him. I want to make sure he's safe, and I want him to have opportunity. I've arranged for him to go to school, as well." Her lips tightened when she thought of Octavius Catto never again being able to lead the Institute for Colored Youth, but she had been assured Jed's position there was secure.

Vincent sat back and shook his head in amazement. "When Morris and I made it to Cromwell Plantation, we thought we would be lucky if we could get out of here alive. We never imagined all this."

Rose felt a pang of sadness as Jed's laughter rang out loud enough for them to hear it.

Vincent pushed himself to his feet. "I'll go tell Jed."

One week after Octavius' death, Carrie, Anthony, and the girls stood on the train platform, waiting to return to Virginia.

"I'm ready to be home," Frances said quietly.

"Me too." Minnie's eyes were full of distress. "I'm sad. Philadelphia is sad."

Carrie put an arm around Minnie's thin shoulders and pulled her close. "I know, honey."

"I'm glad we got to go to Mr. Catto's service," Frances said.

"Me too," Anthony agreed.

Carrie gazed around at the throng on the station platform as she remembered the service the day before. Octavius' funeral had created a moment of mourning that provided a distinct departure from the violence and rioting that led to his death. It was as if the whole city stopped to take a deep breath.

The service, held in the City Armory because he'd been in the National Guard, had been a national event, with people coming in from all over the country to attend. The funeral procession had started at seven in the morning and proceeded through cold, drizzling rain down city streets until it ended at Lebanon Cemetery. It had included regimental guards, students, faculty, and graduates from the Institute for Colored Youth. Preachers, politicians, and more than five thousand mourners had joined them to celebrate the life of an extraordinary man who'd been taken far too soon.

Carrie would never forget the shattered look on Caroline LeCount's face. She had remained stoic throughout the service, but Carrie knew exactly how fragile she was. She'd given her a warm embrace, but she knew Caroline wasn't ready to hear any encouraging words. Carrie planned to write her later, and would visit her the next time she was in the city.

"I'm glad Carter went home yesterday," Frances said. "At least there was one good thing that happened while we were here."

Carrie pushed her thoughts aside. There would be time for rumination when they got on the train. "There was more than *one* good thing," she said.

Frances looked at her doubtfully. "What else good happened, Mama?"

Carrie forced a smile. "Why don't you tell me?"

Frances sighed, but got a thoughtful look on her face. "Well, it was good that Carter went home yesterday. I was afraid he was going to die, but he looked good when he left with his brother."

Carrie nodded. "Yes, Carter is going to be fine. I told him to take it easy for a couple weeks, but he'll be back at work soon." She turned to Minnie. "What other good things happened?"

Minnie blinked up at her, sadness still filling her face. "A good thing?"

Anthony entered the game. "Yes. What good things happened in the last three weeks?"

Minnie chewed her lip. "I was able to spend a lot of time with Sarah Rose and Marcus." She paused. "And Marietta taught me how to make sugar cookies as good as Annie's."

Anthony laughed. "It will be wise to not tell Annie that, my dear."

Minnie shook her head. "Oh, I won't, Daddy. Marietta already told me that Annie won't be happy to know that. She made me promise not to tell. Do you know that Annie taught Marietta how to cook?" Before her father could answer, she continued. "She gets upset, though, if Marietta cooks things as good as hers." She giggled, but then frowned. "I guess Annie won't have to worry about that anymore, since Jeremy and Marietta won't come to the plantation again."

Carrie felt the same surge of regret that she saw on her daughter's face, but she was determined to focus on gratitude. "So, time with the twins and learning how to make sugar cookies as good as Annie's. Those are both definitely good things!" She turned to Anthony next. "What good things happened for you?"

Anthony met her eyes. His expression revealed how challenging the question was, but he forced a smile. "Good things? Well, it was certainly good to have so much time to spend with Jeremy. I also enjoyed getting to know Silas." He grinned slyly. "I especially enjoyed how many times the males beat the females in charades."

"It's only because Mama and Marietta are so bad at giving clues," Frances protested. "We couldn't possibly have won."

"I don't think we're bad at giving clues," Carrie retorted, thrilled to see laughter in her daughters' eyes again. There was nothing wrong with sadness, but she knew how crucial it was to find gratitude in the hard times. "I prefer to think my teammates just weren't very good at guessing."

Frances laughed. "Believe whatever you need to, Mama. I would like to point out, however, that none of you had a hard time guessing the clues Florence and I gave."

"What about me?" Minnie cried.

Frances rolled her eyes. "I'm afraid you are truly your mother's daughter. You were as bad as she was!"

"I was not!" Minnie retorted. She turned to Carrie, evidently eager to change the subject. "Mama, what good things happened for you?"

Carrie forced away the memory of beaten and battered men that filled her mind. For much of her time in Philadelphia, she'd felt like she'd been back at Chimborazo Hospital during the war. Her regular nightmares confirmed it. She smiled through her pain. "Well, I've learned what a miracle worker arnica is. Carter wouldn't be alive today without it. I've had a wonderful time with Florence, and of course, Marietta and Jeremy. I'm grateful I was able to meet Silas and get to know him." She smiled. "And I'm glad you learned how to make sugar cookies, Minnie, despite the fact that I'm sure I gained weight while we were here!"

They were laughing when the train that would carry them to Richmond pulled into the station.

"Thank you, Mama," Frances said seriously. "It's hard to find the good things sometimes when there are so many bad things happening."

Carrie nodded. "I know. Those are the times when we most need to find things to be grateful for."

"Where did you learn that?"

Carrie's smile was genuine this time. "Old Sarah," she said softly.

"Rose's mama?" Minnie asked.

"Yes. I've never known anyone wiser than Sarah." Carrie thought back. "She had more reasons than anyone I've ever known to be bitter and angry."

"But she wasn't?" Minnie asked.

Carrie shook her head. "No. Old Sarah used to tell me that no matter how bad thin's be, there always be some good. You just gotta look for it hard 'nuff." She naturally fell into Sarah's way of talking. "She told me that if I made up my mind to find thin's to be grateful fer, that I would see the goodness all aroun' me."

"Did you?" Frances asked.

"Most of the time," Carrie answered honestly. "Sometimes it's more difficult."

"Like now?" Frances' eyes bored into her.

"Like now," Carrie agreed. She allowed her thoughts to go back in time. "I can remember times when I was very upset about things. I always went to see Rose's mama."

Minnie frowned. "You didn't go see your own mama? Why not?"

Carrie bit back a frown. She didn't think this was a conversation to be had on a train station platform. "How about if we talk about that another time?"

"Alright, Mama," Minnie replied. She took Carrie's hand and squeezed it tightly. "I'm very glad I can talk to you when I'm sad. I wouldn't want to have to talk to someone else."

Carrie felt a surge of gratitude so intense it almost took her breath away. "I couldn't agree more, Minnie." She wrapped her daughter in a hug.

When she straightened, she took hold of both girls' hands. "Sarah used to tell me that the more grateful I be, the more beauty I see." She smiled down at them. "I am so completely grateful for my beautiful daughters."

"And I'm grateful for *all* my beautiful girls," Anthony added. "Are we ready to go?"

Laughing, the four of them climbed onto the train.

Carrie knew the sadness would envelop them again at some point, but she knew choosing gratitude would help them get through it.

Moses insisted Vincent join them for dinner that night. When Vincent looked toward the barn uncertainly, Moses said, "Don't worry about Morris. My mama will send over a big plate of food for him."

His statement made Vincent frown more. "He's not eating very much. He was already so skinny. I didn't think he could get any skinnier, but I was wrong."

Moses could tell Vincent felt uneasy about leaving the next morning. He thought about encouraging him to stay on the plantation, but he also knew it would be best if Vincent could start his job at the factory and get money coming in before winter hit. Vincent and Morris were an unlikely pair, but what they'd been through had drawn them close. "We'll take good care of him," he promised.

Vincent sighed. "I know." He shook his head. "I feel responsible," he said quietly. "If I hadn't been at his house that night, trying to get him to register to vote, none of this would have happened."

"Not true," Moses said firmly. "If the KKK wasn't determined to terrorize black people, none of this would have happened, Vincent. You're not responsible for the tens of thousands of black people all over the South who have felt their wrath." He looked Vincent square in the eyes. "You know the only way things are going to truly change is if black people use their right to vote. You helped give men courage to stand up and be heard." Vincent listened, but Moses didn't see any relief in his eyes.

"Every time I hear Jed talk about his mama, I almost die inside," Vincent confessed. "I saw them shoot her. I still feel sick when I realize that boy watched the Klan beat me and Morris. Jed will never forget it."

"No," Moses said gravely. "He won't." He thought for a moment and then continued, hoping his story would help Vincent. "I was eleven when I watched a group of men kill my father after he tried to escape.

They'd already beaten him badly when they decided to hang him. I hid in the woods so I could watch and say good-bye to him."

Vincent's eyes widened, but he remained silent.

"I'll carry that image with me always," Moses admitted, "but it hasn't kept me from living a good, full life. I know that's what my father wanted for me more than anything. It was the reason he tried to escape. He was coming back for my mama and my sisters so we would have a better life." He stiffened as he remembered the horror of watching his daddy swing from the rope. "That's what Jed's mama wanted for him, too. Jed is smart and has a good heart. He'll be alright in time." He spoke confidently. When Vincent still looked uncertain, he continued.

"Our daughter Felicia is proof of that. I brought her home with me from the riots in Memphis five years ago. She watched both her parents be killed in cold blood. It took her time to heal, but she did."

Vincent straightened. "Is Felicia the one going to school at Oberlin College?"

"Yes. She's determined to make the country better for black people."

Vincent stared at him for several moments and then nodded. "I know you're right. Our people carry so much pain. We all have stories about things that should destroy us."

"We do," Moses replied. "Yet we're here. We're alive. We have a chance to change things for the children who are counting on us to do just that. Go on to Philadelphia, Vincent. Morris and Jed will join you when they can. You going there first will make things easier for them."

Vincent took a deep breath. "Alright," he said reluctantly. "Thank you for taking care of them."

Moses smiled. "There's no reason to thank us. We're happy to do it. Morris will get better in time. Until then, we love having Jed with us. My children adore him." So did Moses. "Did he tell you he went riding in the fields with me today?" He had loved having Jed ride with him and John. Between the two of them, they had given him quite an education on tobacco. The little boy had soaked it up.

Vincent laughed. "It's all he can talk about right now. I've learned more about raising tobacco than I ever knew. I never learned how to ride a horse, either, but Jed seems to do well."

"Jed is a natural," Moses assured him. "He rides with the children and Miles every day after school."

"He told me he loves to ride horses more than he loves Annie's cinnamon rolls," Vincent said with a laugh.

Moses' eyes widened. "That's a mighty big statement. Of course, as much as I love my mama's cinnamon rolls, I would give them up before I gave up riding."

"Those cinnamon rolls are a wondrous thing."

Moses laughed at the yearning in his eyes. "Annie will be up early in the morning to bake you some to take along on your trip." He reached into his pocket and pulled out cash. "This should get you to Philadelphia." He handed him a slip of paper and an envelope. "This is the address to Thomas and Abby's house in Richmond, and a letter to Micah and May. They take care of the house there. You'll stay there tomorrow night and then catch the train the next morning."

Vincent's mouth gaped open. "I can't take this," he protested. "Y'all have already done so much. I'll walk and catch rides. It may take some time, but I'll make it just fine."

"Probably," Moses replied, "but what if you don't make it before Morris and Jed are ready to join you? They won't know what to do, and you won't have a place ready for them." He placed a hand on Vincent's arm. "I make a lot of money, Vincent. I've been lucky and I'm grateful, but it doesn't mean anything if I can't use it to help. I want the world to be a better place for my children. What I do with my money is part of making that happen." He pressed the bills into Vincent's hand. "It would mean a lot if you'll let me do this for you."

"Thank you," Vincent said quietly. "I hope you know how much this means."

"I do," Moses assured him. "When Rose and I escaped the plantation during the first year of the war, we didn't have anything. Before Abby married Thomas, she ran clothing factories in Philadelphia."

Vincent peered at him. "Where I'm going to be working?"

Moses nodded. "Cromwell Factory in Moyamensing is the newest one. She and Thomas started that one together. Anyway, Carrie had met her the year before the war and told her about us. If it hadn't been for Abby opening her home to us when we arrived in Philadelphia, I don't know what we would have done. It's my turn to help others now."

"All of y'all have more stories than I can keep track of."

Moses laughed. "I suppose we do. The bottom line, though, is that we're all family to each other.

Black...white...Navajo... It doesn't matter. We're family."

At that moment, the dinner bell gonged outside the back door of the kitchen.

"Are you really going to pass up my mama's chicken and dumplings?" Moses teased. "You don't look like that big of a fool."

Vincent finally laughed. "I'm not passing up your mama's chicken and dumplings."

"And apple pie," Moses added, his stomach rumbling at the aroma rolling from the front door as they walked in.

"Will you leave any pie for the rest of us?" Vincent demanded, his eyes sparkling.

"My mama always makes extra pies," Moses said casually. "She's been feeding me for a long time."

The sun was dipping toward the horizon the next night, when Matthew and Janie stood.

"Dinner was wonderful, Annie," Janie said warmly, stifling a yawn with her hand as she shifted Annabelle in her arms. "Tell Carrie I'll be by to see her tomorrow after they return."

Rose smiled. "How does it feel to have your own home again?"

"It's wonderful!" Janie replied. "Though I'm going to miss being so close to all of you."

"We're going to miss having you nearby," Abby said. "We love Robert being able to come visit any time he wants."

Matthew lifted his sleeping son into his arms. Robert woke enough to snuggle his head into his father's chest before relaxing back into slumber. "Robert thinks of you as his grandparents. He's a lucky boy."

"Nonsense," Thomas replied. "We're the lucky ones. That little boy is special. He's going to grow up to do something very important."

"He's living up to his namesake," Matthew said somberly.

A moment of silence fell on the porch.

Matthew gazed out over the pastures glowing golden in the setting sun, turning the glimmering coats of the horses into shining orbs. "This was Robert's dream. I wish he were here to experience it."

"We all do," Abby said.

The pulse of the fall evening seemed to throb around them. A soft breeze began to blow, rustling the gloriously colored leaves of the oak trees stationed around the house. In the distance, a coyote howled a mournful call. The horses looked up, their heads carved against the sunset like beautiful statues.

"Robert knows," Rose said quietly. She was certain of that. She could feel him in the air; hear him in the leaves; see him in the horses standing in tribute to him. Tears filled her eyes.

Abby stood and walked to the edge of the porch. "Do you feel him?" Her voice was full of awe as she spun around to gaze at Rose. "I've always been so envious when you say things like that. I believe you, but I've never experienced it." She gulped. "But tonight..."

"I feel it," Matthew said in a hushed voice. "I don't understand it, but I can't deny what I'm feeling."

Moses nodded his head. "It's hard to believe, but I feel it, too." He reached over to take his wife's hand. "I've always wondered what it would be like to feel what you feel."

"What does it feel like to you?" Rose asked, mesmerized by the fact they could feel Robert's presence.

Moses searched for words. "It feels like...a friend is visiting," he finally murmured. "A good friend has come to visit."

Everyone's heads were nodding as the sun finally dipped below the horizon, replacing the gold with a dark pink and purple mass of clouds dancing in the breeze.

When the golden glow was completely gone, Rose knew Robert was no longer there.

Matthew took a deep breath. "On that note, I believe we'll say goodnight."

Rose was alone on the porch as night swallowed the day. Gleaming stars populated a dark sky. She loved full moons, but she also loved the new moon because the dark skies revealed so many more stars. She moved closer to the edge of the porch, peering up at the canvas spread above her. Her breath caught with joy as the Milky Way spread across the sky, its creamy appearance caused by what surely must be millions of stars. Felicia had taught her about it during her last visit. On clear nights, Rose loved to gaze up at it.

Tonight especially, with so much on her mind, Rose needed the wonder and beauty of the Milky Way to embrace her and to remind her there was always beauty in the midst of darkness.

Vincent had departed early that morning. Jed had handled his leaving well, assuring him that he would take good care of his daddy until they could join him.

Rose was on the porch, waiting for Jed to turn out the lantern in the barn apartment. She could see the light glowing in the apartment window, so she knew they were probably playing checkers. Jed would turn down the lantern before he went to sleep. Once he'd known Vincent was leaving, he'd insisted on moving into the apartment with his father so he could care for him. Rose would miss him being in the house, but it was the best decision. She was certain Morris was happy to have his son with him again.

The little boy was extraordinarily responsible, but he was only ten. Unwilling to take a chance on a fire, she wouldn't go to bed until the light went out. Besides, she was enjoying the solitude of a beautiful evening. She pulled her shawl closer around her shoulders, gazed up at the sky again, and then returned to her rocking chair. She could hear laughter inside, as the beginning chorus of hooting owls came from the woods. The sounds wrapped her in a cocoon of contentment.

About twenty minutes later, she saw the barn window go dark. Rose waited a few minutes to make sure Jed wouldn't relight it, and then she turned to go into the house. Just as she reached for the door handle, a strangled scream rent the still night.

"Daddy!"

Chapter Twelve

Rose froze in her tracks.

"Daddy!" This time the call was clearer and sharper. "No, Daddy! Help!"

Moses stepped out onto the porch, his eyes fixed on the barn. "Did I hear something?"

"Go get Janie!" Rose shouted as she dashed to the edge of the porch.

Moments later, she was running up the stairs to the barn apartment. She burst through the door, terrified of what she would find. She had seen Morris that afternoon. He was weak, but he'd been smiling and talking, excited about Vincent going ahead to Philadelphia. He'd seemed energized by the news that they had jobs, a temporary home, and a school for Jed.

"Miss Rose!"

Jed's heartbroken voice ripped through Rose's heart. "What's wrong?" She rushed to the window, lit the lantern, held it high, and looked toward Morris' bed.

"What's wrong with Daddy?" Jed asked, his frightened voice trembling so hard he could barely get the words out.

Rose stepped closer, her heart sinking as she took in Morris' condition. His skin was covered with sweat, but his teeth were chattering. His face seemed to be caving in on itself. "How long has he been like this?"

"He was fine when I done turned the light out," Jed cried. "Just as it went dark, he cried out like he be hurting real bad. Then he started moaning."

Rose wrapped her arms around Jed's shoulder. "Moses has gone for Janie," she said soothingly. "She'll be here soon."

In reality, Janie wouldn't get there for at least thirty minutes. Their new home was a fifteen-minute ride, though she was certain Moses would make it shorter. Janie had to dress, get her medical bag, and return. Janie couldn't ride a galloping horse, so the carriage would have to do.

Rose gritted her teeth. It was obvious, even to her, that Morris had developed a searing fever. She feared he was too weak to survive it.

Abby pushed in through the door, took one look, and whirled around to talk to Annie, who was right behind her. "We need cold water and more rags." She looked toward the basin on the table next to Morris' bed. "There's enough water here for me and Rose to get started. We'll need more. As cold as you can make it."

Annie, her lips set grimly, nodded and disappeared down the stairs.

"What's wrong with my daddy?" Jed demanded again. "What happened?"

Abby met Rose's eyes with a silent message before she turned to Jed. "Your daddy has a fever," she said calmly.

Rose knew the infection Janie worried about had exploded in Morris' body. The infection caused by the lash cuts had buried deep in his body, poisoning his blood. Rose knew they were looking at sepsis. She shoved down the sick feeling that there would be nothing they could do to stop it because Morris' body was too weak to fight.

Rose took Jed's hand. "I'm taking you over to the house so you can sleep in John's room."

Jed wrenched away, tears falling down his cheeks. "No!" he cried. "I have to stay with my daddy. He needs me!"

Rose knelt down so she could gaze into his eyes. "I understand how you feel, Jed. Right now, though, your daddy needs us to take care of him. Janie will be here soon. When he's better, you can come over to visit him."

Jed hesitated, but then shook his head stubbornly. "No." His voice went from frightened little boy to what sounded like a mature man. "My daddy needs me, Miss Rose. I'm not leaving him. I might not can do much, but he'll know I'm here." He walked over to sit down in the chair next to Morris. "I'm gonna sit right here and hold his hand."

Rose recognized a decision when she saw one. She was scared of what Jed was going to witness, but she accepted the right he had to be with his daddy.

"Alright, Jed," Abby said softly. "I know your daddy is happy you're with him." She moved over and dipped a rag into the basin, wet it thoroughly, and wrung it out. "You put this on your daddy's forehead and hold it there."

Jed nodded solemnly, his face calm now that he knew he wouldn't be forced to leave.

The long night wore on.

Janie arrived and immediately began to administer homeopathic drops that would help to reduce his fever, but her expression said what her actions didn't reveal.

Jed didn't miss it. "My daddy ain't gonna make it is he, Miss Janie?" He took a deep breath. "You can tell me the truth."

Rose fought back the urge to scream at Janie not to tell him what they already all knew.

"I'm not giving up hope," Janie said. "Keep talking to your daddy. Your voice is the best medicine in the world for him."

Jed considered that. "Because he don't want to leave me like Mama did?"

Rose's heart almost broke at the vulnerable, frightened look in Jed's eyes.

"That's right," Janie said gently, her own eyes glistening with unshed tears. "Your daddy loves you with all his heart, Jed."

Jed maintained a tight grip on Morris' hand and began to murmur. "Get better, Daddy. I be right here, Daddy. I love you, Daddy."

Rose prayed as Jed begged his father to live.

Janie's face grew more somber as the night edged toward dawn.

Rose could hear Morris' struggle to live in his labored breathing. He had lost consciousness hours earlier.

Jed never relented in his pleading. "Please, Daddy. We got's to go to Philadelphia. We's going north, Daddy."

The breathing turned into a rattling wheeze.

Rose's eyes filled with tears. She knew that sound.

Abby and Annie walked in with fresh bowls of water and froze in their tracks.

"Janie?" Abby finally asked.

Janie shook her head silently.

All they could do was wait.

The sun, still far below the horizon, was just casting a rosy glow on the edge of a dark sky as Morris drew his last breath. The terrible rattling sound ceased as his body fell slack on the bed.

"Daddy!" Jed screamed.

Rose, tears flowing down her cheeks, moved forward to put her arms around the little boy. "I'm sorry, Jed. Your daddy is gone."

Jed shook his head fiercely. "No. Daddy ain't gonna leave me. He be sleepin'. Gettin' that rest you said he needed."

Janie stepped forward and took his other hand. "Jed, honey, your daddy tried hard to stay here with you. He just couldn't. His body couldn't fight the bad infection he had."

Jed stiffened and gazed up at Rose, his eyes full of heartbreak. "Daddy's dead?" he whispered.

Rose nodded, wishing more than anything in the world that it wasn't true. "Yes," she said softly. "I'm so sorry, Jed."

Jed looked up at her wildly and then collapsed into a torrent of weeping.

Rose held him and let him cry. A ten-year-old little boy shouldn't have to experience what he'd been through. Less than a month ago, his mother had been murdered, he'd seen his father and Vincent brutally whipped, and now he had watched his father die.

Rose heard footsteps behind her. Without turning around, she knew it was Moses. Annie had gone for him.

When Jed's cries began to ease, Moses stepped forward and scooped Jed into his arms. Jed, instead of resisting, turned his face into Moses' strong shoulder and sagged against him. Moses gave Morris a sorrowful look and turned to walk down the steps.

Rose knew he was taking Jed to John's room and would hold the little boy until he went to sleep.

They would talk about what to do later.

Rose was waiting on the porch for Moses when he returned from the fields later that afternoon. His eyes revealed his weariness, but his face glowed with satisfaction.

"The last wagons left this afternoon," Moses called when he saw her.

Rose managed a genuine smile, despite her pain. "Congratulations, my dear. It's your best crop yet."

Moses nodded. "The men have done such a tremendous job. Their bonus this year will reflect their hard work."

"After last year, I know they all need it," Rose replied. They had been just a few weeks from harvesting when a flood had struck the plantation, destroying the vast majority of the abundant tobacco waiting to be cut. The men had been paid for their work, but no one had received the bonuses that came with receiving a percentage of the profits. She knew Moses had been counting on an excellent crop this year to help everyone recover, and to rebuild the plantation surplus.

"They're making plans for expanding homes and fields," Moses replied. "No one was willing to count on it until the last wagons actually shipped to Richmond. I won't get the final numbers for another week or so, but I know we're going to make more money than we ever have." His eyes shone. "I'm happy for the men."

Rose watched as the shine in his eyes slowly dimmed and became swallowed by sadness. Coming home had forced his focus away from the crop. "How is Jed?"

Rose sighed. "He slept until almost noon, but he's done very little except cry since then. His heart is broken, Moses."

"I know it is," Moses replied. "Jed loved his daddy."

She glanced toward the window of the room Jed was sharing with John. "I sent John to school, but I stayed here with Jed. I simply held him for most of the afternoon."

"That's what he needed more than anything."

A long silence fell on the porch. Life continued on around them. They could hear Annie laughing with Hope, her husky voice floating through the air. Smoke curled from the parlor fireplace where Thomas and Abby read together in front of the crackling flames. Amber was working one of the foals in the round pen, while Clint hauled hay out to the fields.

In the midst of such normalcy, one little boy had just had his heart shattered, and they were the ones who had to figure out what happened next.

"Carrie, Anthony, and the girls should be here soon," Moses remarked, his eyes set on the horizon.

"Yes," Rose answered, unwilling to bring up the topic that needed to be discussed.

Moses turned around to look over the plantation for a moment and then swung back to her. "I want Jed to stay here."

Rose caught her breath, unable to believe what she was hearing.

Moses peered at her. "We can't send that little boy to Philadelphia, Rose. I know Vincent will be good to him, but he needs a family. We can give him that."

Rose wanted to burst into tears and leap into his arms, but she forced herself to think clearly. She'd been admonishing herself to do it all day. "What if Jed doesn't want to stay here? He knows Morris was intent on him not living in the South."

Moses frowned, thinking through his answer. "That was when he couldn't imagine Jed having any opportunities in the South. We can give him that. We'll support whatever he wants to do as he gets older, like we're doing with Felicia."

"That's true," Rose agreed. Then she said the words she hated to say. "It doesn't change the risk for blacks in the South, though. Morris wanted to get him away from that. What if Jed lives in fear because of what happened to his parents down here?"

Moses moved to sit beside her. "Do you not want Jed to stay, Rose?"

"I want him to stay more than anything in the world," Rose confessed. "I've fallen in love with that little boy. I think of him as my son already." She took a deep breath. "I also know we have to honor Morris' wishes, and we have to respect Vincent. He should have a say in this. We can't just take Jed away from him because we love him." She reached out and gripped Moses' hand. "We should ask John and Hope, as well."

Moses raised a brow. "John and Hope adore Jed."

"I know they do, but they should have a say," Rose responded. "They're old enough to have a voice in what happens. If we want Jed to truly feel part of our family, he has to be sure all of us want him to stay."

Moses considered her words. "You're right." He looked up at the window. "Is Jed sleeping?"

"Yes. He finally drifted off about twenty minutes before you got home. I'm hoping he'll sleep for a few hours. He's exhausted."

"You do know that Cromwell Plantation is the best place for that little boy, don't you?" Moses asked.

"I want to believe that," Rose said slowly. "He could have a good life in Philadelphia, though, Moses. I know Vincent loves him. He'll be able to attend the Institute for Colored Youth, so I know he'll get an excellent education."

Moses shook his head. "Jed needs a family," he said firmly.

"I agree with you," Rose replied. "We need to proceed carefully, however."

Moses clenched his jaw, but then relaxed it. "Alright," he conceded. "What do you propose to do? I know you have this all figured out, so why don't you tell me the plan?"

Rose didn't hear resentment in her husband's voice, just resignation. "I believe we need to send a letter to Vincent. Since the mail is so slow, I recommend sending one of your men to Philadelphia to deliver it. That way we'll know Vincent's answer much sooner."

"I'll send Franklin," Moses said quickly. "He spent quite a bit of time with both Morris and Vincent. Not just when they got here, but during the weeks they were healing. He'll be the best person to deliver the news. Besides," he added, "he's always wanted to visit Philadelphia. He can stay with Jeremy and Marietta while Vincent has time to make a decision."

"Perfect." She looked toward the barn, smiling as John and Hope walked out with Miles. His gray head was bent toward his granddaughter as she talked, waving her hands to emphasize whatever she was saying. "While he's gone, we'll talk to John and Hope. If they agree, and Vincent is willing for him to stay, then we'll talk to Jed and determine what he wants."

Moses turned to meet her eyes. "I knew you had a plan," he said quietly. "It's a good one, Rose." He paused. "It's not what I want to do, but I agree that it's for the best." He grinned suddenly. "While all of this is playing out, I'm going to do my best to make sure Jed knows staying with us is exactly what he wants to do."

Rose laughed. "Once again, we think exactly alike, my dear."

Chapter Thirteen

Carrie smiled at Rose when she walked into the barn. "Good morning!"

Rose returned the smile but looked over her shoulder at the house, which was barely visible in the pre-dawn dark. "I feel odd about going riding on Harvest Celebration day."

Carrie shrugged. "You know everything is ready. Annie, Polly, and the other women have been cooking around the clock for the last week. There's going to be more food than anyone can eat. The arena is ready for the tournament. Tables are in place to hold the food." She cast a practiced look at the sky. "It's going to be perfectly beautiful weather, despite the frost coating the ground. We're in for another Indian summer day. I fail to see what you're worried about."

Carrie led No Regrets from her stall. "Besides, I've hardly seen you since I returned from Philadelphia. If it's selfish to want some time with my best friend, so be it. I won't apologize."

Rose walked over and wrapped her in a hug. "You're completely right. I'm being silly. I can hardly wait to spend some time with you."

"That's more like it." Carrie smirked with satisfaction.

The two friends worked in silence, quickly saddling and bridling their horses. Within a few minutes, they were mounted and trotting briskly away from the house.

Carrie reveled in the beauty of the morning. The sun hadn't risen, so the frosted ground looked like new snow. She knew it would melt quickly, but she enjoyed the magical feeling it gave her. Migrating geese honked overhead as squirrels chattered in the trees, busily working to collect enough nuts for the winter. The oaks, maples, and alders stood proudly in their coats of gloriously colored leaves, their vibrancy somehow more splendid against the frosted ground. Fall wildflowers, snugged beneath trees that sheltered them from the season's few hard frost, called out their own song.

"It's glorious," Rose finally said. "Thank you. I needed this."

Carrie knew that was true. Rose had been extremely busy at school. More children than ever before had arrived as new students at the Cromwell School. While the black and white students were now in separate buildings; Rose's responsibilities had not diminished. Phoebe taught the white students, and Rose continued to oversee everything.

"I know you love teaching, but how are you handling the pressure?"

Rose met her eyes. "It's incredibly gratifying to see the school grow."

"But...?" Carrie questioned.

"But I have so many other things on my mind," Rose confessed.

"Jed."

"Jed," Rose agreed. "He's crying a little less, but he's brokenhearted. I see it in his eyes."

"He's also scared," Carrie said, laying a hand on No Regrets' neck as the bay mare startled at a family of deer that stepped out of the woods, their regal bodies casting shadows on the frost as the sun crested the trees.

"Yes," Rose said sadly. "He keeps asking me what's going to happen to him. He wants to know when he's leaving for Philadelphia."

"What are you telling him?" Carrie asked. "Have you heard from Franklin yet?" She was sure they hadn't or she would have known. "He's been gone almost a week."

"I know," Rose said heavily. "The fact that he didn't return right away means Vincent is struggling with his decision. We told Franklin to give him the time he needed without pressure, but not knowing is difficult. We tell Jed that Franklin has gone to see Vincent and that we should know more soon." Her eyes filled with frustration. "All I want to do is scoop him up into a hug, tell him I'm always going to be his mama, and that I love him." She shook her head. "It's hard," she admitted.

"For everyone," Carrie observed. She could feel the tension vibrating in her friend's body. "Have you talked to John and Hope yet?"

"No. Annie convinced us to wait until we hear from Vincent. I believe the children should know, but Annie is right that Hope is incapable of keeping a secret. I suppose it is asking too much of a very dramatic almost-six-year-old to keep such a big secret."

"I've watched them together this last week," Carrie said thoughtfully. "They already seem like siblings. John and Hope would be sad if Jed left."

"I know," Rose admitted. "I'm probably making more of it than I should." She sighed heavily. "I never had any choices about anything when I was a child."

"You were a slave," Carrie reminded her gently.

"Yes, but never having any control of even the smallest part of my life was difficult. I don't want my children to feel they don't have a voice in their life."

Carrie couldn't help the laughter that bubbled from her lips. She held up a hand when Rose glared at her. "I'm sorry," she gasped in between laughs. When she finally regained control, she pinned Rose with a steady gaze. "Your children have so many choices. Far more than even I had as a child. You know my mother had very strict ideas about how I was to be raised. Except for the times when my father stepped in to save me, I had no say at all."

She brought No Regrets to a halt, waited until Rose did the same with Maple, and took her hand. "Your children know they're loved and respected. John is strong and becoming more responsible by the day. He's smart as a whip. Hope is a complete delight. She's like a ray of sunshine to everyone who meets her." She squeezed Rose's hand tightly. "Your children are who they are because of how you and Moses have raised them. And now? Now you're doing the same thing for Jed. You're not making the decision for him. You're getting the information you need, and you're going to let him decide what he wants to do."

Rose's lips quivered. "I want him to be my son, Carrie. I love that little boy so much. The last week has only made me love him more."

"I know," Carrie said softly. She hoped Jed, if Vincent was willing for him to remain with Moses and Rose, would make the decision to stay, but it had been only a week since his father died. Morris' wish had been for Jed to move north. Surely, that would influence him.

"Thank you," Rose said quietly.

"For?"

"For not telling me Jed will certainly decide to stay. The unknowing is difficult, but being assured of something that has no guarantee is not what I need."

Carrie nodded but remained silent. Their relationship had always been based on honesty. Nothing would ever change that.

A flock of pheasants burst from the tall grass on the side of the road in front of them. The sun reflected off the roosters' gold, brown, green, purple, and white plumage. The less flamboyant females scattered, their dark brown feathers still beautiful, but not as magnificent.

No Regrets shied back, tossing her head in protest.

Carrie soothed her again. "It's alright, girl. The little birds can't hurt you."

No Regrets calmed immediately. She flicked her ears toward Carrie's voice and then pointed them forward again as she watched the flock scurry across the road, disappearing into another rush of thick grasses and brush.

"That mare loves you," Rose observed.

"She's wonderful." Carrie had grown quite fond of the bay mare. She rode her often, but it didn't diminish her decision to wait for Granite.

Something about Rose's eyes made her look more closely. They knew each other too well to hide anything. "Something else is bothering you."

Rose started to shake her head in denial but then sighed heavily. "I'm feeling terribly guilty about something."

Carrie waited for her to continue.

"The day Vincent left..." Rose's voice trailed off as she struggled to admit her feelings.

Carrie remained silent but reached for her hand.

"When he told me Morris wasn't getting well as fast as he had, I was thrilled, Carrie." Rose lifted eyes full of shame. "I was *thrilled*. What kind of person am I?"

Carrie smiled gently. "The kind that wanted him to get well, but was thrilled to have Jed with you longer because you love him." She paused, letting the words sink in. "I believe you would tell me to allow myself to be human. Everyone did everything possible to save Morris, and now you're doing everything possible to make sure Jed has a good life. I believe that makes you a remarkable human being."

Rose met her eyes. "I don't feel like a remarkable human being, but thank you for believing that." She shook her head firmly. "Enough about me. How are *you* doing? You've only been home a week. Are you still having as many nightmares?"

Carrie looked across the empty fields, wishing her mind echoed their emptiness. She and Rose had talked about the horrors of the riots the day after she returned. "They're still there, but not as bad." She thought of all the nights since the riots that she'd sought the security of Anthony's arms to deal with the flashbacks and nightmares. The toughest thing to wipe from her mind was Octavius' senseless death. Besides those who would miss him, she knew all too well that Caroline would never forget how the man she loved had died.

Not wanting to ruin the morning with talk of the riots, she switched the subject. "I got a letter from Elizabeth yesterday."

"How is she? How is Peter? I've read more about the Chicago Fire. How horrible that he had to be there."

"At least he got to go home," Carrie said somberly. "Peter is fine. His burns are completely healed, and he's happy to be back in Boston. He got word about his friend Mark Rivers, though. Mark was killed in the Peshtigo fire along with at least two thousand other residents of the town. Up to five hundred more died in other communities burned by the same blaze."

Rose gaped at her. "Why isn't this more in the news? If it weren't for Peter, we wouldn't know anything about this. They're saying about three hundred died in Chicago, but two *thousand* died in Peshtigo? And another five hundred in the surrounding area?"

Carrie shared her sentiments. "Chicago is a well-known, famous city. Perhaps only three hundred died, but almost four square miles of the city burned. A hundred thousand are homeless, though they're working feverishly to build new homes before winter takes a hard grip. Elizabeth told me money is pouring in from around the world to help provide housing, food, and clothing for those who lost everything."

"And the people in Wisconsin?" Rose pressed.

Carrie frowned. "The news is finally coming through. The few hundred who managed to survive only did so by standing in the river up to their necks for an entire day, while the town burned around them on both sides." She shuddered, well able to imagine their terror, and answered Rose's question. "More than a hundred fifty thousand dollars has been sent to the communities to help them, along with huge quantities of food and clothing. The rebuilding has already begun."

"Humans are so resilient," Rose murmured.

"Yes," Carrie agreed, taking the opportunity offered her to drive home a point. "Humans are resilient. Which means Jed is, too. Just like Felicia was. However this turns out, that little boy is going to be fine."

Rose met her eyes with a look of gratitude and then turned toward the sun stationed in the sky well above the horizon. A warm breeze had already melted the frost. "It's time to get back."

"We've got a big day ahead of us," Carrie agreed. She turned No Regrets and nudged her into a canter. She closed her eyes as the breeze blew across her face.

Carrie was standing outside the arena when Amber rode out, her face flushed with victory. "Aren't you getting tired of winning the tournament?"

Amber laughed. "Did you ever get tired of winning, when no one could beat you and Granite?"

Carrie pushed away the pain that surged inside her as memories flooded her mind. She forced herself to smile brightly. "Not even once," she admitted.

"Me either!" Amber replied. "I love winning!"

Carrie chuckled. "What's not to love?"

John rode up on Cafi just then. He had placed only one ring behind Amber. "I almost beat you!"

Amber raised a brow. "*Almost* and *winning* are two different words," she said loftily.

John's face fell before he turned and rode away.

"Careful," Carrie said quietly. "Pride goeth before a fall. More importantly, it's fine to celebrate your win, but you shouldn't make your opponent feel badly. John came very close to beating you, Amber. Would it have hurt you to congratulate him on a job well done?" Carrie paused. "He's seven years younger than you. The fact that he almost beat you is quite remarkable."

Amber tightened her lips. "He has more time to practice than I do."

Carrie was reminded that in spite of how mature Amber was, she was still a girl. "Did I ever make you feel badly when I beat you, despite the fact that you had more time to practice than I did?"

Amber's eyes flashed, but she frowned and looked away. "I'm acting like a spoiled brat, aren't I?"

Carrie didn't see a reason to lie, so she let silence provide her answer.

"I'm sorry," Amber muttered. "I suppose I should ask John to be King of the Ball again, shouldn't I?"

Carrie smiled. "I don't think that would make John happy, Amber. He barely survived it last year. It's not too late to tell him he did a good job and that you're impressed. Besides," she added, "I think Bart would be quite disappointed."

Amber, who had started to turn away, spun Eclipse around to stare at her. "What did you say? Bart?"

Carrie laughed loudly. "You think we don't know the son of one of Moses' new workers has a crush on you? From what I've heard, he can barely take his eyes off you during school."

Amber frowned, yet her glowing eyes revealing her pleasure. "I can't ask Bart to be my king," she protested.

Carrie lifted a brow. "Why not?"

"He'll think I like him!"

Carrie bit back her mirth when she saw the anxiety in Amber's eyes. "Do you?"

Amber frowned harder and looked away. "He's just a boy," she muttered.

"And you're a beautiful young lady who is also very talented. I wondered who would finally catch your eye. Rose told me Bart is a fine young man. Why shouldn't you ask him to be your king?"

Amber pulled back with a shocked look. "You and Rose talked about me and Bart?"

Carrie made no attempt to cover her laughter this time. "Of course we did, honey. You know how small the plantation is. All of us love you so much. You might as well get used to the fact that we talk about you, because we're always going to. We're not going to let you fall in love with just anyone. Whomever it will be has to meet our very high expectations."

"I have parents for that," Amber muttered, but she couldn't hide the satisfied glow in her eyes.

"Now you have all of us, too," Carrie said blithely. "Consider yourself very lucky that you have so many people who love you."

"I'll try to remember the lucky part," Amber said, a smile twitching her lips. "May I go now?"

"Certainly. I'm assuming you'll be getting ready for the ball in my room again?" She waited for Amber's nod and added, "I'm looking forward to meeting Bart tonight."

Amber rolled her eyes and spun Eclipse, setting off for the barn at a brisk trot.

Carrie leaned against the porch railing, gazing at the crowd of people spread out over the plantation lawn. She could only see the front, but she knew the back of the house was even more congested. The Virginia Board of Education might be able to enforce separate schools, but they couldn't control social gatherings. Equal numbers of blacks and whites, chatting and playing together like old friends, gave her great joy.

Annie appeared on the porch behind her. "You alright, Carrie?"

"Yes, I'm just watching. Everyone seems to be having a wonderful time."

"That be for sure. Folks around here live for the Harvest Celebration." Annie's voice was thick with satisfaction. "I don't reckon there be a thing happening in this state that's got as much good food as we have."

Carrie knew that was true. The tables Moses' men had constructed had bowed under the weight of all the food. It had nearly all disappeared as the lines of people filled their plates. They were now scattered around the grounds, sitting on their blankets as they swapped stories with the families around them.

Carrie smiled fondly. "It's wonderful because they're trying to outdo you, Annie. Everyone knows you're the finest cook in these parts."

"Finest cook in all this state," Annie said flatly.

Carrie controlled her smile. She knew many cooks who were proud of their cooking, but none of them had Annie's confidence. It helped that she had good reason to feel the way she did.

"I couldn't agree more." Carrie was glad her father's housekeeper, May, wasn't there. Carrie had no idea how she would ever explain how *both* of them could be the finest cook in the state. She was happy to praise their abilities, as long as it meant she would never have to feed her family again. Her efforts in Philadelphia had resulted in their hiring a cook so they wouldn't starve or be poisoned.

"Did you see Franklin ride in a while ago?"

Carrie stiffened. "Franklin is back? Do Rose and Moses know?"

"They's upstairs with him right now. I told 'em all them folks out here wasn't gonna miss 'em as long as they were eating."

"That's true."

Annie peered into her eyes. "You know Jed oughta stay right here, don't you?"

"I hope it's what he decides to do," Carrie said carefully. She watched Jed and John race around with a large group of boys in a loud game of tag.

"I been making him cinnamon rolls every morning," Annie confided. "He ain't gonna want to leave my cookin'!"

Carrie smiled. Anthony had commented on the regular supply of delicious cinnamon rolls. She'd suspected it was part of Annie's strategy to entice Jed to stay on the plantation.

"My Miles been takin' him and John riding every single day after school. He's real happy at the idea of another grandson. They meet Moses out in the fields and ride with him until they all be ready to come back."

Carrie almost felt sorry for the little boy. If he truly felt he should go to Philadelphia, it was going to be so hard to make the choice to leave the plantation. On the other hand, she knew he would benefit from the love and life Moses and Rose would give him. She glanced up at the window to their room. "Do you know what Franklin is telling them?"

Annie shook her head, planted her fists on her ample hips, and stared up at the glass reflecting the soft glow of dusk. "Ain't got no idea. Bout to kill me with the need to know."

"How long have they been up there?"

"Almost an hour," Annie said with exasperation. "What's he got to say that be takin' so long?"

Carrie frowned. What was taking so long, indeed?

At that moment, the door opened behind them. Moses, Rose, and Franklin strode out onto the porch.

Carrie fastened her eyes on Rose. The glow of satisfaction she saw in her best friend's eyes provided the answer she needed. Vincent had agreed to let Jed stay.

The final decision would be up to Jed.

Amber took deep breaths to steady her nerves. Having won the tournament for the last three years, she knew it was ridiculous for her to be nervous about the ball, but it did nothing to alter her rapid heartbeat.

Abby walked up behind her in the kitchen and put an arm around her waist. "You look beautiful," she said softly. "The yellow dress looks stunning on you."

Amber managed a smile. "I'm glad Carrie has such an extensive wardrobe. I've got new dresses to wear every year."

"Pure nonsense," Polly muttered. "Me and your daddy told you we would buy you a new dress this year. You don't got to be wearing Carrie's clothes."

Amber's smile was genuine this time. "Mama, what would I do with a new dress? I only wear clothes like this one night a year. What good would a new dress do me in the barn? Besides, I love wearing Carrie's clothes." She didn't finish the rest of her thought. Wearing Carrie's clothes made her feel a little closer to Robert.

The knowing look in Polly's eyes said she understood what her daughter was thinking.

Every year, Amber made Carrie tell her the story of how Robert had chosen her to be Queen of the Ball after he won the tournament at Blackwell Plantation on Granite. She would never quit missing Robert. She loved Anthony, and she was thrilled Carrie was happy, but Robert's death had created a hole in her heart that would never be filled by anyone else. She suspected Carrie felt the same way, but she'd never had the courage to ask her outright.

"Have you decided on your king for this year's ball?" Abby asked.

Amber looked at her sharply. "Have you been talking about me, too?"

Abby's eyes widened. "I'm sure I don't know what you mean, my dear."

Amber's eyes narrowed. "You most certainly do, Abby. You don't lie very well."

Abby chuckled. "No, I suppose I don't."

"That ain't no way to talk to Mrs. Cromwell," Polly scolded. "I taught you better manners than that, young lady."

"I apologize," Amber said quickly, although she didn't release Abby from her gaze. "I suppose Carrie and Rose have been talking to you?"

"They may have been," Abby said evasively.

"Oh, for Pete's sake," Polly said. "Girl, you've got to know that every woman on this plantation talks about you. Mostly, they talk about how proud they are of you, and how talented you are with the horses. But they see you growing up, Amber, and it doesn't take much to know that Bart fellow is sweet on you."

"Mama!"

"Don't Mama me," Polly shot back. "I watch out the window at the clinic sometimes. I see Bart staring at you with his heart in his eyes. You can tell he thinks you're sweeter than any pot of honey he ever tasted."

"Mama!"

Abby laughed. "Amber, those are all good things. Unless you don't like Bart the way he likes you? Then we'll make him leave you alone."

Amber's heart beat faster. "No," she said quickly, not sure she understood her own feelings.

Polly's eyes bored into her. "So you like him."

Amber searched for an answer to a statement that wasn't a question. She didn't know how to understand the feelings rushing through her. She was completely confident on a rambunctious horse, but she had no idea how to make sense of what was in her own heart. "I don't know," she muttered. "Maybe."

Carrie had walked into the kitchen for the last part of the conversation. "Leave her alone," she ordered. "Can't y'all see she's trying to figure out what she's feeling?"

Amber sagged with relief. "Did you ever feel like this?"

Carrie smiled. "Twelve years ago, I was exactly in your shoes. You know that I met Robert the night before the tournament. I hadn't been attracted to any man up until that day. I couldn't put words to what I was feeling, but I knew I was feeling something new." She paused. "I liked it, but it also scared me to death."

Amber listened eagerly. She'd never heard this part of the story before. "What did you do?"

"Acted like a fool, for the most part," Carrie admitted. "I didn't know what to say, so I said nothing. I couldn't even look him in the eye on the way over to the tournament. I just stared at the floor of the carriage so I wouldn't watch him on Granite."

Amber knew that feeling. "At some point, you figured out what to say."

"Not exactly," Carrie said with a laugh. "Right before the tournament started, I realized other girls were giving tokens to the knights who were riding. I didn't have anything, so I borrowed a knife from a man standing nearby and cut a lock of my hair to give to him."

Amber gasped. "You did?"

"Once I'd done it, I felt like the biggest fool in the world. I could see other girls looking at me with pity in their eyes. They felt sorry for me. I've seldom felt more humiliated." Then Carrie grinned. "Robert told me later that when I gave him a lock of my hair, that was the moment he fell in love with me."

"The moral of the story," Abby said, "is that any act can be one of great love when you do it from your heart."

Amber supposed they were right, but she wasn't ready to think about that yet. "I'm only fifteen," she said. "I don't want to get married now."

"That's a good thing," Polly said firmly. "Your daddy and I ain't going to let you do something that foolish. But that doesn't mean you can't have a beau." She smiled broadly. "And a good-looking fella to ask to be your king at the ball."

Amber's nervousness returned. "I don't even know if he'll be at the ball."

"Oh, he's here," Carrie announced. "He's leaning up against a tree close to the kitchen. I figure he's positioned himself so that it will make it easier for him to come forward if you choose him to be king."

Amber could feel the trap closing around her. What shocked her was that it didn't feel unpleasant. "I don't know what to do," she murmured.

"Sure you do," Polly countered. "You asked two other fellas to be your king already."

Amber laughed. "It was Thomas and John! A man old enough to be my grandfather and a seven-year-old boy hardly count."

Abby laughed with her. "Still, you said all the same words. Thomas is going to say the fancy words he always says, then he's going to ask you who you want to choose as king. You're going to swallow all your fears, and you're going to say Bart's name loud enough for everyone to hear."

"Or at least loud enough for Bart to hear," Carrie teased as she took Amber's hands. "You look beautiful."

Amber smoothed a hand down the yellow silk. "Are you sure? I don't think I'm beautiful."

Carrie walked forward and lifted her chin until their eyes met. "You are beautiful, Amber," she said softly. "I know exactly why Bart can't keep his eyes off you." Her smile widened. "I know your mama and daddy are so proud of you. Robert is, too."

Amber's breath caught.

"Robert used to tell me he was horribly nervous the night of that first ball. He was scared I would refuse if he chose me to be queen."

Amber stared at her. "*Robert* was nervous?"

"He was," Carrie assured her. "It's always hard to take the risk of being rejected. However," she said playfully, "every woman in this room can assure you that Bart will say yes."

Rose entered the room. "Bart? He's outside the kitchen. I've been watching him the last few minutes. He hasn't taken his eyes off the door. He wants to be the first one to see you walk through it." She paused. "He's also got on a clean shirt. He seems to have prepared for something he hopes will happen."

Amber took a deep breath. "I suppose this is part of growing up, isn't it?" she asked with a frown. "Still, it's supposed to be the boy asking the girl." Her nervousness returned. She didn't want to ruin her chances by being too forward or eager.

"Usually," Polly conceded. "But that don't mean always. The Tournament Ball is surely an exception. Besides, I figure Bart has done everything he could to make sure you know he *wants* you to ask him."

Amber felt her confidence return as Carrie, Rose, and Abby nodded their heads.

Amber took a steadying breath and walked down the steps, her arm linked through her father's.

Gabe leaned down to whisper in her ear. "You be the prettiest girl out here tonight. I'm real proud of you, Amber."

Amber smiled up into his glowing eyes. "Thank you, Daddy."

As they reached the center of the large circle that had been cleared for dancing, Gabe leaned over again. "Put that Bart out of his misery, girl."

Amber laughed in spite of her nervousness. She had decided to do exactly that.

Thomas Cromwell, dressed in an elegant suit, his silver hair glowing from the bonfire, smiled at her as her father dropped her hand and walked away. "This seems to be somewhat of a tradition, Amber."

Amber smiled when everyone broke into laughter and applause.

"Once more, you have bested everyone in the area as the winner of the tournament. Congratulations!"

More applause, and then an expectant silence fell over the crowd.

Thomas turned slowly in a circle, his eyes sweeping over the faces gazing at him. Close to the tree, the musicians waited to break into song. "Y'all know what is about to happen. Amber, as the victor in today's tournament, will choose her king for tonight's ball."

Amber allowed her eyes to stray toward the tree where Bart had stationed himself. He was staring straight at her, his brow lifted in question. Flustered, she looked away and focused once again on Thomas. She was glad no one could hear how hard her heart was hammering in her chest.

"Once Amber has made her choice," Thomas continued, "the five competitors who came in the next closest to victory will choose the court for the night."

Amber stopped thinking about Bart long enough to wonder who John would choose. She had saved him from choosing last year when she'd selected him to be king, but now he would have to make a decision. She could imagine how tough of a choice that would be for an eight-year-old.

She glanced over Thomas' shoulder and smiled at John. She was glad she'd been able to apologize to him earlier. Carrie had been right about how she had treated him. John's face was glowing with pride now, despite the fact that he looked nervous. She understood how he felt.

"Without further ado, ladies and gentlemen, I present to you Queen Amber!"

The cheering and applause broke out again. When it was quiet, Amber turned slowly, giving everyone a glowing smile. Nervousness gone, she was excited to be proclaimed the winner once more. The crowd surrounding her consisted of family and friends. It was a wonderful feeling. Her final turn left her facing the giant oak tree, the musicians who were eying her expectantly...and Bart.

"I choose Bart Buckley to be my king," Amber said clearly and loudly, relieved beyond measure that she hadn't stumbled over the words.

Thomas smiled. "Bart Buckley," he called. "Do you accept your role as King of the Ball?"

Bart was already moving into the circle, a broad smile making his handsome face glow even more. "I do," he said gravely.

Amber shivered as he stopped beside her and looked down into her eyes.

At that very moment, the music began.

Bart claimed her hand, put his other hand firmly on her waist, and led her into a waltz.

Amber felt as if she could hardly breathe, yet also as if she were floating on air. She was glad that, despite her protests, her father and Clint had insisted she learn to dance. Carrie had encouraged her, as well, telling her the day would come when she would be thrilled to dance with someone. Amber hadn't believed her at the time, but now she understood how right she was. She also understood how Carrie must have felt dancing with Robert that first time.

You look lovely. I'm so proud of you.

Amber caught her breath as Robert's voice seemed to float across the night and pierce her heart with its clarity.

Bart's hand tightened on her waist as he looked down at her with a question in his eyes.

Amber allowed all her joy to blaze through in the smile she gave him in return.

Then she danced. She knew it was a night she would never forget.

Chapter Fourteen

Rose and Moses tucked John and Jed into bed. Both boys were exhausted after the Harvest Celebration, but they had contented smiles on their faces.

"I'm glad you both had a good day," Rose murmured. Her heart swelled with love as she looked at both the boys.

"I ain't never had a day like this," Jed said sleepily.

Rose knew that was true. She longed to tell the little boy that they wanted him to always be part of their family, but now was not the time. "It was special," she agreed.

"Mama?" John asked as he struggled to keep his eyes open.

"Yes, dear?"

"Did I dance alright?"

Moses smiled. "You danced just fine, John. Did you have fun with Missy?"

John shrugged. "I guess. I had to ask *someone.* Amber told me Missy would say yes if I asked her."

Rose exchanged a laughing look with Moses over the boys' heads. John had looked so handsome in his dark pants and white shirt. She'd nearly had to force him to change after a sweaty game of tag, but she'd succeeded. Missy, one of her eight-year-old students who'd had a crush on her son since the new school year started, had been adorable in her bright red dress. Her face had glowed almost as brightly as the bonfire when John asked her to dance with him for the opening round.

"You were wonderful," Rose assured him.

John looked over to get confirmation from Jed, but the boy's slack face said he was already sleeping soundly.

"Mama?" John whispered.

Rose cocked a brow, aware her sleepy son suddenly looked more alert.

"Can't Jed stay with us? Be my brother?"

Rose shot Moses another look and then took John's hand. "Would you like that?" she whispered.

John nodded his head firmly. "Yes. I don't want him to leave and go to Philadelphia. Neither does Hope," he added.

Rose searched for a response. "I'm glad to hear that, but Jed will have to decide if he wants to be part of our family."

John's eyes filled with excited satisfaction. "Then he'll be staying." He sounded very confident.

"How do you know?" Moses asked, keeping his deep voice very low.

Rose looked at Jed in order to be certain he was sleeping, even though she was eager to hear John's answer.

"We talked about it today," John said sleepily. "He told me he wished he never had to leave."

Moments later, he too was sound asleep.

Rose waited on the porch, bundled against the cold breeze that had blown in the next morning. The Indian summer had lasted long enough for the Harvest Celebration to be over, and then it was swallowed by a northern front. A brisk wind rustled the tree leaves as gray clouds scuttled across the sky. She clutched her coat closer as she scanned the horizon for Moses and Champ. She knew he had ridden out to oversee how well the woodcutters were doing in their job to cut enough firewood to last the winter ahead. He'd given Franklin the day off to be with his family after his trip to Philadelphia.

The children were in the barn with the horses, but she'd asked Miles to forego a ride with them today. She didn't think she could wait a moment longer to talk with Jed. She'd barely been able to concentrate during school. She'd caught Hazel looking at her with a question in her eyes several times, but the younger teacher had merely covered for her. She would thank her later.

"He's still not back?"

Rose jerked, unaware until she heard Carrie's voice that she wasn't alone. "No. I don't know how much longer I can wait to talk to Jed."

Carrie reached over and took her gloved hand. "You'll wait as long as it takes," she said calmly. "You know this is something you and Moses have to do together."

Rose sighed. "That doesn't mean I have to like it."

Carrie chuckled. "Certainly not. Is it alright that I'm a *little* glad that Moses hasn't returned yet?"

"Because you want to know what Franklin said?"

"Of course I do. It's been driving me crazy ever since I saw your face when you walked out of the house yesterday. I knew by the look in your eyes that Vincent had agreed to let Jed stay, but I have so many questions."

"Vincent struggled with his decision," Rose said. "He knows Cromwell Plantation is special, but he's not convinced it's anything more than an oasis in a very dangerous desert. He promised Morris he would take Jed to Philadelphia to keep him safe."

"He may be right," Carrie said somberly. "I wish I could argue with that, but after everything that's happened, it would be less than honest. What changed his mind?"

"It took him only a few days to decide Philadelphia isn't the safe haven he expected it to be. He knows it's far better than South Carolina, but he met several of the men who were beaten during the riots. They told him how hard they're fighting for equality in Philadelphia, but that he needed to be careful there, as well."

Rose thought through everything Franklin had told them. "Then Vincent found out what happened to Octavius. He knows the Institute for Colored Youth would provide Jed a great education, but going there won't guarantee his safety. In fact, getting back and forth to school from where he's currently living could be dangerous. The riots have stopped, but feelings are still running high."

"True," Carrie murmured. "I hate how true that is."

"It was Jeremy, though, who really convinced him."

"Jeremy?" Carrie asked with surprise.

Rose smiled. "Jeremy met Vincent the second day he was there. He gave him the job at the factory that he promised, and they also struck up a friendship talking about politics and equal rights. When Franklin arrived, Jeremy invited the two men over for dinner. During the night, Jeremy told Vincent all about Felicia. He told him how safe the plantation is, and how safe Jed would be here."

Carrie listened closely but didn't interrupt.

"He also told him Jed would be well loved."

"How did Vincent respond? As far as I could tell, he really loves Jed, too."

"He does," Rose said somberly. "Franklin told us he broke into tears a few times as they were talking about it. He loves Jed, and he feels responsible to Morris to care for him."

"Was there anything else that altered his decision? I can understand how painful this was for him."

"Philadelphia did," Rose said bluntly. "Vincent knows it's better than the South, but he doesn't want Jed to be in danger. He knows he'll be working a lot. He doesn't want Jed to be alone and have to fend for himself. Even though he's scared of the South, he decided we could be trusted to take care of him." She scanned the horizon again, her heart catching when she saw Moses' silhouette against the horizon. "He only asked that he be able to see Jed anytime we're in Philadelphia."

"Which Jed will want to do," Carrie replied.

"Yes. Jed loves Vincent very much." Rose tried to hide the trepidation in her voice, but Carrie's keen look told her she had failed.

"You're afraid Jed will still want to leave."

Rose saw no reason to deny her fear. "Yes, but John gave me hope last night." She told Carrie what her son had said after the Harvest Celebration as she watched Moses draw closer. As anxious as she knew he was to talk with Jed, he kept Champ at a walk, letting the gelding cool down after a long ride before they returned to the barn.

Carrie smiled. "You're still questioning it? I'm fairly certain John would know."

Rose wanted desperately to believe that, but she'd had time to think about it throughout the day. "Wanting to stay and *choosing* to stay are two different things," she said quietly. "He may feel strongly that he needs to follow his father's wishes, and I'm not sure how he'll feel about not living with Vincent. The two became very close since the night of the attack."

Carrie sat in silence as they watched Moses enter the barnyard and dismount before walking into the barn. "At least you don't have to wait long for your answer," she finally said.

Rose knew that wasn't necessarily true, either. Just as they'd given Vincent time to make his decision, they were going to do the same for Jed. He was only ten years old, but so much in his life had been turned upside down in the weeks since the attack. Felicia had no other options when Moses brought her home after the Memphis riots that killed both her parents. Jed had options.

She and Moses had talked about it last night, after the boys were both sleeping. They wouldn't pressure Jed into a decision.

Moses nodded at Miles when he finished grooming Champ and let him into his stall to eat the bucket of grain waiting for him.

"Alright boys," Miles called. "You too, Hope. A little bird told me Annie has some cookies waiting for you."

The boys whooped with enthusiasm, but Hope stared at him skeptically. "Grandma doesn't let us have cookies before dinner, Grandpa."

Moses bit back his laugh. His daughter didn't miss much. "She's making an exception this time."

Hope still didn't look convinced. "Why?"

Moses thought quickly. Dinner was in less than an hour. His daughter had a valid question. "We're eating dinner a little later tonight, honey. Grandma knew you would be hungry."

"Why are we eating dinner later?"

Moses knew the questions could go on endlessly. He was proud of Hope for thinking and questioning things, but right now he was eager to talk to Jed. He decided to take the offensive. "Are you saying you don't want cookies, Hope? I can tell Grandma you would rather not eat them and spoil your dinner."

Hope narrowed her eyes, seeming to realize she'd walked into a trap. Moses could see her six-year-old mind spinning furiously.

"I didn't exactly say that, Daddy," Hope said carefully.

"Does that mean you want cookies?" Moses looked thoughtful. "Are you certain? I understand if you don't want to spoil your dinner."

"I'm certain," Hope said eagerly. "You don't have to tell Grandma anything." She smiled up at him brightly.

Moses stretched out his hand and took hers, marveling at her beauty and life. "How about if we go over together?"

"Alright, Daddy!"

"Cookies!" the boys yelled.

Miles mouthed *good luck* before he entered one of the stalls.

Moses smiled at Rose as he climbed the stairs with the children.

The threesome headed immediately for the door, but Rose reached out a hand to stop Jed. "Could we talk to you for a few minutes, Jed?"

Jed hesitated. "Did I do somethin' wrong?" he asked anxiously.

"Not at all!" Rose hurried to reassure him. "Moses and I would just like to talk to you for a little while." She understood the look on his face. Smiling, she held up a plate full of warm shortbread cookies. "Would you share these with us?"

Jed grinned. "Sure!"

Moses addressed John and Hope. "You two go on in the house. Grandma has cookies waiting for you." With backward glances full of curiosity, John and Hope went inside. He knew Annie would keep them in the kitchen until they were done talking.

Jed looked at both of them. "Are you real sure I ain't in trouble?"

"I promise," Rose replied as she handed him a cookie. "Will you sit down with us?"

Jed took the chair between her and Moses, but sat stiffly on the edge, his eyes full of questions.

Moses would have felt the same way if it were him. "We want to talk to you about something, Jed." Now that the moment was here, he wasn't sure how to proceed.

Jed munched on his cookie and watched them both carefully. "Alright."

"Are you happy here on the plantation?" Rose began.

Jed nodded vigorously. "I love it here," he assured them.

Moses knew they could talk around the topic for a long time, but he was ready for an answer, or at least something as close to an answer as they might get. "Jed, Rose and I love you very much." Jed remained silent, but Moses saw the happy glimmer in his dark eyes. "How would you feel about staying here on the plantation, Jed? We would love to have you become part of our family."

"We already love you like a son, Jed," Rose said quietly. "We know you loved your mama and daddy very much. We just want a chance to love you, too."

Jed looked between both of them, confusion and uncertainty sparking in his eyes. "What about Vincent? I'm supposed to go to Philadelphia."

Moses spoke carefully. "We sent Franklin to Philadelphia to talk to Vincent when your daddy died," he revealed.

"Vincent knows Daddy died?" Jed's eyes clouded. "He don't want me anymore?"

"No," Moses said quickly. "Vincent wants you very much. He loves you."

"Then why do you want me to stay here?" Jed's eyes continued to mirror his confusion. "My daddy wanted me to move to Philadelphia."

Moses took a deep breath. He had wanted Jed to jump at the chance to be his son, but they had talked about the reality of Jed being uncertain of what he should do. "He did," he agreed.

"Daddy said I shouldn't oughta stay in the South," Jed said, his voice trembling.

Moses was afraid he had messed everything up. He should have said things differently.

Rose stepped in to rescue him. "Jed, Vincent loves you very much. That's why Franklin went to see him. He told Franklin that he thought it would be better if you stayed here with us."

Jed's eyes widened. "He did? Why?"

"Because he believes you'll be safer and happier here," Rose replied. She reached out for the boy's hand. "Philadelphia is safer than South Carolina, but it can still be dangerous for black people."

Jed sucked in his breath. "Do blacks get beat there, too?"

Moses waited for Rose's answer, wondering how she would handle it.

"Yes," she said gently. "Not as much as it happened in South Carolina, but it can happen there. Vincent is going to have to work a lot, so he won't always be there to care for you and make sure you have everything you need. He's scared what might happen to you."

Jed considered her answer. "Did Daddy know it wasn't safe there?"

"No," Moses said quickly. "He believed it would be safe. He didn't know about how dangerous it could be."

"It's so much more than that, though," Rose said. "Vincent knows how happy you are on the plantation. He knows you're getting a good education. He knows you love John and Hope. He knows you love the horses and being able to ride every day." She paused. "You wouldn't be able to ride in Philadelphia, Jed."

Jed's eyes filled with sadness as that reality sank into his thoughts. "No riding?"

Moses took his other hand. As tempting as it was, he didn't want to sway the boy by detailing what he would lose. He wanted him to focus on what he could gain. "It's really very simple, Jed. We love you. We already think of you as a son. We want you to be part of our family."

Jed's lips trembled with emotion as he stared into Moses' eyes. "What about John and Hope? Do they want a new brother?"

"Very much," Rose assured him. "Just last night, John asked us why you couldn't stay and be his brother. Hope feels the same way. They love you, too."

Jed stared at her for a long moment. "You ain't just sayin' you'll keep me 'cause Vincent don't want me no more?"

Moses felt sick as he realized what John had been thinking. "Of course not. We want you to stay because we love you."

Rose slipped from her chair and knelt down in front of Jed so she could gaze into his eyes. "Honey, we sent Franklin to talk to Vincent because we *want* you to stay here. We just had to make sure Vincent would be willing for that to happen. He's made us promise that every time we go to Philadelphia, you'll see him and spend time with him."

A spark ignited in Jed's eyes. "He did?"

"He did," Moses said firmly. "We agreed. We're going to make sure you can visit Vincent, and he's also welcome here anytime he wants to come. He's become part of our family, too."

"Do you think my daddy would want me to stay?" Jed asked.

"I believe your daddy would want you to be happy," Rose replied. "Do you believe you would be happy on the plantation?"

Moses marveled at her controlled diplomacy.

At that moment, a group of horses in the pasture began to race around the field, their heads and tails held high.

Jed watched them and then turned back to Rose. "I love it here," he acknowledged. Then he paused. "I'm always gonna love my mama and daddy, though."

"Of course you are," Rose said softly. "We're never going to replace them, Jed. We're just going to love you for them."

Jed cocked his head and stared at her. "Love me *for* them?" He smiled for the first time. "I reckon they would like that."

"You don't have to decide right away," Moses said. "You're old enough to make the decision about what you want to do. We're not going to pressure you."

Jed thought about that.

The wind began to blow harder. Small drops of rain splattered down on the dry ground, kicking up tiny clouds of dust.

"You sure Vincent wants me to stay here?" Jed finally asked.

Rose reached into her pocket and pulled out a letter. She and Moses had agreed she would only give it to Jed if it seemed he wanted to stay. "Vincent sent you a letter, Jed."

Jed reached for it slowly.

"You don't have to read it right now," Moses said quickly.

Jed shook his head. "I reckon I oughta read it now. I'm getting better at reading, but I might need some help," he confessed, looking at Rose with raw vulnerability.

"Go ahead," Rose said gently. "I'm here if you need me."

Jed opened the letter and began to read.

Moses wished he knew what the letter said, but they'd agreed that since it wasn't written to them, they wouldn't read it. Curiosity was eating at him, but he had to trust that Vincent would have written a letter that would help Jed make his decision. He was a good man.

Evidently, Vincent had written the letter with simple words, because Jed didn't ask for help. He finally looked up, tears pooled in his eyes. "Vincent told me he figures I'll be real happy here. He told me he loves me and that he thinks I'll have the best life down here." He paused. "He also told me that y'all will love me real good."

"We promise to love you like one of our own children," Moses said, and then held his breath. His love for the little boy had grown on a daily basis. His heart was big enough to embrace another child. He wanted it with all his being.

Jed gazed at both of them. "I know you said I don't gotta make a decision right away, but..." His lips quivered. "Is it alright if I do?"

"Certainly." Rose continued to kneel in front of him.

"I'd sure like to stay here," Jed said. "If you be sure...you want me to."

Rose's answer was to laugh and throw her arms around the little boy. "I'm absolutely certain I want you to, Jed! You've made me so happy!"

Moses knelt beside her and wrapped his strong arms around the pair of them. "And I'm absolutely certain, Jed." He laughed loudly. "Welcome to the Samuels family!"

Jed relaxed into their arms for several minutes. He finally looked up with shining eyes. "Does this mean I get a horse of my own? John told me everyone in the family gets their own horse."

Moses laughed even harder. "I believe we can make that happen, Jed. It's a big thing to choose a horse, though. It will take time to find the right one."

Jed nodded. "I reckon I got time now." Then he frowned. "What am I gonna call y'all now?"

"Whatever you're most comfortable with," Rose answered. "You can continue to call us Rose and Moses. If the time ever comes when you want to call us Daddy and Mama, that would be fine, too."

Jed wrinkled his brow. "I reckon I'll stick with Rose and Moses for now."

Moses didn't care what he called them, as long as Jed was going to be his son.

Annie stepped onto the porch, her face wreathed in smiles. "Welcome to the family, Jed!"

Moses grinned. He should have known his mama was listening. Before he could say anything, John and Hope ran out on the porch.

John leapt on Jed and pounded him on the back. "You're going to be my brother, Jed!"

"And *my* brother," Hope cried. "That makes me real happy!"

Moses watched the look of wonder spread across Jed's face. He caught Moses' eyes and grinned widely before he turned back to John and Hope.

Moses locked eyes with Rose. Their family had just grown again. He couldn't have been happier.

Chapter Fifteen

"Get that look off your face, Harold Justin," Carrie scolded. "I promise you Susan will be fine. She's not due for months. Going to New York with your twin brother is not going to endanger her pregnancy."

Harold clearly was not convinced. His blue eyes glittered with concern as he swiped a hand through his red hair. "It's not that important for me to go," he muttered.

"He's been like this for the last two days," Matthew said, his voice a mixture of amusement and exasperation. "Look, brother, you don't have to go. I thought you would enjoy the trip, but it might be better for you to stay here."

Carrie could see the battle being waged in Harold. He very much wanted to go, but he felt guilty leaving his pregnant wife.

Susan suddenly pushed through the door and strode onto the porch. "Harold! I thought we resolved this. You most certainly are not staying home. You've wanted to go on a trip with Matthew for a long time. Now you have the chance, and you're afraid to leave because of me?" She tossed her head, her long blond braid swinging against her barn coat. "Do I look like a damsel in distress? Do I look like a weak woman who can't care for herself?" She glared at her husband, the look softened by the love in her eyes. "What do you think I did before you came along?"

Harold frowned. "You weren't carrying our child," he protested. "Things happen!"

Carrie's heart softened. Harold had lost his wife and two children to cholera six years earlier. He had good reason to be terrified. She walked forward and put a hand on his arm. "Harold, I promise you Susan will be fine. Do you really think I would let anything happen to my partner?" She kept her voice light. "If something happened to her, I'd never be able to run both the stables and the clinic. She'll be right here, working hard, when you get home."

Carrie knew she'd said the wrong thing as soon as Harold's frown deepened. She hastened to correct her mistake. "What I meant to say is that she'll be right here when you get home. Clint and Amber are making sure she doesn't have to do any kind of heavy lifting."

"And they won't let me ride anything that a five-year-old couldn't ride," Susan added. She rolled her eyes. "I think it's ridiculous, but no one is listening to me."

"Oh, we're listening," Miles said as he strode up the stairs to the porch. "We're just ignoring you. It's what you do for people you love."

Susan opened her mouth to argue, but snapped it shut.

Carrie understood. It was hard to argue against love.

Miles rubbed his hands together. "What y'all be doing out on the porch for, anyways? That wind coming in from the north is mighty cold." He narrowed his eyes. "Did my wife throw you out of the house? What'd you do to set her off?"

Carrie chuckled. "Nothing. Annie is fine. We're just waiting on the porch for Janie to come home from the clinic. Everyone is having dinner here tonight before Matthew and Harold leave on their trip." She eyed Harold. "At least, Matthew is going. We're not sure about Harold."

Miles snorted. "What kind of nonsense is that? You figure we can't take care of one hardheaded woman? It ain't like you gonna be gone for months." He eyed Matthew. "How long you boys going to be in New York City?"

"We'll be back in nine days," Matthew answered.

Miles turned to Susan. "You ain't due to have this baby till when?"

"The end of April," Susan answered with a smile.

Miles snorted again and resumed his glaring at Harold.

Carrie choked back a laugh. She was used to that look. All Miles had to do was turn that glare on her as a child, and she would do anything he said.

"Boy, you really sayin' you don't figure a whole plantation of folks, including two fine doctors, can take care of a woman who ain't due for over five months?" Miles waved his hand impatiently. "Go on to New York with that twin of yours. Miss Susan got a whole family here that gonna look after her."

Harold finally smiled and nodded. "Well, since you put it that way."

Annie pushed open the door behind them. "My man has a way with words, for sure. Now, all of you get in here out of the cold. We got us a big pork roast beggin' to be eaten."

Carrie turned when she heard the sound of wagon wheels on the drive. Janie, driven by one of Moses' men, was home.

"With sweet potatoes?" Susan asked hopefully.

"And cornbread?" Harold asked.

Annie chuckled. "And a mess of lima beans and corn that been cookin' all day." She eyed Matthew and Harold. "It ain't enough for you two to be the spittin' image of each other. I reckon it be a good thing you two also got a favorite meal. Makes it a sight easier to send you off on a trip."

Janie climbed from the carriage and joined them on the porch.

"Perfect timing," Carrie said. "We have a feast waiting for us."

"With chocolate cake for dessert?" Janie pleaded.

"You know it, Miss Janie," Annie replied as she rolled her eyes. "How am I gonna send these two boys to New York if I ain't given them some chocolate cake?" She eyed Matthew and Harold sternly. "When you stop in Richmond, you make sure to tell that May that you had the best meal of your life tonight."

Matthew and Harold nodded in unison.

"We'll do just that, Annie," Harold promised.

Carrie was grateful for a large dining room. The room that had seemed so immense to her as a child, when it was just her and her parents, now seemed crowded to the gills. When you added company to the people who lived here already, there was barely room to move your arms enough to eat.

She smiled as she watched the animated conversation and laughter flowing around the table.

Janie raised her hand for quiet. "I have an announcement," she called.

Gradually, the chatter and laughter faded into silence.

"It's really Matthew and Harold's announcement, but they'll never make it, so I'll do the honors," Janie started.

Carrie looked toward Matthew, but all he did was duck his head and look down at the table. Harold was studying his plate, as well. Both men were incredibly modest.

"Harold and my talented, wonderful husband finished their newest book several weeks ago. We celebrated when they sent it off, but something more has happened. We received a letter from their editor today. *It's Not All Bad News* sold out of its first printing before it even hit the bookstores! They're scrambling to reprint more, and they're confident it's on its way to becoming another best-seller! They've asked them to write another one!" Janie's eyes glittered with pride.

Clapping and cries of congratulations broke out around the table.

Matthew finally raised a hand. "We owe our success to the people willing to share their stories with us."

"Not to mention the fact that y'all have scoured the country for people who have good stories to share," Abby chided.

"Not me," Matthew said quickly. "Not anymore. Harold is the one out there getting the stories I have the privilege of writing." He smiled warmly at Harold.

"When we were boys camping in the mountains of West Virginia, we talked about what a great team we would be one day."

"We were right," Harold said loudly. "If I remember correctly, I was the one who began talking about that. Matthew may have been born ten minutes before I was, but he's never had quite as much imagination as I have."

"Nonsense!" Matthew retorted. "You have the ideas, but I'm the one who makes them happen."

It was Harold's time to sputter with indignation.

Susan laughed. "Yes, they're like this all the time. It's a good thing they love each other!"

When the laughter died down again, Thomas asked a question. "Will you meet with your editor while you're in New York City?"

"Yes," Matthew answered. "That's the supposed reason we're going…"

"But we really just want to be there for the opening of Boss Tweed's trial," Harold finished.

"It should be fascinating," Abby agreed. "I'm glad the two of you will be staying with Wally and Nancy Stratford. They're looking forward to having you."

Matthew chuckled. "Nancy is looking forward to us delivering another batch of quilts from the Bregdan Women."

"That, too," Abby confirmed with a grin. "You're certain you don't mind handling their delivery?"

Carrie was impressed with what Abby was doing with women who had joined together to form the Cromwell Bregdan Women. There were now close to fifty members—an almost equal split of black and white women—who gathered on a weekly basis. Once a month, they had a speaker come to encourage and motivate them. They spent their other time together quilting and building relationships.

Abby made monthly trips into Richmond for fabric, returning with wagonfuls each time. The fabric store owner was thrilled to fill her orders.

"How many quilts are you sending out this time?" Rose asked.

Abby's grin widened. "One hundred."

Carrie gasped. "One hundred quilts?"

"Yes. The money the women are making is changing things for their families. The single ones have no other way to create income, and for the married ones, many of their husbands came home from the war wounded."

"Or they can't find work," Thomas added. "They don't want to move into Richmond, but there is little out here for them to do. The women are creating an income for their family."

"Most of the children are helping with the quilting, too," Abby explained. "They're learning a valuable skill and increasing production. That's how we're able to send off a hundred quilts." Her eyes glowed with pride. "They're doing such beautiful work. Nancy could sell far more of them if I sent more, but having a limited supply ensures the women will receive a good price for their work."

Moses chuckled. "Spoken like a true businesswoman."

"Always," Abby assured him with a serene smile.

Carrie turned to Matthew. "I wondered why you and Harold were taking a wagon tomorrow."

"Only way to get one hundred quilts to the train station," Matthew replied. "We'll drop them off at the station, spend the night in Richmond with May,

Spencer and Micah, and then leave the next morning."

"Nancy will have someone at the station in New York City to pick them up the quilts and bring them to her house," Abby added.

"We're really not doing much," Matthew said. He smiled warmly at Abby. "You already know I would do anything in the world for you."

"Just as I would for you, dear boy," Abby said fondly. She gazed around the table. "After my first husband died, I was so alone in Philadelphia. I could never have imagined a family as large as the one we have here. I'm grateful every single day."

Carrie couldn't have agreed more. She opened her mouth to say so, but Jed beat her to it.

"I reckon I know just what you mean, Miss Abby. I been thinking 'bout that a lot. I ain't never forgot what Moses and Rose told me the day they asked me to be their boy. They told me they were gonna love me *for* my parents, since they be dead." Jed looked around the table. "I sure have me a lot of people loving me for them. I reckon that be what family really is."

Carrie's eyes misted with tears. Jed had settled into the plantation remarkably well. He received a letter from Vincent every week. He treasured the letters, but she knew he was content to be here.

A blast of wind rattled the windows.

Miles nodded knowingly. "Good thing you two are leaving in the morning. We got some early winter weather coming. It ain't gonna snow for a couple more days, but it's coming."

"Is it going to be a really cold winter?" Carrie asked.

Miles shrugged. "I don't know that it's gonna be as cold as some others we've had, but it's gonna be long."

"How do you do that?" Abby asked with wonder. "I've been watching you ever since Thomas and I moved back to the plantation. You're never wrong about the weather, Miles."

Miles shrugged casually. "Ain't no mystery, Miss Abby. The weather gonna tell you what it aims to do every single time. You just got to know how to watch and listen. The signs be there for anyone who wants to see them."

Carrie laughed and shook her head. "Don't believe a word he's saying, Abby. Father and I have been trying for all my life—Father before that—to learn how to read the weather like Miles does. We can't do it either."

"That ain't true," Miles protested. "You and your daddy catch some things."

"With *some* being the operative word there," Thomas said ruefully. "Carrie is right. Miles seems to have a direct connection with the weather god." He glanced at Annie. "Please continue to take good care of your husband. I don't know what I would do without him!"

"I'll do that," Annie promised.

Carrie's heart caught at the thought of anything happening to Miles. Miles, like most slaves who didn't know their birthday, wasn't certain how old he was, but he had to be in his seventies. Sam, the plantation butler, had died at seventy-two, leaving a gaping hole in her heart. The place Miles held in her heart was even more special to her. She took a deep breath and reached out to grasp his hand.

Miles looked at her with surprise, his gaze softening as he saw the expression in her eyes. "I love you too, Carrie Girl."

Matthew stepped off the train, gaping in wonder at Grand Central Depot.

Harold stepped off behind him and gave a shrill whistle. "Will you look at this!"

Matthew craned his neck to look up. "The glass ceiling must be one hundred feet high," he breathed with amazement.

"One hundred and twelve feet, to be exact."

Matthew whipped his head around to see who had spoken, and then narrowed his eyes. "Don't I know you?"

The slight man with wavy dark hair, dressed in an elegant suit with a bowtie, smiled. "We've met only once, Mr. Justin. I wouldn't expect you to remember. My name is Thaddeus Courtland."

Matthew's mind raced to place the man with such a pleasant demeanor. "You work for my publisher," he said slowly.

"Yes. I'm surprised you remember. We met only briefly, the day you delivered your first book."

"It's a pleasure to see you again." Matthew smiled and took Harold's arm. "This is my brother, Harold Justin."

"Hello, Mr. Justin. It wouldn't take a genius to figure out that the two of you are brothers, but what no one mentioned is that you're twins."

Harold grinned. "Please call us Harold and Matthew. The Mr. Justin moniker can become quite confusing."

"Please call me Thaddeus."

"Are you here to meet us?" Matthew asked. "I don't recall telling anyone when we would arrive."

"No, I'm just returning from a trip to Baltimore. I spotted you on the platform and decided to say hello."

"I'm glad you did." Matthew returned to staring at the interior of the Grand Central Depot. "I knew it was going to be huge but reading about it and seeing it are two different things."

"Indeed. The Grand Central Depot opened on October ninth," Thaddeus informed them.

"Only four weeks," Harold remarked. "I've never seen anything so impressive."

"I can assure you that was Cornelius Vanderbilt's intention," Thaddeus replied. He waved a hand at the interior. "You're looking at a marvel of modern engineering. The station we're in now is six hundred feet long and two hundred feet wide. The entire structure is supported by iron trusses. There are twelve train tracks, separated by raised platforms to eliminate the need for steps."

Matthew was impressed. "How many trains go through here a day?"

"At least a hundred. You know there used to be a station for each of the railroads."

Harold nodded. "The New York Railroad, the Harlem Railroad, and the New York Central. If I remember correctly, Vanderbilt purchased the first two in 1857. He bought the New York Central just two years ago." He smiled at Thaddeus' raised eyebrows. "I lived in Buffalo before Matthew persuaded me to move south."

Thaddeus looked at him keenly. "How do you feel about living in the South?"

Harold shrugged. "The summers are hotter, but the winters are more bearable."

"And the people?"

Matthew listened closely, wondering how Harold would answer a virtual stranger.

"As you can tell from our books, people are people," Harold responded cheerfully. "There are good people everywhere."

"True," Thaddeus said graciously. He looked like he wanted to say more but held his tongue.

Matthew knew the truth of how much Harold struggled with living in the South. Prejudice and bigotry existed everywhere, but the rampant violence in the South seemed to be eating at Harold's soul. It was one of the reasons he had pushed for Harold to join him on this trip. He needed a break from the reality.

Harold adroitly changed the subject. "Vanderbilt must have purchased a vast amount of land for the depot."

Thaddeus frowned. "That truth is a bone of contention for many New Yorkers. Vanderbilt determined from the beginning that he was going to build the most spacious, elegant, convenient depot in the country. He's achieved it, but not without making enemies."

Matthew waited for him to explain.

"The Grand Central Depot is on thirty-three acres of valuable property. Whenever he encountered resistant property owners not interested in selling, he ruthlessly used seizure rights conferred by the general railroad law." Thaddeus' lips tightened. "I agree that New York needed this station, but Vanderbilt destroyed a beloved market, a hospital for the crippled, the new Church of the Resurrection, and so much more."

Matthew frowned. "He has made enemies indeed."

"Peter Goelet is perhaps his worst enemy."

"Peter Goelet of the Goelet family?" Harold asked. "I interviewed him once. He owns vast real estate holdings in Manhattan. He told me his tradition is to never sell land once it's purchased."

"That's true," Thaddeus confirmed. "He was incensed when he discovered Vanderbilt wanted the entire block between Forty-sixth and Forty-seventh Streets, which he owned. He had no intention to sell, and he told Vanderbilt that. A few days later, he was informed Vanderbilt had taken possession of the block and had already put men to work."

Harold shook his head. "Goelet must have been furious."

"To put it mildly," Thaddeus said. "Goelet demanded his lawyer file a lawsuit for trespass and damages. He wanted Vanderbilt run out entirely."

"Obviously, it didn't happen," Matthew observed as he continued to gaze around at the bustle of people.

"No, Goelet's attorney had the unfortunate task of explaining to his millionaire client that Vanderbilt had used the seizure rights granted under the General Railroad Law of New York State. He advised him it would be in his best interest to negotiate a price before the *courts* decided the price that

Vanderbilt would be obliged to pay him, and nothing more."

Harold grimaced. "That must have been painful."

Matthew, only half listening to the conversation, suddenly realized what was bothering him. "Where are the engines?"

"What?" Harold asked.

"The engines," Matthew repeated. "I see twelve tracks full of train cars, but no engines. How did they get here?"

Thaddeus smiled. "Vanderbilt has no intention of allowing smoke-belching engines to dirty his beautiful glass ceiling."

Matthew listened with astonishment as he explained.

"Engineers have been instructed on a procedure called *flying in*. As they approach the station, the engine is unhitched from the rest of the train. The engineer speeds up to remove the engine from the cars and drives it onto a sidetrack. The passenger cars slide softly into this building, soot-free. The brakeman brings them to a stop."

Matthew's mouth hung open. "Brilliant," he remarked with awe. His eyes continued to absorb everything he could. He couldn't wait to get home and tell little Robert all about it. His two-year-old wouldn't understand much of what he said, but he was still eager to share it with him. "Now that the depot is open, are New Yorkers happy?"

"For the most part," Thaddeus conceded. "It hasn't all been smooth going, however."

"I can't imagine it would be," Harold replied. "This is a massive undertaking. What kind of problems are we talking about?"

"They're still figuring out customer service," Thaddeus responded. "There are bigger problems, however. The rush of hundreds of distracted travelers is fertile ground for thieves and pickpockets."

Matthew patted his inner coat pocket, glad to feel the comforting bulk of his money. He removed it and resecured it in a pocket further inside his thick coat. He watched Harold do the same.

"The deaths have been the biggest issue, however."

Matthew forgot about his money. "The deaths?"

"The layout of the tracks coming south into the station is a rather poor design. The network of tracks is crowded with cars that obstruct the view of approaching trains. Within the last twelve days, seven people have lost their lives by being run over by trains approaching or leaving the depot." Thaddeus looked at them somberly. "Be careful. I'm aware your new book is well on its way to bestseller status. I don't want anything to happen to our valuable authors."

Matthew appreciated the warning, but remained mesmerized by the structure. He'd never seen anything so grand or well-built. "Vanderbilt got his wish. I'm quite certain this is the most spectacular station in the country. Perhaps in the world."

Thaddeus nodded, but he had already moved on to other thoughts. "Your meeting with the publishing house isn't for a few days. Do you have other plans in New York City?"

Matthew nodded. "We're here to attend the beginning of the trial against Boss Tweed."

Thaddeus lifted his eyebrows. "You're here to attend the trial? I hear there will be a limited number of people in the courtroom."

Matthew appreciated their new friend making that observation. He'd assured Harold that being invited to the trial was quite an honor; perhaps now his twin would believe him. "I'm friends with Thomas Nast."

It was Thaddeus' turn to whistle. "The cartoonist who finally brought that thief to justice? Please thank him for me."

Matthew wanted to ask more questions, but a quick glance at his watch told him the Stratfords' driver was waiting for them. He needed to check on the quilts, obtain their baggage, and make his way outside. He smiled broadly. "I will. We must go. Thank you for the information. Will we see you at the publishing house?"

"You will," Thaddeus assured them. "I'm to be part of the meeting."

Matthew tipped his hat and began to make his way forward on the platform. He watched carefully for incoming trains.

Matthew chuckled as he walked into Wally and Nancy's house four days later. "It looks like a quilt factory in here."

Nancy looked up with a bright smile as she arranged the last of the colorful quilts on furniture scattered throughout the house. Her blond hair glistened in the late autumn sun streaming through the bay window in the parlor. "There are so many this time that I thought it would be best for the women to come and choose what they want to purchase. There are quilts in almost every room," she admitted.

Matthew glanced over his shoulder. "How many women are getting ready to arrive?"

Nancy laughed out loud. "You can get that terrified look off your face. I'm only allowing twenty women at a time."

Matthew raised a brow. "I can't imagine the ones in the last group are pleased they won't have first pick."

"True," Nancy conceded. "I had them pick numbers out of a basket at our last Bregdan Women meeting. That way, no one can claim I used favoritism."

Wally appeared in the parlor. He looked every bit the successful real estate mogul. His dark eyes and hair provided a perfect foil for his blond, blue-eyed wife. It was obvious he adored her. "My wife is as smart as she is beautiful," he said proudly.

"Thank you, dear," Nancy murmured. The gonging of the hour from the massive grandfather clock in the far corner of the parlor made her glance out the window. "My goodness, the first ones are here!" She pulled off her apron and stuffed it into a nearby drawer.

Wally eyed her. "Did I hear you say there are quilts in *every* room?"

"Not your office, dear," Nancy assured him. "You and Matthew can escape there."

"Matthew?" Wally asked in invitation.

"Right behind you," Matthew said eagerly. He agreed the quilts were beautiful, but there were things he wanted to discuss with Wally. Harold was having lunch with a fellow reporter from Buffalo. Matthew had declined the invitation to join them, eager to think through what he was witnessing.

Matthew settled into the wingback chair that flanked the blazing fireplace in Wally's wood-paneled study. The rich wood was the perfect setting for the burgundy chairs and sofa that looked out over their back garden. Weak sunshine filtered through the tree limbs, muted even more by the layer of soot and smoke that hovered over the city.

"I'm glad you decided to stay when Tweed's trial was delayed," Wally said as he pulled out his pipe and carefully tamped the tobacco. "I thought you might choose to return to the plantation early."

"I still had to meet with my publisher," Matthew commented. "We had our meeting this morning. I've also enjoyed the time I spent with Thomas Nast."

"New York City owes a great debt to that man. Without his cartoons, I doubt public opinion would have turned so thoroughly against Boss Tweed. Your friend has become quite a hero."

Matthew agreed. "He downplays it, but I believe he knows he played a key role." He frowned. "It's quite discouraging, however, that Tweed was released on bail and allowed to continue his campaign for reelection." He shook his head. "I can't believe he retained his office as a state assemblyman."

Wally shrugged. "Other than the fact that it shows the ignorance of the men who voted for him. Tweed has no power left. A great number of his associates fled the country when the newspapers began reporting exactly what was happening. Tweed was arrogant enough to stay because he believes he is above the law. He's been able to steal so much money from the city because he had such a vast Democratic political machine. That machine has been destroyed, and his career as a political boss is in ruins."

Matthew listened closely. "Do you think he'll ever stand trial and go to jail?"

"Yes," Wally said firmly. "He's out on bail, but his legal problems have only just begun. I work closely with many of the city leaders. We're not going to let this go. He has defrauded the citizens of this city for millions of dollars." His voice was grim. "He'll pay for that."

Matthew felt better. "I came to New York because I wanted to see someone finally be held accountable for their actions. It's quite demoralizing to know he is walking around as a free man."

Wally grinned and held up the newspaper. "Have you seen this morning's paper?"

Matthew shook his head. "I left early." He took the paper Wally handed him. When he looked down, a grin spread across his face. The cartoon depicted Tweed as a jailbird.

"Your friend won't stop until Tweed is behind bars," Wally predicted.

Matthew knew that was true. He and Nast had talked about his commitment to bring Tweed to justice. Nast's campaign had put him and his family in grave danger over the summer. They'd fled to New Jersey for a time because of the death threats, but he had since returned to continue his fight.

"I'm still not quite sure how he did it," Wally said thoughtfully.

"I am," Matthew said. "I write in words, Thomas writes with pictures. His influence is immeasurable.

He's able to reach the learned and the unlearned alike. Many people can't read the articles that are written, while others simply choose not to. There are those who read them but don't fully comprehend what is being said." He smiled. "Then they see Thomas' cartoons. They see them and easily understand them. His depictions of Tweed have opened the eyes of those who were mired in ignorance. I believe an artist with his ability does more to affect public opinion than a score of writers."

Wally listened closely, nodding thoughtfully as he puffed on his pipe. "I see what you're saying." His eyes hardened. "Tweed will pay for what he's done. At last estimate, he has stolen between twenty-five million to forty-five million dollars. I suspect it will eventually be much higher."

"Dear God," Matthew breathed. "I had no idea it was so much."

"He's done immeasurable harm to the city, but now that he's been exposed, we'll work to rebuild what he has destroyed."

Matthew didn't envy the job Wally and his friends would have to do. "We live in a corrupt time," he said quietly, as he watched the skeletal oak trees in the backyard sway with the wind. The grass was brown, but the bare gardens still possessed a distinct elegance. He could imagine how beautiful it was in the spring and summer.

Wally reached behind him and selected a leather-bound book from the shelves that lined the room. "Have you read *The Tale of Two Cities* by Charles Dickens?" He opened the book and pulled a pair of wire-rimmed spectacles from his pocket. "The first line describes the time we live in rather well, I believe."

Before he could read, Matthew spoke the words. "It was the best of times, it was the worst of times." He'd read Dicken's masterpiece more than once since it had come out in entirety two years earlier.

"Yes," Wally said approvingly. "It's how I feel about the time we're living in now. Especially here in the North, we're experiencing an era of rapid economic growth. While there is still inequity, American wages are much higher than those in Europe."

Matthew knew that was true. "The reason for the vast increase in immigration."

"The rapid expansion of industrialization has spurred the need for skilled laborers." Wally frowned. "Unfortunately, when you have that much wealth being accumulated, there are those who will stop at nothing to claim more for themselves."

"Like Boss Tweed," Matthew responded.

"Yes, I'm afraid Tweed defines corruption. He has pressed every boundary he came up against. Yet, he'll pay the price."

"So will the people he hurt," Matthew replied. "Most of those people will never recover."

"I wish I could argue that point, but it's true," Wally agreed. "I have lost money to some of his scams, but not enough to drastically hurt us. I have associates, unfortunately, who can't say the same."

Matthew nodded but remained silent, once again staring into the flames. "The South is struggling. They remain economically devastated."

Wally steepled his hands beneath his chin. "Their economy is tied to commodities, cotton, and tobacco production. They're still suffering from low prices."

"Yes. Cromwell Plantation has done well because we've had such successful crops, but the vast majority of farmers are barely surviving."

"I know that's true," Wally said thoughtfully. "I suspect things won't change substantially until the South abandons its agrarian economy for a modern economy grounded in factories, mines, and mills."

Matthew frowned. "It's not a way of life most Southerners want."

"I fear it won't matter," Wally said bluntly. "Their agrarian society was based on cheap labor through slavery. That's no longer available to them. Their economy can't be sustained by farming alone. If I understand correctly from what I've read, sharecropping and tenant farming are doing nothing but creating a new kind of poverty for both blacks and whites."

"That's true," Matthew sighed heavily.

Wally looked at him keenly. "What's on your mind?"

Matthew told him about Vincent and Morris, detailing the KKK violence in South Carolina. "Morris died from an infection after the beating. His son, Jed, has been adopted by Moses and Rose."

Wally's eyes glittered with anger and grief. "And elsewhere in the South?"

"It's bad," Matthew said bluntly. "The federal government is trying to make things better, but the hatred embedded in Southern society against black people can't be legislated away. In many ways, I believe these trials will represent the culmination of the government's most substantial effort to stop white violence and provide personal security for blacks."

"Why do you say that?"

Matthew thought through his response. "There's been significant federal intervention, along with the suspension of habeas corpus in nine counties in South Carolina. There have been widespread undercover investigations so they can get to the truth. Though many of them have been released with bail, there were several hundred Klansmen arrested. Most were indicted." Matthew sighed. "I appreciate what has been done, but I fear for the future."

"When does the trial start for the men who were indicted?"

Matthew scowled. "Two hundred and twenty were indicted. Only five are being prosecuted."

Wally gaped at him. "Why?"

"Fifty-three of them pleaded guilty. The cases against the rest have been postponed, but I doubt they will ever happen. The five standing trial are charged with violating the Enforcement Act."

"Does the trial start soon?"

"In two weeks, on November twenty-eighth."

"Is there a chance the Klansmen will be held responsible for their crimes?" Wally asked sharply.

"Of the fifty-three Klansmen who pleaded guilty, they've received penalties of three months to five years in prison. Their fines vary from ten dollars to a thousand dollars. Perhaps the greatest punishment is that they have been sent to Northern prisons. No one believed they would actually be treated as prisoners in a *Southern* prison." Matthew shook his head. "They would more likely have been treated as heroes."

"Where are they serving their sentences?"

"Some are in Detroit. Those who received sentences of more than a year have been incarcerated at the federal penitentiary in Albany."

"Here in New York?" Wally sounded surprised.

"I hope they're treated like the criminals they are," Matthew said angrily.

"Do you believe there will be a fair trial?"

Matthew watched out the window as clouds covered the sunshine. The wind began to blow harder. He suspected there would be snow the next day. As he watched, he thought through his response. "I believe both sides recognize the enormous implications of the constitutional questions that will be argued during the trial. I also believe the Constitution of our country is on trial," he said. "There have been other arrests in other states, but not as many as South Carolina. South Carolina is the only place where habeas corpus has been suspended. I suspect the government is using it as a warning to other states." He shook his head. "The only thing I'm certain of is that these trials will have far-reaching ramifications for generations to come."

Wally leaned forward to stare at him. "You believe they are that important?"

"I do. I've already heard that lawyers and judges from all over the country are coming for the trial. Newspaper reporters will flock to Columbia to cover it. This is the first time the government is utilizing their strength to attempt to make things right for freed slaves in the South. If they don't succeed, I'm afraid it will embolden the Klan even more." Matthew tightened his lips. "And if they do succeed…"

"What?" Wally asked after a lengthy silence.

Matthew wondered if he should say what he was thinking. He hesitated to put it into words because of what it would mean, but not saying it wouldn't change the reality. "If they do succeed, all they'll do is put an end to the violence. Nothing will have been done to stop the hatred. Whether it comes out in this generation, or the next, I believe the Ku Klux Klan and other white supremacy groups will continue their reign of terror."

Wally took a deep breath. "There's not much hope in that, Matthew."

"I know," Matthew stated with resignation. His belief had been searing his soul for months. He and Harold had spent hours discussing it. "I'm trying my best to believe in a good outcome, but..."

"But what?" Wally pressed.

Matthew closed his eyes for a moment in an attempt to block out what he was seeing. "If you'd seen the whip marks on Vincent and Morris' backs, you'd realize how terrible the hatred is. I simply don't know what will ever make it end."

Chapter Sixteen

Mathilda Silverson walked slowly through the house, her eyes widening as she took in the lovely quilts draped over chairs, dressers, tables, and sideboards. "How can I possibly choose just one?"

Nancy overheard her as she was talking to another customer. "I know it's difficult," she sympathized. "They're all so beautiful and unique."

Mathilda reached down and held the edge of a quilt done in block pattern, with brilliant hues of red, blue, green, and purple seeming to come alive as the waning sun beamed down on it. "This one," she breathed, obviously mesmerized by the colors. "Definitely this one."

Nancy smiled and walked over. "It's a wonderful choice." She lifted the card she had placed next to it. Abby had prepared one for each quilt. "Sapphire Cross made this one." She turned over the card and began to read.

Thank you for choosing my quilt. My name is Sapphire. I was a slave until I was thirty-two. I picked cotton in Georgia. My husband and I are working hard to create a new life. A good life. I have three children who are in school now. I also go to school in the evenings. Mrs. Rose Samuels has taught me how to read and write. I never thought I could do that. My two girls helped me make this quilt. My husband and my boy keep our cabin warm enough for us to quilt by making sure we have enough firewood. My husband also works on Cromwell Plantation. We hope you enjoy using this quilt. It comes made with a lot of love.

"Oh my," Mathilda whispered. She brushed a tear away. "I was so mesmerized by the beauty of the quilts that I almost forgot real people made them." She picked up the quilt reverently, lifting it to hold a corner to her cheek. "Knowing who made it makes it much more special."

A small group of women had stopped to listen to Nancy read the card. Their faces showed the same emotion that Mathilda's did.

Mathilda looked again at the card. "It seems like such a small amount for so much work," she said quietly. She raised her voice so she could be heard by the rest of the women in the room. "We have so much while they have so little. All of us are Bregdan Women. We just happen to be Bregdan Women who have a lot of money." She paused. "Nancy, I'm going to pay double the price that's marked on this quilt."

Thoughtful looks appeared on the other women's faces.

"Me too," one called.

"And me," another added.

Nancy glowed with happiness as the women collected their quilts and gave her more money than had been asked for. She wished she could be there to see Abby's face when Matthew delivered the funds. She wished even more that she could see the expressions of the women who had worked diligently to create the quilts.

As Mathilda turned to leave, her quilt tucked securely under her arm, she said, "Catherine Bogsworth is in the next group. She's a close friend.

I'm going to tell her what we did and ask her to pass it on to the next group." She paused and smiled. "And have them pass it on to the next group after that."

Nancy laughed with delight. "The Cromwell Bregdan Women are going to be delighted. I'm not sure you have any idea what this will mean to them."

"Perhaps not," Mathilda said thoughtfully. "I've never lived in poverty. I do, however, understand that the Bregdan Principle is true. *Every action I take will reflect in someone else's life. Someone else's decisions. Someone else's future. Both good and bad.*" Her eyes darkened with emotion. "Knowing that I can change someone's life and future with the money I have is vitally important to me. It makes having the worthwhile, because I can use it to make a difference."

Carrie led No Regrets into the barn, exhilarated after a long ride in the frosty air. Miles had been right. Two days after Matthew and Harold left, they'd had snow. Not much, but enough to coat the ground and turn the trees into white-flocked statues.

The clinic hadn't been busy, with the exception of a few patients in the morning. At Janie's urging, Carrie had left early to enjoy a ride. The temperatures remained frigid, assuring the snow hadn't melted. If she understood the message the skies were whispering, there would be more snow that night. She was looking forward to hunkering down in front of the fireplace while she played backgammon with anyone willing to take her on.

"Hello, Amber!" Carrie called as she entered the barn.

"Hello, Carrie."

Carrie frowned, alerted by the dull sound in the girl's voice. She quickly untacked No Regrets and led her into the stall for her ration of grain, and then she turned to Amber. "What's wrong?"

Amber shrugged. "I don't feel good," she mumbled.

Carrie could tell by the shine in the girl's eyes that she had a fever. A practiced hand on Amber's forehead both confirmed it and alarmed her. "How long have you been feeling badly?"

"Since I left school," Amber mumbled.

Just then, Clint strode into the barn, whistling loudly.

Carrie turned to him. "Clint, please take your sister home for me. She's sick with fever."

Clint frowned but didn't ask any questions. "I'll have the carriage ready in a minute."

"I can ride," Amber protested weakly.

"You won't be riding," Carrie said firmly. "I'll be by in a little while with a remedy for you."

"What's wrong with me?" Amber asked.

Carrie took a deep breath. "Tell me what your other symptoms are."

"My body is aching," Amber said slowly. "My head hurts...and I feel weak." She turned her head away and coughed.

Carrie knew her suspicions had been right. "You have influenza, honey. The flu. I know you feel terrible. I'm sorry." She paused. "Were there other children in school who were sick?"

Amber nodded. "I think so." Her voice was tight with anxiety.

Carrie's insides tightened as she shoved away thoughts of relaxing in front of the fireplace. It was obvious Amber knew the ramifications of the flu. She couldn't be Polly's daughter and not have heard the stories from the clinic.

"There were a few that didn't seem to be feeling good when school ended," Amber continued. "There could be more." She paused. "I don't know about the white students, but I suppose some could be sick. Everyone was eager to get home because it's so cold."

Carrie was certain she was right about more students being sick. The plantation had managed to avoid the flu during the last two years, but it seemed their luck had run out.

"Are you sure I don't have a cold?" Amber asked hopefully.

"I'm sure. Cold symptoms come on gradually. Yours have been abrupt. It's rare to have a fever when you get a cold, but yours is already high." She watched Amber carefully, not missing her grimace. "Colds can produce a very slight body ache, but you're experiencing a lot of pain, aren't you?"

Amber closed her eyes briefly. "Yes," she whispered. "I feel like I've been trampled by a horse."

Clint brought the carriage to a stop in front of the barn. Carrie helped the girl into the carriage, positioned her so she could rest her head on the back of the seat, and covered her with a thick layer of blankets. "You're going to be miserable for several days," she said gently, "but you'll get better. You're strong and healthy."

"What if my mama isn't home?" Clint asked in a worried voice.

"She's home," Carrie assured him. "She left the clinic the same time I did. Tell her I'll be by soon with a remedy. In the meantime, keep her well-covered and warm. The chills will be starting soon." Almost as if called forward by her words, Amber began to shiver.

Carrie stepped away from the carriage. "Get her home," she ordered.

As soon as the carriage rolled away, she hurried for the house. If Amber was sick, it was certain there would be more.

Abby looked up as Carrie rushed in through the front door. "It must be cold out there," she called teasingly. One look at her daughter's face froze her smile. "What's wrong, Carrie?"

"Amber has the flu," Carrie said grimly.

Abby's face grew just as grim. "Which means it's going to spread through the plantation and the school."

"Yes." There was no reason to downplay what they were about to face.

"What can I do?"

"I'm going to Amber's house now with some Gelsemium. Will you please find Anthony or Father and have them go to the clinic? Janie should be there for another thirty minutes, and she needs to be aware. We have a large supply of Gelsemium there. I want to treat as many people as we can immediately.

It's the only way to keep it from continuing to spread." Carrie's mind continued to race.

Anthony and Thomas appeared in the parlor doorway.

"We were playing chess," Anthony said. "What can we do to help?"

Carrie was relieved to see both of them. "Anthony, please go to the clinic for Janie. Tell her to stay there." She waited for his nod before she continued. "Father, please go to the school. All the students are gone, but Rose, Hazel, and Phoebe will still be working. They need to know. They may be able to alert us to students who weren't feeling well when they left school."

Carrie wanted to believe she was overreacting, but she knew that wasn't true. The flu, combined with frigid temperatures, could be deadly. Most people who got sick would fully recover, but if they were already weak, or if they developed complications, it could be fatal. She didn't know where it had started, but she knew it would spread rapidly.

She turned when the front door opened, relieved when Moses entered the house, a gust of cold air pushing in behind him. "I need your men."

Moses nodded and waited for her to explain.

"Amber has the flu."

Moses connected the dots quickly. "You need my men to go check the houses of all the students to find out who else is sick."

"Yes." Carrie's mind continued to spin. "Abby, I need you to take the remedy to Amber. Moses, I want all of the men to come to the house before they leave. I'll give them remedy for anyone they find who is sick. It's very easy to administer."

Moses nodded his confirmation before he turned and disappeared back into the cold.

At that moment, Annie appeared in the doorway of the kitchen. "Carrie..."

Carrie knew Annie had the flu as soon as she heard the weakness in her voice. "You're sick," she said gently.

"I reckon I be," Annie said. "I was feelin' fine just a little while ago..."

"You have the flu." Carrie reached behind her for the thick coat Annie had hung on the coat tree earlier that day. "I'm taking you home."

Abby pulled on her coat quickly. "I'll be back when I've given Polly the remedy for Amber. I'll do whatever you need."

Anthony and her father had already left for the barn.

Carrie took Annie's arm and walked outside with her. Before they were halfway across the yard, Anthony, Abby, and her father were riding off in different directions.

Miles' appearance at the door explained how they had readied their horses so quickly. He frowned when he saw Carrie with his wife. "You feeling sick, Annie?"

"Yep, I ain't feeling good," Annie admitted. She looked at Carrie. "You got some of them magic pills that gonna make me feel better?"

"Of course I do," Carrie said soothingly. "I just want to get you in your bed where you can rest while they work their magic."

Once Annie was warmly tucked in, her eyes growing glassy from her rising fever, Carrie pulled the Gelsemium from her medical bag. She poured a glass of water, dissolved a 30c potency tablet in it, and gave Annie a spoonful. "I want you to rest," she said firmly.

She eyed Miles. "I mean it. Annie seems to think being sick shouldn't keep her from doing things. I don't want her up until her fever has broken. She's not to come to the house until I've said she can," she said sternly.

"She ain't going anywhere," Miles promised.

Carrie turned back to Annie. "I mean it, Annie," she repeated. "I'm concerned about you, but I'm also concerned about everyone else. I don't know where you caught the flu, but I don't want you to pass it on to the others."

Annie held her gaze. "I hear you, Miss Carrie. I ain't gonna do nothing to make nobody else sick." She frowned. "I hope I ain't made nobody sick already."

Convinced Annie had gotten her message, Carrie smiled and placed a cool hand on her forehead. "Everything is going to be fine. You just let Miles take care of you. Focus on getting well."

Annie's eyes grew more distressed. "What if I make Miles sick?"

It was a fair question. The odds indicated Miles would also get the flu, but there was a chance he had an immunity to it that Annie did not. "If you start coughing, I want you to make sure you cover your mouth. Every time you get up to use the bathroom, I want you to wash your hands." Carrie was glad evidence was coming out that washing your hands could keep from spreading disease, just as washing her hands before surgery kept bacteria from causing infection.

She turned to Miles. "You can't sleep in the same bed tonight."

"I'll make up a bed on the floor," Miles said calmly. "I'll be fine."

Carrie was convinced both of them understood the seriousness of what they were facing. "I want you to give Annie a teaspoon of the liquid every thirty minutes."

"For how long?" Miles asked keenly.

"Until her fever is gone."

Annie began to shake as chills gripped her body.

"She's going to be fine," Carrie said confidently, "but she's going to be miserable for a little while." She smiled down at her patient. "Focus on the fact that you're going to be fine."

"Thank you," Annie said weakly.

"I love you, Annie. Feel better soon." Carrie squeezed Annie's hand and hurried downstairs.

Carrie had slept only two hours before she made her way back to the barn to check on Annie the next morning. The night had passed in a haze of Moses' men returning with reports of illness they had discovered.

Twenty-five more students had been discovered with fevers. Carrie knew the number would probably be higher today. Every one of the families had received Gelsemium, along with careful instructions. They had received enough medicine for every member of the family in case others became sick as well. All of them had been instructed to stay home until everyone was well.

Every student had also been told to stay home from school for the last three days of the week. They had left Gelsemium with each family as a precaution. If anyone fell sick, they were supposed to alert Janie at the clinic so they could receive more of the treatment.

Carrie had never been more grateful for the large stock of homeopathic and herbal remedies she kept at the clinic, along with the stockpile in the house basement.

"Susan!" Carrie called as she entered the barn. Her partner always arrived at dawn. When Susan didn't respond, she started up the stairs to Miles and Annie's apartment, suspecting she would find her there. She could also be in one of the fields, checking on the horses.

Eclipse snorted loudly and stomped his foot as he poked his head over the stall door.

"Amber isn't here this morning," Carrie called with a smile. "She's sick, but she'll be back soon."

Eclipse snorted more loudly and pawed at the door. His eyes bored into hers. Feeling a sudden sense of unease, Carrie walked over to his stall. She frowned when she realized he didn't have fresh water in his bucket, and every bit of his hay was gone. He could have already eaten the grain Susan gave him every morning, but he wouldn't have gone through the water and hay.

She quickly checked all the other horses confined in the stalls. None of them had water or hay.

"Hello, Carrie." Clint walked into the barn, his tall, muscular frame blocking out the early morning sun as he entered. "How is everything?"

Carrie had considered having him stay home since Amber was ill, but she knew Susan would need his help. She'd told Miles to stay upstairs with Annie, so he wasn't aware the horses hadn't been cared for.

"I need your help giving the horses water and feed," Carrie said.

Clint's eyes narrowed. "Where's Susan? That's always the first thing she does."

"I don't know." Carrie's sense of uneasiness increased. Susan and Harold lived twenty minutes away. With Harold gone, her friend was alone.

Clint's brow furrowed. "The carriage is right outside. Go check on Susan. The mare pulling it had feed and water this morning at the house. I'll take care of things here."

Eclipse pawed the door again.

Clint shook his head. "His highness is fine. I'll take care of everyone." He paused. "Where is Miles?"

"Upstairs with Annie. She's sick, too."

Clint stared at her. "This is going to be bad, isn't it?"

Before Carrie could answer, Anthony appeared behind her.

"What's going on? Is Annie worse?" he asked sharply.

"I don't know," Carrie replied, relieved to see him. She quickly explained the situation. "Will you please go with me to Susan's house after I check on Annie?"

Moses and Rose appeared as Anthony nodded. "How is my mama?" Moses asked, his eyes dark with worry as he felt the tension in the barn.

"I haven't seen her yet," Carrie said quickly, "but I'm sure she's not worse or Miles would have let us know." Her worry for Susan grew as a plan took shape in her mind. "Moses, I'll go check on your mama." She turned to Anthony. "I would prefer to take a wagon to Susan's. If she's sick, I want to bring her back to the house. Will you and Moses get one ready?"

"It will be ready for you when you come down," Anthony promised.

"I'll bring over a load of blankets and pillows," Rose said quickly. "Abby is fixing breakfast. I'll have her fix some ham biscuits for you two."

"Thank you," Carrie said as she turned and hurried up the stairs. Her belief that Annie was better evaporated when she walked into the room. One look at Annie told her she was still burning up with fever. Her heart pounded harder when she looked over at Miles, who had not stirred when she came into the room. His breathing was labored, his face was damp with sweat, and his body shook beneath the thin blanket he had covered himself with during the night.

Carrie wrenched the door open. "Clint, go get Abby!"

Minutes later, she heard Abby and her father pounding up the stairs. Carrie met them with relief. "Miles is sick. He clearly was too ill to give Annie the Gelsemium. They both need to receive a teaspoonful every thirty minutes."

Abby moved over to the bed and began to prepare the remedy.

"Father, please go to the house and bring over blankets and pillows for Miles. Lying on the floor is only making him more miserable. I already know every muscle in his body must be aching." She shook her head. "He must have started feeling badly right after I left."

"Why didn't he come tell us?" Thomas asked.

"It seems to have hit him especially hard. He probably was afraid to leave Annie." She paused. "And then he couldn't." She gazed down at her old friend, her heart pounding with fear. She knew how deadly flu could be, especially for older people. She wanted to stay, but Abby would take excellent care of him.

It was more urgent to find out if Susan was sick.

She feared she already knew the answer.

Carrie, already worried, felt her heart began to pound she and Anthony drew near to Susan's house. There was no smoke coming from the chimney, which could only mean Susan had been too ill to light a fire or keep it going. One look at Anthony's grim face, and she knew he shared her feelings.

Both of them jumped from the wagon the moment Anthony brought it to a stop in front of the house. Not bothering to knock, Carrie pushed through the front door. "Susan!" she called loudly.

Striding through the house toward the bedroom, she dreaded what she would find when she opened the door. "Susan!" she called one more time before she entered.

She couldn't stop the groan that escaped her lips.

Carrie rushed to the bedside. "Susan," she murmured. "Can you hear me?"

A sound behind her told her that Anthony was already preparing the remedy. She knew he would also light a fire as quickly as possible to warm the frigid bedroom.

Susan moaned and opened her eyes slightly. "Carrie," she whispered. She began coughing, her whole body spasming with each cough.

"I'm here," Carrie crooned. "I'm here." She pulled back Susan's covers enough to determine she was shivering uncontrollably, her nightgown damp from the sweating caused by her fever. Carrie would have to wait until Anthony got the room warm before she risked changing her clothes.

"The remedy's ready," Anthony said quietly. "I'll start a fire."

Carrie reached for the glass and spoon, and then poured a teaspoon of the liquid into Susan's mouth. "This will help," she said gently.

Susan moaned again, twisting in the bed.

Carrie took a deep breath. The combination of the fever, chills, and body aches, along with lying in a frigid room all night under blankets damp from sweat, would almost certainly give Susan pneumonia. "I'm here," she said again, not certain Susan was able to understand what she was saying. She stroked Susan's forehead while she waited for the room to warm.

A crackling sound signaled that Anthony had started the fire. She could hear him piling on kindling and logs, coaxing as much warmth into the room as he could.

Twenty minutes later, Carrie decided it was warm enough to put dry clothes on her friend. She gave her another dose of the remedy and then turned to Anthony. "I'm going to need your help. I have to get her out of these clothes, and we need to change the bedding. Please gather more blankets and bedding for me. I'm going to change her while you do that."

Carrie lifted Susan gently, alarmed when her friend sagged like a ragdoll. She propped her in a sitting position while she pulled Susan's nightgown off and wrapped the dry top quilt around her trembling shoulders. From a nearby drawer, she slipped a dry, flannel gown over Susan's head just as Anthony reentered the room.

Together, they changed the bedding and adjusted Susan to create a warm cocoon of sheets and blankets. They lowered her flat again, tucking a pillow beneath her head.

Susan moaned but managed a very weak smile.

Carrie felt a surge of hope. At least she was aware of what they were doing to try to help her.

"We can't move her, can we?" Anthony whispered.

Carrie shook her head. As much as she wanted to take Susan back to the house, it was too risky to take her out in the cold.

Anthony leaned closer to her ear. "The baby?"

Carrie's stomach clenched because she didn't have an answer. Susan had a scorching fever. She didn't know how it would affect the baby. Her friend was barely out of the first trimester, so the risk for a miscarriage was high. All she could do was shake her head silently.

One hour later, after two more doses of Gelsemium, Susan's fever seemed to have dropped a little, and the shaking wasn't quite as bad. For the first time, Carrie felt a surge of hope, but her patient was far too fragile to move.

Carrie beckoned Anthony out of the room. "You need to go back to the house. I know everyone is terribly concerned. Tell them Susan has the flu, but that she has turned a corner. It's going to take a while for her to recover enough to move, so I'm staying with her.

"The baby?"

Carrie sighed. "I still don't know. Her fever was one hundred and four when we arrived. I can only assume it was that high throughout the night…possibly higher. I honestly don't know what that kind of fever can do to a pregnancy. I'm sure it's not good, but there's nothing I can tell you to report to everyone. Please ask them to pray."

Anthony kissed her warmly. "There's a pot of soup cooking on the stove. It should be ready in about an hour."

Carrie's eyes widened with surprise. At the mention of food, she suddenly realized how hungry she was. She'd not eaten since lunch the day before. It had to be almost noon now. "You made soup?" Her eyes narrowed. "I thought you were bringing in firewood. You're just now telling me you know how to cook?"

"If chicken and vegetable soup counts as cooking." Anthony smiled. "It's the only thing I know how to make."

Carrie's stomach growled loudly. "Thank you," she said. "I'll be ready for it."

"There's also some bread in the bread box, and Annie must have given her some of the pound cake she made for lunch yesterday, because there is a plate with some on the counter. I lifted the cover to see what it was."

Carrie's heart clutched at the thought of Harold. He should be home in five days. She had promised him she'd take good care of his wife. How was it possible that she was now praying for Susan to survive?

Chapter Seventeen

Matthew pulled his coat around him more closely as the wind blew in from the east, carrying a damp cold from the New York Harbor. They'd had two inches of snow the night before. The flakes had ceased falling, but the threatening gray sky promised more soon.

"I don't miss this," Harold muttered. "It gets cold in the South, but it's not the type of cold that invades your very being."

"You're getting soft," Matthew teased.

"He's smart," Julie Stratford retorted. A thick cap covered her brown hair, leaving only her sparkling green eyes peering out above the wool scarf that covered her mouth and nose.

Nancy pulled the lap robe up to her shoulders as the carriage made its way through the typically crowded New York City streets. "My daughter-in-law is quite correct. The winters seem to get harder every year. I'm looking forward to spending two weeks on the plantation at Christmastime."

"You and Wally are going to love it," Matthew promised. "Christmas at Cromwell is special."

"I'm sure it is," Nancy replied. "Abby has been trying to get us to come down ever since she and Thomas moved back there." She shook her head. "Wally and I are looking forward to getting away, and to finally meeting all the people we've heard about."

The clanging of streetcars, the whistle of trains, and the clacking of horse hooves on the cobblestones almost drowned out her words. "I can hardly wait to escape the noise," she shouted.

"And I can hardly wait to get home to my wife," Harold said.

Matthew knew that was true. The longer they'd been away, the more anxious Harold had grown to return. His brother had enjoyed the time in the city, but he was ready to go home. Losing his first wife and daughters was something Harold would never get over. Matthew missed Janie, Robert, and Annabelle, but he wasn't afraid they would die while he was gone. He knew Harold had done plenty of traveling for work in the last two years. What made this trip more difficult for him? "One more day," he said reassuringly. "We'll be home soon."

Harold nodded, but his eyes still reflected his anxiety.

"We're going to hate to see you go," Julie said. "It's been wonderful having you here."

"Are you certain you can't come for Christmas?" Matthew asked.

Julie shook her head. "Michael and I would love to, but someone must stay and run the real estate office while all of you enjoy a Southern Christmas," she teased. Her amused eyes turned serious. "I'm glad the two of you are joining us today."

Matthew had considered changing their return to the day before, but Nancy and Julie had convinced them it would be worthwhile to attend an anti-suffrage meeting. It still amazed Matthew that there were enough women opposed to the vote to actually form an association of their own. He had decided it would be valuable to understand why they were so opposed to the vote, and Nancy and Julie were eager to report back to the suffragists fighting so hard to have a voice in the country.

The clamor of the city lessened as they drew close to the meeting hall.

Julie took a deep breath. "May I be honest?"

Matthew looked up to see her eyes boring into his. "Certainly." He was surprised by the intensity of her expression and voice but waited quietly to hear what she had to say.

"I know you're very close to Thomas Nast, but I find myself quite at odds with him."

"Why?"

"Are you familiar with Victoria Woodhull?"

"Of course," Matthew replied, curious to see where the conversation would lead. "She's quite a leader in the women's rights movement. She and her sister are also the first women owners of a stock brokerage firm."

"Are you also aware Victoria is campaigning to be president next year?"

"I heard what I considered to be a rumor. I wasn't aware she had actually entered the election," Matthew said carefully. He knew Victoria Woodhull was quite vocal about her beliefs and passions, but it was impossible for her to be elected in a country where women weren't even allowed to vote.

Julie's eyes sparkled with anger. "We live in a country where women are denied the vote. We can't even enter a restaurant, a store, or an establishment of any kind without being escorted by a man. As if that is a necessity." Her voice dripped with sarcasm.

Matthew raised a brow. "I thought things were changing, at least here in New York City. What about Delmonico's? Isn't that where you hold your Bregdan Women meetings?"

Julie waved a hand impatiently. "They give us a private dining room for our meetings, but they won't allow groups of women to have tables in the main dining room. It's completely absurd."

Matthew agreed, but he wasn't sure what this had to do with Thomas Nast. Or Victoria Woodhull.

Julie sensed his confusion. "I'm sorry, I've gone off topic. Michael assures me I have a habit of doing that. Anyway, Victoria Woodhull is running for president. She wrote a letter to the *New York Herald* saying she was quite aware her decision to campaign would evoke more ridicule than enthusiasm. She also declared this is a time of sudden changes and startling surprises. She believes that what may appear absurd today will assume a serious aspect in the future."

Matthew hoped that was true, but he was still waiting to understand how Thomas Nast fit into the scenario.

Nancy helped lead Julie back to the subject. "Victoria is a close friend of the family. We hate that she has been singled out in the press. We appreciate what Thomas Nast has done to bring Boss Tweed down, but we most certainly don't appreciate what he's done to revile our friend."

Matthew exchanged a look with Harold, but his brother merely shook his head. "I'm afraid I don't know what you're talking about."

Renewed By Dawn

Julie reached beneath her lap rug and pulled out a copy of *Harper's Weekly*, already opened to a page. "This will help you understand."

Matthew took the paper. He frowned as soon as he looked down. Thomas Nast had created a caricature of Victoria Woodhull, depicting her as the devil. He thought back through his many discussions with his friend while he'd been in the city. They had all centered on Boss Tweed. Not once had they discussed women's rights.

Harold took the paper from him. He whistled and shook his head.

"I can't speak for Thomas Nast, but I can certainly tell you I don't agree with this," Matthew said firmly. "I believe women should have equal rights with men, including the right to vote." His frown deepened. "I'm sorry for what this cartoon has done to your friend."

"Will you talk to him?" Julie demanded. "Perhaps he will hear it from you more than he would hear it from anyone else."

Matthew considered his answer carefully. "I am more than willing to talk with Thomas."

"But?" Nancy asked keenly. "I hear a hesitation in your voice."

Matthew sighed. "But my friend is not easily swayed once he's made up his mind. While I appreciate what he's done to bring down Boss Tweed, he and I are on different sides of other things."

"Like immigration?" Nancy probed.

"Yes." Matthew frowned again. "My friend is too often fueled by his own prejudices. Part of why he went after Tweed so hard is because Thomas hates the Democratic Party. He's a staunch Republican, and though Tweed is Scottish, he has strong ties with the Irish Democrats. Thomas dislikes the Irish as much as he dislikes Democrats. Another thing we disagree on – at least the Irish part." As he spoke, he thought about the wonderful Irish people he had met in Moyamensing. There were hardworking Irish immigrants all over the country. He acknowledged there were some—like the police who led the Philadelphia election day riots, as well as the riots in both Memphis and New Orleans—who gave the Irish a bad name, but overall they were merely people trying to create a new life in a new country.

"Until a few months ago, his cartoons were seen to be little more than a personal attack against a man he detests. It wasn't until more evidence came to light to concretely prove Tweed's guilt that his cartoons made him a star in the field of journalism," Matthew added.

"But you'll talk to him?"

"I'll write him," Matthew agreed. "I won't see him again before we leave tomorrow. Writing is probably the best way to approach him, anyway," he said as he watched protest ignite in Julie's eyes. "Thomas is a proud man. If I can give him things to think about, while not pushing him into a corner for his beliefs by making him give an instant answer, I'll have a better chance to change his mind."

Harold nodded. "I agree with Matthew. We talk often about the power of communication to effect change. I believe *how* you communicate is every bit as important as *what* you communicate. If you merely attack someone for their beliefs, you most often end up closing their mind to ever seeing it differently."

Julie nodded reluctantly. "I suppose I can understand that." She turned back to Matthew. "What are you going to say to him?"

Matthew stepped down from the carriage that had come to a stop in front of the meeting hall. "I'll know the answer to that once I fully understand just why these anti-suffragists believe women shouldn't have the vote."

The carriage ride back to the Stratfords' house was silent. It wasn't for lack of things to talk about, but more for the need to be quiet and warm before they dissected the things they'd heard that day.

When they were settled in front of the fireplace with cups of hot tea, Julie was the one to break the silence. "I'm stunned," she admitted. "How does one go about arguing against such ignorance and close-minded thinking?"

Matthew admired her succinct summation of what they'd experienced that day. He was more than familiar with the argument for women's right to vote. He believed with all his heart that women should have not only the right to vote, but equal rights in a country that so depends on them. His experiences with Janie, Carrie, Abby and the other strong women he knew increased his commitment on a daily basis.

Nancy turned to Harold. "You said earlier that *how* you communicate is every bit as important as *what* you communicate. I thought about that during our time today." Her lips twisted. "When I wasn't trying to keep from being sick to my stomach."

Matthew understood her sentiment.

"How can we possibly communicate the necessity of women being able to vote to a group of women who believe that right will destroy the life they know?" Nancy continued. She shook her head heavily. "I'd heard some of those arguments before today, but to sit in a room with three hundred women and men who are virulently opposed to the vote was sobering."

"It was sickening!" Julie said angrily. "I wanted to go up to each of those women and shake some sense into their heads."

Matthew chuckled. "I doubt it would have been helpful, but I'll admit I felt the exact same way." Then he sobered. "Those women are consumed by fear."

Nancy scowled. "Fear of what? All I saw was stupidity." Her eyes, usually full of serenity and humor, flashed with disdain.

Matthew thought through what he'd heard. He'd been analyzing it ever since he left the meeting, just as he would for an article he might write. "First, I'm not sure any of those women looked stupid," he said slowly.

Julie snorted. "You couldn't see beyond their clothing," she declared. "They certainly all look like *wealthy ladies*, but stupidity is at their core. They're evidence that money doesn't equate to good sense."

Matthew tried again. "Perhaps, but do you really think you'll get anyone to listen to you by calling them stupid?"

"They're calling *us* stupid," Julie shot back. She gazed into the fireplace for a moment as she collected herself. "I see your point. Having a name-calling fight probably won't change anything, but I have no idea what will. Those women truly believe that the right to vote will destroy the very structure of American society. They believe their only roles are as wives and mothers, and that men are meant to control everything in this country." She ground her teeth as she glared into the flames.

"Perhaps you'll never change their minds," Harold said quietly.

"We have to!" Julie retorted.

"Do you?" Matthew asked. He knew where Harold was going with his statement. "No one changed Southerners' minds about slavery. No one changed England's mind about American independence."

Julie whirled around to stare at him. "Surely, you're not suggesting another war, Matthew?"

Matthew chuckled. "No," he assured her. "I am, however, suggesting that name-calling and refusal to listen didn't accomplish the end of slavery. Action did. While I never want our country to go through another civil war, I do believe it will take unrelenting action to obtain the vote for women."

Nancy nodded slowly. "What you're saying is that we're probably never going to change their minds, so we have to take more action than they do. Our voices have to be louder."

Matthew answered with a question. "Do you see another way?"

Nancy remained silent for several minutes. "No," she said thoughtfully. "We're not going to change minds that have already been made up. Oh, some may change their viewpoint, but the energy spent trying to change women motivated by fear would be much better spent taking action to achieve women's right to vote. We do that by finding and activating the women who aren't stuck in their fear."

Julie stood abruptly and walked over to the bay window to gaze at the new flakes of snow just beginning to fall. Dusk would cover their descent quickly, but the white curtain covering the world was beautiful. "So I don't have to agree with stupidity?"

Nancy laughed. "I learn a little more each day just why my son loves you so much."

Her statement prompted a smile from Julie. "I'm grateful he can tolerate an outspoken woman."

Michael strode into the room then, his shoulders and dark curly hair covered with the fresh snow. "I don't tolerate you, my dear. I prefer you being outspoken."

"Which is a great relief," Julie said dramatically, "because I would utterly fail at being anything different." She eyed the snow. "Where did you come from?"

"I came in through the back door at the kitchen," Michael explained. He held up a buttered roll. "I knew Mandy would almost have dinner ready. I'm too starving to wait, so I stole this on my way through."

"Stole?" Nancy shook her head. "Mandy has had a soft spot for you since you were a boy. She probably met you at the door with the roll."

Michael shrugged, his eyes dancing. "It might have been something like that," he admitted. He turned to Julie. "What are you being so outspoken about?"

Matthew watched the snow fall as Julie explained. He tried to focus on the conversation, but all he could think about was catching the train home the next day. He was more than ready to leave New York City and be with his family again.

"You just keep fighting," Michael said as Julie finished her recital. "The day will come when women have the right to vote."

Julie took his hand. "Matthew told us that energy spent trying to change women motivated by fear would be much better spent taking action to achieve women's right to vote."

"He's right," Michael agreed. "How old were most of the women there today?"

Julie wrinkled her brow as she thought. "I'd say most were in their fifties or sixties. Some younger, but not many."

Nancy sighed. "It's embarrassing that most of the women were my age." She shook her head. "You're supposed to get wiser as you age, not more ignorant."

"True," Matthew said, turning his attention back to the conversation. "On the other hand, it should give you hope that they're not recruiting many *younger* women."

Julie suddenly clapped her hands. "Which means *we* need to focus on younger women," she said excitedly.

"Aren't you already doing that?" Michael asked.

Julie considered his question. "I suppose so," she acknowledged as understanding filled her eyes.

"Think about it," Matthew said. "Many of these younger women are war widows. They were forced to work during the Civil War. They were forced to provide everything for their family. They see life differently than the older women fighting the vote. They know what they're capable of, and they're tired of not having a voice."

Julie eyes began to shine with excitement. "Which means we need to talk to more and more of *those* women. You're right that we'll probably never change the older women who are set in their ways, but a new generation can change things."

"We're counting on you and that new generation," Nancy said softly. "As long as the day comes when you're able to vote, I'll know I fought the good fight."

Julie shook her head. "No, Mother. You'll be able to vote one day. It won't be long until we have the right to vote."

Nancy smiled lovingly. She loved that her daughter-in-law called her Mother. It spoke of the closeness they had developed. Her son had picked the perfect woman to be his wife. "Perhaps. Perhaps not. The fight for abolition lasted far longer than anyone dreamed it would. There were many abolitionists who never lived to see the slaves set free, yet their part of the fight was necessary. I don't know if I'll ever vote, but I can feel good about the fact that I'm fighting for *your* right to vote. Or my granddaughters'"

A long silence fell on the room as the snow continued to softly fall, blanketing the yard and the bushes snugged beneath the window.

Matthew stopped Harold before he entered his room. "You've been almost silent all night. You didn't say a word during dinner. What's wrong?"

Harold turned troubled eyes to him. "I don't know." He took a deep breath. "But something is." His voice sharpened. "Don't you feel it?"

Matthew shook his head, disturbed by the angst he saw in his brother's eyes. "We're going home in the morning," he said reassuringly. "We'll be back on the plantation in two days."

"One," Harold said firmly. "Our train leaves early in the morning. We'll be in Richmond in the afternoon. We can be home tomorrow night."

Matthew frowned. "It will be dark long before we can reach the plantation if we leave tomorrow afternoon. The weather might be bad. We should stay at Thomas' house in town and leave early the next morning."

Harold set his lips stubbornly. "I'm going home tomorrow. Something is wrong," he said flatly. "You don't have to come with me, but I'm going."

Matthew didn't bother to argue. He knew that when his twin looked like that, nothing was going to change his mind. "We'll go together. Get some rest."

Carrie looked up when she heard a soft knock at Susan's bedroom door. She stood wearily and walked over to open it.

Janie's eyes were full of concern, but she looked over Carrie's shoulder and focused on their friend. "How is she?"

Carrie was grateful Janie didn't comment on her appearance. She hadn't left Susan's side for four days. Janie had come and gone with reports. Rose and Abby had come by, but Carrie had sent them away, telling them others needed them more than she did.

"The pneumonia is worsening," Carrie said softly, as she slipped out of Susan's bedroom and walked into the parlor. "Her cough has gotten worse. Her mucus is thick and green. When she's awake, she tells me she has stabbing chest pain. I can't get her fever below one hundred and two, and she's shaking with chills on a regular basis." She relayed the symptoms in a clinical voice that didn't communicate the angst and guilt eating at her.

Janie saw through her emotionless facade. "It's not your fault, Carrie. You're doing all you can."

It didn't help that Carrie knew Janie was right. She was terrified of losing her friend and business partner. Having to tell Harold his wife had died while he was away was something she couldn't comprehend. "Did you bring more mustard packs? They seem to offer some relief."

"Yes. I also brought some more apple cider vinegar."

"Thank you. Garlic and honey?" Carrie was trying everything to destroy the pneumonia caused by the flu. "I still have plenty of Aconite, Bryonia, and hepar." She'd had Janie bring her plenty of the homeopathic remedies when she realized Susan had slipped into pneumonia.

Janie nodded, but stared at her with keen penetration. "How long has it been since you've been outside?"

Carrie shook her head impatiently. "I'm fine. Anthony brought me some soup earlier, and he brought in plenty of wood for the fireplaces."

"Go outside," Janie ordered. "Susan is sleeping. I'll prepare the mustard packs and build up the fires."

"I'm..." Carrie was interrupted by Janie putting a gentle hand over her mouth.

"It wasn't a suggestion, Carrie. It was an order. You won't be able to help Susan if you get sick, as well. You look like death yourself," she said bluntly. "Go outside and get some air. Wear your coat because it's cold. Do not come back in for at least twenty minutes. When you do come in, I want you to eat some soup and have some cookies."

"When did you get so bossy?" Carrie grumbled, though she knew Janie was right. She also knew Susan was in capable hands. Her reluctance to leave, even for twenty minutes, revealed how guilty she felt.

"When you lost your common sense," Janie said crisply. "Now go."

Carrie managed a slight smile and turned to leave, but something Janie said nagged at her. "There are cookies? Does that mean Annie is better? If not, I'm not sure it's safe to eat Rose's or Abby's cooking."

Janie chuckled with relief. "If you can criticize Rose and Abby's cooking, that's a good sign. Annie is better. She's weak, but she insisted on coming to the kitchen. Abby watched her like a hawk and wouldn't let her stay more than an hour. She made soup while Annie made the cookies. Then she sent her home."

Carrie raised a brow. "I would like to have seen Abby ordering Annie out of her kitchen." She managed a chuckle that faded quickly. "How is Miles?" Janie's deep frown caused Carrie's heart to race. "Is he worse? Does he have pneumonia, too?" She wanted to go to her old friend, but she couldn't leave Susan.

"I think so," Janie admitted. "But he's responding to the treatments better. I won't let him out of their room. The only reason Annie came over to the kitchen was because Miles told her that her hovering was driving him crazy."

Carrie felt a surge of love for the man she'd known every day of her life. "You told him I wished I could be there?"

"I did." Janie rolled her eyes. "He told me that the Carrie Girl he knows is smarter than to leave Miss Susan. He said he's gonna be just fine and don't need nobody else to baby him."

Carrie's laugh was genuine this time as Janie mimicked Miles' voice perfectly. She pulled on her coat and reached for the doorknob. "I'll be back in twenty minutes."

"No less than twenty minutes," Janie said sternly.

"Yes, General Justin," Carrie said, feeling better the moment fresh air hit her face.

Janie smirked and then closed the door.

Carrie walked down the porch stairs, inhaling deeply as she went. Her lungs craved the clean, crisp air. The snow had melted, taking with it the frigid temperatures. It will cold, but not the bone-numbing type. She gazed up at the sky, letting the sun beam down on her face. She would walk to the woods and return. The movement would be good for her body. All she'd done for the last four days, with the exception of stoking the fires and heating soup, was sit in a wooden chair beside Susan's bed.

The exercise and fresh air helped clear her mind. Susan was very ill, but Carrie was certain she would survive. It would be weeks, possibly months, before she would return to full strength, but she would be alright.

Harold was due to arrive home the next day. She didn't have an answer for the question he would ask once he was convinced Susan would recover: *How was the baby?*

Chapter Eighteen

Harold pushed his way off the train and gazed around. Richmond streets were thronged with traffic. Several River City Carriages were pulled up on the side of the road next to the Broad Street Station, but with the congestion on the streets, he could make it to the River City Carriages stable faster by walking.

"Mr. Justin!"

Harold gritted his teeth and kept walking. He didn't have time to talk.

"Mr. Harold Justin!" The call came more loudly.

Swearing under his breath, Harold spun around. He didn't know the name of the man calling him, but he recognized him as a River City Carriages driver. "Yes?" He fought to keep his voice even and pleasant.

"Willard sent me, Mr. Justin." He pointed toward two horses tied to a railing outside the station.

Harold felt a leap of hope. "Willard received the telegram? We weren't able to send it until this morning. I didn't think anyone could deliver it on time."

"Came in about an hour ago. Willard and Marcus got some horses ready real quick. Marcus even packed some food in the saddlebags. I reckon you'll have enough to make it out to the plantation."

Harold breathed a sigh of relief. "Thank you." He scanned the station platform for Matthew, who was waiting for their luggage. "We have some bags coming off the train. Is there a driver who can take them up to Thomas Cromwell's house? We'll have someone from the plantation pick them up at a later time."

"Yes'sir. I'll take care of that for you. I reckon I'm looking for bags for Mr. Harold Justin and Mr. Matthew Justin? I'll get them up the hill for you."

Harold managed a heartfelt smile. "I appreciate it. What's your name?"

"Arthur Ralston, sir."

"Thank you, Arthur." Harold pulled a wad of bills from his pocket and thrust them into the man's hands.

Arthur shook his head and handed it back to him. "Thank you, sir, but no. Willard told me you wouldn't have asked for something like this if you didn't need it real bad. He paid me extra to do this and told me to treat you and Mr. Matthew like family. I ain't gonna let family pay me."

Harold reached out and gripped Arthur's hand. "Thank you again."

Turning, he spotted Matthew standing on the platform. "Matthew!" he hollered, beckoning his brother over when he looked his way.

"I don't have the baggage yet," Matthew said. "You can't have possibly been to the stables and back in this amount of time."

Harold nodded. "You're right. Turns out they received the telegram we sent this morning. Arthur already has two horses ready for us. The saddlebags have food, and he's going to take our baggage to the house. We can leave now."

Matthew grinned and pumped Arthur's hand. "Thank you."

Arthur's smile dimmed as he looked at the sky. "It looks like our sunny day is going to be gone real quick. Rain is coming. The snow just melted, and the roads are going to be muddy. Rain ain't going to help. You sure the two of you want to ride all the way to the plantation? You won't be there until after dark."

Harold saw the hesitation on Matthew's face, but his angst hadn't lessened. He didn't know what was wrong, but his certainty that something was very much wrong was growing. "Thank you, Arthur, but I'm going now."

"Which means I am," Matthew said with a smile. "A little rain never hurt anyone."

Harold gave him a look of gratitude. He suspected they were in for a long, miserable ride.

"Harold?" Susan whispered weakly as she opened her eyes.

Carrie reached for her hand, relieved to find it wasn't quite as hot as it had been earlier. "It won't be long, Susan," she said soothingly. "He'll be home tomorrow."

Susan slumped back against the pillow in disappointment.

Carrie reached out and smoothed back her matted hair. Her friend didn't look like the same woman she'd been when her husband left two weeks earlier. The fever had burned off a lot of weight from a body that hadn't needed to lose a pound. Her cheeks were gaunt, her eyes were still bright with fever, and coughs wracked her body. "How does your head feel?"

Susan frowned. "Hurts," she whispered. "Not as bad, though."

"Your fever seems to be coming down," Carrie told her. "You still have one, but it's not as high." She was encouraged by how much more aware Susan was. She was still very sick, but she was coming back.

Susan gazed around the room for a minute and then reached her hand down to her abdomen, which had not yet begun to show her pregnancy. First moms usually began to show between twelve and sixteen weeks. She looked up at Carrie, her eyes full of apprehension. "How is my baby?"

Carrie wasn't going to let her friend know how uncertain she was. Susan needed confidence and hope more than anything right now. "I have no reason to believe your baby is anything but fine," she said calmly. "It's her mama that I'm worried about."

Susan's eyes searched Carrie's face.

Carrie fought to look back steadily, not flinching away from the probing stare.

Susan finally slumped against the pillows again as a spate of coughing took control of her.

Carrie held Susan's shoulders with one arm while she spooned a tea infused with garlic and honey into her mouth. She'd had the homeopathic remedy thirty minutes earlier. Now that her fever was coming down, she wouldn't need it as often.

When the coughing stopped, Susan took shallow breaths. "How long before my lungs heal?"

Carrie hadn't mentioned the word pneumonia when Susan was awake, but she wasn't surprised her friend knew the symptoms. "I don't have the answer for that," she said honestly. "You've been very sick."

Susan seemed to accept her vague answer for now. "Others?"

Carrie knew Susan's thinking of others was another good sign that she was getting better. "There have been many who caught the flu, but only you and Miles developed pneumonia."

Susan's eyes flew to her face. "Miles? Is he alright?"

Carrie wished she knew the true answer to that question, but she trusted Janie. "He will be," she said firmly, choosing to believe what she didn't actually know. "Neither of you are going to be doing much work for a while, however."

"Amber?"

"She's fine. She got the flu, but she recovered quickly. She was back in the barn with Clint after just three days." She answered the next question she saw on Susan's lips. "Clint never got sick."

"He's been doing everything?" Susan asked.

Carrie knew if she continued to talk, the coughing would only get worse. "I'll answer this question, but no more. You need to rest. Clint is running things, but everyone is pitching in. Father is working. So are Hazel and Phoebe, when they're not checking on sick students. Bart has been at the stable every day. Anthony told Bart he has been invaluable."

Susan managed a slight smile. "Amber must be happy," she whispered.

Carrie grinned "I suspect that is true. Rose closed down the school for a week. Her first day back will be tomorrow. The sick students are on the mend, and no one else has gotten sick for the last two days."

Her determination to get Gelsemium to every family as soon as they'd discovered the flu had lessened its severity. "Sick students can't return to school until their fever is gone, and they've felt good for a week, but things will be back to normal soon."

"Everyone...alright?"

Carrie frowned at the increasing weakness in Susan's voice. "No more questions." She held Susan up as she gave her some water, and then laid her back gently on the pillow. "Get some rest."

Susan opened her lips to protest, sighed, nodded slightly, and closed her eyes. Moments later, she was asleep.

Matthew had anticipated misery but had apparently miscalculated exactly how bad it would be. He tightened his lips as rain dripped off his hat. He appreciated the rain slickers Arthur had brought them, but the cold rain was more miserable than snow would have been. Water dripped around his collar, stinging against his cheeks when the wind blew harder.

The horses were struggling in the mud. Matthew was afraid one of them would slip into a wagon rut in the dark and break a leg.

Harold continued to push ahead.

When his horse slipped yet again, Matthew hollered loud enough to be heard through the rain and wind. "We have to get off the road!"

Harold pulled his horse to a stop and turned in the saddle. "What are you talking about?" he asked impatiently.

Any irritation Matthew was feeling vanished. There was just enough light to see the fear shining in his brother's eyes. "It's too dangerous for the horses," he said as he pulled his gelding to a stop next to Harold's mare. "If one of them breaks a leg, we won't be able to make it. Not to mention the fact that we'll be destroying a valuable animal who doesn't deserve to die this way."

Harold opened his mouth to argue, but snapped it closed as Matthew's logic filtered through his fear. "You're right," he muttered. "What are we going to do?"

"We're going to leave the road and ride up through the fields. They'll be wet, but they haven't been turned into dangerous mud by wagons and carriages. They're all bare now, so we should be able to make better time."

"Lead the way," Harold said. "At least we're headed in the right direction." He tried to peer through the darkness. "Do you know where we are? I thought I knew this road fairly well, but I can't get a feel for how far we've come."

Matthew understood. The rain and the dark confused everything, except the landmark he'd been looking for. "We have about an hour left."

"Are you certain? How do you know?"

"There's an oak tree a few hundred yards back that has a huge stone in front of it. I watch for it every time I make this trip, because I know I'm not too far from the plantation when I see it. We're moving slowly, but we should still make it in an hour or so."

Mathew urged his mount up a small incline on the side of the road. He could feel Harold behind him. He breathed a prayer of gratitude when he felt more solid ground beneath them. They still couldn't go faster than a walk in the darkness, but he was no longer afraid of the horses injuring themselves.

He steeled himself against the cold rain and focused his thoughts on the fact that he would soon be home with his family.

They would also have an understanding of Harold's insistence they return home tonight. He hoped it was unjustified, but his gut told him it was something bad.

Carrie had finally drifted off to slumber on the mattress Anthony had hauled into Susan's room so she would instantly be aware if her friend needed anything. For the first time, she had felt at peace when she fell asleep, confident Susan was on the mend.

The patter of rain on the roof wrapped them in a warm cocoon as the flicker of flames from the fireplace filled the room with gentle warmth.

Granite galloped through the pasture, his beautiful head raised proudly, his tail waving like a silver flag in sharp contrast to his iron-gray body. He ran like the wind, calling out his joy as he floated over the green grass spread beneath him.

Carrie leaned against the fence, laughing as he leapt, bucked, and turned to race back in the direction he had come from. Finally, he slowed down to a high-stepping trot, his dark eyes pinned on her as he drew closer. Slowing to a walk, and then a stop, he snorted loudly and lowered his muzzle for her to stroke his face the way he loved.

With tears in her eyes, Carrie reached out her hand to once again touch her beloved horse...

"Ohhhh...."

A pained cry jolted Carrie from her dream. She blinked as her mind struggled to return to Granite.

"Ohhhh...!" Another sharp cry split the dark room.

"Susan!" Carrie leapt up, lit the lantern quickly and rushed over to the bed.

Susan was clutching her abdomen, her eyes wide with pain and fright. "Carrie!"

"What is it?" Carrie asked, praying her voice didn't betray her own fear. She was achingly certain she knew the answer.

Susan gasped again. "It hurts...so much..."

Carrie pulled back the covers, confirming what she already knew. A pool of blood stained the sheets. Moving quickly, she lit two more lanterns to flood the room with light, and then did a quick examination.

One glance into Susan's eyes told her she understood what had happened.

"My baby..."

Carrie's heart broke at the agonized pain in Susan's voice, but her immediate concern was to make sure she didn't hemorrhage from the miscarriage. She would help her friend deal with the loss of her child once she had ensured she would live. She wished Polly, an experienced midwife, were here to help her, but she was on her own.

The clatter of boots on the porch caused alarm to pulse through her. Harold wasn't due home until the next day. The only reason Anthony would be out on such a blustery night was if something were wrong. She steeled herself for more bad news.

"Carrie?" Susan's whisper was more demanding. She seemed oblivious to the sounds outside.

Carrie wanted to go see who had arrived, but her primary job was to care for her patient. "You've miscarried," she said as gently as possible. "I've got to stop the bleeding."

Susan began to weep, the words removing the final shreds of denial. "My baby," she whimpered.

The clatter of boots ended at the bedroom door. Moments later, the shadows filled with broad shoulders.

"Harold!" Susan cried, before she collapsed in a fit of coughing. "Harold..." The single word came out in a gasp this time.

Harold shot Carrie a panicked look and took two giant steps to Susan's side, grasping her hands as he gazed down at her.

Carrie knew he must be horrified by Susan's condition, but he stroked her hair gently and gave her a soft kiss.

"I'm home. I'm home." His voice cracked on the last word.

"The baby..." Susan's voice broke as the tears began to flow again. *"Our baby..."* The effort sent her into another spasm of coughing.

Harold looked up and locked eyes with Carrie.

He needed an explanation. "Susan has been very sick. She caught the flu and it turned into pneumonia. She had a very high fever for the last four days. She's better now," Carrie added quickly, wanting to alleviate the fear pulsing in Harold's eyes.

"The baby?" Harold asked hoarsely.

Watching the pool of blood grow on the sheets had brought to life her own grief of Bridget being stillborn. There was no room for that tonight. *Carrie knew the two of them needed to express their emotions without dealing with her own sense of loss.*

Carrie kept her voice even. "Your baby has miscarried. Susan was barely through the first trimester, so the baby was vulnerable. I suspect the fever caused the miscarriage." She watched the light die in both Harold and Susan's eyes.

She knew that Susan, shocked by Harold's sudden, almost miraculous appearance, had grabbed onto an unreasonable hope that perhaps the miscarriage wasn't real—that it hadn't actually happened.

Susan began to weep again. Harold leaned in closely, gripped her hand, and stroked her cheek while he kissed her forehead.

Suddenly, Harold stopped and pinned Carrie with another gaze. "Is she really going to recover?"

"She's going to be fine," Carrie said firmly, grateful beyond words that she knew that was true. "The blood you see is from the miscarriage, but she's not hemorrhaging. I'm going to give the two of you a little while, and then I'll be back in to clean up and give her a bath." She gestured toward the table. "Please give her some water."

Matthew rose from a chair in the living room when Carrie emerged from Susan's room. "Should I go get Janie?"

Carrie gasped and held a hand to her heart. "Matthew!" She should have realized he would be there, but she hadn't been expecting anyone else.

"I'm sorry," Matthew apologized. "I didn't mean to frighten you."

Carrie's heart resumed its steady beat. "I'm glad you're here," she said quickly. She glanced out at the darkness and heard the steady drum of rain. "What are you two doing here?"

"Harold knew something was wrong," Matthew said gruffly. "We came in on the train today and rode out here."

Carrie calculated quickly. "In the dark? In the rain?"

"He wasn't willing to wait until tomorrow. He believed Susan needed him."

Carrie glanced behind her. "He was right," she said softly. She explained the situation as lines of sorrow creased Matthew's face.

"Harold was excited about having a new family."

"Susan can get pregnant again," Carrie said. "The fever was too much for a young pregnancy, but she's strong. They can have another child. Miscarriage is common, but most women go on to have successful pregnancies."

"Susan will get well?" Matthew's eyes demanded honesty.

"Yes," Carrie replied confidently. "She's still ill, she's weak, and it will take her time to recover, but I believe she'll be back to herself before spring."

Matthew nodded, relief shining in his eyes. "Should I go get Janie?" he asked again.

Carrie thought for a moment. "No," she said slowly. "I can handle this on my own, but I need some herbs to treat Susan's blood loss. I hate to keep you out any longer than necessary on a night like this..."

"I'll do whatever is needed," Matthew replied before she could ask the question. "From the house or the clinic?"

"The clinic is closest," Carrie answered. "Everything is well marked." She pulled a key from her deep pocket and handed it to him. "I need a bottle of yarrow to help with the blood loss." Her mind raced as she thought of all Polly had taught her about helping with miscarriages. "Bring me a bottle of red raspberry leaves, too." Raspberry tea would nourish Susan's body, help with the blood loss, and maintain good iron levels.

Matthew turned to leave, but then spun back around, anxiety shadowing his tired face. "Janie and the children?"

"They're fine," Carrie said quickly. "I should have told you that already. None of your family has been sick. Most people are on the mend, but Miles is still fighting pneumonia. Janie is confident he will be fine as well. We've been very lucky."

Matthew tightened his lips and looked at the closed bedroom door. His message was clear.

"Matthew," Carrie said gently. "They lost the baby, but Susan will live. That is *good* news."

"Yes," Matthew agreed quietly. He turned, stepped out onto the porch, and closed the door behind him.

Carrie breathed a prayer of gratitude that Matthew was getting her what she needed before she took a deep breath and walked back into the room. Susan was still weeping, but her sobs had turned into a stream of tears. Harold sat on the edge of the bed, stroking her hair and talking gently.

"Are you in pain, Susan?" Carrie asked.

Susan stared at her, confusion clouding her exhausted features. "Pain?"

"Are you cramping? Do you have a headache?"

Susan closed her eyes against the questions but nodded slowly. "Yes," she whispered.

"What can I do?" Harold asked.

Carrie knew giving Harold a task would help him through the night. "Please heat pots of water. I want to give Susan a warm herbal bath and keep hot compresses on her belly. It will help alleviate the pain."

Harold kissed Susan again before he sprang into action.

Twenty minutes later, as the first pots of water were hot enough, Matthew strode through the door with the requested herbs.

"Thank you," Carrie said fervently. "Susan keeps a bag of feed outside in the shed. I'm certain both your horses are hungry. There is also a pail for water."

Matthew nodded and disappeared out into the cold rain again.

Carrie helped Susan ease into a bath prepared with yarrow, rosemary, lavender, sage, garlic, shepherd's purse, and salt. The fragrant water would fight against any infection from the bleeding. She carried the herbal combination in her medical bag at all times.

While Susan bathed, she drank a warm tea made with yarrow and raspberry leaf. Her eyes were dull, and she hadn't spoken since she'd acknowledged the pain.

Carrie remained silent, letting her presence speak as Susan sank into the warm water. It was the first bath she'd taken since she'd fallen ill five days earlier. Her body would feel better, but Carrie knew her heart and soul would take longer to heal. It didn't matter if you lost your child at three and a half months, or if they were stillborn...a part of you was lost forever and you needed to grieve that loss.

Harold entered twice to pour more hot water into the bath. He stroked Susan's wet hair and kissed her, but seemed to also realize that silence was what she needed more than anything.

Each time he left, Susan sank back into the water, her blank gaze fixed on the fireplace.

A quiet murmur from the living room revealed Matthew was staying with his brother.

"How?"

Carrie took a deep breath when Susan spoke for the first time. Her friend wanted to know how to survive the loss of her child. "Very slowly, Susan. You're going to feel fragile. Physically and emotionally." She searched for the right words. "You have to give yourself time to grieve. I know you're a strong woman, but you can't just jump right back into life."

"I don't feel like jumping," Susan said flatly.

"I know," Carrie sympathized. "You're dealing with a double blow. You're having to heal from pneumonia at the same time you're dealing with your miscarriage. I'm sorry."

"I'll heal?"

"In every way," Carrie assured her. "I didn't want to live when Robert and Bridget died. When I lived anyway, I was mad that I wasn't dead." She saw no reason to not be honest. She knew what Susan was feeling. While she acknowledged that losing a child to miscarriage was not the same as having your husband murdered and your full-term baby stillborn, pain was pain. When it came to the heart, there were no *degrees* of pain. There was simply pain. It was human nature to want to avoid it.

Susan shifted her gaze from the fire and looked at Carrie. She remained silent, but she was listening.

"It's still too fresh, but at some point, you'll want to talk about it," Carrie encouraged.

"Did you?" Susan asked.

"No, not for a long time. It's one of my biggest regrets," Carrie answered. "I locked myself in misery, but I also locked the people who cared about me in misery because they couldn't help me." As she spoke, she thought of Caroline, wondering how she was doing since Octavius' murder. "Every time you can talk about how you're feeling, it releases a little bit of the hold it has on you." She smiled gently. "I'm here to listen anytime you want to talk."

Susan nodded slightly and fixed her eyes on the fireplace again.

The wind had picked back up. The rain that had drummed against the roof was now hammering. Either the wind was blowing harder, or the rain had turned to sleet. Carrie suspected the latter.

"I miss my baby," Susan whispered.

"I know," Carrie whispered back. She stepped forward with a thick towel. "Let's get you out of the tub and back into bed." While Susan bathed, Carrie had put fresh sheets and pillows on the bed. There was a pitcher of water and a cup of warm tea for her to drink.

Once Susan was dry, Carrie slipped a flannel nightgown over her gaunt frame.

Susan rubbed a hand down her flat belly, sighed and lay back against the pillows. "Harold?"

"I'll get him for you," Carrie replied. "Be honest with him, Susan. He just lost a baby, too. After losing his two daughters already, please let him be honest with you."

Susan met her eyes, nodded, and slumped back as her eyes fell closed.

Within moments, she was sound asleep.

Carrie laid a hand on her forehead, grateful to find it cool and dry. She had added chamomile and lavender to the last cups of tea to help Susan sleep. She hoped her friend would rest through the night.

"What should I do?" Harold asked anxiously.

"Just love her and be there for her," Carrie answered. "She's lost her child, but she's also still battling pneumonia. Not being able to go to the stables or ride will make her recovery from the miscarriage harder, but she can't even think of going to the barn for at least two weeks," she said firmly.

Harold listened intently.

"Susan's lungs were damaged with the pneumonia. Her body was weakened by the fever. She's lost a lot of weight, but it will come back." Carrie glanced around the house. "I'll have Annie send over lots of soup."

"No need," Harold replied. "I've been making soup for a long time. I'll take care of it."

Carrie felt a twinge of pain as she thought of the years Harold lived alone after his first wife and his two young daughters died from cholera when he was away on an assignment. She felt a flash of gladness that Susan would live. Losing their unborn child was painful, but to lose his wife would have been a blow Harold might not have recovered from. "Susan is going to be fine," Carrie said, certain Harold would need to hear those words often. "She'll be back to herself in two to three months. If she feels like going for walks, go with her. If she needs to cry, let her cry." Carrie paused. "If you need to cry, go ahead." She smothered a smile when Harold looked away, clearly uncomfortable.

"The Justin brothers don't really cry," Harold muttered.

"Speak for yourself," Matthew said. "It doesn't happen very often, but I've decided it's not a sign of weakness. Sometimes it's the only way to get through the hard times."

"Your brother is wise," Carrie said with a smile. "You should listen to him."

Harold stared at Matthew. "How many times?"

"How many times what?"

"How many times have you cried?" Harold challenged. It was obvious he didn't believe him.

"You want me to count them?" Matthew asked incredulously.

"Yep."

Matthew screwed up his forehead. "Five times," he said after a lengthy silence.

Harold raised a brow.

"Twice when both my legs were broken during the Capitol collapse. Twice when I was confined to Rat Dungeon during the war. Once when Janie completely withdrew after the attack on the Bregdan Clinic this spring, and I felt so helpless." Matthew paused. "There are more now that I'm thinking about it, but that should be enough to convince you I mean it. I remember Dad telling us that a real man never cries." His eyes softened. "Abby was the first person who told me that wasn't true. It took me a while, but she convinced me. I'm certain being able to cry when I was in Rat Dungeon was the only thing that got me out of there alive, because I had an outlet for my emotions during one of the toughest times of my life." He smiled. "It got easier after that. I still mostly control my emotions, but when I really need to cry, I know there's no shame in it, brother."

Harold stared at Matthew for several moments before he nodded thoughtfully. "I suppose you have a point."

Carrie hid her grin. That was the closest Harold was going to come to saying Matthew was right. It didn't matter. If Matthew's transparency enabled Harold to help Susan and himself through the months ahead, that's what counted.

Suddenly, fatigue washed through Carrie, almost stealing her breath. Now that Harold was home, he could care for his wife.

"Can I borrow your horse, Harold? I want to go home. You have everything you need to take care of Susan, but I'll be back to check on her tomorrow."

Harold cocked his head. "It's dark, raining, and cold."

"I'm aware. You managed to make it from Richmond," Carrie replied wryly, amusement poking through the fatigue. All she wanted was to curl up in her own bed with her husband. A ride through cold rain was a low price to pay.

"I'll ride to the house with you," Matthew said.

Carrie shook her head. "You've already had an interminably long day, Matthew. You need to go home."

"And I will," Matthew agreed. "Just as soon as I know you're safe at home, as well. The sooner we leave, the sooner I'll be home."

Carrie nodded, grateful for the offer. "Thank you."

Anthony was wide awake when Carrie slipped into the bedroom at midnight. He helped her peel off her wet clothes, toweled her dry, slipped a soft nightgown over her head, eased her into bed, and pulled the covers over her shivering body.

Carrie sighed with contentment when he crawled in next to her and pulled her into his strong arms. She cradled her head against his chest. "I love you," she murmured.

"And I love you."

Carrie was asleep in an instant.

Chapter Nineteen

Rose smiled as she entered the house. She was tired after a long day at school, but the fragrant aroma of greenery revived her spirits. Taking another deep breath, she smelled a delicious whiff of cinnamon rolls and sugar cookies.

Christmas had come to Bregdan once more.

Moments later, John and Jed burst through the front door, their excited chatter filling the air. The boys had gone for a ride with Miles, his first after finally recovering from pneumonia. According to Annie, Carrie had watched over the elderly man like a hovering angel, insisting he stay inside long after he believed he was well.

"Did you have fun?" Rose called.

"Yes!" Jed answered. "Mr. Miles didn't act sick at all. He looked real happy to be back on a horse again."

"Grandpa *has* to ride," John said solemnly. "We didn't go very far, but he sure looked happy. He told me that being off a horse for that long was like cutting off an arm."

Rose suspected that was true. Carrie had refused to let her old friend work in the barn until she was convinced his lungs had healed. Though she had finally let him ride, she insisted he do no barn work until after the New Year. Miles was grumbling, but Annie was enforcing his compliance.

"Mr. Miles said Miss Annie be like a dictator," Jed added.

"Mr. Miles said Miss Annie *acts* like a dictator," Rose corrected. Her son's English was getting better and she didn't always correct him, especially since he worked so hard in school, but she also knew how important it was.

Jed's eyes danced with fun. "Mr. Miles said Miss Annie acts like a dictator," he repeated, enunciating each word clearly. "I believe the two of you are a lot alike."

Rose chuckled and waved a hand toward the kitchen. "The kitchen dictator has some cookies coming out of the oven if my nose is correct."

"Yes!" John yelled. He turned and ran for the kitchen. Moments later, the door swung closed behind him.

Jed stayed where he was, his large dark eyes roaming the hallway and parlor. "It looks different than this morning."

"It is," Rose agreed. "The men brought in big loads of greenery to put around the house. It smells nice, doesn't it?"

"Yep. Looks good, too," Jed replied, his face suffused with longing.

Rose waited quietly, knowing he would say more if she gave him time. Jed had come so far since his father died, but he still had deep moments of sadness. She was grateful he would talk about them when they came. She knew he had long conversations with Moses when they rode the plantation.

"I bet my mama would like this an awful lot," Jed said wistfully. "We ain't never had nothing like this for Christmas. Most times it was just something my daddy carved for me." His eyes grew fierce. "I loved all them carvings."

"They were special gifts," Rose agreed, realizing Jed must be thinking about how they had to be left behind in South Carolina. She thought through her next words. "I remember the first time I saw the house all decorated for Christmas. I just stood and stared, thinking it was the most beautiful thing I ever saw. When I was very little, I would be sent home to my cabin after a day of playing with Carrie. We never had anything like this either, Jed. When I was a little older, I moved into the house to be Carrie's personal maid. I got to see the Christmas decorations every year, but they were never for me." Vivid memories coursed through her. "I thought Christmas finery was only for white people. It never meant anything to me because it wasn't *for* me. It just made me feel bad that my mama and my friends couldn't have something beautiful of their own."

"And now?" Jed asked.

Rose smiled. "Now the decorations are mine. They belong to everyone in the house, Jed. That means they belong to you, too, because you're part of our family. It's alright to feel badly that your mama and daddy never got to experience a Cromwell Christmas."

Jed kept his eyes fixed on her. "*A Cromwell Christmas*," he said softly. "I reckon I like the sound of that."

Rose's love for the little boy grew each day. In spite of all that had happened to him, he had a strong spirit and a ready smile. She knew he loved living on the plantation, but he still held himself apart, as if he were afraid to open his heart too much. Letters came from Vincent every week. He read them avidly, reporting that Vincent liked his job at the factory and was already involved in the Philadelphia Republican Party. Jed loved the letters, but she didn't feel he regretted his decision to become part of their family. It was more that he didn't want to lose contact with his only remaining connection to his daddy, and to the night his mama was murdered.

Rose reached out and took one of his hands. "Christmas is going to be more special this year because you're here to share it with us."

Jed smiled at her statement. He looked like he was going to speak, but he stopped.

Rose waited patiently. When the silence stretched out but he still didn't seem like he wanted to leave, she prompted him. "Is there something you want to say?"

Jed hesitated briefly before forging ahead. "I reckon my mama and daddy would be real glad I'm here for a Cromwell Christmas."

"I believe that, too," Rose said softly, swallowing back her tears.

Jed looked around at all the Christmas greenery and then back at her. "You reckon they know?"

"I reckon they do," Rose replied, believing it with all her heart. "Jed, every parent wants their child to have good things. Your parents gave you the best they could because they loved you so much."

"They loved me," Jed agreed in a cracked voice. He turned piercing eyes to her. "Do you think your mama knows that Cromwell Christmases belong to you now?"

Rose smiled brilliantly. "Yes. My mama knows."

Jed didn't look away. "You sound pretty sure."

"That's because I *am* sure," Rose answered. "I believe my mama knows the life I have now. I also believe it makes her very happy."

Jed considered her words and then nodded, the tension and sadness fading away. He smiled brightly. "I'm real hungry. I'm gonna go get some cookies now."

"I'm *going to* go get some cookies now," Rose said playfully, knowing it was safe to correct him again.

Jed grinned and held out a hand. "You want to come with me?"

Rose swallowed hard and took hold of his small hand. "I would love to."

Three days later, the house was buzzing with activity.

"When will the Stratfords be here, Mama?" Frances asked.

"They should be here in a few hours," Carrie replied. "Their train arrived yesterday. They stayed at Grandpa's house in Richmond last night, but they should be on their way already."

Frances frowned. "Grandpa said it's going to snow today."

"Probably," Carrie agreed. She glanced out the parlor window. "I don't think it will come until later this afternoon, though." She'd watched the snow clouds gather in the distance and cover the landscape, but they weren't heavy enough to start dumping snow yet. "I believe the Stratfords will make it before it starts snowing."

"Daddy is coming with them?"

Carrie smiled. "He is. He's been working in Richmond, but he picked up the Stratfords so he can drive them here."

"And then he'll be home until after New Year's Day?"

Carrie cocked her head. "You know all this, Frances. Why are you asking me again?"

Frances shrugged. "Talking about it makes it seem more real." She gazed around the house, taking deep breaths of the cedar boughs' fragrant aroma. "I love all the red bows, don't you?"

"I do," Carrie replied. "They've always been one of my favorite parts about this time of year. Every time I see green and red, I think about Christmas."

"Me too," Frances agreed. "I guess we're a lot alike."

Carrie smiled happily. "I guess we are."

Frances moved on to a new topic. "When will Felicia be home?"

Carrie, aware her daughter knew the answer, continued to play the game. "Tomorrow."

"And Marcus, Hannah, and Willard are bringing her?"

"That's right. Your daddy has two other people running River City Carriages during the holiday, so they can come out to join us."

"That's good," Frances said somberly. She gazed up at Carrie, her eyes swimming with sadness. "This will be Uncle Willard's first Christmas since Aunt Grace died in the fire. I'm glad he won't be alone."

"So am I," Carrie replied softly.

Frances continued to stare into her eyes. "Do you think Jed will be sad, too?"

"Probably," Carrie answered. "It hasn't been very long since his parents died. I'm sure he will miss them," she said gently, knowing Frances was thinking about her own family.

"Yes," Frances agreed. "I remember my first Christmas after the flu killed my parents. I hadn't gone to the orphanage yet, and Mrs. Sider was very good to me even though she didn't have much, but I still missed my family every single minute."

Carrie stroked her brown hair gently, amazed at how fast her daughter was growing up. "I know you did, honey."

Frances closed her eyes for a moment, and then opened them again, seemingly determined to banish the sad thoughts. "Do you think Mrs. Sider has gotten her Christmas present yet?" she asked eagerly. "I mailed it over a month ago, just to make sure she receives it."

"It should have arrived," Carrie assured her. "It's still ten days before Christmas, though. I believe it will get there if it hasn't yet."

"And you really think she'll like it?"

Carrie smiled, completely confident in her answer. "A collection of the articles you've written for the *Philadelphia Inquirer*? She's going to love them! It will mean so much to her to know you have a good life now."

"I included one of those pictures they made of all of us in Richmond. I wanted her to see my whole family. She only met you and Grandma when you adopted me. I told her all about Minnie and Daddy in the letter. And Grandpa." Her eyes grew big.

"Sometimes it's hard to believe I have a whole family now."

Carrie hugged her warmly. "I know how you feel. It's still hard for me to believe sometimes that you and Minnie are truly my daughters. I'm a very lucky woman."

Frances buried her head in Carrie's shoulder and hugged her back tightly. "Do you have time for a ride, Mama? Just me and you? Before it starts snowing?"

Carrie didn't, but there was no chance she would refuse the invitation. "Definitely," she said brightly.

Frances smiled happily. "Minnie is helping Annie make pecan pies." She wrinkled her nose. "I love eating them, but is it alright that I don't like baking them?"

Carrie laughed. "Another thing we have in common. We both like to eat, as long as we don't have to cook!"

Carrie swung into No Regrets' saddle, watching as Frances settled gracefully onto Peaches' back.

"What are you looking at, Mama?"

Carrie smiled. "Just admiring what a good horsewoman you've become, dear. I'm proud of you."

Frances flushed with pleasure. "Where do you want to go?"

"Your choice, as long as we have time to get back before dark. That gives us a couple hours."

Frances' eyes grew wide. "What if we're not back before the Stratfords get here?"

"Grandma, Grandpa, and everyone else will take care of them until we return. It's not often that I have the chance to go riding alone with you. It's a treat I intend to enjoy."

Frances flushed again, her brilliant smile shining in her eyes. "I want to be just like you, Mama."

Carrie blinked back tears. Susan's miscarriage had brought back so much of the pain around losing Bridget. It had also driven home how lucky she was to have Frances and Minnie. Frances had told her a few days earlier that she wanted to go into practice with her when she became a doctor. Carrie knew her daughter's life and plans could change as she grew older, but the fact that she wanted to was thrilling. "We'll make a good team," she answered. "Nothing could mean more to me."

"Let's go to the river," Frances said eagerly. "I love watching the James River when the snow clouds are coming in."

"Me too," Carrie answered. "Lead the way."

Carrie enjoyed the easy trot and then the rolling canter. She admired Frances' seat in the saddle for a few minutes and then urged No Regrets to pull even with her. The mare hesitated a moment before increasing her speed to catch up to Peaches. Carrie frowned, sensing something in the mare that she hadn't before. There was no indication of lameness. Was she ill?

She was about to call out to Frances to slow down when she realized they had reached the edge of the woods. Her daughter pulled Peaches down to an easy trot and followed the trail through the trees.

No Regrets followed willingly, her body relaxed and fluid again. Carrie stayed alert for several minutes before she decided she must have imagined the problem.

"It's beautiful in the winter woods," Frances called.

Carrie smiled. Miles had taught her the beauty of the winter woods when she was a child. Obviously, he had passed it on to her daughter. For a long time, she had disliked the gray sameness of the trees when they were leafless, until Miles taught her to appreciate the sculpture that every tree formed. He taught her the beauty of splashes of red as the cardinals flitted through the gray and silver branches, and the allure of bright blue as blue jays danced among the limbs. She had learned to watch for the almost invisible gray squirrels, sometimes their twitching noses the only thing that gave away their presence on the side of an oak tree. Green cedars lent color to the scene.

"The whole world seems gray today," Frances said as she pulled Peaches to a walk.

"But look how many shades of gray," Carrie replied. "Every single thing seems to be just a little different, but they all blend together." The gray clouds blended with the tops of the leafless trees, white wisps floating among the lighter and darker clouds as they pressed closer to the earth.

They broke out onto the banks of the James River. The flowing water mirrored the snow clouds.

"It's going to snow soon, isn't it?" Frances asked eagerly. "Grandpa and Miles are teaching me how to read the signs. The clouds are getting heavier and heavier, and it's gotten colder since we left."

"You're getting good at reading them," Carrie said proudly. "It will be snowing before we get home."

Frances tilted her head up to the sky eagerly. "Do you think the snow will still be here for Christmas?"

Carrie shrugged. "How long it will last is something no one can predict ten days out. It could get warm enough to melt it, but I believe it will snow again before Christmas."

Frances frowned, but it faded away into a smile immediately. "I'll just enjoy it while it lasts," she said philosophically.

"That's one way we're not alike," Carrie teased. "You're much more patient than I am."

It was Frances' turn to frown. "Not really, Mama. I learned to pretend a long time ago. Pretending I'm patient makes it easier when I can't control what's going on."

Carrie tilted her head and marveled at her daughter's wisdom, while also feeling sad that she had endured so much pain. "You learned that on the wagon train trip to New Mexico?"

Frances looked sad as she thought about her brother who had died during the blizzard that almost claimed her entire family, but she shook her head. "Before that. Things were very hard during the war. We were hungry a lot and my mama cried every night. It didn't get easier when Daddy came home. It seemed to get harder, and then we left for New Mexico because he thought life would be better. We all almost died in that blizzard. We probably would have if it hadn't been for you. I thought things would get better when we went back home, but then everyone died anyway."

Carrie sucked in her breath when she listened to her daughter recount the massive losses of her young life in such a calm voice.

Frances smiled. "You don't have to look so sad, Mama. Life got better." Her voice faltered. "So much better than I could have imagined. I guess you have to wait out the really hard times long enough to reach the better times. When I'm pretending to be patient, I'm waiting out the hard times until the better times come."

Carrie sucked in her breath, thinking about all the hard times they'd been through in just the past few months. As Christmas came to Cromwell, she prayed it was the beginning of the better time.

"I love you," Carrie said softly. "You're very special."

Frances smiled back, but her eyes widened as she looked down. "There it is!"

Carrie followed her gaze but saw nothing to elicit Frances' exclamation. "There *what* is?"

Frances slid down from Peaches and knelt on the beach. "You know how much Minnie loves to gather rocks on the beach?"

Carrie nodded. Her youngest daughter had a collection of rocks from all over the plantation that lined her windowsills. She was content to search for them for hours.

"I've been looking for a white quartz to give her as a Christmas present," Frances explained. Still kneeling, she found a smaller stone and dug in the riverbank. A few moments later, she held up a piece of quartz. "It's even bigger than I thought!" She grinned as she held up the fist-sized piece of quartz. "Minnie has some quartz, but nothing this big. It will be beautiful when I wash it."

Suddenly, her grin faded. "Mama!"

Carrie stiffened, looking around with alarm. There hadn't been an attack on the plantation for a long time, but they all knew it wasn't safe to lower their guard. Nothing but stillness met her searching gaze.

"Mama! Something is wrong with No Regrets!" Frances remained on her knees, staring at the mare's underside.

Carrie slid from the mare immediately. Her eyes widened as soon as she knelt beside Frances and looked up. "Well, I'll be," she muttered.

"What's wrong with her?" Frances asked fearfully.

Carrie chuckled. "Nothing. No Regrets is going to be a mother soon." She shook her head in amazement. "We were assured none of the mares we bought this fall were pregnant. Evidently, they were wrong."

"She's going to have a *baby*? How do you know?"

"Let's head home. I'll explain on the way." Carrie was suddenly anxious to have No Regrets in a stall deep with fresh straw.

Frances sprang into Peaches' saddle, waited for Carrie to mount, and then turned to her eagerly. "She's really going to have a baby? When?"

"Soon," Carrie said, letting the realization seep into her mind. "The normal gestation for a mare ranges from three hundred and twenty to three hundred and sixty-two days. Susan and I watch the mares very carefully when they're due to foal. Clint, Amber, and Miles watch with us. Most changes in a mare occur in the last month of her pregnancy," she explained as her mind spun with the surprise. "They're subtle in the beginning, but we missed all the signs because we had no reason to look for them."

"And now?"

"No Regrets has already developed an udder and her teats are swelling. That's what you saw when you thought something was wrong."

Frances listened closely. "When do you think she'll have her baby?"

Carrie knew her daughter wanted a more succinct answer than her cryptic *soon*. "Within the next two weeks."

"Two *weeks*?" Frances looked as astonished as she felt. "Why doesn't she look pregnant?"

Carrie answered her question with a story. "When I was fourteen, Miles brought home a mare for me to learn jumping."

Frances grinned. "The secret jumping lessons your mother and Grandpa didn't know anything about?"

Carrie returned her grin. "Yes, those were the ones. Anyway, I loved riding Sunny Girl. She was smart and willing and could jump anything. I never jumped very high on her, but it was wonderful fun. One day, she seemed hesitant to go over the jumps that Miles had set out. I wasn't feeling very well that day anyway, so after a little while, we went back to the stables. I groomed her, fed her, and let her out into the pasture." She shook her head. "The next morning, she didn't come for her feed. Miles went out into the pasture and found her with her colt."

Frances gasped. "She had a baby the same day you were taking her over jumps?"

Carrie nodded. "We couldn't believe it either. She never looked pregnant, and she never acted pregnant. It doesn't happen often, but Miles assured me it could. And obviously, it did."

"Was Sunny Girl alright?"

"Perfect," Carrie confirmed. "You would have thought she leapt over jumps and had a foal every day. It didn't faze her a bit, and her colt was fine. We kept them both for four years, until Grandpa sold them."

"Why?"

Carrie frowned. "Because Grandpa knew America was going to war soon."

Frances met her eyes. "It was after Miles had run away with the other slaves?"

"Yes," Carrie acknowledged. "With no one to take care of all the horses, Father sold them."

"Except for Granite."

"Except for Granite. Father would never have broken my heart by selling him."

"I'm glad," Frances said softly. Then her brow furrowed. "Will No Regrets be alright? Isn't it awfully cold to be having a baby?"

"It's not ideal," Carrie admitted, "but now that we know the baby is coming, she'll stay in her stall where we can watch her carefully. I'll teach you how to test her mammary secretions each day. She'll let us know when it's about to happen."

Frances nodded eagerly. "You'll be with her, won't you?"

"I'll do my best," Carrie promised. "We never let a mare foal on her own if possible. It usually happens without a hitch, but we want to be there just in case. With it being so cold, the foal will be more at risk."

"Can I be there, too, Mama?"

Carrie nodded.

"Any time, day or night?"

Carrie chuckled. "I promise I'll have someone wake you up when it happens. Mares can give birth at any time, but it's usually at night."

As they broke out of the woods, the snow began to fall. Huge, fluffy flakes floated from the sky, dancing as the wind swirled them in a white waltz.

"It's snowing!" Frances cried. She held out her hand and watched as flakes landed on them.

The flakes fell faster. Carrie wanted to hurry, but now that she knew the truth of No Regrets' condition, she wasn't willing to push her. She allowed her to move forward at a ground-eating walk, but wouldn't let her go faster. They would still get home before dark.

Chapter Twenty

Susan stared at Carrie with amazement when she delivered the news the next morning. "No Regrets is pregnant?"

"*Very* pregnant," Carrie answered. "As in, I believe she'll give birth in the next two weeks pregnant."

Susan's eyes widened as she absorbed the news. "We're going to have a foal from Lexington?" she asked with awe.

Carrie grinned. "Once I got over the shock of her being pregnant, that's all I've thought about. I can hardly wait to see her baby."

Susan stood and paced around the room. "How much longer are you going to keep me a prisoner in my home?" she asked impatiently.

Carrie eyed her friend. She knew she was being overcautious, but Susan didn't realize just how close she had come to dying. She'd gained back most of the weight she'd lost. Harold had plied her with soup, bread, and vegetables canned during the summer. Her breathing sounded strong, and if irritation was a sign of good health, she was ready to be set free. There were still moments her eyes filled with sadness, but that was to be expected.

"Quit staring at me like you think I might faint away at any moment," Susan demanded with exasperation.

Carrie laughed. "I'm not, actually. I'm wondering if I clear you to return to the barn, whether you'll refrain from any physical work for another month, and then only light work through the end of February. I realize you're better, but it really is going to take you another two months to build your strength back. If you push too hard right now, especially in this weather, you'll keep your lungs from healing." She paused and fixed Susan with a steely gaze. "Your pneumonia can come back."

"I know. I know," Susan said. "I can follow your orders."

Carrie bit back a grin at her compliant tone. Her friend's snapping eyes told the truth.

"Besides," Susan added. "Do you really think Clint and Amber will let me do anything? Amber has been to see me several times. She's even worse than you are. Evidently, Polly has convinced her I came close to dying."

"You did," Carrie said quietly.

Susan took a deep breath. "I know it's true, but I prefer to not focus on that." She walked over and stared out the window. "I'm going crazy here, Carrie. I need to be back in the barn with the horses, even if all I do is breathe in the smells. I need Silver Wings. I truly do know how close I came to dying. Since I prefer to live, I'm not going to anything stupid. I promise."

This time, Carrie believed her. "You'll keep drinking the yarrow and raspberry tea every night and morning?"

"I promise," Susan said solemnly.

"You'll rest in the house if you get tired?"

"I promise."

"You'll eat everything Annie cooks for you?"

Susan hesitated before answering. "Carrie, you know Annie will want me to eat the same amount of food Moses eats. I don't think it's humanly possible for me to do that."

Carrie laughed. "I know. I just wanted to see if you would agree to something absurd."

Susan glared at her. "Well? If it were up to me, I would ignore you and go back to work. However, Harold made me promise to do whatever you say."

Carrie knew the dark shadow in Susan's eyes revealed how frightened Harold had been when he returned home. If nothing else, Susan would never do anything to cause her husband pain.

Carrie remained hesitant, but the pneumonia was only part of her decision. Susan would heal more quickly from the miscarriage if she returned to the barn and the horses. Praying she wasn't making a mistake, she nodded slowly. "Okay."

Susan cocked her head. "Okay? Really? You're releasing me from prison?"

Carrie laughed. "I'm releasing you from prison," she confirmed. "I'll have Clint deliver a carriage in the morning. Harold can bring you over." When Susan opened her mouth, Carrie knew she was about to protest that she could ride over. She snapped it closed quickly, obviously not wanting to press her luck.

"Silver Wings has missed you," Carrie said softly. The big black mare with a white star pushed her head over her stall door every time someone walked in the barn, grunting with disappointment each time it wasn't Susan. She'd been out in the pasture for exercise every day, and Amber and Hazel had both ridden her, but the longing had never left the mare's eyes.

Susan sighed. "I've missed her, too. I've never gone this long without seeing her." She strode across the room and gripped Carrie's shoulder. "Thank you for saving my life, Carrie. I'm not sure I've ever really said thank you, but it comes from the bottom of my heart."

"You're welcome," Carrie replied as she stood and gathered Susan to her in a warm hug.

Rose smiled happily when she walked into the kitchen. Felicia, John, Jed, and Hope perched on chairs in front of the roaring fireplace, steaming mugs clasped in their hands as they talked and laughed with their grandma. Frances stood next to the window, watching the snow continue to gather as she ate a thick biscuit. Minnie, her face flushed from the heat and her red ringlets escaping her ponytail, was pulling a pan of biscuits from the oven.

"Mama!" Hope squealed. "Grandma made us hot chocolate!"

"And we're having pancakes this morning!" John added.

"And bacon!" Jed called.

Rose looked toward Felicia.

Her daughter rolled her eyes but smiled broadly. "Good morning, Mama."

Rose walked over and hugged her, thrilled to have her daughter close enough to hold. "I'm glad you're home, honey."

"Me too, Mama."

"I'm glad you're home too, Felicia," Jed said shyly.

Felicia smiled and reached over to ruffle his dark curls. She'd fallen in love with Jed instantly. It was easy to love the little boy, but Rose knew the reality of their shared experiences gave them a unique connection.

"Are you leaving for school now?" Felicia asked.

"Soon. This will be the last day before the Christmas break, though."

Annie slipped another pan of biscuits into the oven and then turned. "I reckon that be another good reason for a celebration," she said brightly. "With Felicia home, the Stratfords visiting, and Susan back on the mend, I figure I'm gonna cook all day so we can have a feast."

"What kind of feast, Grandma?" John asked eagerly.

"How about a giant pot of chicken and dumplings, some of them fancy rolls you like, and some apple pies?"

"Yummy!" John shouted.

Felicia grinned. "Since I'm part of the reason for celebration, can we add a pumpkin pie to the mix?"

"Pumpkin pie is for *Christmas*," Hope told her seriously.

"Christmas and *celebrations*," Annie assured her youngest grandchild. "Apple *and* pumpkin pie tonight."

Rose's stomach rumbled in advance of the feast.

Annie heard it and laughed. She held out a cloth-wrapped package. "I got you some sausage biscuits already made up."

Rose smiled gratefully. "Thank you."

"Can I go with you today?" Felicia asked.

Rose hid her surprise. Her daughter had been exhausted when she arrived home the day before. She'd expected Felicia would sleep in late, not dreaming she would want to accompany her to school. "I would love that."

"I've already eaten," Felicia revealed. "I came down early so I could spend some time with Grandma."

Rose met Annie's eyes over Felicia's shoulder. Her expression revealed she had been surprised too, but there was nothing in her eyes to indicate there was anything to worry about.

"Quit worrying, Mama," Felicia chided.

Rose widened her eyes in what she hoped would pass as an innocent expression.

Felicia laughed. "I know you're worried because you expected me to sleep in today. I simply want to spend as much time with my family as I can while I'm here. I miss all of you while I'm at school."

Rose hugged her again, relishing the feel of her daughter in her arms. "I'll quit worrying," she promised. "It's time to head to school."

"Did Daddy leave for the fields already?" Felicia asked as they pulled on their heavy coats, gloves, and hats.

"Your Daddy is still asleep in bed," Rose told them, anticipating a response.

Felicia's eyes sharpened with concern. "Is he sick?"

Rose laughed. "No. He's a plantation owner who had a very successful harvest, knows his men are doing what they're supposed to be doing, and simply didn't want to get out of bed on a cold, snowy morning." She didn't add that Moses had made it very difficult to leave the cocoon of their bed.

Annie's laughing eyes revealed she knew the truth.

Snow continued to fall as the carriage rolled down the road toward school, but it had lessened dramatically. Horses cavorted through the fields, their flashing hooves kicking up sprays of snow. Clint and Amber called to each other in the barn, their voices floating in the still air.

"Amber isn't going to school today?" Felicia asked with surprise.

Rose shook her head. "I reluctantly agreed to let her take off from school until we start back in January. With both Miles and Susan sick, it wasn't possible for Clint to do all the work himself. Even with Amber working, they're still behind, but at least it's not foaling season. Hazel and Bart come over after school to help, too."

"Bart?"

Rose raised a brow. "You haven't talked to Amber?"

"She has no time," Felicia complained. "I went to the barn yesterday afternoon before dinner to talk to my best friend, but she was doing a million things." She returned to her question. "Who is Bart and what does he have to do with Amber?"

"Don't the two of you write during the school year?" Rose didn't want to be the one to tell Amber's secret.

Felicia's response was to stare at her. "Mama?"

Whether they corresponded or not, it was evident Amber hadn't chosen to tell her closest friend about Bart. "You should ask Amber," Rose finally said. "You haven't even been home twenty-four hours. I'm sure you can talk to her after school."

Felicia shook her head with frustration. "Why won't you tell me?"

Rose met her eyes. "Because I don't gossip," she said evenly. "Would you want me to reveal your confidences?"

Felicia sighed with defeat. "I suppose not," she admitted. "Can you just tell me if Amber is okay?"

Rose smiled, letting her dancing eyes portray all the message she was willing to give. "Amber is very much okay. I'm certain she'll tell you herself as soon as she has time."

Rose was glad to have some time alone with Felicia. They exchanged letters regularly, but it wasn't the same as talking in person. "How is school?"

"It's good," Felicia said quietly.

Rose frowned, her heart quickening. "That's not a very enthusiastic response," she observed.

"It's not an *unenthusiastic* response." Felicia refused to meet her eyes.

"What is it?" Rose asked as she took Felicia's hand. They had fifteen minutes before they would reach the school. At least they could start a conversation, even if it had to be finished later.

"I'm going to be seventeen next year," Felicia said.

Rose nodded, shocked at how fast time was flying. She could hardly believe the confident young woman sitting with her was the same frightened girl who had arrived at the plantation five years earlier after losing both parents. "Does that bother you?"

Felicia considered the question. "I've always loved that people thought I was older than I am. Or that they were so impressed with how smart I am. Or surprised by the fact that I'll be finishing college about the same time other students are beginning..."

Rose waited to see if she would continue, but Felicia remained silent. "And now you're not loving it as much?"

"I still love Oberlin, but I'm realizing that very soon I'll have to do something more than go to school," Felicia said slowly. "I've talked for so long about wanting to make a difference. Pretty soon, I'm going to have to actually *do* something."

"You still have another full year of college after you finish this year," Rose reminded her, though she completely understood how she felt. "You don't have to know all the answers right now." She looked deeply into Felicia's eyes. "What aren't you telling me?"

Felicia looked away and sighed heavily. "I wish you didn't always know."

Rose was glad her smile was hidden behind the thick scarf wrapped around her face. She used to say the same thing to her mama, but every single time, she was glad her mama knew what was really going on with her. She waited quietly, just like her mama had.

"I've been asked to do something very important."

Rose squeezed Felicia's hand for encouragement.

Felicia finally looked up and met her eyes. "Sojourner Truth came to Oberlin right before I left for home. She met with me and asked if I would travel with her this summer." She gulped. "She wants me to speak with her, and also chronicle the things she's doing."

Rose was once again glad for the scarf covering her mouth. She didn't want Felicia to see it gaping open with surprise. When she could form words, she lowered the scarf and smiled. "That's quite an honor," she said calmly. Since her daughter wasn't jumping up and down with joy, she had to assume she wasn't excited. "How do you feel about it?"

Felicia stared at her with disbelief. "Mama, it's *Sojourner Truth*. How do you expect me to feel about it?"

Rose wondered briefly if her mother had struggled as hard as she now was to let her daughter come to her own conclusions. "I don't know that I can have any expectations, Felicia," she said gently. "Only you know how you feel about it."

Felicia shook her head and kept her eyes on the road.

Jeb's broad shoulders outlined against the snow gave no indication he was listening to their conversation, but Rose knew he could hear every word. She and Jeb had become close during the years he'd driven her back and forth to school, keeping guard over the schoolhouse while she taught. Moses had offered to let him switch out with other workers, but he insisted he was happy doing what he was doing, and that he didn't trust anyone else to watch over Miss Rose as well as he could.

Rose waited quietly, wondering if they would have to finish the conversation after school.

"I'm scared," Felicia finally murmured. "Excited. Overwhelmed." Her voice grew smaller. "Mostly scared."

"What are you scared of?"

Felicia turned disbelieving eyes to her again. "Mama, I'm *sixteen*."

"You mentioned that before," Rose said evenly, praying she would speak the right words.

"Who listens to a sixteen-year-old black girl?" Felicia demanded.

"Evidently, Sojourner Truth believes the people she speaks to will listen to you. What did she tell you when she asked you to join her?"

"She told me that the people she speaks to need to hear it from both age groups," Felicia replied. "She said when people come to hear her, they're hearing from a very old woman who doesn't have much longer to live."

Rose was sad that Sojourner was probably right. She was seventy-four. How much longer did she have?

"She said they need to hear from someone who is very young, so that they can see the world has to change for my generation of black people in America. They need to know there are young people willing to take up the fight."

Rose knew the best thing she could do was to continue asking questions. "How do you feel about that?"

"Is that all you're going to do? Ask me questions?"

Rose smiled. "I know how frustrating it is," she admitted. "My mama did the same thing with me."

Felicia stared at her. "I suppose now you're glad she did," she said flatly.

Rose chuckled. "My mama knew me well enough to know I had to come up with my own answers, because I probably wouldn't believe anyone else." She paused. "I believe my daughter is just like I was."

"You were teaching a secret school in the woods, risking a beating every single day."

"I was," Rose agreed.

"You were much braver than I am," Felicia declared.

Rose allowed a full-throated laugh to escape. "Braver than *you*? Honey, I don't know any other girls who would have chosen to stay behind in Ohio when we returned to the plantation, just to could get the education you wanted at Oberlin. You've gotten a lot of support at Oberlin, but I know you've been lonely without us. It took great courage to keep pressing through to realize your dream."

Felicia eyes shimmered with vulnerability.

"I mean it, Felicia. You're very brave."

"Brave enough to travel with Sojourner Truth?" Felicia's voice wavered nervously.

"What do you think?"

Felicia groaned with frustration, clasped her hands tightly and closed her eyes.

Rose remained quiet, letting her daughter wrestle with her own doubts and fears.

"I *want* to be brave enough," Felicia finally whispered. "I want to let people know there's a whole generation of young black women who are willing to fight to make things better."

"It's what you've always wanted to do," Rose reminded her.

"Wanting to do something and actually *doing* it are two different things."

"You're so right," Rose agreed. Felicia's admission that she wanted to do what Sojourner Truth had proposed freed her to say more. "Honey, you're an extraordinary young woman. There are not many sixteen-year-olds who could do what Sojourner is asking, but I believe you can."

Felicia searched her eyes. "Mama, Sojourner Truth is a very famous woman. I know how much you respect her. She told me one of the reasons she chose me was because of you. She's very impressed with what you're doing with the school down here."

Rose swallowed her surprise. She was thrilled, but this wasn't about her. "What were the other reasons she chose you?"

"She told me my teachers said I'm a wonderful speaker. That I'm very passionate if I believe in something," Felicia replied. "She told me my age and my intelligence are something she wants others all around the country to experience because it will help change how others see black people."

"What else did she say?"

Felicia managed a smile. "She told me my story will encourage others, especially other black girls. She said the fact that I've accomplished so much, even after witnessing my parents' murder in Memphis, will help other people believe they can do things, even if they've had bad things happen to them."

Rose kept her expression neutral. "Do you believe she's right?"

Felicia blinked and then slowly nodded. "I suppose I *want* her to be right." Her expression tightened. "But what if she's wrong?"

"There's only one way to find out," Rose said gently.

The schoolhouse came into view, a number of children already milling around in the schoolyard.

"You and Daddy would agree to me going?"

Rose took a deep breath. This was the hardest question yet. "Felicia, I would be happiest if I could keep you right here on the plantation with me for the rest of my life. Your Daddy feels the same way. We've known for a long time, however, that your life is meant to be something much more. You will never fulfill all you're meant to do by staying here with us." She smiled. "I will miss you and worry about you every single minute you're on that trip, just as I do when you're at Oberlin. But your daddy and I would never stand in your way. We'll simply be your biggest supporters."

Felicia threw her arms around Rose as the carriage drew to a stop. "I love you, Mama," she whispered.

"I love you, too," Rose whispered as she swallowed her tears. She would make it through the school day, and then she would attempt to process the amazing conversation they'd just had.

Carrie smiled when she walked into the barn. Susan was standing in Silver Wings' stall, stroking the mare's muzzle while she whispered in her ear. Deciding not to interrupt them, she turned and went to No Regrets' stall. The bay mare snorted and swished her tail to indicate her unhappiness at being confined to the barn. She looked longingly toward the pasture.

"You can go out for a while," Carrie said soothingly. She slipped into the stall and knelt down. "As long as you're not about to become a mama." A single look confirmed it wouldn't be today.

"She won't give birth today."

Carrie looked up when Susan's voice sounded above her. "You're right. Welcome back, partner. I didn't want to disrupt your time with Silver Wings."

Susan smiled brilliantly. "I can't tell you how good it is to be back. I feel like I've come home."

"I understand completely," Carrie replied with a frown. "It's extremely cold today. You've got to keep that scarf around your face to protect your lungs from the cold air."

Susan pulled the scarf above her nose obediently. "Better?"

Carrie smiled at the gleam of fun in Susan's eyes. "You can't stay out here all day."

Susan's sigh was loud enough to be heard through the scarf, but her eyes continued to dance. Clearly, nothing could dampen her happiness. "Annie sent soup over for me and Miles. I'm going up to be with him in just a little while. I'll get warm, have soup, and rest until I'm ready to come back down. He's already made me promise to spend a lot of time playing checkers with him."

"That sounds like an excellent plan," Carrie conceded, and then remembered what Annie had told her to ask Susan. "Will you and Harold stay for dinner tonight? There's going to be a celebration meal."

"Celebrating what?"

"You being well enough to come back to the barn, for one. Miles' recovery, the last day of school, Felicia's homecoming, and the Stratfords' visit." Carrie chuckled. "Annie is going all out. I suspect the feast will be as lavish as what she'll fix for Christmas."

Susan hesitated. "You're going to let me stay here that long?" she asked skeptically.

Carrie grinned. "As long as you and Harold agree to sleep in the guesthouse."

"We'd love to," Susan agreed. "It sounds wonderful!"

"It's settled then," Carrie said happily, grateful life was returning to normal. "I'll let No Regrets out into the pasture for exercise. Miles can bring her inside after a few hours."

"That will make her happy," Susan responded. "I don't think this mare has any idea she's about to give birth. She doesn't act pregnant at all."

Carrie eyed the mare speculatively. "This must be one special foal. I'd love to know how she ended up pregnant. Most breeding facilities run a very tight ship. I've checked all the other mares we bought in September, and none of them appear to be pregnant."

"I went back and read all the letters between me and the seller. No Regrets had only been at his barn for five months. She came directly from the breeding facility where Lexington is a stud."

"That's why he didn't know she was pregnant," Carrie mused. "The breeders didn't know." She looked at No Regrets with admiration. "You were one determined lady."

No Regrets looked back at her calmly, snuffled and bobbed her head.

Carrie and Susan laughed loudly.

Carrie snapped on the lead line and led No Regrets from her stall. "I'm putting her out and then heading to the clinic. I have a lot of patients coming in today."

Susan frowned. "More flu?"

"No," Carrie said with relief. "Just a few colds, some broken bones and caring for a couple wounds. I'm looking forward to a completely boring day."

"Are you enjoying the plantation, Nancy?" Carrie had gotten her hoped-for boring day, and was now ensconced in front of a blazing fire in the parlor with a cup of hot tea completing the thawing out she needed after a ride home in the cold.

Nancy Stratford smiled brilliantly. "It's even more wonderful than all of you told me. The plantation is stunningly beautiful. I feel completely isolated from the world, while also being wrapped in endless amounts of love and warmth. And incredible food," she added.

"Wait until dinner," Minnie announced as she walked into the parlor with a plateful of cookies. "Annie's chicken and dumplings are the best things you ever ate!"

Nancy reached for a cookie. "I hear you're quite a cook yourself, Minnie. Did you help make these?"

"I made them all by myself," Minnie said proudly. "And I helped with the chicken and dumplings. Annie has promised to teach me everything she knows."

Carrie knew what a remarkable thing that was. Annie had only reluctantly taught Marietta to cook. Carrie was convinced Annie hadn't taught her everything. Annie's kitchen was her kingdom. She didn't share it with many people, and she wasn't eager to reveal her secrets.

"Have you always liked to cook, Minnie?" Wally asked from his place in a chair across the parlor where he was talking to Thomas.

Minnie frowned. "I don't really know," she confessed. "My mama was a very good cook, but she could never teach me because we never had much food at home. She would just bring home meals she cooked for Mama and Daddy." She hesitated, realizing how confusing she sounded. "I suppose I should say the food she cooked for Carrie and Anthony. Anyway," she said with a shake of her head, "I never did much cooking, but Annie tells me I must have gotten my mama's gift."

Wally knew the story. "Well, she must be right. I was talking to Annie, and she told me you're one of the finest cooks she's ever seen."

Minnie beamed with pride. "Thank you, Mr. Stratford. Would you like a cookie?"

"Just one. I don't want to ruin my appetite for the chicken and dumplings."

"Not just chicken and dumplings," Minnie replied. "We're having hot rolls, green beans, and apple and pumpkin pies."

Wally groaned with pleasure and rubbed his belly. "Thomas, you should have warned me I was going to leave the plantation a fat man."

"It's only fair that we share the hazards," Thomas said nonchalantly. "Are you up for losing another game of backgammon before dinner?"

Wally chuckled. "I've beat you three games in a row."

"Which means it is surely time for the tide to turn," Thomas replied. He reached under the table and pulled out the backgammon board. "It's your turn to lose, my friend."

Carrie watched the two men for a moment, before she turned back to Minnie with a smile. "You can leave the cookies, dear. I know you're eager to get back to the kitchen."

Minnie grinned. "Thank you, Mama. Miss Annie is teaching me how to roll out pie crusts today!" She laid the plate of cookies down on the table and disappeared in the direction of the kitchen.

"She's charming," Nancy said as she turned to Abby. "You have delightful grandchildren."

Carrie knew Nancy and Wally had met Frances when she returned home from school and extended an invitation for her to visit New York City. Frances had been eager to share the news as soon as she had arrived home. Carrie had willingly promised her a few days in New York on the way home from Elizabeth's wedding in Boston.

"My grandchildren are perfect," Abby agreed. "I'm the luckiest grandmother in the world."

"Only until Michael and Julie give me *my* first grandchild," Nancy teased.

"Believe what you want," Abby scoffed. "I will always know the truth."

Carrie chuckled at the old friends' banter. She closed her eyes and leaned back into her chair. The day hadn't presented any new crises, but all the days leading up to it had left her exhausted. Now that everyone was healthy and safe, she was tired to the bone.

"Are you alright, Carrie?" Abby's voice was warm with concern.

"I couldn't be better," Carrie assured her, too exhausted to open her eyes. "I'm just tired."

"You should be," Abby said sympathetically. "Pretend we're not here. If you fall asleep, I'll wake you in time for dinner."

Carrie decided that sounded like a fine idea. Moments later, she could feel her body slipping into slumber, lulled by the crackle of the flames, the wind blowing against the windowpanes, and the sound of laughter from the card games being played at the dining room table. The house was full, and everyone was safe.

Rose pulled back the covers and dove beneath them. She peered at Moses as he added fresh logs to the fire. "You won't be the only one who can sleep in tomorrow morning," she said contentedly.

Moses placed the final log on the flames, pulled the screen in place to keep embers from shooting out, and then crawled in next to her. "I'm happy about that, but I'm more interested in what you need to tell me. You had a funny look on your face all during dinner."

Rose explained the conversation she'd had with Felicia earlier that day.

Moses raised a brow in astonishment. "Our daughter is going to travel with Sojourner Truth?"

"Evidently," Rose replied. That fact was still working its way into her mind. Now that she'd had a day to think about it, she was no less astonished than she'd been that morning. She would never forget the thrill of being granted her diploma from Oberlin College by Sojourner Truth. She savored the fact that Sojourner's opinion of her had helped lead to this opportunity for Felicia. She'd admired the influential woman since she had learned about her in Philadelphia after her escape from the plantation.

"What an amazing opportunity," Moses said and then frowned. "But absolutely terrifying." His frown deepened. "Our daughter will be putting herself in front of so many people. Some of them will hate her and want to hurt her because of what she represents."

"I know," Rose said quietly. "I've thought about that all day."

Moses stared into the flames, thinking deeply. "It's what she's wanted ever since I brought her home from Memphis. All she has wanted is to make a difference. It's why she's worked so hard and learned so much." He turned to look at Rose. "Do you think she's ready?"

"I think I'm going to be terrified every single day," Rose said helplessly. "I suppose I'm counting on the fact that Sojourner believes she's ready. I'm also counting on Sojourner keeping her safe. She's stayed safe all these years, and she has powerful friends all over the country."

"Whom Felicia will meet," Moses said slowly, his voice filled with awe. "Our little girl is growing up."

Rose reached for his hand. "I believe Felicia has *grown* up," she corrected.

Moses cocked his head. "She's going to finish school after the summer of traveling, isn't she?"

"She promises she'll finish," Rose assured him. "I believe she will. Not because she's doing it for us, but because she's doing it as a way to make sure her dreams come true. I believe after a summer with Sojourner, she'll be even more committed to having a major influence over what happens in America."

Moses remained silent for a long time, gazing into the flames. "I'd say we did pretty well with our daughter," he finally said. "Her birth parents raised a remarkable child, and we've helped them by finishing the job. Felicia is an extraordinary young woman."

"I'd say you're right," Rose murmured. "I'd also say that calls for a celebration," she added coyly.

Moses turned to her, his eyes shining with desire. "A celebration? That's a fine idea, Mrs. Samuels."

Rose moved into his arms and let his kiss erase any lingering concerns about Felicia.

Chapter Twenty-One

"Hazel!"

Hazel stopped in her tracks on her way to the barn. When she saw Rose beckoning to her from the porch, she altered course and joined her. "Good morning. It's freezing. What are you doing outside?"

"Good morning," Rose said warmly. "I come outside for some fresh air every morning." She held up her mittened hands. "Some mornings are a little colder than others, but layers of clothes solve the problem. Are you working in the barn today?"

"Yes. I'm going to help as much as I can during the next week." Hazel's eyes shone with excitement. "I never get tired of being with the horses. Amber is going to have me ride some of the three-year-olds she's training."

Rose loved her twenty-two-year-old assistant teacher. Phoebe's best friend, Hazel was tiny but fierce. The five-foot-tall recent graduate of Oberlin College was loved by her students, as well. They had connected instantly with her easy smile and constant good humor, even when she was reprimanding them for something. She was an excellent teacher, and she'd become a good friend. "What else are you going to be doing?"

Hazel's smile brightened even more. "Well, I suppose there are a *few* things to be done before the wedding on Christmas Eve." Suddenly, she laughed and spun in a circle like a little girl. "Can you believe it, Rose? I'm about to become Clint's wife."

"Clint is a smart man. I can easily believe he chose you to be his wife, Hazel." Rose frowned and brought up the reason she'd called Hazel over. "Are you really at peace with your family not coming? Clint said he would go to Ohio to marry you if that's what you wanted. It's not too late to change your mind."

Hazel shook her head firmly, her finely carved features set in determination. "I'm not changing my mind. I love my family, and we'll go to Ohio to meet them as soon as we can, but my home is here on Cromwell Plantation now. Amber would be heartbroken if she couldn't stand up with me during the wedding. Gabe is going to give me away to his son. Polly is helping me finish my dress." Her eyes misted with tears. "I have an additional family down here. I want to share the happiest day of my life with them, and I want Clint to be able to share the day with them, as well."

Rose was convinced. "I'm thrilled you're getting married here," she confided. "I would have hated to miss it."

Hazel looked toward the parlor window. "I'm really getting married in the same place you and Moses did?"

Rose nodded, memories flooding her. "I met my daddy for the first time that night."

Hazel's eyes widened. "What?"

"My daddy was sold right after I was born. My twin brother, Jeremy, was also sold."

Hazel nodded. "Because he looks white. I remember."

"Anyway," Rose continued, "no one knew where my daddy was. Mama hadn't seen or heard from him since the day he was sold." That knowledge still filled her with sadness. Her mama and daddy only had one good year together before John passed away beside her in bed. She shook her head, casting away the sorrow. "Carrie found the plantation where my daddy was a slave. She bought him and then gave him his freedom. It was her wedding gift to me."

Hazel whistled. "That's quite a wedding gift."

"The best she could have given me," Rose agreed. "She kept my daddy hidden in the room above the barn for three days. It was empty after Miles escaped, so it was the perfect place. While I was in Carrie's room getting dressed, she went over and got him."

Hazel listened intently. "Was that the first time your mama saw him, too?"

Rose grinned. "No, Carrie made sure they had two days together before the wedding. When I walked to the top of the stairs, I looked down and saw a strange man with my mama. That's when Carrie told me who it was. He gave me away to Moses."

Hazel cocked her head. "I'm confused," she confessed. "If Jeremy is your brother...and he's white..."

Rose smiled. "I didn't know then that John wasn't my actual father, or that I had a twin brother. Mama hadn't told me yet about being raped by Thomas' father. Carrie didn't know either. For the year John was with us, he was the best daddy anyone could have had. He will always be that to me."

Hazel shook her head. "There are so many stories on this plantation," she said softly.

Rose shrugged. "Hazel, every person is a story. I remember Matthew telling me that every person is a book if you only take the time to learn their stories. I've decided he's right." She paused. "You have quite a story as well, my friend. Born into slavery in Georgia. Escaping to Oberlin, Ohio when you were twelve. Four months of travel on the Underground Railroad. Educating yourself and finishing college at Oberlin to be a teacher. And then you come down here and fall in love with a tall, handsome stable manager for one of the most successful stables in America."

Hazel laughed. "When you put it that way, I suppose I do have quite a story." She returned her gaze to the house. "And now the former slave is going to marry her tall, handsome stable manager in a magnificent Southern plantation mansion." She spun around again and clapped her hands. "It's all so romantic!"

Rose glanced at the barn. "Amber has told me several times how much she loves having you help her in the barn."

Hazel's eyes softened. "I love that girl. She's the little sister I always wished I had when I was growing up. I was the youngest of five, so I always dreamed of having a younger sibling. Amber is such a joy."

"She loves you, too," Rose assured her, then thought of something new. "You're positive you won't mind her wearing the yellow gown she wore at the tournament ball for your wedding? Gabe and Polly had talked her into a new dress. They were going to take her into Richmond, but then the flu hit. There's been no opportunity for her to leave."

Hazel waved a hand. "I don't care if she wants to wear her *breeches*," she said nonchalantly. "At the end of the ceremony, I'm going to be married. That's all that matters to me."

Rose chuckled. She knew Hazel meant that. "We'll at least get her out of her breeches," she promised. "How is your new house coming?"

Hazel's smile faded. "The flu certainly slowed things down. Clint was making good progress on it, but when Susan and Miles got sick, he had to stop working on it all together." Her frown melted into a smile. "I don't care, though. It will get built. In the meantime, we'll stay with Gabe and Polly. Phoebe offered to move into this house for a while so that Clint and I could use the guest house, but I don't feel right about that. It will be fine," she said firmly. "It's enough that we'll be married. I'm used to sharing. Once everything gets back to normal, Clint tells me he can finish the house within a month or so."

A series of ringing neighs split the cold morning air.

"I have to go, Rose. Amber needs my help feeding."

"Of course," Rose said quickly. She stood and moved toward the house. "I have some things to do, too. Have a good day." Her mind was spinning as she hurried into the house.

Carrie was concerned about Susan. Her friend seemed to be recovering from the pneumonia, but her sadness had increased over the last week.

"You look worried, Doc. Did I mess up my leg real bad?"

Carrie smiled, pushing aside her concern so she could focus on her patient. "No, Nathan. You're going to be fine." Carrie continued to stitch the wound she was working on. The cut was deep, but since Nathan had come in immediately after the wood-chopping accident, there was no worry of infection. "You did the right thing by coming in so quickly."

Nathan snorted. "My Lulu made me. She told me you talked to all the women at one of them Bregdan Women meetings about how to take care of things when you get hurt. I told her it weren't no big deal, but she made me come anyway."

"Your wife is much smarter than you are, Nathan," Carrie teased gently. "If you hadn't let me take care of this, it could have become badly infected. I'm assuming you're not interested in losing this leg?"

"No ma'am!" Nathan said with wide eyes. "I kept it all through the war. I don't figure on losing it now."

"Then you should go home and thank your wife for being a smart woman," Carrie retorted as she placed the final stitch and straightened her back.

"Can I bandage that for you, Mama?" Frances asked. Her daughter had been watching intently as she treated the cut.

"Yes, thank you." Frances was working at the clinic since she was out of school. "Frances, I have something I need to do. Would you help Janie through the afternoon? I'll come back and ride home with you at the end of the day."

Janie overheard the conversation. "No need. Annie is making Robert and Annabelle some of the gingerbread cookies they love so much. I promised to come by and pick them up before I go home. Frances can come back to the house with me."

"Wonderful!" Carrie changed out of her dress, slipped into warm, soft breeches, and shrugged into a heavy coat. She stepped out onto the porch once she'd added a hat, gloves, and scarf to her attire. There had been no snow for three days, but a strong, northerly wind made it brutally cold.

Janie joined her on the porch. "Is anything wrong?"

Carrie hesitated. "I'm concerned about Susan. Since Frances is here to help you, I'm hoping I can spend some time with her."

Janie's eyes filled with sympathy. "She's very sad."

Carrie nodded. "Thank you for taking care of things here and for bringing Frances home. How about if I return the favor tomorrow?"

Janie grinned. "That would be perfect. Robert and Annabelle are begging Matthew and me to go out into the woods for a Christmas tree. Since we'll be at the house for Clint and Hazel's wedding on Christmas Eve, we're going to put the tree up tomorrow night. Matthew was going to take the children..."

"But they'll be thrilled if you join them," Carrie finished for her. "It works out all the way around." She gave Janie a hug and went to saddle All My Heart. The plantation men had built a snug stable with six stalls behind the clinic.

All My Heart whinnied when Carrie stepped into the stable. "I know you're ready to go back to your mama. We talked about this on the way over. Amber asked me to ride you because she's busy at the barn. She wanted you to have more exercise."

All My Heart snorted loudly.

"Yes, I know I'm not your first choice. Things will be back to normal soon. You'll be able to go back to being Amber's spoiled favorite." Carrie slipped on the saddle and bridle as she talked. "You really are a special horse, All My Heart."

The dark bay mare with a perfect white heart on her forehead pawed the ground and snorted again.

Carrie let out a laugh before she opened the stall door, mounted and headed down the trail that led to the plantation. She held All My Heart to an easy walk until she was sure her muscles were warmed up in the frigid cold, and then let her break into a gentle canter. Carrie snuggled down into her thick coat, grateful for the bright red scarf that protected her mouth and nose. The temperature had dropped even more since she'd left the house that morning. A glance up told her they were going to get more snow before the night was over.

"What are we doing?" Susan asked.

Carrie cast her a sideways look. "I'd say we're walking down a tunnel."

Susan looked at her with exasperation. "I wasn't asking about the obvious. *Why* are we walking down Cromwell Plantation's secret tunnel?"

Carrie held up the basket Annie had hastily thrown together for her. "It's the easiest way to have a picnic."

Susan stared at her. "Carrie, it's freezing outside. This isn't exactly picnic weather."

Carrie shrugged. She was well aware of that, but she couldn't think of a single place where she could have Susan to herself, except for the riverbank. The house was crawling with people, as was the barn. She'd thought about riding with Susan back to her house, but she preferred neutral territory that didn't remind her friend of her loss. "Life is all in how you perceive it," she said lightly. "*Any* weather can be picnic weather."

"Fine," Susan retorted. "Don't tell me. But you'd better have plans to build a fire on the riverbank. I hardly think cold, blowing wind and sleet can be good for my pneumonia."

Carrie frowned. She knew exactly how true that was. She continued to think as they walked down the tunnel. It was cool, but certainly not cold. Being underground protected the bricked-in tunnel from the frigid wind blowing outside. Sleet had started to fall just before they entered the tunnel. She knew Janie would close the clinic early so both she and Frances could arrive home safely. This whole escapade was rather extreme, but she couldn't shake the worry she felt over her friend.

Carrie made her decision before they reached the end of the tunnel. When she spotted the door to the riverbank in the distance, she sank down to the floor and leaned against the tunnel wall. "This is good."

Susan stopped and stared down at her. "What are you talking about?"

Carrie smiled as she patted the cobblestones. "You're right that it's too cold outside. We're going to have our picnic here instead." She understood the incredulous look Susan gave her.

"We walked all the way down the tunnel to sit underground for a picnic?" Susan demanded. She sighed heavily as she joined Carrie on the tunnel floor. "I've played your game long enough. It's time to tell me what's going on."

Carrie opened her mouth to explain but remained silent when Susan held up a hand to stop her from speaking.

"Let me help you out. You're worried about me, so you brought me down here to share some of your great wisdom."

"You're partly right," Carrie admitted, glad to hear resignation, not resentment, in her voice. "It's true that I'm worried about you. I did not, however, bring you down here to impart my great wisdom. I know bringing you into the tunnel is rather extreme, but I couldn't think of another quiet place. I had hoped to spend time on the riverbank, but you're right that it's far too cold and windy. Taking you out there would be tantamount to signing your death warrant." Carrie shrugged. "So here we are."

Susan shook her head. "I know we're not just here to have a picnic, Carrie."

Carrie could tell by the tone of her voice that her friend was running out of patience. She couldn't blame her. "I have something I want to read to you," she confessed as she pulled a thick sheaf of papers out of her pocket. "May I?"

Susan's eyes filled with curiosity. "Do I have a choice?"

"Yes," Carrie responded seriously. "I won't read it if you don't want me to."

Susan sighed. "Go ahead and read it."

Susan watched her but remained silent.

"I'm worried about you," Carrie repeated "I thought being back in the barn would bring you peace, but you seem to keep getting sadder."

Susan didn't refute her observation.

Carrie could sense her wanting to say something, so she leaned back against the wall and waited.

"I know you told me to talk about it," Susan said slowly. "I can't find words…" Her voice trailed off as tears flooded her eyes. She blinked them back furiously.

"I understand," Carrie said softly.

A long silence fell on the tunnel again.

"I feel so stupid," Susan finally blurted.

"*Stupid*? How?" Carrie was mystified.

Susan's face filled with frustration and grief. "Lots of women have miscarriages. I know it's common, but I prayed it wouldn't happen to me." She took a deep breath. "Carrie, I'm thirty years old. I had given up hope of having a baby, until I met Harold. I want so much to have a child with him." She twisted her hands in her lap. "What if I'm too old to have another baby?"

"Susan, thirty is not old. You have a lot of time left. I believe you would have carried this baby to term if you hadn't gotten so sick. You can get pregnant again."

Susan seemed to sink into herself. "I wanted *this* baby," she whispered. She lifted agonized eyes. "I wanted to know *this* baby. I wanted to hold *this* baby. I wanted to teach *this* baby how to ride. I wanted to teach *this* baby how to swim in the river." Her voice choked and she fell silent.

Carrie felt every bit of the pain etched on Susan's face. She knew she'd been right to force this time together. She held up the sheaf of papers. "Biddy Flannagan sent me this letter after Robert and Bridget died. It was the catalyst that brought me back to life." She turned up the flame on the lantern and began to read.

My Dearest Carrie,

I have asked Abby and Rose to not give you this letter until the end of July because I don't believe you will be ready to hear anything I have to say until then. You may still not be ready, but I fear waiting any longer would not help you.

"Robert and Bridget had been dead for almost three months when I read this letter," Carrie explained.

You know my story, so there is no need to remind you while you are buried in your own grief.

Carrie glanced up again, knowing she needed to provide some explanation. "Biddy lost so much. She lost her husband before the war. All her sons, and all but one of her grandsons, were killed in battle."

Susan held a hand to her mouth. "That's terrible," she breathed.

I'm sure at this point you're wondering how I survived it all, because you are questioning why you should survive your own loss.

Carrie understood when Susan gasped. She remembered wondering how the old woman had so clearly articulated her own thoughts.

No one's grief is alike, Carrie. All of us have a different life, and we are all different people. We all lose our loved ones in different ways. There are many who are certain they understand your grief, but those are the ones who probably understand it the least. I certainly understand grief, but I'm not so arrogant to say I understand your grief. You do not need to explain your grief to anyone. It is mostly important for you to know that your pain is unique to everyone else's. You can merely do the best you can to survive it.

Carrie paused, remembering how comforting it had been to be given the space to do things her own way. She and Susan were alike in that need.

There will be people in your life who may feel you have grieved long enough, or that it is time for you to move on with your life. They will think about the strong Carrie they know, and expect you to behave in a certain way. Sometimes, my dear, our very strength means our grieving is even deeper because our hearts are so passionate about everything. It can be both a blessing and a curse. Most days, four years after the loss of my final grandson, I can walk through life fairly normally, but then something will happen that awakens all the pain and makes it all seem fresh and new. All I can do is grit my teeth, wait for the worst of the agony to pass, and pray for my breath to come a little easier.

Carrie, no one can dictate how you deal with the loss of Robert and Bridget. We all must find a way to embrace life again, though I'm quite certain that seems impossible to you right now. For so long, I simply didn't care to try to make meaning or sense of all the death. There is no real sense in it, after all, but humans strive to find a way to move on since we are the ones still alive. You never truly get over it, because the deaths leave a hole in your life that nothing else can fill.

She stopped reading again, giving Susan time to absorb the words. Susan had her eyes closed, tears streaming down her face, but Carrie could sense her listening avidly. After a long pause, she continued.

There are people who will tell you that you have to let go of your loved ones. What rubbish!

I've never told anyone that I have Faith fix birthday cakes every year for my husband, my sons, and my grandsons. The children in Moyamensing have no idea why Faith bakes so many cakes, but they know what the smells from the kitchen mean, and they are always lined up to eat them. Many would tell me I'm being maudlin, but it is simply my way of honoring their existence in my life. I treasure the memories of each one, even while I strive to live life each day and move into the future, however much more of it I have left. The day is coming soon when I will be with all those I have lost. You do not have that same knowledge, so do whatever feels right to you to honor the lives of Robert and Bridget.

Now, I'm going to tell you something I am quite sure you don't want to hear, and you may not be ready to hear, but still I am going to say it. We are enough alike that I know your first thought is to shut everyone out and endure the pain on your own. Carrie, my dear, you will never move through your grief unless you experience it. Hiding it or denying it will only prolong it. Talk about it, Carrie. Talk about it with Abby. Talk about it with Rose. Talk about it with anyone who will listen—even Granite, who may be the best listener of all!

Carrie looked up to see Susan gazing at her. She pushed away the painful memories the letter was evoking and continued to read.

Talk, Carrie. Talk about Robert. Talk about Bridget. Talk about the pain ripping through you. Talk about how you feel like you are a failure for not saving them. Talk about how you believe it is your fault.

"Did you?" Susan asked.

Carrie knew what she was asking. "Yes, I believed it was my fault. I know now that it wasn't, but it didn't change anything about how I felt then."

"I feel the same way," Susan admitted shakily. "If I hadn't gotten sick. If I'd been able to keep the house warm so it wouldn't develop into pneumonia."

"Your miscarriage was *not* your fault," Carrie said, and then continued to read, knowing Biddy's words were far more powerful than any she could manage to say.

I already know what you are thinking, Carrie. How do I know you believe it is your fault? I know you, dearest one. I've watched you go long, sleepless days and nights to save everyone you can possibly save. I've watched you fight the grain of society to help others because you believe it is the right thing to do. I watched you save so many here in Moyamensing from cholera. How it must ache that you could not save your husband and daughter. I'm not going to try to convince you it is not your fault, though it is most assuredly not. I'm just going to tell you to talk about it. Every time you do, you will breathe a little easier. It's okay that you don't believe me, but I urge you to at least try. You have so many people who love you so deeply. Let them love you, Carrie. Please let them love you.

Tears blurred Carrie's eyes and made it impossible to continue reading, precisely as they had the first time. She took a deep breath, regained control, and picked up the letter again.

I fear I may have already tried to say too much, but I don't know how long it will be before I see you again. I wish we could sit in my parlor and talk for hours, but I understand why you don't want to leave the plantation. Grieving is a process, dear one. There will be days when it doesn't hurt quite so badly, and then it will come roaring back with an intensity you are sure will destroy you. There are days when the sadness consumes you, and then anger will make you want to lash out at every person around you. You will feel crazy at times. There will also be days when you will almost feel normal…but then you will feel guilty, because how could you ever hope to feel normal again? The spiral of feelings will seem to spin you around until you feel there is no life within you.

Now, do I believe it will get better? Yes. Though I will never quit missing the loved ones I have lost, my life is also full and good. The things I am doing will never replace what I have lost, but I have wonderful people that make the loss not quite so terrible. You are one of them. I have no idea how long it will take for you, Carrie, but there is one thing I encourage you to do. Every time you think of Robert dying in your arms, also try to pull forth a memory of you dancing together. Remember your first kiss. Remember laughing together. Accept the pain of the horrible memory, but also welcome the other memories that make you miss him so very much. Remember him the way he is hoping you will remember him.

I love you, Carrie. You are constantly in my thoughts and prayers.

Biddy

Susan wiped at the tears streaming down her face. "I never knew my baby," she whispered. "I have no memories to bring me joy."

"I understand," Carrie answered. "I could remember Robert, but there were no memories of Bridget. There was only a black hole of emptiness that could never be filled. Until I realized I did have memories. I had the memories of the moments Bridget had been conceived, and I had the memories of feeling her life inside me." Susan had never felt her child kick, but Carrie was certain she'd felt the life inside her. Carrie's throat locked as memories threatened to choke her. "I never saw my baby either, Susan. She was already buried before I regained consciousness five days later. I never got to hold her. I was told she was beautiful, but I'll never know for myself."

"I miss my baby," Susan cried as she collapsed into a spasm of weeping.

Carrie moved over, wrapped her in her arms, and let her cry. It was the greatest gift she could give right now. She hoped Biddy knew how much her letter was helping another grieving woman.

Carrie didn't know how much time had passed before Susan fell silent. She continued to hold her friend, allowing all the emotions and feelings to flow through her.

Susan finally looked up. "Thank you," she said softly.

Carrie felt a surge of relief as she saw the beginning of peace in Susan's swollen, red eyes for the first time since the miscarriage. She knew the pain and peace would come in opposing waves, but it was enough to know it had begun.

Susan straightened and took deep breaths. "What's in that picnic basket? You'd better not say it was simply part of your ploy to get me here."

"How about roast beef sandwiches, fresh carrots from the greenhouse, and gingerbread cookies?"

Susan responded by pulling the basket closer. "I'm starving," she announced.

Carrie glanced toward the door. "Are you sure you don't want to go outside?"

Susan raised a brow as she unwrapped a sandwich and took a bite. Even with the door closed, they could hear the wind howling down the river. "For someone so brilliant, you can be awfully dumb," she mumbled with a smile.

Chapter Twenty-Two

Nancy took a deep breath when she entered the barn. "I thought it would smell bad," she admitted. "It's wonderful. What am I smelling?"

Amber poked her head over Eclipse's stall door. "Nothing smells better than a barn, Mrs. Stratford! You're smelling horses, hay, feed, saddle soap, and saddle oil."

"Good morning, Amber," Nancy said, and then gasped when Eclipse thrust his head over the stall door. "Oh my goodness!" She clasped a hand to her heart. "Are you safe in there with that huge animal?"

Abby chuckled. "You're sounding like a city girl, Nancy."

"I *am* a city girl," Nancy retorted. "I grew up in New York City. I've spent my entire life there. The closest I've been to horses are during carriage rides." She still had her eyes latched on Eclipse's massive head. "She's so beautiful!'

Amber shook her head. "Eclipse is not a *she,* Mrs. Stratford. This handsome fella is the Cromwell Stables stallion. He's the daddy of every one of the young horses you see. Eclipse is the reason Cromwell horses are known all over the country."

Susan strode into the barn. "Well, Eclipse is part of the reason." She smiled. "Cromwell Stables also has some of the finest mares in the country, but our true secret weapon is Amber. She's become known as one of the finest trainers in the country. The horses she trains earn a premium that other stables will never receive. We're lucky to have her."

Amber grinned and ducked back into the stall. Moments later, she rolled out a wheelbarrow full of soiled straw and manure.

Nancy wrinkled her nose. "Ugh!"

"Don't turn your nose up at valuable compost," Abby chided playfully.

Nancy stared at the wheelbarrow doubtfully. "Compost?"

"City girl," Abby scoffed again. "The straw and manure break down into soil. It's called compost. It's used during the winter to feed the plants in the greenhouse. Next summer, it will be added to our gardens."

Nancy glared at Abby. "Don't keep calling me a city girl. I'm not the only one. You spent decades in Philadelphia."

"I did," Abby agreed. "But not before I grew up on a Virginia plantation."

Nancy's eyes widened. "Really? We've never talked about it!"

"I'll remedy that while we're riding over to the greenhouse."

Nancy started to nod, but then froze. "Riding?"

"Why do you look surprised?" Abby demanded. "I told you we were going riding. Why do you think you're wearing breeches for the first time in your pampered life?"

Susan laughed. "Do the two of you always go at each other like this?"

"Only when she's being silly," Abby replied smugly.

"And when Abby does dumb things in New York City." Nancy raised a brow. "We've had to save her more than once because she has no idea how to stay safe."

Abby shrugged, her eyes dancing with fun. "I suppose there could be some truth to that, but now it's my turn to teach you some things."

Nancy shook her head as she turned her eyes toward Eclipse. "I'm not going to get on an animal that huge," she sputtered.

Susan opened a stall door and led Maple out. The small mare was already saddled and bridled. "You're right, Nancy. Maple will be perfect for you. She's small and very gentle. All you have to do is sit in the saddle. She'll take care of everything else."

Nancy started to shake her head, but then stopped and moved closer to the buckskin mare who was gazing at her with large, soft eyes. "Aren't you pretty?" she cooed.

Maple snuffled a response and reached out her nose to sniff at the hand Nancy had extended.

Nancy smiled with delight and turned to Abby. "You really believe I can ride her?"

"Absolutely," Abby said. She turned to Amber. "Who would you like me to ride today?"

"Morning Joy," Amber replied. "She's coming along nicely and is eager to please. You won't have any trouble with her. She'll be glad for the exercise."

Nancy took a shaky breath as Maple walked away from the barn. "You're certain this is safe?"

"Perfectly," Abby assured her. "Maple is a dream." She spent the next few minutes telling Nancy how to guide her horse, and how to sit easily in the saddle. She was impressed with how quickly her friend's nervousness eased.

Ten minutes from the barn, Nancy looked at her with a brilliant smile. "This is wonderful!" She shivered. "It's cold, though."

"At least the snow stopped," Abby replied, raising her face to the sun. "It's beautiful today!"

Snow shimmered like diamonds under the bright sunlight. It was still too cold for the snow to melt, so it crunched beneath the horses' hooves as they broke through the top layer. Both Maple and Morning Joy had plumes of white blowing from their muzzles.

Nancy finally relaxed enough to look around. "It goes forever!" she gasped.

"Cromwell Plantation is two thousand acres," Abby told her. "It was carved out of the wilderness by Thomas' family back in the 1700s."

"It's beautiful. Everything is so wide open."

"The fields are all buried in snow," Abby explained. "In four months, Moses will start planting the next tobacco crop. Instead of white, it will be an ocean of green swaying in the breezes."

Nancy eyed her speculatively. "You love it here," she said softly. "I was concerned about you leaving the city and living out here, but I see I needn't have worried."

"I was worried myself in the beginning," Abby admitted. "I wasn't sure that slower plantation life would suit me, but I'm almost as busy as I was in the city." She knew her face was glowing. "I love every minute of my life here."

"Because of the Bregdan Women?"

"That's certainly a large part of it," Abby agreed, "but it's much more. I never dreamed I would be a grandmother." She chuckled. "I never dreamed I would be a *mother*! To have Carrie here, and also have two beautiful granddaughters, is more than I fathomed. Every moment with them is pure joy."

"Thomas seems so happy here," Nancy observed.

"He is," Abby assured her. "He is grateful for his years in Richmond, but Cromwell Plantation has his heart. He doesn't have to worry about all the hard work, though he loves to ride the fields with Moses. He reads copious amounts and maintains correspondence with many friends and former colleagues. He's content here on the plantation, but he hasn't given up his determination to have an influence. He believes far too many governmental decisions are made from ignorance. He spends hours researching issues and then sends deeply thought-provoking letters to communicate his opinions."

"Do you read them?"

"Every one of them," Abby said promptly. "He and I work together on the letters he sends to congressmen about suffrage for women."

"I didn't know the two of you did that."

"It's only been in the last month. We have you and Julie to thank," Abby revealed, smiling at the surprise in Nancy's eyes. "When Matthew returned from New York City, he told us about the meeting of anti-suffragists. We also discussed how we need to mobilize more and more of the younger generation to join in the fight. Thomas and I are sending letters to the youngest members of Congress. We spend many evenings in the library, doing research and writing letters. I find it quite fulfilling."

"That's magnificent!" Nancy exclaimed. "Julie and I are inviting many young women to our Bregdan Women meetings. Everyone is welcome, but we're discovering just how many influential *young* women there are in New York City. I had no idea! We're meeting journalists, educators, doctors, businesswomen..." Her voice trailed off as she looked into the distance, her blue eyes gleaming almost as brightly as the sky spread above them. "We have a dream that next year we can invite some of the leaders in the suffragist movement to speak to our group. Our goal is at least two hundred women for that meeting."

Abby knew that when Nancy had that determined shine in her eyes, nothing would keep her from her goal. "You'll do it."

"I have another dream," Nancy confided.

"And that would be...?"

Nancy grinned. "To have Sojourner Truth speak to us. We've been inviting a growing number of black women to our meetings. Some of them were born free, but many escaped slavery, or were set free after the Emancipation Proclamation. I can easily get Susan Anthony, Elizabeth Stanton, or Lucy Stone to speak to us because they're friends, but I want a voice that will speak to these young black women." She shook her head. "I haven't been able to get in touch with Sojourner Truth."

Abby smiled. "I might be able to help with that." Her smile changed to a grin when Nancy turned skeptical eyes toward her. "Don't doubt my reach just because I live on a Southern plantation," she chided. She told Nancy about Felicia's invitation to tour with Sojourner.

Nancy took a deep breath. "Moses and Rose will let her go?"

"They've told her that it's her choice. Please don't say anything to anyone. Rose told me about it because she wanted my opinion, but Felicia has not yet decided if she'll accept the invitation."

"Do you believe she will?"

Abby shrugged. "I'll be surprised if she doesn't, but she may not be ready to take such a huge step. The time will come, however. Every person on this plantation knows Felicia is going to do something special with her life. It will be fascinating to watch what she does as she grows up. I hope I live long enough to know a portion of it."

"You and me both," Nancy replied. "I hope she accepts the invitation. It would be thrilling to have both Sojourner *and* Felicia speak at our meeting. The two of them will be quite powerful."

Nancy's mouth gaped open as they rounded the back of the largest tobacco barn. "Oh my..." she gasped. "You would never know this was back here. It's huge."

The Cromwell greenhouse hugged the backside of the tobacco barn. The glass panels, supported by a sturdy wooden frame, extended two hundred feet down the length of the barn, pushing out forty feet toward the woods. There was a large clearing on the far side of the greenhouse, allowing full southern exposure. Several stovepipes pushed toward the sky, allowing smoke from the constantly burning woodstoves to escape.

Abby nodded proudly. "We expand it every year. We've also built a large one down near the workers' quarters, and most of the original twelve plantation hands have added one to their land. It's been wonderful to have fresh produce year-round."

"Cromwell Plantation is a marvel," Nancy murmured. "This was Felicia's idea?"

"Yes, she sent a letter from Oberlin about greenhouses and suggested we build one. Anthony was familiar with them, so he played a big role in buying the supplies. It's been interesting to transport glass from Richmond. Not all the panels made the journey without breaking," she said wryly. "Still, enough did. Moses' men have built all of the greenhouses."

Nancy peered toward the building, cocking her head as shadowy figures moved behind the moisture-fogged glass. "Who are those people?"

"Bregdan Women," Abby replied. "They work in the greenhouse in exchange for produce for their families. The men keep the fires burning around the clock to keep the greenhouse warm." She was proud of the operation. "Each woman takes the extra produce home. They sell it to their neighbors, or barter for other things they need. Everyone wins."

Nancy eyed the building hungrily. "Is it warm in there?"

Abby smiled. "Come find out for yourself."

Nancy smiled with delight as they entered the greenhouse. The warm, moist air enveloped them like a cloud of comfort.

"Take your coat off," Abby told her. "You'll be cold when you go back outside if you don't remove it in here."

"Hello, Abby!"

"Howdy, Miss Abby!"

Abby called greetings to the women hard at work in the greenhouse, and then waved them over to join them. "Ladies, I would like you to meet Nancy Stratford. She's my friend from New York City."

One of the ladies stepped forward excitedly. "You're Mrs. Stratford? The one who sells our quilts to your friends?"

Nancy smiled and nodded. "It's such a privilege to sell your beautiful work!" Her gaze encompassed all the women who were looking at her with broad smiles.

"I'm Sapphire," the same woman said. "You don't know what the money means to my family. Thank you."

Nancy stepped forward and grasped Sapphire's hands. "Your quilt made a dear friend of mine very happy. The story you wrote on the card meant even more to her. It was because of your story that all the women paid more for the quilts than what you asked."

Sapphire beamed with pride. "Thank you for letting me know that, Mrs. Stratford. My daughters and I work hard on those quilts."

Each woman stepped forward to shake Nancy's hand and then drifted back to their work in the greenhouse, talking excitedly in low voices.

"These women are special," Nancy told Abby.

"Don't I know it," Abby replied warmly. "They give me far more than I give them. Now, let's explore the greenhouse."

Nancy's mouth gaped open with amazement as they walked through the raised beds. "You're growing everything in here, Abby!"

"If it can be grown, it can be grown in here," Abby agreed. She stopped in front of a plant that reached almost six feet tall. "Do you know what this is?"

Nancy cocked her head and walked closer. Suddenly, her eyes widened. "Are those pineapples?" She reached out a hand to touch the spiny fruit. "Are they really pineapples?"

Abby chuckled. "They are. Anthony convinced us to give them a try. When he was growing up, his family was invited to visit a friend who had built a greenhouse modeled after the one George Washington built at Mt. Vernon. Anthony told us it was quite possible to grow tropical plants."

"What else do you have?" Nancy asked eagerly.

"English grapes. Oranges. Limes. Lemons." Abby pointed them out as she walked Nancy through the rows of plants, some stretching almost as high as the ceiling.

"Extraordinary," Nancy said. "I've never seen anything like it." She eyed her friend. "No wonder you were eager to leave the chaos of New York City this summer."

Abby frowned, remembering how terrified she'd been during the Orange Riot near the end of July. "I find my heart demands peace and quiet more and more," she revealed. "New York City is always loud. It didn't use to bother me, but now I can hardly think there. There are certainly times I miss the North, but I never want to go back to living in a city."

"If I lived at Cromwell Plantation, I would probably feel the same way," Nancy admitted. Her expression grew serious. "Do you fear losing your way of life?"

Abby cocked her head. "What do you mean?"

"I've listened to the conversations while we've been here. I know the Ku Klux Klan and other white supremacy groups are determined to strip blacks of the rights the Fourteenth and Fifteenth Amendments have given them. From what I can tell, they've determined that terror is their best weapon. If they can't strip them of their Constitutional rights, they're going to make them too frightened to use them." Nancy shuddered. "I hate what happened to little Jed's parents. I also met Angel Blue a couple days ago. Amber told me about her mother and four siblings being murdered in North Carolina last year by the Klan. Will they stop at nothing?" Her voice was a mixture of pain and outrage.

Abby's heart clenched, but she kept her voice even. "I don't know," she said slowly. Thomas and I talk about it on a regular basis," she confessed to her friend. "We've had plenty of trouble on the plantation, but it's been peaceful for a while. At least for now, the Klan has decided the cost of attacking Cromwell is too high."

Nancy stopped and gazed at her friend, her eyes narrowed with worry. "And when they determine to take the risk again?"

Abby managed a smile. "We deal with it," she said calmly, hoping the nervousness she felt every day wasn't revealed in her voice.

The look in Nancy's eyes told her she had failed.

Annie cleared her throat after Moses and Anthony brought in two huge pots of beef vegetable soup and placed them on opposing ends of the table. The fragrant aroma, blended with the delicious smell of freshly baked bread, filled the dining room. Plates of freshly churned butter waited to be spread over thick pieces that had already been cut. "I got me an announcement to make."

Everyone ceased talking and turned their attention to her.

"I ain't cooked none of this meal tonight," Annie declared. "Minnie made everything you gettin' ready to eat. She even churned the butter for me yesterday. She went out to the greenhouse and brung back all the vegetables. She cleaned and cut them. She made the soup, and then she went right on and baked all the bread." She paused and then smiled. "I tasted all of it to make sure it be good. It ain't just good. It's some right fine cookin'. I'm real proud of you, Minnie."

Applause and cries of congratulations rang out around the table.

Carrie gripped her daughter's hand and leaned over to hug her tightly. "I'm proud of you too, honey. Well done."

Minnie's face flushed almost as red as her hair, but her eyes shone with excitement and satisfaction. "I hope you all enjoy it," she said.

The voices telling her how delicious everything was fell silent.

When dinner was finished, Carrie leaned over again. "I'd say that since every bite was devoured, you can be sure the meal was enjoyed."

Minnie grinned and stood. "I have one more surprise," she announced. "I picked the first lemons from the lemon tree in the greenhouse. I've only had lemon cake once before. Annie has never made it, so Felicia helped me find a recipe from one of the cookbooks in the library."

Annie snorted. "I ain't never used a cookbook in my life. Don't see no reason to start now."

"Well, you wouldn't be having lemon cake tonight if I hadn't, Miss Annie," Minnie replied with a smile. "I couldn't have made it, though, if you hadn't taught me everything I know."

"I reckon that be true enough," Annie allowed.

Carrie swallowed her smile. Minnie was not only turning into an excellent cook, she was also a budding diplomat.

Minnie turned her eyes to Frances. "I decided lemon cake was a good way to celebrate, Frances."

Frances looked confused. "What are we celebrating?"

Minnie's answer was to look at Matthew. "I believe that's your cue," she said as she sat down.

Carrie looked between the two, completely mystified. She knew nothing about whatever was about to happen. She'd been surprised Matthew, Janie, and the children had decided to stay for dinner. She was always thrilled to have them, but they would have a cold carriage ride home.

Matthew cleared his throat and reached for a newspaper on the table behind him.

Frances stiffened and latched her eyes on the paper. "Is that what I think it is?"

"A newspaper?" Matthew asked. "I would say that is an astute observation, Miss Wallington."

Frances rolled her eyes. "You know what I'm talking about."

Matthew smiled, opened the newspaper, folded it to the page he'd chosen, and began to read.

I was in Philadelphia in October for Election Day. I'm not a man, so I couldn't vote. Many people reading this may think I'm also too young to have an opinion on what happened that day. You would be wrong. I may only be fourteen, but I know the difference between right and wrong.

I certainly know that what happened in Philadelphia on October 8, 1871 was wrong.

You see, my mother is a doctor. Dr. Carrie Wallington. I want to be a physician, as well, so she allows me to work with her as much as possible. We were visiting Philadelphia on Election Day. We had been warned there would be trouble, so we were working at the Moyamensing Clinic that my mother helped found, ready to treat patients if anyone was injured.

I'll never forget the black patients that streamed through the door all day. There were men who had been beaten. They were cut with rocks and sharp objects. Men had been shot. We were able to save most of them, but others died.

Why? Because they wanted to vote. They wanted their voices to be heard. They wanted to exercise the rights the Constitution gives them.

There were many white men not willing to give them that right. They did whatever it took to make sure they couldn't vote.

They were wrong.

A man I greatly respected died that day: Mr. Octavius Catto. I shared meals with him when we visited Philadelphia. He was always kind to me. He always took time to listen to my ideas, even though I'm a child. I listened to him, as well. I learned from him. I became a better person because of him.

He was killed because he was a black man who wanted to vote. He was killed because he was a black man who encouraged other black men to vote. He knew it was dangerous, but he did it anyway because it was the right thing to do.

I will always miss Mr. Catto. The world was robbed of a very good man that day.

Something else wrong happened on Election Day.

Women were not allowed to vote. I may not be old enough to vote yet, but I'm old enough to know that it's wrong that women can't vote.

I'm old enough to know women should have the same rights as men.

I'm old enough to know women's interests should be represented and safeguarded.

I'm old enough to know women should have control of how they live their lives.

I'm old enough to know that if women have to obey laws, they should have a voice in framing those laws.

I'm old enough to know that if women have to pay taxes, they should have the right to vote on how they are spent.

I'm old enough to know that America will never be a democracy until every citizen has the right to vote.

It's really very simple. Every American should have the right to vote.

One day I will be old enough to vote. I'm starting to fight for that right. I'll keep fighting until I can go to a polling station and let my voice be heard. I'll keep fighting until my mother and all the other strong women I know are able to vote. I'll keep fighting until it's safe for black men to vote.

I'll keep fighting, with the hopes the day will come when I won't have to spend Election Day stitching up wounds and praying that people live.

I'm fourteen now, but I will grow up. All the other children my age will grow up. When we do, we want an America that will allow us to have a voice in the country we are helping to create.

We want a country that will do the right thing.

A long hush fell over the table as everyone absorbed the powerful words Frances had written.

Carrie didn't bother to control the tears that rolled down her face after Matthew read the article. She was quite certain her heart was about to burst with pride.

"I guess it's a good thing my lemon cake is delicious," Minnie finally said. "All of you look like you've been struck by lightning. Maybe cake will help."

Carrie laughed through her tears as Minnie's words broke through her emotions. She jumped up and rushed around the table to where Frances was seated. Anthony beat her by a mere second. They wrapped their arms around their daughter together.

"I am so proud of you, honey," Carrie said softly. "So very proud."

"We're both proud of you," Anthony said huskily.

"Thank you." Frances whispered.

Abby, seated next to Frances, had a firm grip on her hand. "You're a powerful writer, Frances."

Frances looked at her grandmother. "Do you believe my words will make a difference?"

"I do," Abby said firmly. "I'm so proud of you."

"Welcome to the fight," Nancy said. "With young women like you fighting for the vote, I'm confident the day will come when we have it. Never let anyone diminish your voice or tell you that you're too young."

"Or too old," Felicia added. "That was an amazing article, Frances. Sojourner Truth is in her seventies, but she's still fighting the battle. She told me she's going to keep fighting until she dies."

Janie stared at Felicia. "Sojourner Truth *told* you that? You talked to her? When?" she asked eagerly.

Suddenly, all eyes were on Felicia.

Felicia looked to Rose for help. "Will you tell them, Mama?" she asked shyly.

"I'd be happy to," Rose replied as she took a deep breath.

Carrie knew how much Rose was fighting to accept the next step Felicia was taking with her life. They had talked about the equal mix of terror and pride that she'd felt every moment since learning the news.

"Sojourner Truth came to Oberlin right before Felicia came home. She asked her to travel and speak with her next summer. She believes her audiences need to hear from an older woman still fighting the battle for equality *and* a brilliant young woman who has overcome great challenges to create a new life. Moses and I agree this is a wonderful opportunity for her."

"What?!" Annie cried. "When was somebody gonna tell me that my baby girl gonna be traipsing around the country with that famous woman? Ain't I got the right to know anything around here?"

"Of course you do," Rose said quickly.

"I asked Mama and Daddy to not say anything until I decided what I wanted to do," Felicia said earnestly. "We weren't trying to keep anything from you, Grandma! They told me I could do it, but I had to decide if I *wanted* to."

"Well, of course you wanna do it," Annie said indignantly. "You figure the good Lord saved your life back in Memphis just so you could do somethin' little? Nope. Girl, you got big things gonna happen in your life. I reckon I be so proud I could about pop."

Annie paused as she shook her head in amazement. "And you, Miss Frances. That be one powerful piece of writin' in that newspaper. You be two years younger than Felicia, and you already havin' your words read all around the country. I reckon I ain't *about* to pop, I suppose I done popped wide open!"

Everyone laughed as congratulations and accolades continued to flow around the table.

"That's enough," Minnie finally said, clapping her hands to get everyone's attention. "If all of you aren't going to eat the lemon cake I baked, I'm going take it back in the kitchen and eat it all by myself!"

"Oh, no you're not," Anthony said. He stood up and reached the kitchen door in one long stride. "You're not going to get it away from me, daughter." He pushed his way through the swinging door.

Minnie giggled and ran after him. "You're being silly, Daddy."

Moments later, Minnie hanging like a monkey from one of his arms, Anthony reappeared with the cake platter. "I bring forth the Lemon Cake," he intoned dramatically.

The laughter continued around the table as every crumb of cake was consumed.

Chapter Twenty-Three

Rose stood to the side, watching Jed as Moses helped four of his men bring a towering cedar tree into the parlor. She smiled when she saw his eyes widen with awe and delight as the tree, nailed solidly to a large base, was placed in the corner of the room. Chairs and tables had been moved to make room for it.

When Jed noticed her and grinned, Rose walked over to join him. "It's beautiful, isn't it?"

Jed nodded enthusiastically. "It looks so different here than it does in the woods, Miss Rose. John, Hope, and I rode with Mr. Moses to pick it out yesterday. He let me pick this one out!" His eyes glowed with pride.

Rose listened closely, not revealing that Moses had told her last night that it took forever to find a tree because the three children couldn't agree on which was the biggest and most beautiful. He had finally decreed that Jed would choose the tree because this was his first Cromwell Christmas. John and Hope had reluctantly agreed that was fair.

"It's a beautiful tree, Jed," Rose said warmly.

Jed didn't take his eyes from it. "What happens next?"

Rose nodded toward a stack of crates in the hallway. "Those crates are full of decorations. Polly and Annie made new candles that will go in the candleholders. Everything will go on the tree to make it even more beautiful."

Jed's eyes grew larger. "There will be candles on the tree?"

Hope walked in just in time to hear his question. "*Lots* of candles," she told him dramatically. "It will be the most beautiful thing you ever saw when it's all decorated. We'll be working on it all day," she said importantly.

"Who will?" Jed demanded.

"All the children," Hope replied. "Ain't you ever decorated a tree before, Jed?"

Rose cleared her throat.

"I mean, *haven't* you ever decorated a tree before, Jed?"

Jed frowned, his face a mixture of embarrassment and defiance. "No," he said shortly.

"A lot of people don't have Christmas trees," Rose said soothingly, knowing the little boy was doing the best he could to adjust to his new world. "It just happens to be important here at Cromwell Plantation. Would you like to help decorate it, Jed?"

Hope looked up at her with surprise. "Mama, it's tradition. Jed has to help us because he's one of the children," she said earnestly.

"No," Rose said gently. "Jed doesn't have to do anything." She would explain more when she was alone with her daughter, but she wanted to alleviate Jed's discomfort. "Jed picked out an absolutely beautiful tree. If that's all he wants to do for his first Cromwell Christmas, that's perfectly fine."

Hope looked uncertain, but she finally seemed to understand some of the message Rose was trying to send with her eyes. "You did pick out a real beautiful tree, Jed. We'll decorate it if you don't want to help."

Jed gazed at the tree, looked at the crate of decorations, and then turned his eyes to Rose.

Rose understood the combination of uncertainty and desire. "You don't have to decide right now, Jed. If you want to help decorate, you'll be welcome. If not, it won't be a problem." She had a sudden brainstorm. "Would you like to help decorate for the wedding tomorrow night? We could use some more help."

Jed's frown deepened. "John told me wedding decorating is a girl's job."

Rose chose to not correct his perception, concentrating instead on her intent to make decorating the tree a better option.

Jed stared at the tree again and nodded. "I'll help decorate the tree." Once he'd made his decision, the excitement returned to his eyes.

Rose hid her smile of satisfaction.

Hope clapped her hands happily. "We have to go out in the woods before we start decorating," she told him.

"What for?"

"We have to collect lots of pinecones and dried flowers," Hope explained. "We use them to decorate the tree."

Jed looked at Rose again. "Christmas trees are a lot of work."

"They are," Rose agreed. "They're worth it, though," she assured him. She could hardly wait to see the look on his face tonight when the candles were lit for the first time. They usually waited until Christmas Eve to light it, but since a wedding celebration was going to happen the next evening, they'd decided to light it early.

The sun had dipped below the horizon and the stars were just beginning to glitter in the clear evening sky when Felicia walked out onto the porch. She was surprised to see Jed standing alone at the far end beside one of the columns. She watched his stiff figure for a few minutes and then walked over to join him. "Do you mind if I stand with you?"

Jed remained silent but shrugged his permission.

"I remember my first Cromwell Christmas," Felicia said, instantly understanding what the boy was thinking. "It was hard."

"I felt like I didn't belong," Felicia admitted. She knew what Jed was feeling, but she also understood his feelings had to be stronger than what she'd felt five years earlier. She had arrived on the plantation in the spring, giving her more than half a year to adjust to everything before Christmas arrived. Still, it had been overwhelming for her.

Jed looked up at her but still didn't say anything for a while. When he finally did, his voice was small. "You did?"

"I did," Felicia assured him. "My parents didn't have much. I'd never seen a Christmas tree. We never had a feast. We never had cookies, because we couldn't afford to make them. Some years, my daddy would bring home an orange, and the three of us would split it." She smiled as she remembered. "I loved it because it was such a treat. Nothing about my childhood prepared me for a Cromwell Christmas, though."

"Me neither," Jed muttered.

Felicia kept talking. "That first Christmas, I felt guilty about enjoying it."

When Jed's head shot up, she knew she was right about what he was feeling. "I thought I was dishonoring my parents if I allowed myself to enjoy such an amazing Christmas," Felicia confessed. "I thought it meant that I didn't appreciate what they'd done for me."

A long silence followed her words, but it wasn't uncomfortable. Felicia looked out over the fields as the sky grew dark. The horses not in the barn were all huddled together under the large lean-tos in the pastures, munching on the mangers of hay. Though it was cold, their thick fur and their shared body heat kept them warm. There had been a time she'd worried about them, but Carrie had convinced her they were fine living life the way God created it. Shelter and hay were more than they would have had out in the wild.

"You don't feel that way anymore?" Jed finally asked.

"No," Felicia responded. "I have a new life now. I finally realized that enjoying my new life didn't mean that I wasn't happy in my old life."

Jed thought some more and then asked, "You saw your parents get killed?"

Felicia took a deep breath. The memory still brought her pain, but she realized she could relate to Jed in a way none of the rest of the Samuels family could. "I did, Jed. It was the most awful thing I ever experienced."

"What happened?"

Felicia fought her urge to leave the porch. She knew telling her story was something Sojourner wanted her to do on the stage. She supposed she could start practicing with her new little brother.

Jed looked up when the silence stretched out. "It be alright if you don't want to talk about it."

Jed's voice was steady, but Felicia could read the disappointment in his eyes. "It was during the Memphis Riot almost six years ago," she began. "There were policemen involved in the riots." Her voice shook, but she kept talking. "We knew there was going to be trouble, so we were home. Actually, I was determined to go to school that morning. I went, but Moses sent me home again."

Jed's eyes widened. "Moses?"

"Yes. He was in Memphis with Matthew." She decided to leave Robert out of the story because she wasn't sure if Jed knew what had happened to Carrie's first husband. Now was not the time for that story. "I had met him the day before when he visited my school. He knew there was going to be trouble, so he told me to go home. I did. My daddy stayed home that day, too." She shook her head. "It didn't matter. The trouble came to us."

Jed stared at her, waiting silently for her to continue.

"The policemen called for my daddy to come out of our little house. He didn't want to, but he knew they would break into the house if he didn't. He thought going out would keep me and mama safe. When he went outside, they shot him." Felicia shuddered with the memory. "I saw it through the door. My mama screamed and ran out to him. They shot her, too." She blinked back tears.

"What did you do?" Jed whispered.

"I ran out to both of them. My mama had begged me to stay inside, but I didn't care what happened to me. Both my parents were dying in front of me. I saw both of them take their last breath."

"The policemen didn't hurt you?"

Felicia flinched. "They were going to, but Moses saved me." She wasn't sure how much of the story to divulge at the moment. Matthew and Robert had appeared and knocked out the policemen with chunks of wood, but all of that could be revealed later. "Moses saved me and carried me back to the fort where he was staying. Since I didn't have a family anymore, he brought me back here to be his daughter."

Jed absorbed the story. "I'm real sorry that happened to you," he muttered.

"And I'm sorry your mama was killed, and that your daddy died from the beating they gave him," Felicia said softly, realizing how fresh Jed's pain was.

Another long silence stretched out. Felicia shivered but chose to stay where she was. She'd put on a coat but didn't have a hat or gloves. She pulled up the collar on her coat and tucked her hands under her armpits.

"Is that why you call him Daddy?" Jed finally asked.

"What do you mean?"

"Moses saved your life," Jed answered. "Is that why you call him Daddy?"

Felicia understood. "I call him Daddy because he's a father to me. I loved the father I was born to, but I also love Moses. It's the same reason I call Rose, Mama. It was hard for me in the beginning because I thought it meant my real parents wouldn't still be my parents. When I finally realized that Moses and Rose were loving me *for* them, I decided they were my mama and daddy, too."

"That's what they told me," Jed said quietly, once again looking out into the darkness. "They told me they were gonna love me *for* my real parents."

Felicia stood quietly, letting him wrestle with his feelings.

"My daddy only been dead for two months," Jed said.

"I know."

"Mr. Moses be a real good daddy," Jed muttered.

Felicia reached down and took his hand. Jed stiffened but didn't move away from her.

"Miss Rose be a real good mama, too," he added.

Felicia remained silent until he looked up at her with pleading eyes. "Jed, your parents loved you a whole lot, didn't they?"

Jed nodded hard. "Yes," he whispered.

Felicia could hear the unshed tears in his single word. "All your parents wanted was for you to be happy and loved," she told him. "I can promise you they would be happy you're here on Cromwell Plantation with Moses and Rose."

"You really think so?" Jed demanded.

"I do." Felicia had never been more certain of anything.

Another long silence passed. "How long before you felt right about being here?"

"Longer than it's going to take you," Felicia said, forcing a lightness into her words.

Jed jerked his head up again. "What do you mean?"

"It means you belong here," Felicia replied. "You love horses as much as Moses and John do. I've watched you ride. You're really good. You love riding in the tobacco fields with Moses."

"You don't like those things?" Jed asked with astonishment.

Felicia chuckled. "I learned how to ride a horse because it's what everyone does here, but all I really wanted to do was study in the library."

Jed made a face. "Why?"

Felicia chuckled again. "Because I've decided that the only way to make sense of my parents' deaths is to learn as much as I can and make the world a better place. That's why I'm at school in Oberlin. I want to be as educated as possible."

Jed thought about that for a few minutes. "Is it alright if I'm just happy riding horses and being in the fields with Mr. Moses?"

"Absolutely," Felicia answered. There were times when she wished that was enough for her, but she'd long ago accepted that she yearned for something different.

Jed changed the subject. "Is the Christmas tree going to be real pretty?"

Felicia smiled, knowing he had released some of the burden he'd been carrying. "It will be the prettiest thing you ever saw. You helped decorate it, didn't you?"

"Yep. I reckon it's the prettiest thing I've ever seen already." Jed looked toward the parlor window glowing from the lantern light inside.

"Wait until you see it with all the candles," Felicia told him, relieved to see a new peace shining in the boy's eyes. What she'd said must have helped him work through what he was struggling with. "Are you ready for some of Annie's famous sugar cookies and hot chocolate?"

Jed nodded eagerly. "I reckon I am." He started toward the door and then stopped. "Thank you," he said quietly. "I reckon you're going to be a real good big sister."

Felicia grinned. "And I reckon you're going to be a good little brother." She wrapped an arm around his shoulders and walked inside with him.

Thomas cleared his throat after everyone finished eating. "It's time."

Hope and John leapt up from the table and dashed to the parlor, Minnie on their heels.

Jed stared after them with a confused look shining in his eyes. "Is running into the parlor part of the tradition?"

Moses chuckled. "Only if you want it to be," he assured him.

"We're not going to miss anything," Frances told him. "Grandpa won't light the candles until we're all in there."

Jed nodded and then sidled next to Moses when he stood. Without saying anything, he slid his small hand into Moses' massive one.

Rose smiled at the picture the two of them made.

Moses smiled down at Jed. "Are you ready, son?"

Jed looked up. "Yes, Daddy," he said clearly.

Rose couldn't stop the gasp that escaped her lips. She could tell by the look in Moses' eyes that this was a moment he would never forget.

Moses knelt and pulled the boy into his arms. Jed didn't resist. In fact, he seemed to melt into him. "I love you, Jed," he said quietly, his deep voice reverberating through the room.

"I love you too, Daddy," Jed said shyly, his head buried into Moses' shoulder. After a long moment, he looked back. "I love you too, Mama."

"I love you, Jed," Rose answered, a brilliant smile on her face. She was aware that the smiles around the table mirrored her own.

Rose blinked back her tears and looked at Felicia. The look of triumph on her daughter's face confirmed her suspicion that Felicia had talked to Jed while they were on the porch together. When Felicia looked at her, Rose winked. *Well done*, she mouthed.

Felicia grinned and linked arms with her mother as they walked into the parlor.

Thomas looked around the parlor, his heart so full it felt as if it would burst. The children were sitting cross-legged in front of the tree, their faces tilted upward as they waited for the splendor of the lights.

Abby waited quietly at the piano, her loving eyes fixed on him.

Carrie and Anthony sat hand in hand on the couch closest to the fire, while Rose nestled into Moses' side on the opposing couch. Wally and Nancy watched expectantly from the wingback chairs flanking the fireplace. Hazel and Phoebe had joined them for the evening, their faces glowing with contentment. Thomas knew Hazel was thinking about her wedding that would take place in the parlor in less than twenty-four hours.

"It's Christmastime again," Thomas said. "It's a joy that all of us can be together." He nodded to Abby, lit a long stick of wood by thrusting it into the fireplace, and then began to light the myriad of small candles adorning the branches of the cedar tree.

Abby began to play the piano, the sounds of *Silent Night* filling the room as the Christmas tree came to life.

When Thomas had reached high enough to light the last candle, he stepped back.

"Oh!" Hope cried. "It's beautiful. The most beautiful Christmas tree I've ever seen."

Thomas chuckled. From the moment she had begun to speak, the little girl had said the same thing every year.

"It is beautiful," Jed said softly, his face filled with awe.

Thomas smiled and placed a hand on the boy's shoulder. "Welcome to your first Cromwell Christmas, Jed. We're so glad you're part of the Cromwell family now."

Jed grinned happily. "I reckon I'm real glad too, Mr. Thomas."

Abby continued to play as the tree twinkled in the corner. Flames leapt in the fireplace as a strong wind blew against the windowpanes.

Peace filled the room, wrapping each of them in its embrace.

Thomas had loved Christmas at Cromwell since he was a boy, but as he grew older, each of them seemed more special than the one before. A glance around the room told him that each one *was* more special, because each Christmas their family expanded.

When Abby finished the last song, Thomas sat down in the chair he had placed close to the tree and turned up the light on the lantern resting on the table next to him. Usually, he read a portion of *A Christmas Carol* aloud to the children, but he had decided to do something different this time. He was quite certain they would still demand *A Christmas Carol*, but he could read it to them on Christmas Day.

Thomas adjusted his spectacles on his nose and began to read...

A Visit from St. Nicholas

'Twas the night before Christmas, when all through the house

Not a creature was stirring, not even a mouse;

The stockings were hung by the chimney with care,

In hopes that St. Nicholas soon would be there;

The children were nestled all snug in their beds;

While visions of sugar-plums danced in their heads;

And mamma in her 'kerchief, and I in my cap,

Had just settled our brains for a long winter's nap,

When out on the lawn there arose such a clatter,

I sprang from my bed to see what was the matter.

Away to the window I flew like a flash,

Tore open the shutters and threw up the sash.

The moon on the breast of the new-fallen snow,

Gave a luster of midday to objects below,

When what to my wondering eyes did appear,

But a miniature sleigh and eight tiny reindeer,

With a little old driver so lively and quick,

I knew in a moment he must be St. Nick.

More rapid than eagles his coursers they came,

And he whistled, and shouted, and called them by name:

"Now, *Dasher*! now, *Dancer*! now *Prancer* and *Vixen*!

On, *Comet*! on, *Cupid*! on, *Donner* and *Blitzen*!

To the top of the porch! to the top of the wall!

Now dash away! dash away! dash away all!"

As leaves that before the wild hurricane fly,

When they meet with an obstacle, mount to the sky;

So up to the housetop the coursers they flew

With the sleigh full of toys, and St. Nicholas too—

And then, in a twinkling, I heard on the roof

The prancing and pawing of each little hoof.

As I drew in my head, and was turning around,

Down the chimney St. Nicholas came with a bound.

He was dressed all in fur, from his head to his foot,

And his clothes were all tarnished with ashes and soot;

A bundle of toys he had flung on his back,

And he looked like a peddler just opening his pack.

His eyes—how they twinkled! his dimples, how merry!

His cheeks were like roses, his nose like a cherry!

His droll little mouth was drawn up like a bow,

And the beard on his chin was as white as the snow;

The stump of a pipe he held tight in his teeth,

And the smoke, it encircled his head like a wreath;

He had a broad face and a little round belly

That shook when he laughed, like a bowl full of jelly.

He was chubby and plump, a right jolly old elf,

And I laughed when I saw him, in spite of myself;

A wink of his eye and a twist of his head

Soon gave me to know I had nothing to dread;

He spoke not a word, but went straight to his work,

And filled all the stockings; then turned with a jerk,

And laying his finger aside of his nose,

And giving a nod, up the chimney he rose;

He sprang to his sleigh, to his team gave a whistle,

And away they all flew like the down of a thistle.

But I heard him exclaim, ere he drove out of sight—

"Happy Christmas to all, and to all a good night!"

Carrie and Frances walked through the night together, their frosty breath rising up to dance against the clear sky as the wind caught it and pulled it away.

"Each Christmas just seems to get better," Frances said.

Carrie agreed. "I believe that's because each year brings us more people to love," she mused.

Frances nodded thoughtfully. "That's true. I'm sad, though, that Marcus and Hannah couldn't join us. Especially Willard. I thought about Grace all day today."

Carrie wrapped an arm around her daughter as they drew close to the barn. Frances had been close to Grace. "I know you miss her."

Frances nodded. "I try not to think about Grace burning up in the fire last year, but it's hard," she admitted. "She and Willard were sad to have to go back to Richmond so she could work at the Spotswood Hotel on Christmas Eve." She swallowed. "It still doesn't seem like she's really dead, sometimes."

"I know," Carrie replied softly. "We all miss her."

"You're sure Marcus, Hannah, and Willard will be here tomorrow?"

"I'm certain," Carrie assured her. "I know they wanted to be here longer, but they had some things come up at Riverside Carriages that needed to be taken care of. That's why they sent another driver to bring Felicia home. They wouldn't miss Hazel's wedding."

"I bet they just don't want to miss Annie's Christmas cooking," Frances said with a giggle.

"That, too," Carrie agreed. She fell silent as they entered the barn. Even though No Regrets hadn't shown the signs of being within twenty-four hours of giving birth, she was still checking on her every night. Since none of them had guessed she was pregnant, she might also bypass the normal signs and have her foal when no one was paying attention. If it were spring, she wouldn't be so concerned. December's brittle cold changed the scenario completely. If there were a problem, the foal could freeze to death.

The barn was cold, but being out of the wind felt wonderful. Most of the horses were sleeping, but a few snuffled a greeting. Carrie held up the lantern as they approached No Regrets' stall. She frowned when the mare didn't stick her head over the stall door.

"Mama?" Frances asked, her voice echoing the nervousness Carrie felt.

Chapter Twenty-Four

Carrie relaxed a little when she saw No Regrets standing against the back wall of the stall. "Wait here," she told Frances.

No Regrets looked up at her when she entered, her tail swishing in silent protest about what was going on inside of her. She gazed at her side and then back at Carrie with pleading eyes.

"It's alright, girl," Carrie said soothingly. She moved to No Regrets' head, stroking her nose gently as she gazed into her liquid eyes. After several minutes of talking to her, she knelt down and looked up. Wax-like beads clung to both teats.

"What do you see, Mama?" Frances asked quietly.

"There are droplets of colostrum on her teats," Carrie told her. "They usually appear twelve to thirty-six hours before foaling." She thought backwards. "I last checked on No Regrets six hours ago. The droplets weren't there."

"So she's going to have her baby tonight?" Frances asked, careful to keep her excited voice very quiet.

Carrie stood again and moved to the mare's head. "Tonight or tomorrow," she said. There was no way of knowing for sure.

"What are you going to do, Mama?"

"Stay with her until she gives birth." Though it was possible it would be tomorrow night, her gut told her it would happen sooner. Carrie patted No

Regrets' neck and strode across the stall. "I'm going to change out of this dress," she said crisply. "I have breeches in the tack room." She thought as she walked across the barn. "Go over to the house and change your clothes, dear."

"Do I tell everyone?" Frances asked.

"You can tell them No Regrets is beginning her labor, but ask them to not come to the barn. She doesn't need an audience. It will only upset her and cause the other horses to be restless."

"But I can be here?"

Carrie smiled. "Of course. I promised you could. I remember the first time I saw a mare give birth. It's something I'll never forget." She was excited to share No Regrets' birth with her daughter. "Ask your father to give you two blankets and ask Annie to prepare a basket of food. It could be a long night."

"Should I tell Miles to come?"

Carrie considered the question and then shook her head. "Not now. I think it's going to be a while before she gives birth, but since No Regrets hasn't done anything the way I would expect, I'm not willing to count on that. I suspect Miles will join me sometime during the night, but there's no reason to pull him away from the Christmas celebration now."

Frances nodded somberly, only her glistening eyes revealing how excited she was. "I'll be back soon!"

Carrie changed quickly, shrugged into a thick barn coat, and shoved her feet into sturdy barn boots. She should have asked Frances for thick socks, but this would do.

"Hey, girl," Carrie crooned as she moved back to the stall. Respecting No Regrets' need to be alone, she leaned against the door and looked in.

No Regrets swung her head to meet Carrie's gaze.

Something about the mare's penetrating stare was discomfiting, but Carrie couldn't identify what she was sensing. She felt ridiculous wondering if No Regrets was sending her a message. "You're going to be just fine," she said gently. "Take your time. I'll be here with you."

Twenty minutes later, Frances appeared, her arms laden with supplies. She had changed into warm breeches, boots, and her father's thick barn coat. The coat swallowed her, but Carrie was certain there was a thick layer of sweaters filling the bulky space beneath it. Abby wouldn't have let her out of the house again without ensuring she would stay warm.

Carrie smiled and silently emptied her daughter's arms, placing the items on the barn floor. She'd already pulled over a large wooden trunk they could sit on while they waited.

"How is she?" Frances whispered.

"I know she's wondering what's going on, but she's fine." The documents from the sale had revealed this would be No Regrets' first foal. "Just like women rise to the occasion during their first birth, so do mares. God equipped them to handle it."

Frances pulled a pair of thick socks from a deep pocket. "Daddy sent these for you."

Carrie grinned and sent him a silent blessing. She pulled off her boots, slipped on the wool socks, and put her boots back on. She felt instantly warmer.

"And a canteen with coffee," Frances added as she set down the large basket of food Annie had prepared.

Carrie reached for it eagerly. She wanted to drink it before it cooled. She was certain Annie would bring her more when she was finished working at the house.

"Are you hungry, Mama?"

Carrie chuckled. "I'm still stuffed after our huge meal. I couldn't possibly eat anything."

Frances eyed the basket. "Annie sent a lot of food."

"Annie always sends more than enough, but we'll be hungry before this is all over," Carrie assured her.

Frances looked over the stall door. "She's still just standing there swishing her tail."

Carrie nodded. "She's just begun labor. The birth will happen at her own pace."

Frances looked uncertain. "What if she has trouble?"

"Then we'll help her," Carrie said calmly. "Don't worry, honey. Most mares give birth without any trouble at all." It wasn't necessary to tell Frances about the few times it hadn't gone smoothly. If No Regrets got in trouble, that would be soon enough to explain how they would assist her.

Frances continued to look nervous. "It's awfully cold, Mama. The foal is going to be born all wet."

"That's true," Carrie agreed, pleased Frances was thinking ahead. She pointed toward a stack of supplies she'd brought out from the tack room. "We'll use those towels to dry the foal off as quickly as possible. Once it's mostly dry, we'll keep it warm with a blanket Chooli made," Carrie explained. "The Navajo are famous for their horse blankets. Chooli used to help her grandfather make them before she left the reservation. I told her I was concerned about this birth, so she made a blanket."

Frances tilted her head. "How are you going to keep it on?"

Carrie held up several large blanket pins. "Blankets aren't uncommon, Frances. We hardly ever use them here because our foals are born in late spring, after the weather has warmed. The first commercial blankets were manufactured by Troy Woolen Mills in New Hampshire, back in 1857. Miles told me all about them. The stables he worked at in Canada used them often for their foals because the weather was so unpredictable."

"So, the foal will be alright?"

Carrie nodded. "Clint added more straw to the stall today. The foal will have a wonderful place to rest."

Frances' eyes cleared of trouble for the first time. "You sure you don't want a biscuit, Mama?"

"I'm fine," Carrie assured her. "Eat whatever you want." She stood and looked over the stall door again. Her heart quickened when she realized No Regrets' neck and flank were now damp.

Frances edged in beside her. "Why is she sweating?" Her voice was alarmed again.

"Shhh..." Carrie cautioned in a soft voice. "We want to be calm. Our being nervous will make her nervous."

"I'm sorry," Frances whispered contritely.

"Don't feel badly," Carrie said as she squeezed her daughter's hand. "I understand how nerve-racking your first birth can be." She looked over the stall door again. "Sweating is a normal part of birth," she explained. "No Regrets is positioning her foal so it can be born. The foal has been on its back in her womb, but now the baby is rotating until its head and forelimbs are extended in the birth canal. The outward signs for the mother are sweating and restlessness."

As if on cue, No Regrets began to move, walking to one end of the stall and then turning. She stared at her flanks and pawed the ground.

"The baby is coming tonight, isn't it?" Frances whispered.

Carrie nodded and smiled, suddenly very eager to see their Christmas baby. She sat back down on the trunk. "No Regrets knows what to do. The end of this stage is marked by rupture of the allantois membrane and a sudden release of allantois fluid. It usually takes one to four hours after the mare starts to sweat."

Frances listened closely. "How do you know so much, Mama?"

"I helped Miles as much as I could when I was young, but most of this I learned from books," she admitted. "When Robert was murdered, and I was suddenly the owner of a breeding stable, I realized I needed to know far more than I did."

"Felicia says you can learn anything from a book," Frances said. "Is that true?"

Carrie considered the question. "I believe you can learn just about anything that is *known* from a book. That doesn't mean it's true, though," she cautioned.

"Not true?" Frances asked in a confused voice.

"Just because someone wrote something doesn't make it true. People can put untrue things in a book as easily as they can speak untruth. You always have to keep learning, and you have to make your own decisions." Carrie knew the importance of what she was saying. She was glad for this time in the barn with her daughter to have this conversation. "New things are always being learned. What may seem like knowledge today could very well be proven wrong tomorrow. You have to keep an open mind, and you have to keep looking for the most recent information."

"It sounds very hard to know the truth," Frances said.

"It can be," Carrie agreed. "Do you want to be the best doctor you can be, Frances?"

Frances nodded immediately. "Of course, Mama."

"Then you will need to do the hard work of being educated. I learned a lot of things in medical school, but since then I've discovered that many of the things I was taught weren't true."

"They made it up?" Frances' eyes were large in the lantern light.

"No," Carrie said quickly. "They taught us what they knew at the time, but medicine is constantly evolving. If I want to help my patients the best way I can, I can never stop learning."

Miles appeared at the door of the barn. He walked over, glanced into the stall, and then settled on the trunk next to Carrie. "She's pushin' her baby into place," he said quietly. "She seem to be havin' any trouble?"

Carrie shook her head. "No. She's doing well."

Miles eyed the blankets and basket of food. "I reckon you and Frances plannin' on being here till that baby be born?"

"Yes," Frances replied excitedly. "It's going to be my first birth."

Miles chuckled. "Something you ain't never gonna forget," he assured her. His eyes took in the wool blanket and the towels, and he nodded his satisfaction. "You know where I be. You need anythin', just let me know."

Carrie squeezed his hand. "We will."

Miles stood slowly. "I'm goin' on up. Annie be over right soon. She wouldn't hear of not gettin' some things ready for breakfast."

Carrie heard the weariness in his voice. He was doing well but was still recovering from his bout of pneumonia. "Good night, Miles," she said tenderly.

Three hours later, Carrie heard No Regrets grunt as she lowered herself to the floor of her stall. Carrie grinned and looked over the stall door again, checking to make sure the mare hadn't positioned herself too close to the wooden wall. The foal would need space to slip from the birth canal. No Regrets was in the far corner but was positioned perfectly. Carrie remained where she was, content to watch for now. The mare didn't need her help.

She smiled tenderly as she gazed at Frances. They'd talked for almost two hours before she had curled up in a mound of hay Carrie had created for her, covered herself with a blanket, and fallen fast asleep.

No Regrets' head stayed up, staring back at her flank as she shifted around in an attempt to get comfortable.

Carrie knew the foal had begun its journey down the birth canal.

As soon as No Regrets laid down flat and extended her legs, Carrie knew it was time to wake her daughter. "Frances," she whispered. Carrie shook her shoulder gently. "It's almost time, honey."

Frances bolted upright immediately, her eyes instantly awake. "Is it happening, Mama?"

"It is," Carrie replied as she moved back to the stall door and beckoned her daughter to join her.

Frances was beside her in a flash. "Is she alright?"

"No Regrets is doing fine," Carrie said quietly. "She's lying down like that because it makes it easier to push the foal out."

No Regrets strained, grunting as she struggled to give birth. For just a moment, Carrie was gripped with a sadness that she would never know that feeling. She'd been unconscious when Bridget was born, and would never have another opportunity. The feeling of Frances' shoulder against hers snapped her out of her memories. She had two beautiful daughters whom she adored.

Frances gripped her hand tightly and leaned forward. "Mama!"

Carrie smiled as the tip of the foal's nose appeared, enclosed in the bluish-white amnion. "It won't be long now."

No Regrets grunted again as she pushed. The foal's head, front legs, and shoulders eased out onto the straw.

Carrie winced with pain as Frances grabbed her hand in a death grip, but she understood. Seeing the miracle of birth for the first time was intense. She felt Frances' body tighten when No Regrets sighed and flattened her head on the straw. "She's resting for a moment," Carrie whispered. "Everything is fine."

No Regrets closed her eyes for several moments. When she opened them, she was staring directly at Carrie. She didn't look away as she grunted and strained again.

Carrie shivered as the mare communicated a silent message that she still didn't understand.

Moments later, the foal, still encased in the amniotic membrane, slid all the way out onto the straw. The membrane broke, revealing its dark bay color.

Carrie wanted to jump into the stall and start toweling the foal dry immediately, but she forced herself to stay where she was, because the baby was receiving essential blood from the placenta via the umbilical cord.

"Why isn't the foal moving?" Frances' whisper was frantic.

"Everyone is resting," Carrie whispered back. "It can take up to an hour, but I'm not going to give the foal more than ten minutes because of how cold it is." She kept her voice calm, determined not to let her daughter know how anxious she was about the weather conditions. The outside temperature was in the teens. She didn't want to prematurely rupture the umbilical cord, but she also didn't want the foal to freeze.

Carrie kept an eye on her pocket watch, breathing a sigh of relief when the foal began to move at minute eight. She continued to watch carefully as the foal, who she could now identify as a colt, continued to struggle. The umbilical cord broke when the colt managed to raise himself to his knees.

Carrie caught her breath with appreciation when the colt lifted his head. Even though he was just a few minutes old, she could tell he was an exquisite specimen; a true representation of No Regrets and Lexington. She had seen enough pictures of the famous stallion to know his son carried the conformation of his famous Thoroughbred sire.

"Can I help towel him dry?" Frances asked.

"I'm sorry, honey, but no. Both of us in there at the same time will make No Regrets nervous, and could also frighten the colt." When Frances nodded her understanding, Carrie grabbed the towels and blankets and eased her way into the stall.

"Hello," she crooned tenderly, walking slowly over to the colt. The colt froze briefly before it met her eyes and relaxed. Carrie, expecting more alarm, was puzzled but grateful. "I'm going to dry you off, little boy. You've chosen a terribly cold night to be born." The colt kept his eyes fixed on her as she began to rub him gently. She switched to new towels, until the last one collected no moisture.

No Regrets watched her closely but showed no concern. It was obvious she knew Carrie was helping.

When the colt was dry, Carrie stepped back. She wouldn't blanket him until he had stood and eaten. He needed his mother's colostrum. The effort and warm milk would protect him.

The colt watched her intently for a moment and gathered his front legs beneath him. He shook his head, blinked his eyes, and gave a light whinny.

No Regrets whinnied back, folded her legs beneath her and stood. Once standing, she lowered her head and nudged her foal encouragingly.

Carrie remained kneeling but edged her way back to give the new mama and baby the space they needed. She looked over her shoulder at Frances, who was grinning with delight as her eyes devoured the new foal.

"He's beautiful," Frances said, her voice trembling with awe.

Carrie started to respond but was distracted by the colt lurching forward to try to stand. She heard Frances' giggle when he wobbled for a moment and fell over on his side. The colt whinnied to his mama, rested for a moment, and pushed forward onto his front legs again. Carrie resisted the temptation to help him. His efforts to stand were making him stronger, but she also knew if his bones were not fully formed, her attempt to help could do permanent damage to his joints.

Carrie watched quietly as the colt gathered his strength and lurched upward again. This time, he managed to stand on all four hooves, though he swayed as he fought for his balance.

"That's a mighty fine colt."

Carrie smiled at Miles when he appeared next to Frances. She could barely glimpse the breaking of dawn through the barn door. Until that moment, she hadn't realized the entire night had passed. Energized by the birth, she didn't feel fatigued at all.

She turned back to watch the colt stagger toward his mama in search of milk. She was surprised when he continued to sway slightly but turned *away* from No Regrets, and instead turned toward her.

The colt stood quietly for a few minutes, allowing his legs to grow steadier, and wobbled slowly through the thick straw toward Carrie, his dark eyes fixed on her.

Carrie held her breath, a deep sense of wonder creeping into her mind and heart. Was it possible?

The colt continued forward to where she was kneeling and stopped just short of her. Slowly, his eyes still fixed on hers, he thrust his head forward until his forehead touched hers.

Carrie's eyes filled with tears. She reached up and let her trembling hands hold the colt's head. "Granite?" Her words came out in a broken whisper. She had told him that if he returned, he would have to let her know it was him.

Her mind spun back to the first moment she'd seen him when she was fourteen; a prancing, rambunctious gelding whose gray coat glistened and gleamed in the sun like burnished pewter. He had immediately calmed when he saw her, lowering his head to come over and accept her caresses. Everyone had been astonished when he'd pressed his forehead against hers with a gentle nicker.

The colt stood quietly, his forehead pressed to hers, and then nickered gently.

Tears spilled from Carrie's eyes as she kissed his soft muzzle tenderly. "Welcome back, boy. Welcome back."

Her heart filled with a joy that she knew could never be described with mere words.

The colt whinnied again and walked carefully back to No Regrets, found her swollen teat, and began to greedily drink.

Carrie sank back into the hay and devoured him with her eyes.

"Well, I'll be," Miles said quietly, his voice filled with the same awe she felt.

Carrie looked up at him, her vision blurred with tears of happiness.

"That's him, ain't it?" Miles' eyes blazed in the lantern light.

Carrie nodded silently, not sure what she should say.

"Mama?" Frances asked. "What does Miles mean?"

Carrie searched for words to express the miracle that had happened. How could she explain what she didn't understand herself?

Miles did it for her. "Do you figure miracles can happen at Christmastime, Frances?"

Frances furrowed her brow and nodded. "Christmas seems to be the perfect time for miracles, Mr. Miles."

"Well, girl, you're lookin' at a miracle. Sometimes God knows a connection be so strong that it just ain't meant to be broken. Your mama and Granite had that kind of connection. I reckon God knew that, so He sent him back to be with your mama."

Carrie held her breath, wondering how her daughter would respond to the revelation.

Frances, her eyes wide with wonder, stared back and forth between Carrie and the colt for a long moment as she considered Miles' words. Then her face split with a broad smile of happiness. "Merry Christmas Eve, Mama."

Carrie laughed loudly, her heart pulsing with vibrant joy.

The colt released his mama's teat for a moment, turned his dark eyes toward her with a knowing gaze, and then went back to feeding.

Carrie stayed where she was, envisioning the years ahead that she would share with her beloved horse.

When the colt stepped back, she moved forward and wrapped the warm blanket around him, pinning it securely in place. The colt rested his head on her shoulder as she worked. Carrie felt as if her heart were going to burst.

"What are you going to name him, Mama?"

Carrie shook her head. "I don't know." It didn't make sense to name a dark bay colt Granite, but it would take time to come up with a new name. No matter what she called him, she knew he would always be Granite to her.

Miles slipped into the stall and walked gently to the colt. Instead of showing alarm at a new human, the colt turned eagerly and whinnied again.

No Regrets watched calmly, evidently knowing her baby was in good hands.

"Well, hello again, boy," Miles said softly. He stroked the colt's nose as he examined his body. "Yep," he finally said.

"Yep, what?" Carrie asked. "What are you looking for?"

Miles continued to stroke the colt's muzzle. "See those gray eyelashes?"

Carrie leaned forward and nodded.

Miles pointed to a place high on the colt's forehead next, just beneath the thin forelock. "There be a few gray hairs. Yep," he repeated, "this colt is going to be gray. Just like Granite."

Carrie shook her head. "Miles, that isn't possible. He has two bay parents. No Regrets is a bay.

Lexington is definitely a bay. Two bays can't produce a gray foal."

"You're right," Miles agreed, "but this foal is going to be gray," he said with complete certainty. He stepped back and stared at the foal speculatively. "I don't know who his sire is, but it for sure ain't Lexington. He's a perfect specimen, but his sire ain't who we think it is."

Carrie shook her head in amazement, not caring who his sire truly was. "He's really going to be gray?"

"If I don't miss my guess, he's going to look just like Granite. See the black stockin's on all four legs? They gonna stay black, but the rest of him will be gray."

Carrie knew better than to argue with Miles when he was that certain.

Carrie lowered her head to the colt again, almost melting when he pressed his forehead into hers eagerly. "Welcome back, Granite," she said joyfully.

Granite nickered softly, lay down in the deep hay, and fell asleep.

Chapter Twenty-Five

Rose looked up when Carrie pushed through the front door. "I wasn't sure we would get you out of the barn today."

Carrie gave her a look of pure delight. "I wasn't sure you would, either." She laughed as she shrugged out of her coat and hung it on the hall tree. "It would take something like Hazel's wedding to get me to leave Granite."

Carrie had refused to leave No Regrets and Granite all day long. The mare seemed fine with sharing her foal, not minding when Granite curled up next to Carrie after feeding.

"What's it like?" Rose asked curiously.

Carrie searched for words to describe the feelings that had ranged from disbelief, to awe, to stunning joy. "It's like a piece of my heart has been returned to me," she said slowly. "It's more than that though..." Her voice trailed away for several moments. "I've seen a miracle happen, Rose. I believed he was coming back..." She stopped again. "I guess I should say I believed he *told* me he was coming back. I was holding onto that belief because it was the only thing giving me hope that one day my heart wouldn't hurt so badly."

Speaking her thoughts was helping her make sense of what she'd experienced. "When it happened... when I realized it was *Granite*... I thought my heart would explode with joy and disbelief. Every time he came up to me today and pressed his forehead into mine, I could feel another piece of my heart healing."

"It's been a hard year," Rose said quietly.

Carrie nodded. "There have been so many difficult things that have happened. I've learned so much about having the courage to press through, but I was struggling with feeling joy, because I was focusing on all the pain life has thrown our way."

"And is going to *continue* to throw our way," Rose replied tersely.

Carrie saw the pain shining in her friend's eyes. "What's happened?" she asked quietly.

Rose shrugged. "Nothing new. Jed is doing his best to embrace a Cromwell Christmas, but I see the pain lurking in his eyes. I hate what happened to his parents. I *hate* what is happening in our country." She shook her head, her voice immediately contrite. "I'm sorry, Carrie. I'm not trying to ruin your perfect day."

"You're not," Carrie assured her. She walked over to where Rose was standing by the window and slipped an arm around her waist. The dining room was miraculously empty, giving them an opportunity to talk.

"I know I shouldn't be thinking about these things at Christmas, but I can't keep them out of my mind," Rose admitted in a trembling voice. "Morris is dead. Jed will always remember seeing his mama shot in front of him. Vincent will always carry the scars of the beating. Octavius is dead. Caroline is grieving. ..." She shook her head. "In the beginning, I believed life would get better when slavery was abolished, and my people were free. It's not happening, Carrie."

Carrie squeezed her hand tightly. Rose fought hard to stay positive in the face of pain, but there were times when it became more than she could bear. "What brings you joy, Rose?"

Rose swung around and stared at her, anger sparking in her eyes before it faded to a resigned sadness. "Joy?"

Carrie understood the discouragement and disbelief in her voice. "Last night, when I went to the barn, I was feeling much of what you're feeling. It started when I thought about Grace. Just a year ago, she was laughing with us on Christmas Eve morning. She was dead within twenty-four hours." She shook her head to clear the memory. "We've had so many hard things to endure. I remember something your mama told me one time."

Rose sighed. "If you're getting ready to quote my mama, then I suppose I'm going to have to decide to feel better."

Carrie laughed and squeezed her best friend's hand more tightly. "Your mama told me one time that when I be hurtin' more than I think I can bear, I got to find a place inside where there be joy. The joy will burn out the pain."

The sound of children's laughter bubbled through the house. Jed's laughter rang louder than the rest as it forced itself through the cracks around the kitchen door.

Rose smiled slightly. "I guess Jed is letting joy burn out the pain."

Carrie thought again about Granite. "Dawn was breaking outside the barn when Granite was born,

Rose. I could see the rosy glow through the barn entrance when I realized it was him." She paused, trying to identify what she'd been feeling. "I felt... I felt like I was being renewed by the dawn." She stopped again, searching for words. "After so many difficult things, it felt like a new time was dawning."

"Renewed by the dawn..." Rose repeated quietly. "I like that." Her voice grew more intense. "Do you really think that will happen, Carrie? We've had hard things for a terribly long time. Just when I think it's going to get easier, it seems to get harder." She pressed her forehead against the cold windowpane.

Carrie understood the desperation in her voice. She'd felt it many times, but she'd also just witnessed a miracle. "I believe joy can burn out the pain," she said softly. "We have to look for joy every single place we can, Rose."

More laughter floated to them.

Rose smiled. "It's so much easier to find joy when you're a child," she said wistfully.

"Is it?" Carrie asked seriously. "John fought to find joy again when Rascal was killed in the flood. Felicia fought to find joy when her parents were killed in Memphis. We'll probably never know how hard that was for her." She paused. "Frances had to find joy after her entire family died from the flu and she was forced into an orphanage. Minnie lost her entire family last year in the fire. I can't believe finding joy was easy for any of them."

Rose looked into her eyes thoughtfully. "You're right," she admitted. "I suppose joy has to be a choice." She frowned and then laughed. "What am I talking about? My mama told me for most of my life that I had to choose joy in the midst of pain." Her frown turned into a scowl. "Why is it so hard for me?"

Carrie shook her head. "You choose joy more than anyone I know, Rose. That doesn't mean you aren't human. It doesn't mean there aren't times you're struggling. You're not feeling badly because of your own pain. You're feeling badly because of a little boy that is suffering more than he should." She took a deep breath. "It's up to us to teach the children..."

"Teach them what?" Rose asked.

"Teach that each day is a new beginning. Each dawn brings the promise of a new day." Carrie said firmly as she turned and looked toward the barn. "We're teaching them that every dawn brings the possibility of a miracle."

Carrie's bedroom was crowded with women. Polly worked on Hazel's hair, with Amber standing close by to hand her the pins she needed. Rose was sewing the final buttons on. Frances was creating a flower bouquet made from beautiful, fresh blooms she had gathered in the greenhouse earlier in the day. Phoebe sat on the window seat, observing everything with amusement. Carrie knew nothing was required of her, so she was content to gaze at the barn and remember the miracle curled up in the straw.

Annie, Abby, and Minnie were hard at work in the kitchen, finalizing the meal that would be served after the ceremony.

Thomas and Wally were replacing the candles on the Christmas tree, ensuring they would burn safely through the evening.

Carrie frowned suddenly. "Where is Moses?" She hadn't seen him all day or afternoon. As soon as she said his name, she realized something else that she'd been oblivious to because of Granite. "And where is my husband?"

Rose shrugged. "I'm sure they're busy with something," she said casually, keeping her eyes fastened on Hazel's gown.

Carrie's eyes narrowed. Rose sounded *too* casual, but nobody else in the room seemed to notice. She started to open her mouth to demand more information, but Rose turned to her and shook her head slightly, her eyes dancing with fun.

Carrie narrowed her eyes but remained silent. The expression in her friend's eyes revealed some kind of surprise was in the works. She wouldn't be the one to spoil it, but as she looked back toward the barn, her mind spun with anticipation as she tried to imagine what the surprise could be.

Polly put a final pin into Hazel's hair and stepped back. "It's done," she said with satisfaction.

Amber smiled brightly. "You look beautiful, Hazel!"

Hazel gazed into the ornate gold mirror that hid the Cromwell family secret, her surprised expression revealing she recognized the truth of Amber's statement. Her dark hair was swept into a bun high on her head. Fresh flowers created a halo of blooms that glowed in the lantern light.

Carrie wondered how many weddings the mirror had witnessed. When it traveled from Europe, wrapped securely inside a large crate deep in the bowels of a ship, it could never have imagined what it would experience. She was grateful for all the wonderful events that had played out in her bedroom, witnessed by the beautiful mirror.

Rose pulled the dress off its hanger and carried it over to Hazel. "It's time," she said softly.

Hazel blinked her amber eyes and held her slender, caramel-colored arms in the air.

Polly stepped in to help Rose slide the gown over Hazel's head, protecting the bride's hair as she did.

Phoebe stepped forward and buttoned the back. "It's lovely," she said softly.

"Oh!" Amber cried. She clapped her hands excitedly. "You are so beautiful, Hazel. Clint is going to be so excited when he sees you." She lowered her voice. "My brother is real nervous, you know."

Hazel turned away from the mirror and looked at Amber with wondering eyes. "What could he possibly be nervous about?"

Amber smirked. "I might have told him that he's not good enough for someone as beautiful and wonderful as you are."

"Amber!" Hazel's voice was shocked.

Amber laughed and waved her hand. "Don't worry. I told him this morning that I wasn't sure *you* were good enough for someone as handsome and wonderful as *he* is. That made him feel better. He doesn't need to know that I meant what I said in the beginning. Abby has been teaching me about male ego."

Laughter filled the room.

Phoebe stood and walked over to her best friend. "Amber might be right, you know. I'm not sure anyone is good enough for someone as beautiful and wonderful as you are, Hazel. You are the most beautiful bride I've ever seen." She looked at Polly next. "You've made the loveliest wedding gown in the world, Polly."

Hazel turned back to the mirror and slowly slid her hands down the white silk, twisting and turning as the glow from the fireplace brought the fabric to life in swirling colors. "She's right, Polly," she whispered. "I never imagined having such a beautiful gown." Tears filled her eyes as she spun and wrapped Polly in her arms. "Thank you!"

Polly laughed as she stepped back quickly. "You're welcome, Hazel, but I ain't gonna let you put any wrinkles in that dress." Her black eyes flashed with pleasure. "My son is getting a real special woman. I hope the two of you will be as happy as Gabe and I have been."

"Me too," Hazel murmured. "Me too."

Hazel linked her arm through Gabe's and moved to the top of the sweeping staircase that led to the parlor. Boughs of fragrant cedar, adorned with red ribbon, wrapped around the shining banisters. She was other lucky women who had walked down this staircase to start a new life with the man they loved. In the short time she'd been a part of Cromwell Plantation, she'd grown to understand just how special a place it was.

"What you thinking?" Gabe asked quietly.

Hazel gazed at her almost father-in-law. "I'm thinking that right now I feel like the luckiest woman in the world. When I rolled onto Cromwell Plantation for the first time, I knew my life was going to drastically change." She smiled. "I had no idea just how drastically, however."

Gabe returned her smile. "Clint told me he fell in love with you the instant he laid eyes on you."

"The same thing happened to me," Hazel replied as she envisioned the moment she saw the tall, handsome stable manager.

"It was when he saw you ride a horse that he knew he couldn't live without you," Gabe added.

Hazel grinned. "It definitely gave me an advantage." She would never forget the long ride that had ended with a picnic on the banks of the James River, or how Clint had declared his love for her.

Gabe eyed her. "He would have married you that first week, you know."

"I know," Hazel agreed. "I should have," she acknowledged. "I knew I loved him, but it seemed foolish to make such a fast decision. In retrospect, I should have."

Gabe squinted and shook his head. "Retrospect? Girl, you got lots of fancy words."

Hazel chuckled. "So does your son," she assured him. "He just uses most of his in relation to horses. He reads as much as I do." She eyed Gabe. "He told me you were the one who made sure he had all the magazines and books he needed to learn about horses. He's aware how much you sacrificed to get them for him."

Gabe shrugged, but his eyes shone with pride. "Ain't no use doing something if you ain't gonna do it right. I reckon my boy knows a whole lot about horses, sure enough."

"He's amazing," Hazel said. "Susan has told me many times that she couldn't run the stables without him."

Down below, Abby began to play the piano. The quiet strains of music flowed through the parlor door and swirled up the staircase.

Gabe squeezed Hazel's hand as he tucked it more firmly in the crook of his arm. "And Clint tells me he can't live his life without *you*. Let's go down and put that boy out of his misery."

Clint took a deep breath as the music started. The night he had long awaited had arrived. He found it almost impossible to believe Hazel Rollins was going to be his wife. He had dreamed of this moment since he'd first seen her in the barn six months earlier.

The parlor was the perfect place for their wedding. The Christmas tree glowed with candles whose light glimmered off the decorations and ornaments. Candles adorned every windowsill, the fireplace mantle, and every table. Cedar garlands provided a rich aroma that blended with the smells wafting from the kitchen. Dining room chairs, in addition to the sofas and parlor chairs, provided just enough seating for the people who had joined them.

Clint looked over the group, his eyes resting on Willard. Willard had agreed to come to Cromwell with Marcus and Hannah for Christmas, but Clint knew his friend had to be haunted by the fact that his beloved wife had died in the Spotswood Hotel exactly one year ago. He appreciated him being here but didn't think he could have done the same if the roles were reversed. Willard looked up, met his gaze, and smiled broadly. Clint returned his smile, recognizing the soul-searing sadness in his friend's eyes.

Clint's only regret was that he hadn't been able to finish the cabin he was building before the wedding. The flu had disrupted all his plans. When the entire barn operation became dependent upon himself and Amber, he'd been forced to put his free time into more hours at the barn. He hadn't been back to the cabin in over two weeks. He'd hoped to accomplish more, even if it wouldn't be finished in time for the wedding, but Miles, still healing, had needed help. He would never disappoint the man who was both a role model and a mentor, so he'd not mentioned anything about his desire to finish the cabin. It would happen. In the meantime, they would be fine living with his parents.

At least he had tonight to look forward to. Miles and Annie had offered to move over to the house and give the newlyweds the apartment above the barn for their wedding night. Clint had accepted eagerly.

A sudden rustle of cloth jolted Clint out of his thoughts. He latched his eyes on the parlor door as the music played louder. Just as the song reached a crescendo, Hazel appeared in the doorway.

Clint caught his breath and stared at her with wonder. Was it truly possible this beautiful woman was becoming his wife? She shone with exuberance and life, her glistening eyes fixed on his with a look of adoration. He wondered if the pounding of his heart could be heard over the music, and decided he didn't care.

His smile matched hers as she glided across the floor toward him.

When they came to a stop in from of him and the minister Thomas had persuaded to officiate on Christmas Eve, Gabe leaned over and spoke to him in a low voice. "Boy, you better treat her like the jewel she is."

Clint met his father's eyes. "You can count on it."

Hazel smiled and stepped forward to stand beside him.

The minister looked out over the assembled group and began. "We are gathered here tonight…"

Moses pushed back from the table and smiled at the scant residue of their dinner celebration. The food had disappeared almost magically, leaving nothing behind but stray crumbs of the cake Minnie had insisted on making. Much to her delight, everyone agreed it was delicious.

"I'd say it's time for the last announcement," Moses said. "If I'm right, there's a wedding couple eager to have some time to themselves."

Clint and Hazel laughed along with everyone else as they exchanged puzzled looks.

Moses' smile broadened as he turned to look into Clint's eyes. "Did I ever tell you about the night Rose and I were married right here in this same parlor?"

Clint shook his head.

"Marrying Rose was the best thing that ever happened to me," Moses said, letting his eyes rest lovingly on his wife. Rose beamed back at him, her eyes shining with excitement. "I only had one regret," he continued. "I wanted a home to take her to, but all we had was the little shack her mama had lived in." He paused and smiled. "Until Carrie decided that just wouldn't do for her best friend."

Clint and Hazel stared at Moses, their expressions revealing they had no idea where this story was going.

"Carrie had a special wedding gift for us," Moses told them. "Without us knowing it, she'd had a new cabin built for us, and she'd filled it with furniture." He shook his head, remembering just how he'd felt when he and Rose realized what she'd done for them. "She made our wedding night something we never forgot...not to mention the rest of the time we lived in that cabin before we escaped for Philadelphia."

He looked back at the couple. "Rose came to me two weeks ago, Clint. She told me you hadn't been able to finish the cabin because of the flu."

A look of wonder began to dawn in both Clint and Hazel's eyes.

Moses grinned. "Have you been wondering why Miles kept finding more things for you to do around the barn?"

Clint smiled but remained silent.

"Clint and Hazel, aside from the fact that all of us love you, the two of you are incredibly valuable to the plantation. It was the very least we could do to make sure you have a home on your wedding night. A group of my men have been working to finish your cabin." Moses grinned, feeling the same excitement he saw shining in the couple's eyes. "It's waiting for you."

Cheers and clapping exploded around the table.

Hazel was the first who spoke, her voice wobbly through her tears. "I knew when I arrived at Cromwell Plantation that I'd come to a special place. At the time, I couldn't know *how* special." She took a deep breath. "Thank you." She looked around the table, her eyes resting on Rose at the end. "Thank you all."

Rose grinned. "There is a carriage waiting for you out front. Jeb will be driving you to the cabin."

"You done got lots of food waitin' for you," Annie added. "Minnie and I made sure of that."

"There are a whole bunch of quilts to keep you warm," Polly added. "The Bregdan Women made them special for you." She smiled. "We would have been real happy to have you and Clint stay with us for a while, but I'm glad you got your own place."

Tears flowed freely down Hazel's cheeks.

Clint took her hand and stood, lifting her to stand beside him. "There aren't words to say how much this means to us. Thank you," he said hoarsely. "We love all of you."

He grinned widely. "Now, if you don't mind, I'm taking my wife home."

Chapter Twenty-Six

New Year's Day, 1872

Carrie and Rose, arm in arm, led the way through the tunnel door out onto the shores of the James River. As they broke out into the early morning cold, Carrie thought back over the years she and Rose had celebrated the beginning of a new year on a large rock in the river, further west of where they stood now. For many years, it had been just the two of them.

Slowly, it had begun to grow. Now, there were fifteen women and girls taking seats on the logs Moses and his men had placed in a large circle around a towering bonfire they would light as soon as the sun rose.

New Year's Day was a Cromwell tradition they all treasured.

The snow clouds from the night before had blown further north. A few bright stars still dotted the dark blue horizon when Carrie looked west. The blustery wind from the south had pushed the snow away and then died down to complete calm, but not before bringing in warmer temperatures.

Carrie snuggled into her coat. It was still cold, but not quite the brittle cold that made her fear her frosty breath would crack apart in mid-air. A smattering of clouds visible in the eastern sky promised a glorious sunrise. She fixed her eyes on the horizon and thought about the year she had just lived.

Silence reigned as everyone sat with their own thoughts. It was tradition that no one spoke until the sun had fully risen, giving each person time to ponder the year just lived, and also to contemplate the new year that was beginning.

Intermingled with hard memories of the year were wonderful memories. She had long ago learned that life was always a mixture of hard and good. While there had certainly been hard things in 1871, the last week of joy had eased the pain.

Carrie sighed happily as she thought back over the days since Granite had returned. She'd spent many hours with him every day, slipping out of bed extra early every morning so she could be with him before heading to the clinic. She loved the predawn hours because they were alone in the barn. The long-legged colt was a youngster in every way, except his eyes, which shone with an expected wisdom.

Anthony, Frances, and Minnie slipped into the barn several times a day to see him. They were his other favorite people, though he always greeted everyone with a shrill whinny.

She spent hours grooming both Granite and No Regrets. She was content to sit quietly in the straw while the colt fed and slept. Carrie had told him everything that happened in the months he'd been gone. She swore she could detect both sadness and joy in his eyes as he listened.

Carrie smiled as she thought of his first morning outside in the snow with No Regrets. He had danced and pranced with the same exuberant joy he'd always exhibited. He leapt and bucked, delighting in the sprays of snow he kicked up. No Regrets watched with a look of gentle indulgence. When he had finally tired of the snow, he trotted over to where Carrie stood, his tail and head held high. When he bounced to a stop, his eyes had bubbled with happiness.

It would be three years before she could ride Granite, but her mind was full of the adventures they would have while she waited for him to grow.

When Carrie pulled her thoughts away from Granite and looked around the circle, she saw Abby watching her with a tender, knowing look. Carrie grinned, knowing her mother was reading her thoughts, as usual.

Her eyes caught the horizon glowing behind Abby. The dark blue had brightened to a softer, warmer hue. The sun, still tucked beneath the horizon, gently kissed the clouds scattered across the sky with hints of pink, orange, and purple.

Carrie pointed quietly, alerting the others to turn around and watch the final minutes before the sun exploded into a new year. Everyone turned to face the eastern horizon. Carrie could almost feel the deep breaths of anticipation erupting from each woman.

As the sky lightened, more clouds seemed to race onto the canvas of the new year, each one turning more brilliant colors. The pink and purple faded as the clouds became infused with a brilliant golden orange color, striated with ribbons of purple that made their appearance even more spectacular. It was as if the whole sky had been set on fire and pulsated with new, vibrant life.

Carrie gasped, not certain she'd ever seen a more glorious sunrise. Surely, it was a sign they were entering a more joyful year. She absorbed the beauty, fiercely believing 1872 was going to bring joy to each woman and girl sharing this moment with her.

The sun was still several minutes from making its appearance when Felicia spoke quietly.

"I know we're supposed to remain silent until the sun is all the way up, but I have something I believe I'm supposed to read to you now," Felicia said tentatively.

Carrie and Rose exchanged a look, both nodding. They knew instinctively that it was important.

"Go ahead, dear," Rose said.

Felicia reached into her pocket for a folded piece of paper. She opened it but didn't lift it to read. "I know this year has been hard for most of us. It's easy sometimes to believe life is nothing but hard." She paused. "I was reminded recently that I have to find the joy in life."

Carrie and Rose exchanged a look.

"I overheard my mama and Carrie talking on Christmas Eve. I wasn't trying to eavesdrop, but I've thought about what they said all week. Last night, I wrote a poem." She cleared her throat and began to read.

Darkness surrounds.
Engulfs.
Swallows the light.
Darkness smothers.
Entraps.
Blocks out hope.
Darkness is pain.
Agony.
Searing the soul.

Yet in the darkness,
Hope resides.
Hope shimmers,
Looking for a way to shine.
Waiting.
Waiting for something to burn the darkness.
It waits.
Waits for joy.
Joy bright enough to burn the pain.
Hope waits.
Waits for dawn.
Waits for the sun to burn away the darkness.
It comes.
Joy.
Light.
Hope.
A new sun.
A new dawn.
A new day.
Darkness recedes.
Pain dissolves.
Life begins,
Renewed by dawn.

Felicia stopped reading, and then repeated in a soft voice, "*Renewed by dawn.*"

Carrie caught her breath, the power of the poem reverberating in her as the top of the sun edged above the horizon. She saw Rose wrap her arm around Felicia as everyone stood to welcome the sun. Carrie understood the pride glowing on her face.

Carrie walked over to Frances and Minnie and wrapped her arms around their waists. The girls grinned at her, their faces bright with joy. Frances slipped her free arm around Abby and pulled her close.

Carrie caught her breath again, realizing she was seeing the renewal of life in each of her daughters.

She gazed around the circle as the sun rose higher. Each life here had endured darkness during the last year. Each expectant face spoke of their determination to cast aside the darkness in order to embrace hope. To embrace joy. To embrace life, which at this very moment was being renewed by the dawn.

As the sun climbed slowly, casting its brilliance on the snowy landscape and sparkling on the blue water of the river, Carrie felt the joy growing explosively in her heart.

Carrie released her daughters, walked to Rose, and grabbed her hands. Just as they did every year, the moment the sun cast aside the pull of the earth, they raised their voices and shouted, "Happy New Year!"

Holding hands, they spun in a dance of joy.

The echo of everyone's voices rose into the morning air as they joined in the dance. Leaving a year of darkness and pain behind them, they whirled their way into joy and light...into a new dawn.

"Happy New Year!"
"Happy New Year!"
"Happy New Year!"
1872 had arrived.

To Be Continued...

#17 in The Bregdan Chronicles!

Journey To Joy Is coming to life!

Summer 2020 Release Date!

Would you be so kind as to leave a Review on Amazon?

Go to www.Amazon.com
Put Renewed By Dawn, Ginny Dye into the Search Box
Leave a Review.

I love hearing from my readers!

Thank you!

The Bregdan Principle

Every life that has been lived until today is a part of the woven braid of life.

It takes every person's story to create history.

Your life will help determine the course of history.

You may think you don't have much of an impact.

You do.

Every action you take will reflect in someone else's life.

Someone else's decisions.

Someone else's future.

Both good and bad.

Renewed By Dawn
The Bregdan Chronicles

1 - Storm Clouds Rolling In
1860 – 1861

2 - On To Richmond
1861 – 1862

3 - Spring Will Come
1862 – 1863

4 - Dark Chaos
1863 – 1864

5 - The Long Last Night
1864 – 1865

6 - Carried Forward By Hope
April – December 1865

7 - Glimmers of Change
December – August 1866

8 - Shifted By The Winds
August – December 1866

9 - Always Forward
January – October 1867

10 - Walking Into The Unknown
October 1867 – October 1868

11 - Looking To The Future
October 1868 – June 1869

12 - Horizons Unfolding
November 1869 – March 1870

13 - The Twisted Road of One Writer
The Birth of The Bregdan Chronicles

14 - Misty Shadows of Hope
1870

15 - Shining Through Dark Clouds
1870 – 1871

16 - Courage Rising
April – August 1871

17 – Renewed By Dawn
September 1871 – January 1872

Many more coming... Go to DiscoverTheBregdanChronicles.com to see how many are available now!

Other Books by Ginny Dye

Pepper Crest High Series - Teen Fiction
Time For A Second Change
It's Really A Matter of Trust
A Lost & Found Friend
Time For A Change of Heart

Fly To Your Dreams Series – Allegorical Fantasy
Dream Dragon
Born To Fly
Little Heart
The Miracle of Chinese Bamboo

All titles by Ginny Dye
www.BregdanPublishing.com

Author Biography

Who am I? Just a normal person who happens to love to write. If I could do it all anonymously, I would. In fact, I did the first go 'round. I wrote under a pen name. On the off chance I would ever become famous - I didn't want to be! I don't like the limelight. I don't like living in a fishbowl. I especially don't like thinking I have to look good everywhere I go, just in case someone recognizes me! I finally decided none of that matters. If you don't like me in overalls and a baseball cap, too bad. If you don't like my haircut or think I should do something different than what I'm doing, too bad. I'll write books that you will hopefully like, and we'll both let that be enough! :) Fair?

But let's see what you might want to know. I spent many years as a Wanderer. My dream when I graduated from college was to experience the United States. I grew up in the South. There are many things I love about it but I wanted to live in other places. So I did. I moved 57 times, traveled extensively in 49 of the 50 states, and had more experiences than I will ever be able to recount. The only state I haven't been in is Alaska, simply because I refuse to visit such a vast, fabulous place until I have at least a month. Along the way I had glorious adventures. I've canoed through the Everglade Swamps, snorkeled in the Florida Keys and windsurfed in the Gulf of Mexico. I've white-water rafted down the New River and Bungee jumped in the Wisconsin Dells. I've visited every National Park (in the off-season when there is more freedom!) and many of the State Parks. I've hiked thousands of miles of mountain trails and biked through Arizona deserts. I've canoed and biked through Upstate New York and Vermont, and polished off as much lobster as possible on the Maine Coast.

I had a glorious time and never thought I would find a place that would hold me until I came to the Pacific Northwest. I'd been here less than 2 weeks, and I knew I would never leave. My heart is so at home here with the towering firs, sparkling waters, soaring mountains and rocky beaches. I love the eagles & whales. In 5 minutes I can be hiking on 150 miles of trails in the mountains around my home, or gliding across the lake in my rowing shell. I love it!

Have you figured out I'm kind of an outdoors gal? If it can be done outdoors, I love it! Hiking, biking, windsurfing, rock-climbing, roller-blading, snow-shoeing, skiing, rowing, canoeing, softball, tennis... the list could go on and on. I love to have fun and I love to stretch my body. This should give you a pretty good idea of what I do in my free time.

When I'm not writing or playing, I'm building Millions For Positive Change - a fabulous organization I founded in 2001 - along with 60 amazing people who poured their lives into creating resources to empower people to make a difference with their lives.

What else? I love to read, cook, sit for hours in solitude on my mountain, and also hang out with friends. I love barbeques and block parties. Basically - I just love LIFE!

I'm so glad you're part of my world!

Ginny

Join my Email List so you can:

- Receive notice of all new books
- Be a part of my Launch Celebrations. I give away lots of Free gifts!
- Read my weekly BLOG while you're waiting for a new book.
- Be part of The Bregdan Chronicles Family!
- Learn about all the other books I write.

Just go to www.BregdanChronicles.net and fill out the form.

Made in the USA
Columbia, SC
13 November 2020